Rogue Warrior
GREEN TEAM

Photograph By Roger Foley

ROGUE WARRIOR

GREEN TEAM

Richard Marcinko
and
John Weisman

POCKET BOOKS

New York   London   Toronto   Sydney   Tokyo   Singapore

Many of the Rogue Warrior's weapons courtesy of Heckler & Koch, Inc., International Training Division, Sterling, Virginia

 POCKET BOOKS, a division of Simon & Schuster Inc.
1230 Avenue of the Americas, New York, NY 10020

ISBN: 0-671-89671-7

First Pocket Books hardcover printing March 1995

10 9 8 7 6 5 4 3 2 1

POCKET and colophon are registered trademarks of
Simon & Schuster Inc.

Printed in the U.S.A.

Once again, to the shooters

And to the memory of Colonel Charlie A. Beckwith, USA, a true Warrior, and a good and valued friend

—Richard Marcinko
—John Weisman

The Rogue Warrior series by Richard Marcinko and John Weisman

Rogue Warrior
Rogue Warrior: Red Cell
Rogue Warrior: Green Team

Also by John Weisman

Fiction

Blood Cries
Watchdogs
Evidence

Nonfiction

Shadow Warrior (with Felix Rodriguez)

Blessed are the true believers.

—Koran 23:1

THE TEN COMMANDMENTS OF SPECWAR

According to Richard Marcinko

- I am the War Lord and the wrathful God of Combat and I will always lead you from the front, not the rear.

- I will treat you all alike—just like shit.

- Thou shalt do nothing I will not do first, and thus will you be created Warriors in My deadly image.

- I shall punish thy bodies because the more thou sweatest in training, the less thou bleedest in combat.

- Indeed, if thou hurteth in thy efforts and thou suffer painful dings, then thou art Doing It Right.

- Thou hast not to like it—thou hast just to do it.

- Thou shalt Keep It Simple, Stupid.

- Thou shalt never assume.

- Verily, thou art not paid for thy methods, but for thy results, by which meaneth thou shalt kill thine enemy by any means available before he killeth you.

- Thou shalt, in thy Warrior's Mind and Soul, always remember My ultimate and final Commandment: There Are No Rules— Thou Shalt Win at All Cost.

OFFICE OF THE CHAIRMAN
THE JOINT CHIEFS OF STAFF
WASHINGTON, D.C. 20318-9999

Definitions of Joint Chiefs of Staff [JCS] Terrorist Threat
Conditions [Threatcons] for Operational Units

The four Threatcons, which may be suffixed with the specific
geographic area deemed at risk, are defined as follows:

a. Threatcon Alpha. This condition applies when there is a general
threat of possible hostile activity against installations and personnel, the nature and extent of which are unpredictable. The measures
in this threat condition must be capable of being maintained
indefinitely.

b. Threatcon Bravo. This condition applies when an increased and
more predictable threat of hostile activity exists. The measures in
this threat condition must be capable of being maintained for weeks
without causing undue hardship, without affecting operational
capability, and without aggravating relations with local authorities.

c. Threatcon Charlie. This condition applies when an incident
occurs or when intelligence is received indicating that some form of
terrorist action against installations and personnel is imminent.
Implementation of this measure for more than a short period will
create hardship and will affect adversely the activities of the unit
and its personnel.

d. Threatcon Delta. This condition applies in the immediate area
where an hostile attack has occurred, or when intelligence has been
received that an hostile action against a specfic location or person is
likely. It makes normal activities virtually impossible to pursue.

Contents

Part One

ALPHA

Chapter

1

THE FIRST TWO FLOORS WERE EASY—NO ONE IN SIGHT, NO BOOBY traps, and no cats, rats, bats, goats, sheep, or other miscellaneous animals to make our presence known. I crept up the dusty concrete stairs one by one, my black, knee-length Pakistani "pasha" tunic covering the carbon-colored, custom-suppressed Heckler & Koch USP 9mm in its ballistic nylon thigh holster. The rest of my outfit was also basic black—from the thong sandals to the Maharishi-styled trousers, to the titanium-framed Emerson CQC6 combat folder clipped to my waistband next to the Motorola beeper, to the lead-and-leather sap secured by a thick, black Ace bandage to the inside of my right wrist.

My beard was full—reaching almost halfway down my chest. My mustache drooped Fu Manchu–like way below my upper lip. My shoulder-length hair, restrained by a thick black cotton band, was wild and crazee. If anybody ever looked the part of Islamic fundamentalist rogue warrior—the kind of maniacal mujahideen you used to see on the TV news shows when they sent camera crews into Afghanistan—it was me. Which is precisely why I'd volunteered as point man on this little jaunt, prowling and growling up the unlit stairwell of a Cairo slum at 0-dark-hundred to catch my quarry napping on his bedroll.

I wasn't alone, of course. You do not meander into Islamic Cairo, home to some of the meanest Muslim fundamentalist sons of bitches in the world, without some fundamentally mean sons of bitches of your own to backstop your ass. That's why, half a yard behind me, Senior Chief Nasty Nicky Grundle, his suppressed Heckler & Koch MP5K-PDW submachine gun at the ready, rested a huge paw on my shoulder. A yard behind him, Master Chief Boatswain's Mate Howie Kaluha's well-muscled Hawaiian back (not to mention his well-maintained Kraut submachine gun) brought up the rear.

A few streets away, cruising in the limo—it was actually a baby blue Peugeot 504 station wagon, but in Cairo, as the saying goes, almost anything that runs can be considered a limo—Doc Tremblay, handle-bar-mustachioed master chief corpsman and supersniper, waited, a Manurhin PPK/s loaded with seven rounds of .380 MagSafe frangible manstoppers tucked in his waistband and a disposable syringe filled with two hundred milligrams of Dr. Nostradamus's best Ketamine Love Potion Number 9 in his hand. Behind the Peugeot's wheel sat Grandma Syde's favorite Peck's bad boy, Machinist's Mate First Class Stevie Wonder, on indefinite leave from his classified job at the Washington Navy Yard. Wonder's carrot-colored hair was covered by a dark, knit fellahin cap, and his tight frame was hidden by a shapeless gallebiyah. He was, however, wearing his trademark wraparound shooting glasses with lenses in the color named especially for him—bastard amber.

Wedged under Wonder's right thigh was a nineties hush puppy—a suppressed Heckler & Koch 9mm USP semiautomatic—loaded with Doc Tremblay's best hand-loaded, subsonic hollowpoint. To his nightshirtlike garment was pinned a throwaway receiving device about the size of a pack of gum. When I pressed a Chiclets-sized button in my pocket, his gizmo would vibrate for thirty seconds. The tickle would tell him he had one minute to get his mick ass in gear and pick me and the rest of the team up.

There's more: while Nasty, Howie, and I crept up the stairs, Chief Gunner's Mate (Guns) Duck Foot Dewey and Commander Tommy Tanaka were making their way up along a precarious path of irregular stonework, spindly balconies, laundry lines, and drainpipes that ran alongside the target's third-story dormer windows. I knew it would take every bit of their mountain-climbing expertise

4

to clamber up thirty-five feet of brittle brick without snapping anything off and raising a ruckus.

I know, I know—you're asking, what the fuck? What the hell's going on? What's Dickie doing back in the Third World when he should be home at Rogue Manor, just climbing out of the Jacuzzi clutching a tall, frosted glass of Bombay on the rocks in one hand, and something warm, wonderful, and remarkably full-breasted in the other.

Believe me, if there'd been time, I'd have been asking myself the same question. And as soon as I get a couple of minutes, I'll tell you everything. But at the present, there was no time for anything but the matter at hand. To wit: scratching and snatching, then whopping and popping.

Translation: our mission was to sit around and *scratch* our asses until the time was right, then *snatch* one Mahmoud Azziz abu Yasin, Islamic fundamentalist and terrorist asshole, from his beddy-bye. Whereupon, I'd *whop* him upside the haid with my handy little sap, knock him cold, and hustle his ass down to the Peugeot, where Doc would *pop* that two hundred milligrams of Dr. N's Ketamine right into his upper deltoid, which would drug the shit out of ol' Mahmoud for a few precious hours.

Then we'd spirit the tango Adam Henry (that's radio talk for terrorist asshole for the uninitiated among you) out of Egypt on a thirty-two-foot fishing trawler Doc had rented in Alexandria, and after a pleasant ocean cruise, we'd rendezvous with a guided-missile frigate that had orders to be standing by, 75 miles off the Egyptian coast during a six-hour window. From the frigate, we'd chopper to a carrier task force that sat another 125 miles out to sea. Then we'd use a Grumman C-2 Greyhound carrier onboard delivery plane to COD us all to Sigonella, Sicily.

There, we'd quietly slip Azziz aboard his own C-141 StarLifter aircraft and fly him back to CONUS (or the CONtinental United States in civilian speak), where we'd drop him off in such plain sight that even the FBI would be able to find him. We would then disappear back into the shadows from which we'd come, leaving the feds to take all the capture credit when Azziz finally stood trial for his lethal part in a series of bombings across the United States that had cost sixty-five lives in all and disrupted the cities of New York, Chicago, Houston, and Washington, D.C., for more than a month.

Sounds easy. A clockwork op. Guess again. Snatch-and-grabs (or, as the Brits call 'em, cosh-and-carrys) are precarious, risky operations. Probs and stats? Bad. Goatfuck likelihood? High.

GF factor 1: you're operating in a hostile environment with no back-up.

GF factor 2: your government will disavow your actions if you're caught.

GF factor 3: if the locals do get their hands on you, the odds are that you'll end up being dragged behind a car or truck for a few hours while they cut off significant pieces of your anatomy joint by joint.

So, you ask, how did I feel right now?

Brief answer: I felt as happy as *un grand porc en merde*, although you probably couldn't get something the width of a hairpin up my sphincter because the pucker factor was off the charts.

Above me, something moved. My hand went up. We stopped. I gave signals, and Nasty pressed himself against the stairwell wall, giving himself the greatest field of fire. His free hand grasped my shoulder. That way I'd know where he was all the time. Knowing where everybody is all the time is an important element of operations such as these. It's altogether possible to kill your own man if he's out of position by as much as a few inches. I know—because it has happened during training.

I kept moving in the same steady pace I'd set two floors below, progressing inch by inch, the fingers of my left hand sweeping carefully, caressing the stair treads and risers as carefully as if they were virgin pussy. These fundamentalist assholes were SUCs—smart, unpredictable, and cunning. And they fucking *owned* this part of town—even government troops stayed away from this particular neighborhood unless they were being deployed by the hundreds.

We'd learned this fact—and others—during the past week and a half as we'd begun the deadly business of target assessment. We'd infiltrated commercially. Nasty Nick, Tommy, and I came through Rome, Messina, and Cyprus, catching a ferry from there to Port Said and busing the dusty road from Ismailia to Cairo eleven days ago. Howie, Duck Foot, and Wonder came commercial—TWA from Dulles to Frankfurt, a change of planes for the hop to Athens, then southeast over the Med to Cairo. They arrived eight days ago.

Doc Tremblay'd had the toughest commute. He had had to come through Cairo traffic from his house in Maadi, six miles from Tahrir Square in central Cairo. Doc was on a two-year assignment here. You don't want to know what he was doing, or who he was doing it for—because if he told you, he'd have to kill you. Anyway, glutton for punishment that he is, he'd volunteered to come along for the ride when I'd called him on the secure line and told him we'd be visiting.

That was a-okay with me. I always like to have a mole—a covert operator no one knows about—to wheel and deal for me. So, Doc took some accumulated leave and disappeared from the Military Assistance Group offices. He told the embassy people he was taking vacation time in Alexandria, Suez, and Ismailia. Instead, he'd slipped into Cairo's back alleys, and by the time Nick, Tommy, and I arrived here, he'd assembled weapons, ordnance, bought a junker Peugeot and a pair of half-decent motorbikes, and arranged rooms at a local tourist hotel. All, I might add, without alerting the Egyptian secret police, the local Christians in Action station—Navy talk for CIA agents—or the State Department's Foggy Bottomed apparatchiki.

Once we'd arrived and set up shop, it hadn't taken us long to locate Azziz. Why? First, because we already knew where he lived. The Defense Intelligence Agency—DIA—had provided my boss, the chief of naval operations, with a detailed map of the area. And second, because, as cops are fond of saying, a perp is a perp is a perp (actually, cops say that everywhere but New York, where they say a poip is a poip is a poip). Translated into English, that means perpetrators are creatures of habit. And Azziz the perp's habits were centered around politics and prayer.

Moreover, Azziz enjoyed a certain celebrity status on the local fundamentalist scene. No matter how low he may have wanted to keep his profile, the local mullahs singled him out, citing ol' Mahmoud as an example of righteous dedication to Islam's cause. He had defied the infidel. He had waged war against the Great Satan on the Great Satan's turf—and he'd won. So they showed him off. They displayed him at their rallies. They stood him at attention during their sermons.

So, finding our Muslim needle wasn't going to be hard—not in *this* here haystack. The challenge would be to snatch him up without creating a ruckus, in the same sort of low-key, quick-and-dirty kidnap operation I'd perfected more than a quarter century ago in Vietnam.

We called them parakeet ops back then. We'd take four or five guys and hit a village, nabbing a VC paymaster or political cadre out of his hooch in the middle of the night with such quiet efficiency that the people in the adjacent hooch wouldn't hear a thing. They'd wake up the next morning, and Binh or Phuong or Tran would just have *di-di maued*—that's disappeared in Vietnamese slang. His bodyguards would still be there—dead, of course, and nicely, cunningly, lethally boobytrapped. It was unnerving. It was intimidating. It was wonderful.

Parakeet ops took split-second timing. They also took good operational intelligence—you had to know how, and where, the bird lived before you could snare him.

So, when Doc had showed me the latest *Cairo Weekly*—a newsletter published by the embassy's personnel office—and I read the listing titled "Security Advisory," which said, quote, "AMEMB [translation: AMerican EMBassy] personnel should avoid the areas adjacent to the Rifai, Saiyida Sukayna, and al-Hambra mosques next Wednesday—five days hence—as DIPSEC [translation: DIPlomatic SECurity] has been advised that Islamic rallies have been planned," a hundred-watt lightbulb went off in my thick-as-rocks Slovak skull.

All three mosques were in the general area where Azziz's family lived—the southern section of Islamic Cairo adjacent to the City of the Dead and below the Citadel. Odds were that Azziz would be featured at one or more of the rallies.

My plan was KISS simple. Duck Foot and Howie would surveil one mosque, Wonder and Nasty would cover the other, and I'd handle the third with Tommy. We knew what Azziz looked like—his red hair and broken nose made him easily distinguishable. We'd shadow him at a discreet distance, check out the opposition, see what patterns he established, and once we could be reasonably certain of them, we'd go in and grab his ass. DIA's locals had no need to know we were in the city—which would protect their butts, bureaucratically, and our asses on the operational level.

I'd done time in Cairo back in the late eighties and was familiar with the city. It's not an easy place to learn. There are thousands of unpaved streets and muddy alleyways that run together in labyrinthine mazes. There are cul-de-sacs from which it's impossible to escape. There's the City of the Dead—six square miles of cemeteries turned slums, where more than half a million people live in mausoleums and mud-hut shanties with open-trench sewers.

Doc Tremblay, whose passion is shopping, knew it like the back of his hairy fucking hand. But my youngsters had never been here before. I knew they'd have to get the feel of the place before they felt confident operating with the split-second timing the mission required.

There's a philosophical point about clandestine operations I should mention at this juncture. It is that you can't send a SEAL off to Cairo, Kabul, or Kinshasa and say, "Just do it." SEALs have to be able to blend in. Just as we learned how to use camouflage in Vietnam to render ourselves invisible to Mr. Charlie, you have to be able to hide in plain sight when you're in an urban jungle, too.

One thing that often helps immeasurably is the ability not to sound like a Yankee. Me? I speak French and Italian and get along in gutter Arabic, Spanish, and German. Tommy T is fluent in French, German, and Russian. Howie's Spanish is better than his English. Nasty Nick and Wonder *hablan español*, too. Duck Foot can pass as Polish if he has to. He reads Arabic better than he speaks it, however. Doc Tremblay? His Arabic's fluent, his Farsi's passable, and his French? *Superbe.* Those linguistic abilities are what help make them dependable shooters overseas.

You send someone sounding like an American farm boy out in the Azerbaijani boondocks, and he's gonna stick out like a sore *szeb*. That will compromise your mission. Then there's the operational gestalt. You have to be able to blend in—whether it means passing as a tourist or a truck driver. If you "read" like US GOVT ISSUE, you'll probably be dead-meat body-bag material before you get to shoot or loot.

So the boys and I spent the next four days playing our own brand of tourist—familiarizing ourselves with the warp and weave of this huge, gawky city. We'd started at the trio of mosques where Azziz was likely to make his appearance. All three sat in the shadow of the Citadel—the fortified complex built by Salah al-Din in the twelfth century. The Citadel still dominates Cairo's skyline, accented by tin mosque domes that reflect the sunlight and a series of needlelike minarets that look skyward like ready-to-launch SAM-7 missiles.

Each two-man team, dressed like tourists and equipped with the requisite cameras, guidebooks, and maps, worked outward through concentric circles, charting alleyways and narrow passages, making mental notes about the decrepit three- and four-story apartment houses that sat cheek-to-jowl on narrow streets, laundry fluttering like flags from shuttered windows and shaky balcony railings.

Nasty and Duck Foot (and their sweet teeth) hit the neighborhood teahouses. They sat at window tables, Duck Foot tried his Polish on the waiters, and they maintained cover by sampling dozens of honey-covered cakes. Tommy and Howie wandered the Khan al-Khalil—Cairo's huge market district—munching grilled meat wrapped in hot Arab bread, seasoned with fiery green pepper and chopped onion and sold by voluble street vendors dressed in the kind of sweat-suit pajamas common to backstreet Cairo. (Whether the kabobs were cat or rat they couldn't tell, but they're snake eaters, so what difference would it make anyway?)

Wonder, Doc, and I poked our noses inside small grocery stores, reveling in the pervasive smells of cardamom, cumin, allspice, and cinnamon. I tried my backstreet Arabic and was gratified to discover I could still make myself understood. Doc Tremblay, whom I first met back in Naples when he was a second-class corpsman in search of a good time and I was working for the legendary Frogman Everett E. Barrett, chief gunner's mate/guns, at UDT-22, was positively loquacious, much to the delight of the natives. Doc reminds me of Jim Finley, my utility man from Bravo Squad, Second Platoon, in Vietnam. We called Jim "the Mayor," because no matter where we went, he'd be out pressing the flesh, making friends, within minutes of our arrival. Doc's much the same—he's the kind of guy who looks like he just belongs, whether he's in Chicago, Cairo, or Kathmandu.

While the rest of the men learned the streets, Doc and I worked out escape routes, logging hundreds of miles—at least it felt that way—bouncing along in the decrepit station wagon he'd bought. We should have used the motor bikes, because the rusty, dented Peugeot was a joke. I'd told Doc I wanted something that could pass for a Cairene's car—and did I ever get it. The damn thing kept crapping out on us no matter how Stevie Wonder played with its innards.

We finally pulled it off the pavement and into a quiet alley behind our hotel. "Once and for all, fix the damn thing," I told Stevie. He'd saluted me with his middle finger and gave me a confident "Yes, sir."

That had been on Tuesday. The next day, Tommy T and Duck Foot sighted our quarry coming out the back of the Sidi Almas mosque just north of Saleh ed-Din Square.

Azziz, they said, was flanked by a pair of bodyguards who looked as if they were packing heat. Azziz was in deep conversation with a huge black guy—could have been Sudanese or Somali, but they'd dubbed him the Nubian—dressed in flowing robes and cowboy boots. The quartet had climbed into a huge Mercedes limo with blacked-out windows and driven to a coffeehouse, where the Nubian and Azziz sat for two hours in deep conversation, while the bodyguards waited just outside the doorway.

Tommy and Duck Foot gave them a loose tail when they left. Azziz was dropped right here at his apartment house. He was patting his pocket as he got out of the car, which told Duck Foot he'd been given something valuable—perhaps documentation or money, or both. Tommy stayed with Azziz, watching as he and his shadows climbed the three flights of stairs to his flat.

Duck Foot followed the Mercedes, which wove its way downtown, finally pulling up on the long driveway to the Cairo Meridien. The Nubian disembarked there. Duck Foot, ever patient, walked into the lobby and plunked himself down at the bar, watching as the Nubian took the elevator to the sixth floor. Six minutes later, the tall black man reappeared, now dressed in a fashionable Western suit and carrying an overnight bag. He paid his bill in cash, tipped the concierge handsomely, and climbed back into the Mercedes, which Duck Foot followed out to the airport.

I'd listened to their report and immediately initiated a twenty-four-hour stakeout at Azziz's apartment. I had Duck Foot shinny up the power pole that also held the phone line and drop a passive device in place. We couldn't overhear Azziz's conversations, but we knew he was making lots of overseas calls from the number of blips we heard as he dialed. Moreover, as soon as the Nubian had departed, Azziz started to receive a continuous stream of visitors.

The signs told me Azziz was about to skedaddle. We had to move first—even though we weren't as ready as I might have wanted us to be. So, I faced Rome, Jerusalem, and Mecca and prayed to every deity I could think of. I even made the old religious sign the priests had taught me when I was an altar boy: spectacles, testicles, wallet, and watch. *Please, sir*—I prayed to the Diety—*let the fucking car work.*

The chain of events that had led me to this current and potentially precarious circumstance had actually begun roughly six months ago, when the feds grabbed Mahmoud in a grocery store in Brooklyn and charged him with being the ringleader of an alleged tango group that had pulled off six separate bombings all across the U.S. Usually in these cases, the accused is defended either by a William Kunstlerlike rad-chic, or a public defender.

Not so in Azziz's case. The thirty-five-year-old Egyptian national who had no visible means of support was somehow suddenly represented in court by one of New York's most prestigious Wall Street firms, whose $1,000-an-hour attorneys used the old-boy network to select the most liberal federal judge currently serving on the bench to preside at the arraignment.

After half an hour of "May we approach the bench, Your Honor" legalese double-talk and triple syllables, Let-'em-Loose Bruce allowed young Mahmoud to take a walk on $5-million bail, which the lawyer produced immediately—in cash. And, of course, not three hours after the Most Happy Fellah sauntered out of the Federal Detention Center in lower Manhattan, he'd forfeited the money by climbing on a plane to his hometown, Cairo, using a false passport that he'd somehow (?!?) obtained.

And why not? Azziz (and those azzisting him) knew all too well that the United States had neither the will nor the balls to bring him to justice from overseas. He also understood (given the tenuous political situation here in the land of the pharaohs) that the Egyptians, nervous over the intensifying influence of homespun Islamic fundamentalism, would turn a blind eye to his return and leave him alone unless he committed some heinous act of domestic aggression.

Heinous act? you say. You want an example? Okay—gang-banging the Egyptian president's wife and daughter at the Giza pyramids at high noon would probably (although by no means certainly) prompt the local authorities to take a closer look at Azziz and his activities. It would take something more serious than that to make them actually act.

In fact, the Egyptian foreign minister, a Turhan Bey look-alike if ever there was one, had only three weeks ago oozed over to the American embassy in dramatic response to a vapid State Department démarche on said tango's whereabouts and personally assured G. Throckmorton Numbnuts Jr., or whatever our current ambassador's name is, that Mahmoud Azziz abu Yasin was nowhere in Egypt. He had personally looked into the matter, and said conclusion was the result of his investigation.

Of course Ambassador Numbnuts Jr., a heel-rocking, change-jingling, striped-suited, no-load pencil-dicked Foggy Bottomed foreign-service diplo-dink cookie pusher, who believes in the tooth fairy, Santa Claus, and Barney, took him at his word.

Sure. Right. *Absolument.* Just the way the same Foreign Ministry swore back in October 1985 that the Palestine Liberation Front *Achille Lauro* terrorists who'd murdered wheelchair-bound Leon Klinghoffer had left the country, when in fact they were still safely holed up in a four-star hotel just outside the Cairo International Airport perimeter fence, drinking mint-fucking-infused tea, eating honey-and-nut fucking *baklawa,* and waiting for their first-fucking-class Egyptair flight back to Tripoli.

We at DOD, of course, knew better. But the Department of Defense doesn't write démarches—not in this administration at least. So the State Department performed as usual: the Foggy Bottom apparatchiki held long meetings, wrote internal memos to the file, wrung their hands, and finally resolved to do—absolutely nothing. Meanwhile, Ambassador Numbnuts Jr. sat at his Texas Instruments laptop and composed directives forbidding his political officers, mil-group advisers, or rezident intel gumshoes from scouring the streets in search of the missing MIQ, or Muslim-In-Question.

"We do not," he opined in bits and bytes on embassy letterhead, "wish to offend our generous Egyptian hosts by appearing to doubt their good word."

Unfuckingbelievable, right? Well, I know he wrote it, because I've seen the goddamn thing.

But not everything at AMEMB/CAIRO was a total clusterfuck. Under quiet orders from an anonymous, modern, fourteen-story building in Rosslyn, Virginia, just across the Potomac from Washington, Defense Intelligence Agency assets (they're called assets in the trade because you *sets* dey *asses* on de street) were told to keep loose tabs on our man Mahmoud from the time he stepped off the plane from Frankfurt into his Muslim mummy's loving arms. They did their jobs successfully.

They backchanneled their data to headquarters by sending it via courier, not cable or telephone, because they knew there's not a single fucking communication posted from an embassy—not a secure fax, not a scrambled phone call, not even a goddamn code-word secret CIA cable—that an ambassador can't get a copy, tape, or transcript of, if he so desires.

Anyway, DIA's intel nuggets caromed around the chain of command until they reached Chief of Naval Operations Arleigh Secrest's antique walnut desk on the fourth-floor E-ring of the Pentagon. CNO, one of the few admirals these days who can actually be designated a warrior, not a manager or a technocrat, decided it was time to do something militant and military. He lobbied his fellow service chiefs, stroked SECDEF—that's the SECretary of DEFense—and wheedled, needled, and diddled the folks at CIA until they all saw things his way.

When the ducks finally came up in a row, he picked up the phone and called my extension.

Two weeks after that, me and my guys were on our way here. We'd paid for our tickets with the counterfeit credit cards and traveled on the ersatz Irish, German, British, U.S., and Canadian passports we'd received from a USG—that's U.S. Government— employee I'll call Freddie the Forger, whose very classified shop sits in plain sight about a thousand feet from the State Department's main entrance.

Freddie's a gem. He looks like Bob Dylan, circa 1967, and he only takes a shower once a month or so. Who cares—his work is perfect, and his documents are all genuine and up-to-date. There's not an ultraviolet scanner, magnetic-strip decoder, or bar-code reader in the world that can tell one of Freddie's IDs, passports, credit cards, or driver's licenses from the real McCoy—until the bills come in and nobody pays 'em.

Still, we needed the best documentation we could get. After all, I had personal orders from CNO to maintain, as he put it to me in technical language, "a completely Stealth fucking profile."

I understood all too well the reasons for CNO's stricture. First and foremost was the Egyptian government, which frowns on foreign military operations conducted on its sovereign soil. Second was our own American ambassador and his superiors at State, most of whom frown on American military operations, period.

But while CNO, a man I have come to like and respect, warned me to be discreet, he also ordered me to get the goddamn job done. "Dick—do not fail to bring this bastard back" is what he said in his booming foghorn basso.

CNO's choice of phrase struck a chord deep within my soul. He used virtually the same words as another CNO I respected, Admiral Black Jack Morrison.

"Dick, you will not fail," was what Black Jack said the day he'd ordered me to design, build, equip, train, and lead the most effective and highly secret counterterror force in the world, SEAL Team Six.

Of course the world was simple in those days. There were the good guys—us, our allies, and our surrogates—and there were the bad guys—the Soviet Bear, its allies, and its surrogates. Yin and yang. Black and white. Us or them.

Yesterday's villains were known quantities. Today's bad guys are faceless assholes like Azziz; members of self-contained cells, or loners who say they represent some fragment of the underclass. Most often, we have no idea who they are, how they operate, or what their targets are going to be. What worried CNO and me even more was the possibility that half a dozen groups of these tangos would coalesce—form a loose syndicate and operate in concert. That would make them PDMPs—Pretty Dangerous Motherfucking People indeed.

Except, the only people who seemed to appreciate this nasty factoid were CNO and me. This, after all, was the nineties—when Americans turned inward. The polls all showed it, too. Crime. Health care. Welfare reform. Those were the popular problems to be concerned about, and the White House, which was ruled by pollsters, followed the public lead. Americans, they'd decided, couldn't care less what was going on in places whose names they couldn't pronounce.

And yet, CNO and I knew that what happened in those corners of the world was going to affect us in a big way. All those KGB and GRU veterans for hire. All those old Soviet nukes and chemical/biological warfare canisters. All those guns and bullets, grenades, land mines, rocket-propelled grenades, plastic explosives, and shoulder-held surface-to-air missiles—all just waiting to be used against us.

So we waged our own unconventional little war. CNO did covert combat on the Pentagon's E-ring, where the service chiefs have their offices. He skirmished at meetings of the Joint Chiefs of Staff. He staged hit-and-run strikes during day-long strategy sessions in the Office of the Secretary of Defense. He left behind philosophical time bombs during visits with the White House national security adviser.

On the overt side, he dropped tactical tidbits to half a dozen favored reporters and hammered the subject in all of his public appearances. He made quite a name for himself on the TV talk shows—volubly promoting the right to pursue those who murder Americans if they take flight overseas and return them to justice here, and defending the concept of counterterror—which means doing it to them before they do it to us. And every now and then, when he won his battles on the home front, I got to fight mine in places like this.

Today's mission, for example, had been approved in the Oval Office, by the Leader of the Free World himself. Seventy-two hours before we'd gone wheels up, I was snuck into the White House through the East Wing, looking like one of the first family's Hollywood friends—I wore Reeboks, blue jeans, and a chambray shirt, my long hair tucked under a po' boy cap. CNO arrived through the West Wing basement entrance in a dark suit. We linked up in the NSC adviser's office and went the roundabout route to meet the commander in chief.

It was obvious the president wasn't happy about my mission. But CNO had worked him over pretty good. He'd explained that any indigent tango who could throw away $5 million cash in bail money and spend a grand per hour on lawyers was worth going after, if only to find out who was funding him.

More to the point—i.e., politically—he convinced the president that the only way to deter this particular genus of terrorists was to take the sort of explicitly violent, yet deniably clandestine action, which would force them to reconsider further acts of aggression within our borders. And he wasn't about to let the president weasel out of it now: "If they perceive you as indecisive or weak, Mr.

President, they'll only hit us again," CNO insisted. "That could jeopardize your reelection substantially." Indeed, he gently reminded the president that virtually every foreign-intelligence profile we'd intercepted, from both allies and adversaries, made the point that the leader of the free world had been a Vietnam War protester and was probably inherently resistant to using force.

The president asked for my opinion. I told him I concurred with my boss. I added that we somehow had to show the Egyptians that they couldn't lie to us about harboring terrorists—but that we couldn't do it overtly.

The president nodded in agreement. He may have not had a military molecule in his body, but he was 100 percent a political animal. Instinctively, he knew there was no way we could allow a country receiving almost $3 billion in American aid to provide terrorists with a safe haven. "But isn't there a less, ah, brutal way of convincing them, Captain?"

I was about to use the dreaded F-word when I saw the look in CNO's eye. I bit my tongue. "No, sir. No way at all."

The president sighed. "I still don't like it, Admiral Secrest. But I'm gonna bow to your wisdom—and my wife's. She insists we have to act decisively."

It was nice to hear that someone in the White House actually has balls.

So the supreme CINC gave us his blessing, although he refused to sign a national-security finding in the matter. Well, I could see his point. It's not the kind of mission where you want to leave a paper trail. In fact, the political aspects of this assignment were lose/lose, so far as CNO and I were concerned. If I screwed up, the White House would jettison CNO—maybe even court-martial him. If I succeeded, only CNO and the president would know what I'd done. There were no medals in this for me or my men, only the knowledge that we were doing what we were born to do, for the country we loved so much.

CNO and I left together, hustling out the West Wing into his car. We rode back to the Pentagon in silence. There's a term for what CNO had just done. It's called leading from the front.

I admire and respect an officer who takes the same risks as his men—and while CNO wasn't coming with us, his ass was on the line no less than mine was. So my response to him was the same as it had been to Black Jack Morrison back in 1980.

No way would I fail. "Aye, aye, sir," I said.

My fingers discovered something—a single strand of monofilament ran six inches above the stair tread, attached to the wall on one side and threaded through the filigree iron railing on the other. I drew the line in carefully. It was attached to a series of small, empty tin cans. What I'd discovered was the same sort of simple, effective intrusion device I'd first seen used in Vietnam. Some big-footed American trips the wire, the cans go clank-clank, and Mr. Charlie shoots you dead before you know what's happened.

The hair on my neck stood up. *If there was one, there'll be another.* These things always ran in pairs—or even triples. I stopped to let my fingers do the walking.

Bingo—monofilament number two was three steps above number one. And wire number three ran at chest level, two feet above that.

Each had to be disposed of. First, I made sure Nasty and Howie knew what, when, where, and how. Then I flipped the Emerson out of my waistband, and as Nasty took the cans into his big hands one by one, I clipped the line. Then we set them all on the landing below us. We repeated the sequence for the next two without incident.

Two apartments were on the third floor. From our surveillance, I knew Azziz lived with his mother and younger brother behind door number one—the one on the left that looked out on the back alley. Across the hallway were the bodyguards. Two at a time they accompanied Azziz whenever he left the house.

We had two options: the first was to break in and do our job without alerting the watchdogs. The second involved breaking into both apartments simultaneously, allowing Howie to wax the bodyguards while Nasty, Tommy, Duck Foot, and I silenced Mom and baby bro, grabbed Azziz, and skipped. I preferred option number one.

Inshallah, it was not to be.

The ever present Mr. Murphy of Murphy's Law fame had accompanied us on this little adventure. As I came up to the third-floor landing, the right-hand door opened, spilling light down the stairwell. A shaggy-haired kid in sweats peered out, his face quizzical.

I froze, hoping he wouldn't see me.

The expression in his eyes said otherwise. Nasty didn't wait to be coaxed—a quiet *brrp* from his HK and a three-round burst took the kid down before he could react. You could hear the hollowpoint, frangible rounds impact, cracking bone and cartilage in the tango's chest.

I bolted the last two yards and caught him before he hit the ground, took him by the shoulders, and dragged the body out onto the landing. Howie moved into the bodyguards' flat, his HK in close-quarters-battle ready mode, his round, brown face impassive. He knew what he had to do.

Nasty and I took the left-hand door. I hit it hard enough with my foot to pop it off the hinges.

Inside. I went left. Nasty went right. There was motion at the window in front of me—Duck Foot and Tommy T coming through the shutters, right on the busted-door cue. From somewhere, a woman screamed—the cry was cut off.

Now it was all moving so fast that things happened in flash-time sequence. I hit the left-side bedroom door. Azziz rolled over, grabbing for something under the mattress. "Fuck you—" I wrestled his hand from under the mattress, breaking a finger or two in the process, and slid the pistol he'd been trying for out of reach. Then I swatted him back against the wall, covered him with my body, and applied a liberal helping of leather sap behind his ear. He went spongy.

I grabbed the roll of surgical tape in my pocket; Tommy already had his out. We trussed Azziz's hands and feet quicker than any cowpokes ever hog-tied a dogie, then flipped him onto the floor, facedown.

We did a quick sweep of the room. I turned the mattress. There was a pistol there. And a heavy, thick, brown envelope. I grabbed it and looked inside—it was stuffed with English fifty-pound notes and a few documents. It went into my big inside pocket. Then I plucked the tango from the floor and threw him over my shoulder. It was time to get the hell out of Dodge. "Go-go-go."

Tommy bolted toward the landing. I followed him, my left hand fumbling for the transmitter in my pocket. I finally got it, squeezed it hard, and—*smaaaack*—caught the edge of the bedroom door right in the middle of my forehead at full speed. I bounced backward, Azziz's weight pulling me off my feet. His head hit the floor with a thunk as I sat down hard, stunned. Bad juju, Dickie.

"Skipper, Skipper?" Tommy wheeled, grabbed my arm, and pulled me to my feet.

"What? What?" I shook my head. It didn't help—I still saw nothing but stars. Then I came to my senses. We were behind fucking schedule. "Go—move! I'm okay, I'm okay!" My lip was split, my nose was bleeding. But what the fuck—no pain, no . . . pain.

I ran back through the living room. I saw two doors leading to the hallway—double vision is one sign of a concussion. Fuck me—I picked the one on the right and managed to stagger through without hitting myself again.

Howie was already on the landing, an urgent expression on his pockmarked, copper-colored face. "We're clear," he said, his head inclined toward the other flat. "We're behind sked, Skipper."

I already knew whose fault that was—mine. I motioned for him to get his ass in gear. "Go-go-go—" Howie charged down the stairs to run interference. I followed him unsteadily, keeping as close as I could with Azziz's inert form bouncing on my shoulder like the proverbial sack of shit. I misstepped on the ground-floor landing and turned my ankle but kept moving. I love pain—it makes me realize I'm still alive.

I came out the front door and discovered empty street. More bad juju. Doom on me. Where the hell was Wonder? I looked up and down. Nada. Nothing. You can never find a fucking taxi when you need one. I hit the call button again, praying as I did so.

There is a technical phrase for our condition: it is known as goatfucked. Think of it as a painting, entitled *Five Assholes and a Tango Waiting for Shit to Happen.*

Fuck that. Inaction breeds failure. "Move out." There was a single streetlight about 150 feet to my left, casting nasty shadows. Five hundred feet behind that, the narrow, unpaved street came to a dead end. Somewhere close by, a pack of dogs howled. I started jogging to my right, hobbling toward an intersection I knew Wonder would have to pass.

I heard the growl of Duck Foot's and Tommy T's motorbikes. They roared past me, spitting dirt as they took point. The rest of the team fanned out in a rough diamond pattern around me. At least we'd die together.

Movement on my shoulder. Azziz woke up and started screaming in rapid Arabic. That's all I needed. I flipped him onto the ground, applied a choker hold, and he went limp again. But not before half a dozen lights came on in half a dozen windows.

I have a vivid imagination. The things I was doing to Wonder in my head at this moment would have made Torquemada queasy. I gritted my teeth and kept moving.

We reached the intersection and jammed ourselves into a doorway, sweating. Tommy went right, Duck Foot sped off left, up the hill toward the Citadel, to search for Doc and Wonder.

It seemed like an eternity—like the endless waits during ambushes in Vietnam when I'd lie soaked and cold in the jungle waiting for Charlie to show himself. Back then, we'd sometimes wait for two or three hours. We couldn't afford more than a couple of minutes here.

I heard a car. Lights doused, Wonder careened into the intersection and did a bootlegger's turn, coming to a full stop fifty feet from us, his right foot pedal to the metal gunning the engine in neutral. "Yo, Dickhead—over here!"

We were at the Peugeot in less than five seconds. Doc already had the rear gate up. I hobbled up. Doc grappled Azziz by the shoulders, then Howie tossed my ass unceremoniously northward, crammed his bulk next to me, and pulled the gate shut from inside. Nasty rode shotgun, his HK on his lap. Wonder slid the wagon into gear, accelerating steadily so as not to disturb Doc, who was already popping Azziz in the upper arm with the syringe.

"What the *fuck*, Wonder?"

Wonder's face turned toward me. It was bathed in sweat. "Goddamn motor died, Skipper. This piece of shit ain't worth the bald, pus-filled tires it's running on. Doc had to push so's I could jump-start the cocksucker."

I wasn't in the mood for any goddamn excuses. "Weren't you supposed to fix the sucker, asshole?" I pulled both sets of rear-window curtains shut, giving us some privacy. By now, Duck Foot and Tommy would be heading for the rendezvous spot we'd picked just past the Giza circle. There, we'd ditch the bikes, roll our cargo into a nice camel rug I'd bought at the Khan al-Khalil market, transfer him into the trunk of Doc Tremblay's car, which had the luxury of diplomatic plates and a decent engine. Then we'd head both cars up to Alexandria for our exfiltration to sea *en convoy.*

The air was cool—midfifties—but I was still sweating buckets. My heart was pumping a steady 160 or so. My ankle ached. My lip hurt like hell. I felt my temple, where a huge, painful, spongy knot about the size of an egg had begun to materialize. I wiped the blood from my face, cleared my bloody nose on my tunic, then inhaled slowly and deeply to slow my respiration.

Was I happy? Is the Pope Polish? Do wild bears shit in the forest?

I caught Wonder staring at me in the rearview mirror, a hurt expression on his face. What the fuck, we were alive. I threw him the bird so he'd know I forgave him. He gave me an exuberant, relieved wink. I returned it with as much energy as I could muster and a hearty, "Fuck you, dipshit no-load worthless ex-Marine asshole," which brought a broad smile to his ugly face.

Doc ran a quick check on the now comatose Azziz. He splinted the tango's broken fingers, checked for fractured ribs, and held his eyelids open while he checked pupil dilation. When he'd finished, he peered at my bloody features critically. "What the hell happened to you?"

I told him. He stifled a giggle and shone a penlight in my eyes. *"Entiymah feeshmok*—you have no brains." He turned my face left, then right, clucking like an Arab *emeq*—hen. "You've gotta be the clumsiest son of a bitch who ever lived, y'know? You're lucky you don't have a friggin' concussion." He slipped tape and dressing out of his vest and tended to my battered features. "You know, Dick," he said, "you're like a gawddamn bad penny—you just keep coming back."

"Doom on you, Doc," I said affectionately, telling him to go fuck himself in Vietnamese. "You're the one who's always willing to make change."

After he'd finished his ministrations, I knelt like a Muslim in prayer, rested my elbows on the front seat, and peered out through the windshield. We were making good time as we raced through the empty streets, snaking past the occasional lorry.

We chugged along the es-Sayala, past the Salah ed-Din mosque, and onto the el-Gami'a bridge. Just on the far side of the bridge was a broad, six-lane avenue that ran south past the university to the circle where we'd bear right and head toward the Alexandria Road.

Except, there was a roadblock halfway across the bridge. A

sandbag maze had been built. I could see two machine-gun positions. Behind them sat an armored personnel carrier with 20mm cannon pointed in our direction.

"What the fuck—"

"Roving spot check."

"Like I said, what the fuck?"

"They set these up randomly at night. Looking for fundamentalists, I guess," Doc Tremblay said.

We were about to be clusterfucked by Mr. Murphy. Doom on Dickie.

I considered the possibilities. If we turned and ran now, we'd only draw attention to ourselves. The only thing to do was bluff our way through.

I tapped Stevie. "Keep moving. Go slow. And take that stupid Egyptian hat off."

The fellah cap disappeared. Quickly, we rolled Azziz onto the floor just in back of the front seat. Nasty and Howie put their feet on top of him.

We eased into the bright, generator-driven lights of the roadblock. An officer in fatigues, flak jacket, and Beretta M-12 submachine gun slung horizontally over his right shoulder waved for us to slow down.

Stevie waved back.

The officer held up his hand. Wonder brought us to a halt. The Egyptian peered into the car. We five grungy gringos stared back. I saluted. "Hi."

Doc said, "How're ya doin?"

"What's happenin'?" Stevie asked.

The officer waved a second man over and they conferred in Arabic. Nasty and Howie leaned forward, the better to camouflage Azziz's body with their own.

The Egyptian asked Stevie something in Arabic. Wonder's palms went up and he shrugged: "I'm American. I speak English."

"You *Ameerica?*" The Egyptian looked down at Wonder critically and spoke haltingly. "Where you are go?"

Wonder shifted slightly behind the wheel. "We are tourists," he explained as if speaking to a three-year-old. "Pyramids. We are go to pyramids."

The officer considered what Wonder'd said. He smiled. He nodded. "Pyramids," he repeated.

"Right."

He hooked his thumb toward the opposite bridge railing. "Getting out."

"Huh?"

"Outing. Show passport, please." He backed away from the car slightly. As I watched, the Beretta on his shoulder came level with the windows, and his finger slipped from the trigger guard onto the trigger itself. I knew that six pounds of pressure was all he needed to make hamburger out of us all. I started making mental calculations about how many of the ten soldiers at the roadblock we could take out if it became necessary.

We'd hit the two officers and four machine gunners first—they posed the greatest threats. The other four, who were carrying AK-47s, looked like your average conscripts. We could do 'em on the second go-round.

As for the APC—well, I hoped Doc had at least one grenade hidden somewhere on his person.

My hand moved down my leg toward the USP. I held my breath. I'd take the officer with a double tap—then the second one.

"Doc—"

Doc Tremblay's lips barely moved. "I'll do the right machine gun."

"Nasty—" I tapped Grundle's shoulder. "You've got the left one."

"Check."

Stevie opened his door. I hoped he'd concealed the hush puppy.

He stood up. He stretched. He lifted the hem of his gallebiyah, dug into his jeans pocket, and extracted a well-worn blue passport, which he handed to the officer.

The guy held it upside down, which gave me a pretty good idea about his command of written English. Still, he pawed through it with dogged determination until he came to the Egyptian visa. He studied the writing. Then he smiled and handed Wonder the passport back.

"Tourist," he said with a big smile on his face. "American tourist. Welcome to Egypt." He actually embraced Wonder, kissing him on both cheeks. Then he stood back and saluted.

Stevie returned the gesture, a big smile on his face.

"I guess that means we're on our way to the pyramids," I said loudly. "Let's go, Stevie boy."

That's when the fucking Peugeot died.

"Stevie . . ."

"I know, I know." He hit the ignition. Nothing.

He turned the key again. This time we got a weak groan as the starter coughed, wheezed, coughed again, then finally caught. He revved the engine, slid the car into gear, and we moved off, waving like assholes and grinning Louis Armstrong smiles at the Egyptian soldiers.

By the time we cleared the university circle, the sky was changing—from the blue-black of night to the distinctive purple-rose glow that presages sunrise in the desert. I took the big manila envelope from my stowage pocket and examined its contents.

There was an Egyptian passport. I flipped through it. He had recently received a Pakistani visa. I counted the money. Azziz had been given fifty thousand English pounds—$75,000. What was it for? Had he already earned it, or was it a down payment for services to be rendered? Well, he'd tell us, sooner or later.

I put my back up against the rear door, tucked my chin against my knees, closed my eyes, listened to the throbbing of tom-toms in my head, and thought about the possibility that I might be getting too old for these kinds of full-contact diversions.

Moi? Too old? No fucking way.

Chapter

2

I TOOK A FIFTEEN-MINUTE COMBAT NAP ONCE WE LEFT GIZA AND HIT THE desert highway to Alexandria. Despite the occasional brush with Mr. Murphy, things had gone pretty smoothly to this point. Score one for the SEALs.

Yeah—that's us. Navy SEALs. We're on the books as Naval Special Warfare SEa-Air-Land units, although I've always believed the acronym stands for Sleep, Eat, And Live it up. The little brood of killers I command, however, isn't on anybody's books.

I'd created it myself—carved three platoons—that's forty-eight men—off from SEAL Team Six and disappeared into the ether. Vanished off everyone's organizational charts, into the black hole of covert operations.

Why? Because America needs a unit like this to do jobs like the one we'd just done. Frankly, there are too many SpecWarriors these days—more than ten thousand of them when you count the Army's Special Forces, the Air Force Special Operations Air Wing, U.S. Marine Expeditionary Units' SOC (Special Operations Capable) forces, and the Navy's SEAL teams. There are so many SEALs at SEAL Team Six these days that it takes the unit a full day and a half to mobilize, instead of the four hours from call to out-the-door when I was in charge.

Moreover, because there are so many, and they're so versatile, the system tends to forget the sole reason SpecWarriors were created in the first place. Which is, to kill. We are not armed guards or peacekeepers; we do not pacify a region or occupy a zone.

My job is to infiltrate a hostile area and kill as many of the enemy as I can, without his knowing that I'm even around, then get away without leaving any fingerprints.

But don't tell such things to the folks who run the Pentagon these days. Most of 'em believe that killing's a bad thing—unless you do it with words.

In point of fact, the system has almost always used us special-operations types as shock troops—in other words, as rapid-deployment forces. That's akin to employing a team of neurosurgeons to inoculate cattle. Sure, they can do it—but what a waste of talent.

Knowing the system's flaws, I created SEAL Team Six. At the moment of its birth, Six was made up of seventy-two seasoned shooters with a well-defined, single-purpose mission: counter-terror. Translation: hit the bad guys before they hit us. How many times has it been used that way? The answer is classified. But it's less than the fingers on one hand.

Five years later, I created Red Cell, a fourteen-man unit with a two-tier responsibility. Red Cell's primary mission was to test the vulnerabilities of naval installations worldwide against terrorist attack. Our other assignment—code-word secret at the time—was to slip away in pairs and neutralize bad guys before they had a chance to hit American targets.

But those days are gone now. Red Cell was disbanded late last year. Not cost-effective, according to the new powers that be at the Pentagon. And what have the more than five hundred SEALs at SEAL Team Six been doing instead of waxing bad guys? The unhappy fact is that, most recently, they've often been used as an extension of the State Department, assigned to the Bureaus of Diplomatic Security, and "Thugs and Drugs."

That means they do such things as teach African cops how to establish SWAT teams, run after cocaine smugglers in Peru and Bolivia, or train a professional presidential bodyguard corps in Turkey. Shit, in Turkey they were pulled off bodyguard training so they could go help locate earthquake victims.

Well, so far as I'm concerned, if you want to train policemen in

Kinshasa, join the Agency for International Development. If you want to chase cocaine smugglers in the Andes, apply to the DEA or FBI. And if you want to deploy as a rescue worker, become a goddamn Boy Scout.

Luckily for me, CNO thinks the way I do. He fought hard to get me the authority I needed to create Green Team. That meant a lot to me. But he went the extra mile: he fought even harder to keep me and my men outside the normal Navy chain of command. I report to CNO, and through him, to the secretary of defense and the president. No one else.

In conventional warfare, a well-defined chain of command is all-important. In Somalia—remember Somalia?—the chain of command for U.S. forces was a clusterfuck, because there wasn't one. At one point early in the Somalia escapade, for example, a platoon of Marines discovered a huge arms cache belonging to one of Mogadishu's top thugs, Mohammed Aideed. They were under orders to blow all the arms caches they found, but an Aideed aide on the scene convinced the young platoon lieutenant to call the U.S. embassy, where some asshole staffer told him that one of our special ambassadors in Mogadishu had indeed made a side deal with Aideed—they'd agreed that if the warlord kept his arms caches locked up in warehouses, we wouldn't destroy them. "Don't blow it up," the staffer ordered.

What the lieutenant should have answered was, "If you're not wearing railroad tracks [captain's bars], [colonel's] eagles, or [general's] stars on your collar, you can go fuck yourself, sir." Then he should have pulled the pin on the willy-peter grenade he held in his hand, popped the spoon, counted to three, and rolled it into the warehouse.

Then, he should have said to the Somali asshole, "If you can unscrew the fuse out of that fucking grenade in the next four seconds, go ahead and do it. And if you can't, your fucking warehouse is about to blow, because those were my goddamn orders."

But the lieutenant didn't do that. He spared the warehouse. After half a dozen similar instances, Aideed was able to convince a lot of Somalis that he was actually just as powerful—perhaps even more powerful—than the Americans with all their troops and sophisticated weaponry. They believed him. And when they did, the assignment in Somalia began an inevitable descent from humanitarian mission into absurd clusterfuck.

Why? Because, when you diagrammed the chain of command in Somalia, it looked like a goddamn Rube Goldberg design. There were U.N. military commanders and American special ambassadors and U.N. political types and generals from the Pentagon, all vying for control of forces that used different radio frequencies, ammunition, and spoke in half a dozen languages. For a while, the pretty boy White House communications director issued rules of engagement by long-distance phone to the American forces that patrolled south Mogadishu. There was a so-called unified command, but it was composed of Italians, Nigerians, Pakistanis, Americans, Brits, and French—with no one taking responsibility for anything.

At one point the Nigerians and Italians went out on a joint patrol. The Nigerians got hit by snipers—lost half a dozen men.

What did the Italians do? They watched.

So who suffered the most? Not the generals, admirals, or ambassadors, believe me. Nor the folks at the White House, whose participation was never reported. It was grunts who got killed. And why did they die? They died because no one took fucking responsibility. They were commanded by committee.

If there had been a well-defined chain of command, like the one we'd set up during Desert Storm, things would have worked better. Not perfectly, because war is an imprecise goddamn science, filled with that unpredictable "fog of war" that Clausewitz, the great Prussian philosopher of warfare, called *"la friction."* But fewer soldiers would have died, fewer families would have had to bury their sons. Chain of command is important. End of sermon.

Having said that, let me now add that in SpecWar, you can't utilize the normal chain of command, because there are too many levels, which slows down reaction time to an unacceptable velocity. Unconventional warfare demands a swift-reaction, unconventional chain of command, which is exactly what CNO and I devised for my unit. My chain of command is simple: the president or the secretary of defense talks to CNO, and CNO talks to me.

CNO engineered this unique chain of command on my behalf despite the absolute, clear, and emphatic opposition of his deputy, the newly frocked vice admiral Pinckney Prescott III, A/VCNO, or

Assistant Vice Chief of Naval Operations. But that was to be expected.

Pinky da Turd, as I like to call him, is the son and grandson of admirals. Pinky da Foist was foisted on the Navy because, as a pseudo-aristocrat from a Philadelphia Main Line family sans benefit of trust fund, he had to make a living. So they sent him to Annapolis. Little Pinky II followed in his daddy's black-shoe steps twenty-five years later, and—as if to prove the Peter Principle once and for all—Pinky da Turd, Annapolis '72, brought up the rear. Luckily for the nation, Mrs. Pinky da Turd, the former Harriet Lickadick Suckacock of Blue Balls, Pennsylvania, has whelped no children. Anyway, somehow, after Annapolis, Pinky managed to survive BUD/S training and become a SEAL. Well, let's be honest. He wears the same trident that I do. But he's never been in combat. He's never led men from the front. He's never done anything in the military but fight paper wars, which makes him the epitome of the Can't Cunt CO—a lard-assed, worthless, shit-for-brains turd-bucket staff puke. Am I making myself clear yet?

He's been the bane of my existence since I commanded SEAL Team Six, and he was grand panjandrum of NAVSPECWARGRU TWO—that's the commodore of NAVal SPECial WARfare GRoUp TWO to the uninitiated among you. A by-the-book officer whose forte lies in memo writing, Pinky tried everything in his power to get me court-martialed for insubordination when I was CO of Six. When that failed, he spent $60 million of the Navy's money to investigate me. When nothing turned up and I retired with a full pension, he gave my files to the U.S. attorney general's office.

I thought once I'd retired from the Navy, Pinky would be purged from my life. But roughly two years ago, he—and, as I discovered much later, CNO—engineered my unwilling recall to active duty. I was shanghaied to solve a slight problem: a batch of missing nuclear Tomahawk cruise missiles. It was only temporary, they said at the time.

Well, my "temporary" assignment has lasted more than a year. Sure, Pinky was able to disband Red Cell. But he wasn't able to stop me from creating another small unit of real shooters to satisfy the critical counterterror mission in which CNO and I believe so strongly. Indeed, despite all da Turd's clout I slipped down to Dam Neck, Virginia, where SEAL Team Six is currently based, and made off with four dozen old-fashioned shoot-and-looters.

Moreover, regardless of Pinky's absolute, categorical and un-equivocal orders to the contrary, Green Team operates out of my two-hundred-plus acres of snakes and lakes behind Rogue Manor, where I've built a passable kill-house and functional twenty-five-yard pistol and hundred-yard submachine-gun ranges. I've got room for fifty shooters in the converted barn, a weight pile outdoors, and a universal machine with half a ton of iron in the basement next to my sauna. There are two Jacuzzis—indoor or outdoor, take your pick—a twenty-four-foot wet bar, and no less than twenty cases of Coors Light and Stroh's on hand at all times.

I get away with it because CNO doesn't mind where we bunk, just so long as we get the job done. Pinky, on the other hand, gets hemorrhoids just knowing that I'm off the reservation. He deserves each and every one of them. After all, it was Pinky who took all the credit for solving the Case of the Missing Tomahawks. He got himself frocked for another star—frocking means that he wears three stars but gets paid as a rear admiral because he hasn't gone through Senate confirmation yet.

Simultaneously, he engineered the A/VCNO billet for himself and said, "Thank you for everything, Dickie," by putting Red Cell, the unit I conceived and designed to test the Navy's antiterror capabilities, out of business permanently. He got frocked, and I got frucked. Typical.

Wonder threaded the Peugeot into Alexandria shortly after 0800, and we linked up with Doc Tremblay and the others on the eastern edge of the Corniche 26 July, which runs along the Med. The boat we'd chartered was tied up below the Maritime railroad station in the Western Harbor, about two miles and six minutes away. I knew it was six minutes away because we'd driven the route twice at this same time.

Except today, Alexandria was in gridlock. Nothing was moving. It took us six minutes to go half a block—eight lanes of traffic crammed into a four-lane street. Fifty minutes later, we'd inched another three blocks and were now embedded in the middle of a humongous traffic jam halfway around Midan Tahrir (Tahrir Square) directly in front of the central bus station. Since then, despite the wild gesticulating of half a dozen traffic police in black uniforms, and a cacophony of horns that made all conversation impossible, nothing had moved.

I was getting nervous. What the hell would happen if Azziz, rolled in the rug in the trunk of Doc's car, suffocated from exhaust fumes—the fucking square was blue with diesel smoke, and catalytic converters are unknown in Egypt. I didn't need a corpse on my hands right now.

Worse, what would happen if he regained consciousness and started banging on the trunk lid? We didn't need that problem either.

Doc's sedan was two vehicles ahead of me, but the cars on either side of us were so close I couldn't open the door. I climbed out the hatchback of the Peugeot and threaded my way past a horse-drawn wagonload of carrots and a huge tank truck to where Doc's Mercedes idled.

Doc rolled down the window. "What you want to do?"

"I'm worried about our package."

He nodded. "Me, too. I'd like to slip him some water."

Now, I wished I'd kept the motorcycles instead of jettisoning them just outside Cairo—Tommy could have gone ahead to see what the hell was going on and found us an alternate route. Now, we were just fucking stuck.

"What do you wanna do, Skipper?"

There wasn't much we could do. "Wait and pray," I said.

I was halfway back to the station wagon when my beeper went off.

I pulled it from my waistband and checked the digital readout. The number I saw was attached to the phone on Pinky Prescott's desk.

He had no authority over me, so screw him—let him wait. I hit the cancel button. Ten seconds later, the fucking thing went off again.

Six calls and three minutes later, I decided to let him have his way with me. Shit—our fucking car wasn't going anywhere.

I pointed toward the bus station. "I'm going to use the phone before this asshole gets us all caught."

Why not just turn the goddamn thing off? you ask. Good question. The answer is because I can't turn it off. CNO had it designed specifically for me. He knows that I like to operate UNODIR, which means I take my shooters and go off after leaving a message behind that says, more or less, "Dear Officer in Charge:

UNODIR [UNless Otherwise DIRected], I'm gonna kill a few bad guys today."

Well, this little Motorola on my hip is the leash that keeps me chained to CNO. If he doesn't like my UNODIR, he can get hold of me—anytime, anyplace in the world—and shut me down.

It doesn't always beep. If I'm in the middle of something delicate, I can change the fucking thing from a beeper to a vibrator. But I can't turn it off. I tried losing it about six months ago, but CNO had an answer for that, too. He said that if I lost the goddamn thing, I'd lose my captaincy and my men would be scattered to other units. That made me sit up and take notice. See, I don't give a shit about rank or the salary attached to it. Hell, *Rogue Warrior* made me a dump-truck-load of cash, and the sequel, *Rogue Warrior: Red Cell*, did even better. So, I'm not doing this for money.

I'm doing it because Pinky, whose vocabulary is filled with words like *downsizing* and phrases like *doing more with less* was only too happy to follow the secretary of defense's directive. Hence, he decommissioned Red Cell six months ago as part of what he called a cost-cutting measure at Naval Special Warfare. I believe he was dead wrong to do so. The only way to prove it was to stay active, work for CNO, and fight for my point of view.

Counterterror—CT in Navyspeak—so far as Pinky is concerned, is a nonstarter. His view—shared, incidentally, by many of today's Navy hierarchy, and Pentagon bosses—is that CT is not cost-effective, so it can be jettisoned without losing efficiency. CT is expensive and disruptive. It requires expensive, intensive, danger-ous training. People die. And you spend a lot of money without seeing tangible results. What Pinky doesn't seem to understand is that a "tangible result" is when some fucking tango doesn't blow up an aircraft carrier at Norfolk or passes on assassinating some four-star asshole in Naples or decides against hijacking a plane from Point Mugu Naval Air Station.

Anyway, when Red Cell was disbanded, the Navy's capability to train base commanders to defend against terror was—for all intents and purposes—lost. It was lost because Pinky had ensured that there would be no counterterror "institutional memory" left. No one to tell base commanders, "Well, we ate you alive in 1990, came back and chewed you up in 1994, and now we're back to show you the latest in tango infiltration techniques and how to counter them."

CNO, bless him, saw merit in my argument that we still needed a CT capability. That's why I was able to take my Red Cell shooters out of Dam Neck limbo and form the nucleus of Green Team. He knows I don't work for money or glory. He knows I'm not interested in making admiral or guaranteeing my pension. He knew I was doing this because I believed in the mission, and I believed in my men, and if I had to swallow a little shit to keep my mission on track and my unit integrity integral, I'd close my eyes and chew. CNO knows me well enough to know that I adhere to the same commandment I make my men obey. The one that says, "Thou hast not to like it, thou hast just to do it."

I shouldered my way inside the station and found the Téléphone et Télégraphe Centrale desk. There were two hundred people in line. I charged back outside. Off to my left I saw a hotel marquee. I dashed inside and went straight to the desk. A corpulent clerk, cigarette in an onyx holder, looked up at me. The bored face of the petit bourgeois staring at a television set on the counter behind him.

"*Min fadlaak. Fee telefoon?*—Please, do you have a telephone?"

He turned toward me. "Are you a guest?"

"No."

He shook his head. "*Asif*—I'm sorry. The telephones are for guests only."

"It's an emergency."

He shrugged. "I am sorry."

The picture on the screen caught my eye because it contained a Navy vessel. It looked familiar—an aircraft carrier I'd seen before. I pointed. "What's that?"

"CNN." Carefully, the clerk flicked the end of his cigarette into a brass ashtray. "An incident somewhere in England." He shook his head. "Bad."

"Could you turn it up, please?"

He shrugged. "Of course." He waddled the six feet to the set and slowly, slowly rotated the volume knob. The camera reverse-zoomed, and I realized that I was looking at the main dock at the Royal Navy base at Portsmouth. CNO was there this week as a guest of his old friend Sir Norman Elliott, Britain's Admiral of the Fleet, to participate in the decommissioning of the aircraft carrier HMS *Mountbatten*, aboard which CNO had served during an

34

exchange tour with the Royal Navy in the early seventies. A lot of smoke was still evident. It must have been a hell of an explosion.

". . . extent of the damage. The bomb exploded under the *Mountbatten*'s gangway just as the American chief of naval operations and the Admiral of the Fleet made their way aboard. In all, thirty-six were killed, sixty-eight wounded . . ."

I realized why Pinky'd been beeping me.

I guess I looked pretty bad when I told the guys what had happened, because Doc suggested I might need something to calm me down. I waved him off and called for a rapid head-shed right in the middle of the fucking traffic jam. Despite my orders to complete this mission, we'd split up. Nothing was going to keep me from going after CNO's assassins. So—Tommy would handle the rendezvous and tango transfer. I'd haul balls for London and find out who'd done CNO. Then we'd assemble and kill the assholes, soonest. The list of suspects wasn't all that long—the IRA was topmost, followed closely by the same fundamentalist sort of Muslim stashed in Doc's car.

It didn't matter. Whoever they were, they were going to die.

We made arrangements to link up in London within seventy-two hours. "Call Command Master Chief Weber at CINCUSNAVEUR," I told Tommy. Hans Weber, an old friend and a master scrounger, was the senior enlisted man working for the Commander-IN-Chief, U.S. NAVal Forces, EURope. He'd be able to get them on a flight from Sigonella once they'd dropped Azziz off. And he'd always know where I was.

I grabbed a change of clothes and a nylon rucksack and jogged away from the traffic jam to find a cab to Alexandria's small airport. If I could grab a flight to Cairo by 1100, I knew I'd be able to catch the 1400 Egyptair to London and be there by nightfall. The goddamn beeper went off again. Well, there'd be plenty of time to call Pinky from Cairo International. Frankly, I didn't give a flying F-word about what he wanted.

Chapter

3

THE PLANE BANKED AND DESCENDED OVER WINDSOR CASTLE THROUGH sheeting rain and bounced three times before it finally settled down on the runway at Heathrow, reversed its thrusters, and taxied to the gate. I came up the bridge to find the impeccably turned-out, even-featured, perfect 38-short frame of Lieutenant Commander Randy Rayman waiting for me, holding a black-covered diplomatic passport with my picture in it. He proffered it between the first two fingers of his right hand, probably so he wouldn't have to touch me. Well, I *was* pretty ripe.

Randy is another of those pretty-boy Annapolis staff puke SEALs who's never been blooded in battle, but loves to talk tough, swagger, and flaunt his Budweiser when he's prowling and growling outside the SpecWar community. He's also a legend in his own mind where women are concerned. I say in his own mind because just about a year ago, his wife of eight months up and left him for an enlisted man at SEAL Team Four.

When I formed SEAL Team Six, Randy'd been a young pup lieutenant who'd come to Papa and begged to be included—as an administrative officer. I turned him down—after all, I had no admin slots, only shooter positions. Besides, he wasn't my type. He was a weak-chinned, five-o'clock-shadowed whiner who always had an excuse for not getting something done. He thought he was better than his men, when it was his men who'd always made him look good. Most significantly, he wanted to be part of Six not because he wanted to kill bad guys, but because he thought the assignment would look good on his record. I gave him a no-shitter that more or less went, "So solly, sailor, we don't have any tickee-punchee billets," and booted his ass out the door.

I may have rejected him. But a subsequent CO didn't. Currently, he's the duty DEVGRP SEAL at CINCUSNAVEUR—in English, that means that Randy's the SEAL Team Six detailee to the office of the Commander-IN-Chief, U.S. NAVal Forces, EURope. CINCUSNAVEUR is located across Grosvenor Square from the U.S. embassy, in General Dwight D. Eisenhower's World War II headquarters building on North Audley Street. His detail, or assignment, is to advise the CINC on SpecWar and counterterror options, to interface with his corresponding numbers, encourage tactical and strategic cooperation, maintain active liaison in the field, and report fully on all activities.

That's what it says on the books. As for advising the CINC about unconventional warfare and terrorism, Randy couldn't design the scenario for a picnic. And according to the gossip back at Dam Neck, his self-described "duties" included lunching at clubs with foreign service and Foreign Ministry types, making small talk at embassy cocktail parties, and serving as a charming partner for unaccompanied females at the ambassador's twice-a-week diplomatic dinners.

Instead of looking on his assignment as a challenge, he'd taken it as a vacation. So, once every four weeks or so he had a formal meeting with his SpecWar counterparts at the British MOD, or Ministry of Defense. Every six months he spent three hours with SAS 22 Regiment at Hereford and scheduled three hours with the Royal Marines' Special Boat Squadron unit at Poole.

When he finishes his assignment here, he's slotted to be given command of a SEAL team. Maybe he'll be able to teach his men how to waltz and eat hors d'oeuvres.

I'm familiar with the type. When I was the naval attaché in Phnom Penh back in the seventies, I spent thirteen months in Cambodia and logged 287 days of combat. One of my successors, a socially minded chap I'll call Lieutenant Lounge Lizard, logged zero days in combat. On the other hand, he spent 314 consecutive afternoons at the *cercle sportif,* the city's most exclusive swim club, chatting up the local gentry and posting MEMCONs—those are MEMoranda of CONversations for you nondiplomatic types out there—filled with his version of intelligence factoids and info-bits back to Washington. Guess which one of us made admiral and which one they spent $60 million to investigate.

"Thanks." I slid the passport into the breast pocket of my leather jacket and clapped Randy on the shoulder by way of greeting since he didn't appear to want to shake my hand. We headed down the long passageway leading to Immigration and Customs. "What's up? I need a real no-shitter."

"Bad juju, Dick. The Admiralty's batshit—they don't know what the hell happened. No one's even claimed responsibility. Our office is going crazy, too—CINC's back at Bethesda. Gallbladder surgery. He's out of commission for a month. But things'll sort themselves out: A/VCNO arrived by Concorde this afternoon with a dozen of NIS's top-grade security investigators. They're gathering intel, writing reports, and trying to make sense out of what's happened."

Sense? They'd screw it all up. Pinky'd wasted $2,500 a ticket to bring in a bunch of no-loads from the Naval Investigative Services Command, when he should have brought worker bees—DIA analysts and SEAL shooters. Naval Investigative Services? The name is a fucking oxymoron. This is the very same NIS, gentle reader, that has managed to clusterfuck every investigation in which it's been involved, from the Johnny Walker/Jerry Whitworth spy ring, to the Moscow embassy fiasco, to the Jonathan Pollard case, to spending *$60 million*—yeah, you heard me, 60 million—of your tax dollars to witch-hunt yours truly.

This is the very same Naval Investigative Service that is called the Admirals' Gestapo, because admirals use NIS to settle political scores and turf wars by tapping each other's phones, reading each other's mail, and launching investigations of each other, the way Mafia capos use hit men to settle la Cosa Nostra's internecine power struggles.

I shook my head. "Where is Pinky?"

"He's using the CINC's office. When I left, he was on his way to dinner with Sir Aubrey Hanscomb Davis."

"The monocle man from MOD?"

Randy's eyebrows rose in surprise. "You *know* Sir Aubrey? I can't even get an appointment with him."

Knowing Randy, that figured. "We've met." Sir Aubrey Hanscomb Davis was the supergrade spook from the Ministry of Defense who carried the SpecWar portfolio. I'd been introduced to him at former secretary of defense Grant Griffith's house just about a year ago. He had all the warmth of a kipper and a personality to match. He and Pinky must be getting along like long-lost brothers.

I gave the British immigration officer a hard time. Well, I didn't—my picture did. The diplomatic passport Randy'd given me had an ancient photo—whitewall haircut and dress uniform. I guess that's what they had on file at CINCUSNAVEUR. The immigration lady looking over the narrow countertop didn't see much spit and polish. What she got instead was shit and Polish: a maniacal-looking wild man, with a golf-ball-sized black-and-blue knot on his forehead, foot-long pigtail, and certain ripeness of body.

I grinned and pointed at the passport. "That's not the real me," I said, leaning closer. "This is the real me."

She retreated as much as her stool allowed. *"Hmmm."* She wasn't convinced. She waved a supervisor over. They conferred. They checked the computer. Finally, she stamped my passport and waved me on.

I met Randy, who was obviously smirking in a no-smirking zone on the far side of the gate, and we headed out toward the taxi stand, where an embassy car sat, creating a small logjam in the light evening traffic. He gave me his version of events during the forty-minute ride, although in point of fact he knew precious little. CNO had arrived three days ago. He'd traveled light—three aides and two security men. They all checked into the Marriott on Grosvenor Square, so they could be close to the embassy and right next door to CINCUSNAVEUR.

The night he'd arrived, CNO hosted a cocktail reception in his suite for his friends in HM's armed forces and a select number of resident U.S. military personnel. He'd seemed to be enjoying himself immensely. The second day, he'd met for three hours with his British counterparts at the Admiralty on Whitehall, then had a lunch of poached Scottish salmon, *haricots verts*, buttered boiled new potatoes, and Pouilly-Fuissé with the former prime minister in the Grill Room at the Connaught Hotel. He'd met privately with Sir Aubrey Davis for three hours in the afternoon at the Ministry of Defense, then been guest of honor at a formal Royal Navy reception that lasted late into the evening at the huge Naval and Military Club on Piccadilly.

He'd been in a sunny mood at 0600 this morning when Randy'd escorted him to his car. CNO was driven into Hyde Park, where Admiral Sir Norman Elliott, the Admiral of the Fleet, sat in a Royal Navy chopper that had landed on a two-acre plot of greensward cordoned off by Special Branch. The two old friends flew off together, and that was the last Randy saw of him.

That was all very good if I'd been a social columnist. What about some intel I could use? Who were the pus-nutted motherfuckers who'd killed him? What were the Brits really doing? What were we doing? "What the hell's going on, Randy?"

Randy didn't know. Nothing was certain. On the one hand, the IRA hadn't taken credit for the bombing, so it was unlikely they'd done it. On the other hand, no one else had claimed responsibility either.

"What do your friends at MI5 say? What about Special Branch?" MI5 was Britain's domestic intelligence-gathering and law-enforcement agency. Special Branch was responsible for Scotland Yard's antiterror activities.

The look Randy gave me told me that he had no "friends" at MI5—or anywhere else. What the fuck this no-load shit-for-brains can't cunt had been doing here besides sipping sherry, I couldn't imagine.

"Hereford?" That was headquarters for the 22 SAS Regiment. The Special Projects team at SAS, a forty-eight-man unit devoted to fighting terrorism, had to be working full-time on this.

"I called down there this afternoon—talked to the duty officer. He said they didn't have anything for me right now—they were still developing information."

That made sense—why share intelligence with an asshole. "What about Poole?" That was where the Royal Marines Special Boat Squadron units were headquartered.

"I called down there, too. The CO's a friend of mine. Geoff Lyondale."

"And?" I was getting fucking impatient.

"He hasn't gotten back to me yet."

I made up my mind to do my own intel gathering. Obviously, young Randy Rayman wasn't going to be any help. In fact, he'd probably muddied the waters already. That didn't make me very happy. We pulled up on Grosvenor Square. We extricated ourselves from the limo. I took a gander at the huge American embassy building, then wheeled toward the CINCUSNAVEUR entrance on North Audley. "I want a suite at the Marriott," I told Randy. "I want an office, a secure fax and phone, three cars, and six Heckler & Koch USP nine-millimeter pistols. I've got half a dozen men on their way already."

"Suite? Cars? Guns? Dick, that's impossible."

I wasn't in the mood for "impossible." I took him by the lapels of his impeccably pressed uniform blouse, jammed him up against the decorative eight-foot wrought-iron spikes that bordered Ike's old HQ building on the Square, and pulled his face close until we were touching noses. "Hey, shit-for-brains, I don't think you heard me. I want a suite at the Marriott, a secure phone and fax, three cars, and six USP nines, or I'm going to fucking break you into little fucking pieces and stuff you into the fucking storm drain right now—do I make myself fucking loud and fucking clear?"

The look in my eyes must have convinced him I was serious, because his Adam's apple went up and down like a fucking bobber, and he gulped, "Y-y-y-yes, sir," at me. He even spelled it s-i-r, not c-u-r.

I released him and he squirmed out of reach. "I'm glad we understand each other, Randy. Now get the fuck out of my sight, you worthless cockbreath, and get me checked in—I have real work to do."

I hustled my ass around the corner to North Audley Street. I flashed my ID at the plainclothes Marine behind his bulletproof glass, received a visitor's ID, slid it through the electronic turnstile, and marched inside. I took the elevator to the second floor, where CINCUSNAVEUR's command master chief had his goat locker.

The name on the door plate read MMCM H. WEBER. I knocked thrice and waited.

An impatient growl emanated from inside. "Come."

I stuck my head through the doorway. "I'd come if I could, but I'm not breathing hard yet, Hansie, you no-load dipshit motherfucker blackshoe fucking Nazi."

A yard of smile spread across the ugly face behind the desk on the far side of the office. "Captain Dickhead—sir."

It was nice to be treated with such respect. He came around his desk and grabbed me—lifted me clear off the deck, waltzed me around again, Willy, hugged the hell out of me, then put me back on the ground.

Hans Weber is one of the chiefs in the informal network of old Navy fleet sailors I refer to as my Safety Net. He's a master chief machinist's mate now, but when I served with him on the DD-1030—the USS *Joseph K. Taussig*—he was a shy, gangly twerp E-3 fireman. And that, friends, is one step up from being a smudge of soot.

The *Taussig*, a small destroyer escort, was my first assignment after Organized Chicken Shit, which is how I refer to Officer Candidate School. As an ensign, the lowest shape of officer life, I was assigned to the fireroom, where I worked as a snipe, or engineering officer, overseeing the ship's boilers. Unlike most of the ensigns before me, I did my own boiler and hull inspections. After all, I'd gone to OCS as an enlisted Frogman. That meant I could dive as well as brawl and drink beer. And I knew how machinery worked because instead of just reading textbooks about what makes a boat work—like the assholes from Annapolis—I'd actually had to tear things apart and put them back together again in the Teams. And unlike most ensigns, I didn't mind getting dirty. So instead of a neat tan uniform I wore green Team fatigues and climbed all the hell over my boilers and swam under the keel before signing off on any work I'd ordered to be completed.

Hansy was maybe eighteen or nineteen then, a first-generation American—a New Yorker from Manhattan's Yorkville neighborhood. For a New Yorker, he was a rarity: an introverted, quiet kid who did only what was demanded of him. He showed no initiative. He kept to himself. His self-imposed isolation caused friction in the fireroom because the other men believed Hans thought himself superior to them.

Then, over coffee in the mess one day, I discovered why Hans was remote: as a kid he'd been harassed in school because of his

German ancestry. See, in New York City, lots of Irish, Polish, and Hungarian kids from Yorkville who'd lost their fathers, uncles, brothers, or cousins in World War II didn't have much empathy for a large, awkward, blond kid who spoke English mit a Cherman eggscent because his parents shtill spoke nussing but *Deutsche* at home.

I encouraged Hans to come out of his shell. He'd dropped out of school and enlisted in the Navy because he wanted to show he was a "good" American. "Hey, asshole," I told him, "I'm a high-school dropout, too—and look at me. So cut the shit. If you really want to be a 'good' American, don't just fucking talk about it—prove it."

By the time I left the *Taussig* to report to SEAL Team Two, Hans had signed up to get his GED. After he'd gotten his high-school diploma, he'd enrolled in every correspondence course he could find. We stayed in touch. I kept track of him as he progressed through the fleet, and through the ranks.

Now he was an E-9, which is as high as any enlisted man can go. He'd been posted to London as CINCUSNAVEUR's command master chief. The CINC's quarters down the hall may have been more luxurious, but it was Hans who occupied the corner of the building where Ike's actual office had been. He ran the admiral's HQ and the admiral's staff—there were those who said that Hans Weber *was* CINCUSNAVEUR. Whenever I passed through London, we'd catch up on gossip at the Goat, a smoky little pub on Stafford Street where they didn't seem to mind Hansie's ten-for-a-dollar cigars, and the bratwurst was as good as anything in Yorkville.

He ran a hand over his graying flattop. "It's been a fucked-up day so far. That's why it's good to see you, Dick. I was hoping you'd show." He jerked a thumb in the direction of a pint-size fridge under a table. "Brew?"

"Thought you'd never ask." I retrieved a can of Coors, popped it, and sucked deeply. "Damn, that's good."

I dropped myself in an armchair facing Hans's desk. "Gimme a dump, Chief—I've spent the last hour with Randy Rayman and I don't know any more than when I climbed off the fucking plane."

It didn't take him long to fill me in. Basically, the situation was FUBAR—Fucked Up Beyond All Repair. CNO's deputy, the vice chief of naval operations, had taken temporary command back in Washington. The first thing he'd done was send Pinky Prescott here—to keep him out of the way, Hans surmised. VCNO probably forgot that Pinky did a three-year tour in London in the late seventies and still thought he had friends in high places over here, because when he arrived, he installed himself in the CINC's cabin and started "running" the investigation. "Just like fucking Prince John in *Robin Hood*," Hans said bitterly. "The king is dead. Long live the king."

Things were clusterfucked. So, on his own, Hansie'd started working the phones. He'd ascertained that the hit hadn't been IRA. From the way the explosion went, he said—at least the way a Royal Navy chief gunner's mate he knew explained it—it had to be a limpet mine of some kind, set off by radio control. "According to him, the fuckin' thing put a thirty-foot hole in the aircraft carrier's hull, but it was tamped or shaped to explode up as well as in. Had to be set by a diver, right, Skipper?"

"Or divers, Chief. That's one of the things I want to see for myself." I explained I was planning a solo trip to Portsmouth to eyeball the scene of the crime and gather some intel firsthand.

"Sounds good to me." Hans took a pull of coffee from a huge white mug on his desk and continued his brief. Pinky and the assholes from NIS were running amuck. Pinky had insisted on being briefed by the Brits without either an intel liaison or CINCUSNAVEUR's POLAD—POLitical ADviser—present. He wasn't sharing the information he'd received, either. Currently, said Hans, there was no plan. There was no action. "We're sitting with our thumbs up our asses, waiting for someone to tell us what to do. Fuck it all, Dick, we lost one of the best goddamn sailors we've ever had. And what are we doing about it? We're fucking talking about it." He looked at me. "What can I do to help?"

I told him what I'd asked Randy Rayman to do. Hans shook his head. "Won't happen—not him. He'll just go running to Admiral Prescott."

Well, I still had a crew of six coming within the next thirty-six hours and I'd need accommodations and supplies for them. Hans made a note on his pad and murmured, "Done and done."

"Tougher request, Chief: I'll need you to scrounge me a diving rig and wet suit, size forty-six long, by morning—without anybody knowing about it."

Hans's stick scratched paper again. "No prob, sir, can do."

I told him I'd be sending for the rest of my Green Team shooters—two platoons total. They'd probably be flying into the joint Spec Ops air base at Mendenhall. They'd need bunks, too. Hansy made another notation on his pad.

Most important, I said, I'd need real tactical intelligence— information from outside the normal loop—so we could find the tangos who'd killed CNO and kick some ass. I'd already considered calling around to my friends in the British SpecWar community and had rejected the idea. It was too high-profile. I wanted to operate on my own.

"Aren't you gonna coordinate this with the Brits?"

Frankly, I hadn't thought about coordination. Admiral Secrest was my CNO, so I saw this as a unilateral action until otherwise ordered and told Hansie so.

"I'm not sure that's wise, Dick." He flipped me another Coors. "The Brits don't like rogue ops on their turf—it offends their innate sense of order."

"I thought 'innate sense of order' was one of your Kraut characteristics."

He smiled. "Yeah—but they have it, too." Then he got serious. "And watch your step. Admiral Prescott is pissed that you're even here—and he doesn't mind who knows it."

So, the knives were already out. Well, I was used to it. "I'll kiss him on the lips when I see him. Randy said something about his being out for dinner."

Hans made a face. "With Sir Aubrey Davis, the twit who carries the spook portfolio."

"Twit? I thought he was supposed to be pretty hot shit."

"Maybe *twit*'s the wrong word, but he sure looks like an asshole with that stupid monocle wedged in his face. Still, he's a fuckin' deadly political animal, no doubt about it. Don't underestimate him, either, Captain, he's a regular goddamn Machiavelli, and he gets everything he wants from the prime minister—everything. He's the most cold-blooded son of a bitch I've ever run into. He's not afraid to take casualties, believe me—rumor has it he's turned dozens of poor assholes into cannon fodder just to prove some political point or other."

"For example?" I was dubious.

"For example, the SAS guys who killed the IRA tangos on

Gibraltar. Sir Aubrey sent 'em out with orders to kill the T's on sight. But to keep things kosher on the political front, he had the SAS censured and the four shooters demoted."

I remembered the incident. If Hans was right—and there was little chance he wasn't—Sir Aubrey was a proper viper.

Hansie was still waxing eloquent. "And he has no use whatsoever for enlisted pukes like me. CINC introduced us once—at last year's Christmas party—and I thought he was gonna order me to shine his shoes or wipe his ass or both."

I laughed. "Sounds about right. Isn't that what chiefs do?"

"Fuck you. If it wasn't for a chief, you'd still be a know-nothing Team asshole."

He was right of course. The size-10 boot of my platoon chief at UDT-21, the legendary Everett E. Barrett, was the only reason I'd received my GED high-school certificate. He'd booted my ass until I did the work and got it. Ev Barrett was my first sea daddy. I still hear his Froggish growl in my mind providing advice during times of great stress. He and his wife, Del, took me in when I was but a tadpole. Ev battered me. He hammered me. And he tempered me, until he'd made me over into the kind of Frog he was himself. And when he'd done that, he sent me out into the world with a kick in the ass, a hearty "Fuck you very much," and the exhortation to do unto others as I'd had done unto me.

The principle was simple. "What you learn," Ev said, "you gotta pass on to others. It doesn't matter whether you work with a guy once or you serve with him for years—you gotta treat him the same. You gotta help him do his job." He called it Barrett's First Law of the Sea. I simply call it Barrett's Law.

It was Barrett's Law that had caused me to try to turn Hans's life around back on the USS *Taussig.* And it was chiefs that ran the Navy. But I wasn't about to give Hansie any satisfaction about those truths now. "Listen, if I were still in the Teams, *you'd* still be a goddamn third-class no-load dip-dunk shit-for-brains fucking Nazi fleet sailor."

"Touche." Hans laughed, too. He jotted something more on his desk pad. "Tell you what, Dick—you let me deal with AVCNO. You just go about your business. I'll handle paper flow."

"Aye, aye, Chief." I liked that. The chiefs who control the paper flow can manipulate the system just about any way they want.

Admirals can order anything they fucking want to—but all the paperwork would still have to be routed through a master chief like Hans. And by the time Master Chief Weber allowed his exalted highness Pinckney Prescott III to see even a single sheet of paper concerning me, I'd have sneaked and peeked in Portsmouth, my men would be in place and ready to go, my equipment would be in order, and I'd have figured out a plan.

Hans looked me over critically stem to stern. "You bring a uniform with you?"

"Nope. Just the clothes on my back." I explained that I'd been on assignment. Hans knew better than to ask where.

"Okay—I'll send something over to you. They wear dress blues here at CINCUSNAVEUR. And go to Marks and Spencer tomorrow at oh nine hundred and buy yourself a suit, a few shirts, a couple of ties"—he looked at my thong sandals and bare feet—"and a decent pair of shoes and some black socks might not hurt, either." Hans looked at my shoulder-length hair and threw up his hands in surrender. "I'm not gonna even start on the military acceptability of your hair."

"What are you, Chief, my fucking mother or my fucking butler?"

"I'm your fucking MACPOC, *Mister* Marcinko," said Hans, using the Navy's verbal acronym for command master chief. "This is London, Dick, not Virginia Beach. They put a lot of weight on style here."

That's one reason I wasn't particularly fond of London. Despite the pink-Mohawked punks on the underground, and the tangerine-tressed lasses on Oxford Street, official London tends toward chalk-striped suits and chalk-striped minds. Old Etonian ties (both the literal and the figurative kinds) can mean more here than how good you are at what you do. The formula for success is the same whether you're a conservative right-wing Tory or a left-wing Labourite: attend a public school like Eton or Harrow (in Britain, their exclusive private schools are called "public"), followed by Balliol College, Oxford, for a PPE, which is what they call a degree heavy in politics, philosophy, and economics.

The current prime minister had graduated from Balliol. So had the leader of the opposition. The head of MI6, Britain's intelligence service, was an Eton/Balliol product, too. I guess it made it easier for them all to talk to one another, because they'd all shared the same cold showers and bad food. But their traditions also held them back. Most of the Brits I'd ever met who'd followed the public school/Oxford route were bad warriors—just like Naval Academy "ring-knockers."

Oh, like Annapolis-trained officers, a few broke through. But the vast majority were pompous and closed-minded. They were class conscious. They'd been taught to debate, and they had sharp minds. But they lacked killer instinct. Equally important, these overeducated, by-the-book types lacked individuality, the character trait most necessary for unconventional warfare. These were not wolves or eagles. They were herd animals, slow moving and deliberate.

I waved Hansie off. "Okay, okay. I'll buy a suit. Right now I'm going to check into the Marriott and grab a combat nap."

He gave me a thumbs-up. "Hold on—I've got something for you to take with you." He produced a huge bunch of keys on a long chain attached to his belt, selected one of them, unlocked a closet, reached inside, and handed me a fifth of Bombay. "Sleeping potion."

I rolled the bottle in a newspaper and gave Hans an offhanded salute. "Thank you, Chief. You still know how to take care of your men, don't you?"

"God knows I try, Captain." He threw a salute back in my direction. "See you at oh six hundred. I'll have some results for you then."

By 0430 I was up and feeling almost human. At 0500 a bellman rapped on my door, interrupting my sit-ups. He was carrying a heavy wood hanger, on which sat a set of 46 long dress blues— inseam 32, cuff 35—regulation white uniform shirt and tie, and a plastic bag containing a pair of 11EE dress black shoes, and one pair of USG Issue Socks, Stretch Nylon, Black. The hat in his other hand fit perfectly, too.

God bless all chiefs.

I showered, shaved, trimmed my beard, braided my hair into a neat, single French braid, and presented myself at CINCUSNAVEUR at 0600, headed for Hans's office. But it wasn't the MACPOC office I went to. A Marine in dress blues met me at the security booth, escorted me to the second floor, marched me down a long, carpeted hallway, and opened a pair of paneled oak doors that revealed a sumptuous office suite. We walked past secretaries and aides' offices, to a single, intricately carved doorway flanked on one side by an American flag, and on the other by a blue pennant on which floated three huge gold stars.

Randy Rayman was standing outside the door. The smirk on his face vanished when he saw I was in proper uniform. It didn't disappear from his voice, however. "A/VCNO wants to see you now," he said, and opened the door for me.

The office was cavernous. There were nautical oil paintings on the walls. On one side of the room, a camel-backed sofa in striped chintz and an inlaid coffee table were flanked by a pair of Empire side chairs. On the other, an antique sideboard that must have been three yards long held a display of miniature sailing vessels and Victorian silver.

Straight ahead, Vice Admiral Pinckney Prescott III was waiting, his scrawny ass parked behind CINCUSNAVEUR's ornate Victorian partner's desk in a well-worn tufted leather judge's chair. Behind him, through gossamer curtains, bulletproof glass, and anti-grenade-screened windows, I could see Grosvenor Square.

I'm happy to report that he looked terrible. His pallor, normally the sickly, whiter shade of pale common to bean counters who spend their entire existences under fluorescent lights, was so tallowy this particular morning as to look almost jaundiced. His gray hair hadn't been combed, giving him a definite wild-man Dagwood Bumstead appearance. His lined face either drooped or sagged—I couldn't make up my mind. An untrimmed tuft of nose hair protruding from his left nostril completed the picture.

He didn't bother to rise. He pointed at a straight-back chair with a bony index finger and, by way of greeting, said, "Sit."

I sat.

"Where have you been?"

I wasn't about to say. "That's classified."

"I'm the goddamn A/VCNO," Pinky bawled. "Now tell me where you've been and what the hell you've been doing."

"I can't tell you, sir," I said, spelling it with a *c* and a *u*. I couldn't, either. My assignments were all need-to-know, and Pinky didn't have the need. CNO had wanted things that way.

Pinky sighed audibly. He fidgeted in his chair. He cracked his knees and his knuckles. "I will make it a point to find out. And when I do, you will suffer." He opened his pen and wrote himself a note.

Pinky sipped from a CINCUSNAVEUR mug of coffee that sat on a CINCUSNAVEUR coaster. He took his time, too. Finally, he replaced it and stared at me. "You n-n-never answered your pager," he whined. "Now you turn up here, uninvited. I wanted you back in Washington or wherever the hell you base these days, waiting for orders, not here, running around like a b-b-bull in a—a d-d-damn china shop."

I was delighted to see he'd started to develop a stutter in the six weeks since I'd last seen him. I decided to encourage it. "I t-t-t-thought I c-c-c-could h-h-help."

Pinky didn't find my attempt at humor comical. "Don't d-do that, goddammit—don't mimic me." He stopped, caught himself, took another sip of coffee, and tried to regain his composure. "And as for your helping, the idea itself is ridiculous. P-p-pathetic."

Randy Rayman sidled into the room. I caught him in my peripheral vision, leaning against the wall, a smug expression on his face. I decided to give him a floor show. After all, I was in as sunny a mood as Pinky. "Thanks for the vote of confidence. And fuck you very much, too, Pinky."

Pinky's eyes went wide, and his face flushed in embarrassment. "Don't you talk to me like that," he protested. "I'm in charge here."

I started to answer him but he cut me off. "You don't have CNO to protect you anymore. And vice chief doesn't like your methods any more than I do. So sit down and shut up, Dick, or I'll have you removed under custody."

He pouted. He shot his cuffs. He played with his bureaucrat's pen—a hundred-dollar, burgundy Montblanc rollerball—while he waited for me to begin squirming.

I wasn't about to squirm. I have the goods on Pinky: an NIS—Naval Investigative Services Command—SLUDJ (for Sensitive Legal [Upper Deck] Jurisdiction) file code-named Foxhunter. Those of you who read *Rogue Warrior: Red Cell* will remember that I stole it from NIS headquarters. For those of you who haven't, SLUDJ is NIS's top-secret witch-hunting unit. Its agents are known as Terminators. They specialize in obtaining political dirt on admirals.

The Foxhunter file is typical of their efforts. It contains pictures of

Pinky in flagrante delicto with a female Japanese agent. It contains telephone transcripts of Pinky and said bimbette engaged in aural sex. If anyone from the Senate Armed Services Committee ever saw it, Pinky's third star would get flushed down the tubes.

The problem was, the file was concealed under the kitchen floor back at Rogue Manor, and no one but me (with the possible exception of Stevie Wonder) knew how to get at it. But the knowledge that I had a SLUDJ sledge to pop Pinky with kept me from getting nervous about his threats. So I didn't squirm or fidget or look nervous. I did the most obnoxious thing I could do to him—I smiled beatifically and sat as still as Buddha.

And when it finally became obvious—even to Pinky—that I wasn't about to play his game, he started up again. He said that Randy Rayman had come to him and complained about being manhandled. That alone provided grounds for my immediate arrest. But there was more. I'd asked for guns. Guns, in Britain, where they are illegal. Another black mark had gone next to my name.

"Does that mean my request for weapons is being denied?"

That sent him into another spasm of stuttering. When he recovered, he d-demanded to know where the six men I'd mentioned to Randy Rayman were coming from. I told him they were on their way from Sigonella.

"What were they doing there?"

When I told him that the information was sensitive and that he wasn't cleared to know, he went off into another paroxysm.

Then he ran down the usual list of complaints. He b-b-bitched about my long hair. He screamed that I was an uncontrollable m-maverick. It was quite a performance, filled with the heretofores and whereupons and whatwithals bureaucrats love to use.

In fact, it reminded me of the time in Vietnam when, as a green-behind-the-ears ensign on my first combat tour, I'd taken two STABs (the SEAL Tactical Assault Boats we used in Vietnam) and run a free-fire operation at Dung Island, which was just down the Bassac River from Juliet Crossing, the area's top hotbed of VC activity. Bravo Squad spent two hours there, raking the island with every fucking round of ammo we carried. I even called in a Spooky—one of the old C-47s equipped with Vulcan Gatling guns that could spew out 6,300 rounds per minute—by waking up the

PROCOM (the local Vietnamese PROvincial COMmander) and convincing him to authorize it.

The wrinkle was that I did everything without prior authorization from the ops boss, a rule-abiding, ship-driving lieutenant commander named Hank Mustin. When we finally got back to our base at Tre Noc, Mustin was waiting for us on the end of the dock, jumping up and down like a fucking organ grinder's monkey.

He was going to have me court-martialed. He was going to have me shot. It took the base commander, a lanky captain named B. B. Witham, to get him off my back. And then, lo and behold, it turned out that we'd—quite by accident—interrupted a humongous VC operation the night in question, and we were all going to receive commendations, Hank Mustin included. From then on, I had old Hank by the balls.

And when Pinky finally got around to the bottom line, I realized I had him by the short and curlies, too.

"I don't know why, Dick, but Sir Aubrey has insisted that you work with his people on this. I have tried to convince him otherwise. After all, we have Lieutenant Commander Rayman over here—he's the kind of new-generation SEAL I prefer—but Sir Aubrey wants you, and this is his operation."

I tried to look glum, but the prospect of being thrown back into the briar patch must have put a distinct smile on my face, because Pinky's thin lips distorted as if he'd just licked a styptic pencil. "Don't smile like that," he said. "This is serious."

He rapped his pen on the desk surface. "There will be no UNODIRs in the U.K. I am assigning Lieutenant Commander Rayman TAD to your unit. He will be your liaison with me."

I turned toward Randy Rayman. "You know what TAD stands for?"

"Temporary Additional Duty," he recited.

"Not to me it doesn't. On my team it stands for Traveling Around Drunk, Randy, and don't you fucking forget it. You flunk lunch with me, you're dead meat."

Pinky rapped his pen again. "Quiet, goddammit. I *will* be kept informed. I'll be watching you."

I dropped the pager on his desk.

He pushed it back at me. "You can't take that off."

"CNO gave it to me, not you, sir," I said, spelling it c-u-r again. I didn't wait for him to react further. "Now, if the admiral will excuse me, I'd like to go and set up a meeting with my counterparts."

"Dismissed." Pinky sighed. He looked horrible.

His reedy voice pursued me as I quick-marched out the door followed by his asshole acolyte, Randy Rayman. "Don't forget— you are to keep me informed. That is an order."

Oh, I'd keep him informed. After a fashion. *My* fashion.

Chapter

4

WHEN I GOT BACK TO MY SUITE AT THE MARRIOTT, A BLACK BALLISTIC nylon duffel bag was sitting in the middle of the living room. I hefted it. It weighed, I estimated, just under one hundred pounds. I opened it up and discovered a fully charged U.S. Divers OXY-NG, bubbleless, self-contained O_2 rig, weight belt, inflatable SEAL combat safety vest, U.S. Divers best fins, diving hood, Kevlar-reinforced socks and gloves, knife, waterproof flashlight, mesh bag for holding souvenirs, compass, depth gauge, two hundred-foot lengths of strong, lightweight nylon line, and a forty-six-long cold-water wet suit in dull black neoprene.

God bless all chiefs. You will see this material again.

By 0730 I'd changed out of my dress blues back into real work clothes—my rancid jeans, thong sandals, a sweat shirt, and an old leather jacket I'd bought in Pakistan. Then I called down to Hereford, to contact my old friend Mick Owen, but was told he wasn't about.

Damn. Mick's an SAS shooter. He's a bad boy from Wales who enlisted in the paras, only to discover that throwing himself out of planes was too tame. So he put himself through SAS selection and was badged, as they say, by 22 Regiment.

We'd met just after the Princes Gate incident. Mick was part of the Pagoda Troop team that took the Iranian embassy back from a bunch of tangos. I was CO of SEAL Team Six at the time and visited SAS for a debrief on the operation. Mick—he was a junior lieutenant then—conducted it. Afterward, we hit all of Hereford's pubs for a series of quadruple gins and pints. It must have been love at first sight, because we were inseparable for the entire ninety-six hours I spent with the regiment. He bunked me in his BOQ (that's Bachelor Officers' Quarters for the nonmilitary among you). He took me shooting and looting at the SAS kill-house. We fast-roped from Sea King choppers. We jumped HALO—High Altitude/Low Opening—from C-130s. Talk about your whirlwind tours.

Ever since, we'd stayed in touch on an irregular basis. These days he was a captain, in command of his own twenty-four-trooper Special Missions detachment. Translation: he was one of the select few allowed to go hunting on his own, tasked by the top echelon at SIS—the British Secret Intelligence Service—much the same way my own Green Team operated. So he was probably off somewhere trying his best to slot—that's SAS slang for kill—some poor tango sod.

I left my name and my number, gave Hansie's extension as a backup, and rang off. Then I threw the duffel over my shoulder and slipped out the Marriott's service entrance, took the blind curve on George Yard, and worked my way around to Weighhouse Street, a narrow thoroughfare lined with red-brick apartment houses that probably hasn't changed a hell of a lot since Victoria was queen. I bought a newspaper, then sat down to an English breakfast of percolated coffee, lard-fried eggs, limp bacon, beans, and fried tomatoes at an Italian luncheonette filled with taxi drivers. So far as I could tell, I wasn't being followed.

Fortified, I walked two and a half short blocks to the New Bond Street underground station, bought a 70P ticket, took the escalator down to the Central line, grabbed the first train, and rode one stop to Oxford Circus. There, I changed trains. In another ten minutes, I was at Waterloo Station.

There was an express to Portsmouth leaving in six minutes, according to the flip-flop-card train-information board high above the gates. I bought a round-trip ticket, marched down the platform, opened a coach door, heaved the gear atop the divider, and plunked myself onto the upholstered seat. The trip would take about an hour and a half. And guess what—I'd forgotten to let Randy Rayman know where I was. Pity. I closed my eyes.

Portsmouth was cold and there was a slight drizzle as I trudged out of the Portsmouth and Southsea Station. From somewhere behind me, a ferry to the Isle of Wight sounded its foghorn, a mournful, gloomy bellow that fit the day's mood. The decommissioning ceremony had been held at the Royal Navy's Portsea dock, across the wharf from HMS *Warrior*. *Warrior*, built in 1860, was the first of the ironclad warships. It was one of Portsmouth's foremost tourist attractions.

I caught a taxi to the naval dockyard and climbed out about one hundred yards from the main entrance. An eight-foot, chain-link perimeter fence ran along the side of the road, which dead-ended at Victory Gate—the gate leading to HMS *Warrior*. Just past Victory Gate, another eight-foot fence—this one topped by three strands of barbed wire—ran parallel to a street named the Hard Park Road. A quarter mile away, I could see the Portsmouth central bus station and the ferry terminal. To my right, beyond the fence, lay a series of one-story sheds. There was no traffic. I tossed my bundle over the top, climbed the fence, heaved myself over the barbed wire without incident, and landed on the other side.

Just like that? you ask. What about sensors or other goodies meant to keep intruders out? What about Royal Marines with guard dogs patrolling the perimeter? What about TV cameras sweeping the area? What about jeeps with fifty-caliber machine guns on pintles?

Fiction, my friends. All that sci-fi crapola is the stuff of fiction. In actual fact, in the real world, most military bases—from San Diego to Sigonella, from Norfolk to Naples, and from Pensacola to Portsmouth—are wide open and ripe for plucking. And I was the mean motherplucker about to do it here and now.

I jimmied a shed door with my Emerson CQC6 folder and slid inside. The place had the musty smell common to storage facilities worldwide. I shed my civvies and shrugged into the wet suit. I pulled the vest on, attached all the accoutrements, put my fins under my arm, and grabbed the Draeger by the harness. Then I snuck a peek outside to make sure all was clear, and—Frog that I am—headed for water.

I could feel the chill as I submerged—the water temp was probably somewhere in the low forties. It was going to be real invigorating until the outside water seeping into the wet suit was trapped and heated by my body and started to provide insulation against the cold. Well, you don't become a SEAL because you like to stay comfortable. During my UDT training back in Little Creek, the instructors would sometimes muster us at about 0400, when the air was in the high forties and the water slightly cooler, and stand us naked outside for an hour and a half or so while they hosed us down every fifteen minutes. Swim buddies were allowed to keep themselves warm by pissing on each other.

It's the sort of harassment-slash-bonding experience the Navy frowns on these days. But lemme tell you—it works, both to build character and to create unit integrity. Indeed, something that the nonwarriors in charge of things these days never seem to realize is that bonding between men in combat units doesn't just happen. It is created.

In the old Navy, it was done by chiefs like Ev Barrett, who rode the men hard and impelled them to new and higher limits every day, through a mixture of tough love, intimidation, and physical abuse. Or it was done by officers like my mentor Roy Boehm, the godfather of all SEALs, who pushed the edge of the training envelope by proving to his men that the word *impossible* does not exist.

These days, if you rough up a man, you're history. If you call him names, he can put you on report. And as for realistic training, well, these days, an accident can mean the end of an officer's career. So unit commanders—all of whom want to make flag rank—tend to take it easy on their men. The result is that we bleed less in training—but we die more in battle.

The water wasn't just cold—it was dirty, too. It smelled like a goddamn sewer—and so would I. Well, I'd purify my body with Vitabath and Dr. Bombay later. Right now, it was S^3 time. That stands for swallow, swim, and shut the fuck up.

Even close to shore, the current was pretty strong—over a knot. But it was moving in my direction, so I lay back and went with the flow. The hard part would come on the return trip, when I'd have to struggle against it. A one-knot current is about all that most swimmers can handle. I can go against a one-and-a-half-knot current, but my life had better depend on it. And two knots? You can hold the fucking world record in freestyle, and you'll still look like you're treading water. To play it safe, I ran seventy-five feet of my route line from a piling, so if Mr. Murphy was swimming along with me, I could pull myself hand over hand the last twenty-five yards.

After twelve minutes underwater, I turtled to grab a look-see. I was about three hundred yards north of HMS *Warrior*. It was another two hundred and fifty yards beyond that to the *Mountbatten*, which was surrounded by barges and pontoons. I'd have to be careful working my way around *Warrior*. It was past midmorning now and there'd be tourists aboard. I could also make out TV lights and cameras set up on the docks, and reporters holding hand mikes, opining.

Fucking television was going to be the death of us all. Interview the Special Operations Teams as they landed at Mogadishu? No problem. Turn the cameras on to show the Iraqis exactly where their SCUD missiles were hitting Tel Aviv? Absofuckinglutely—why not. Broadcast the Pentagon briefings live and ask exactly when and where the next air strikes were going to take place? But of course. Cover firefights from the Kuwaiti border as they happen? Can do.

I'll tell you the logical conclusion to this kind of mindless shit: it is when some blow-dried, air-bag, pretty-boy correspondent does a live, split-screen remote from the home of a Marine lance corporal, who's being covered by a CNN Minicam crew while he goes on patrol in Lower Slobovia. The Marine is blown away by a land mine, and Pretty Boy turns to the camera and says, "How does it feel to see your son waxed, live, on CNN? We'll find out after these commercial messages."

I submerged, went deep, and swam with a slow, steady pace, counting kicks until I reached my objective.

Underwater searches are usually performed with two, four, or even six men. The three most common methods are known as the running jackstay search, the checkerboard jackstay search, and the circle-line search. The first two require a minimum of two divers, four buoys and four weights, and two grid lines. In the running jackstay search, the divers work their way through a 250-by-50-meter course, which they traverse lengthwise. The checkerboard jackstay search requires nine separate grid lines and weights. It can be swum by one or two divers.

The least complicated is the circle-line search. You set a buoy, attach it to a weight, and run the search line around the buoy line. Then you swim in circles, working your way concentrically to the end of the rope.

Of course, I didn't have a buoy or a weight, so I'd have to improvise. It occurred to me that my one-man circle search could easily turn into a one-man circle jerk.

It took me almost half an hour to work my way one hundred yards beyond the *Mountbatten*'s charred hull. I threaded my way around the barges, under the pontoons, and three small police boats that patrolled the dock area to keep onlookers away. That left me roughly another hour and a half of O_2. The Brits had obviously gone over the hull and the area below it, so I began my first search pattern just off the end of the dock. I tied my rope to a piling and started circling. It quickly became obvious that here, too, the bottom was clean—in fact, in the flashlight beam it looked as if it had been raked. They'd probably gathered all the fragments they could find and taken them to forensics.

Okay, it was time to move. I switched locations, moving toward the center of the harbor by fifty yards, attaching the end of my rope to an old tire I discovered on the bottom. The channel got deeper here, and the water was moving faster, too. I checked my depth gauge. I was bottoming at about forty-five feet now—roughly four yards below the Draeger's published safety specs. What the hell, I'd taken Draegers to sixty feet and I wasn't dead—yet. My second search was unfruitful, too. So I dragged the tire fifty yards to my left—east-southeast on my dive compass—and began all over again.

As I moved farther and farther away from the piers, the bottom began to look like a fucking obstacle course. Sludge had settled atop the silt. On the one hand, that was good, because it kept the silt from clouding as I poked, probed, and prodded. On the other hand, that was bad because the fucking sludge stuck to everything— including me. Obviously, the Brits hadn't dredged the harbor in some time, because there were timbers, tires, bottles, and other assorted chunks of junk all half-buried in the slimy silt. My vision was obscured by the murky water—visibility was about six yards at best—and despite the flashlight beam I kept bumping into things I didn't particularly want to touch.

After forty-five minutes and four circle jerks, I still hadn't found anything suspicious. Shit. I knew there was some piece of the fucking puzzle I hadn't figured out yet, and it made me mad. I was overlooking something—something as obvious as the fucking Slovak nose on my face. But I was just too stupid to see it.

I stopped dead in the water. Hold on a fucking second. I was searching the way Frogmen are taught to search. That's taught—as in "by the book." I was breaking one of my own SpecWar commandments—the one that goes: "Thou shalt never assume."

Ev Barrett's paternal growl rumbled inside my head. *"Every time you* assume, *Seaman Marcinko, you shit-for-brains no-load dipshit blankety-blanking bleeper-blanking asshole geek, you make an ASS of U and ME."* I went dead in the water. I'd assumed that the best way to search for some piece of evidence was to go about it the way Pinky would have wanted me to. Well, shit, I was a fucking unconventional warrior.

Okay, class, let's think unconventionally.

How, for example, would Roy Boehm have hit the target?

Roy? He'd have come a-calling in an SDV—a Swimmer Delivery Vehicle—or a minisub. Roy would bottom it in the deepest part of the channel, where there's the most traffic. Then he'd swim to the target, using the current to help him carry his goodies—no need to tire himself out when the water'd do the work for him.

When he'd finished committing mayhem—planting the bombs, setting the booby traps, or whatever—he'd swim back to the SDV or minisub, climb aboard, and haul balls outta Dodge.

Doom on me indeed. I surface-turtled carefully (I didn't want to make a guest appearance on the nightly news) and got my bearings. Then I dove and swam due south. I didn't give a shit that I was running out of O_2. I *knew* how the *Mountbatten* had been hit.

I worked my way into the middle of the channel, right under the route taken by the Isle of Wight ferryboats. It put me about three hundred yards from the carrier. The bottom was real messy—filled with the nasty sorts of things that can damage boats. The current was bad—almost two knots by my estimation, and I had to fight my way down. Then, straight ahead, just about where I would have launched from, given the current and the harbor configuration, I saw something in the dark water. It was a shard of concrete piling about eight feet high and three feet across, and it stuck out of the harbor bottom like a pylon. It had probably come off a barge and wedged itself in like this. Next to it, half-buried, lay a piece of black metal, about three feet by four feet, shaped roughly like a shark's dorsal fin.

I swam down and flipped it over to get a better look. Bingo. It was the stabilizer from a minisub, broken off at the stem end. It had probably been lost when the sub hit the concrete piling. Hot damn. I was ecstatic. I was so ecstatic I never noticed when Mr. Murphy arrived and perched on my shoulder.

When did he do that? you ask. He dood it when I ran out of O_2. I sucked, and nothing happened. Doom on Dickie. I could see the headlines now: "SEAL Drowns During Unauthorized Probe of Friendly Harbor. U.K. Declares War on U.S."

Nah. I turned the emergency valve. That gave me five minutes of grace. But it didn't help me with the stabilizer fin. I hefted it. Guesstimation? Eighty pounds. Normally, you carry an inflatable bladder with you if you expect to find something that large and that heavy.

I had rope. Maybe I could tow it. I tried. It was like trying to make headway with a sea anchor out. Now I was getting frantic.

Lightbulb. My safety vest.

Quickly, I shed the vest, tied it to the stabilizer, and fiddled with the internal O_2 valve until I achieved negative buoyancy. I quick-released my weight belt, climbed back into the Draeger harness, and taking hold of the fin and vest, swam for the surface. I came up just in time to see one of the Isle of Wight ferryboats one hundred yards from me and closing fast.

Okay, Dickie, go back where you belong. I bottomed like a lead weight and sucked silt. Even so, I thought the ferry's twin screws were going to give me a crew cut as it *chugga–chugga–chugged* steadily over me. I hugged the bottom as best I could, just like the days when, as an enlisted Frog at UDT-21, we played Zulu-5-Oscar, or Z/5/O, exercises in Norfolk harbor.

They used to make us play hide-and-seek during the E&E (evade and escape) training. The instructors would dump us in the water and put boats out to search for us. So I cheated. That's what E&Es are supposed to be about anyway—evading and escaping, by any means possible. Anyway, I used to swim to the slip where the Norfolk-Kiptopeke ferry berthed, then dive and hang on to a slimy piling for dear life as the ferry docked above me, its diesels going *chunka–chunka–chunka*, just like the ferryboat above me now.

The noise and turbulence subsided. It was time to try again. This time I checked my compass and swam out of the channel before I surfaced. Now I really was out of O_2. I pulled the Draeger mask off and, spitting dirty water, looped the rope around my shoulder and side-stroked my way toward the shore, just over five hundred yards away. Except now I was swimming against the current, which (thank you, Mr. Murphy) had increased to about a knot and a half. So it took me almost an hour of painful swimming to get back to my point of departure.

Oh, did I hurt. I was about twenty yards from shore when the security detail finally decided to make an appearance. So, instead of hauling my ass out of the water, I got to wait as a jeepload of bored Brits cruised slowly around the sheds, smoking cigarettes. I hung on to the route line and whimpered imprecations at the god of goatfucks. Finally—it seemed like hours, but wasn't longer than five minutes—they chugged off and I was able to haul myself up onto the shore.

Cold almost to the point of hypothermia, I dragged my piece of evidence into the shed and collapsed, retching wretched water. My arms and legs burned like hell. My shoulder was rubbed raw where the rope had cut into it. Somehow, I'd cut myself behind the left ear and was bleeding into my wet suit. Trust me—this is no way to make a living.

But I had something concrete. Evidence. The first road sign in a long trail that would bring me to avenge CNO. I ran my hand along the smooth metal of the stabilizer fin. *It* was worth the pain.

I got back to the Marriott to find a stack of messages longer than my lizard. Most of them were from Vice Admiral P-P-P-Prescott. Then there were three from Hans, and singles from Sir Aubrey Davis and Major Geoff Lyondale. I took a twenty-minute shower and a double dose of Bombay on the rocks, then returned Hans's call first. After all, he outranked everybody else.

"Yo, Hansie."

"About time you decided to show up. Have a nice swim?"

Nice swim indeed. "Fuck you, Chief. What's up?"

"Got a call from Sigonella. Your people will be here tomorrow morning before noon. I got 'em rooms at the Marriott."

"Great."

"And I charged the rooms to the embassy."

Even better. Let the fucking State Department pay. "Who called?"

I heard Hans sip his coffee. "Guy named Tommy. Oh, he said to tell you the package didn't make it."

I didn't need to hear that. You're not supposed to lose prisoners —especially when you've worked as hard as I had to snatch him in the first place. Especially when a fucking frigate (or is that a frigging fuckit?) and an aircraft carrier are involved. They are not cheap to deploy. And—more to the point—deploying ships of the line creates a paper chain that admirals like Pinky Prescott can follow.

So now, there were going to be a lot of questions, and no answers. After all, only CNO and the president knew what my mission was about. But CNO was dead, Pinky Prescott wanted nothing more than to haul my ass into a court-martial, and the Leader of the Free World wasn't about to sacrifice his butt to protect mine by going to the Navy and saying, yes, Dickie actually was operating under a Presidential Number One Priority.

There was also something larger at stake: Green Team. Losing Azziz was like blood in the water to a political shark like Pinky, if he ever found out. If Pinky smelled failure, he'd do his best to chew me and my men up. The son of a bitch would come after us, and without a rabbi like CNO to protect us, we were all vulnerable. This was not good news.

There was nothing to do but play poker. "Tommy say anything else?"

"Nope. Just to tell you he'd explain when he saw you."

Explain? There was nothing to explain. Doom on me. Still, there was a small—very small—bright side. We'd reduced the number of tangos worldwide by one, and the experience had provided some real-world training for the men. And as for Mahmoud Azziz abu Yasin, well, I rationalized, if he was as fundamental a Muslim as he said he was, he'd be just as happy making prayers in heaven as he was making bombs on earth.

"Any other news?" I asked Hans.

"I phoned around for you on the bombing."

"Learn anything we don't know already?"

"Nope."

"I did."

"What?"

"Come pay me a visit and see. I don't wanna talk on an open line."

"Aye, aye, cur." I heard him chuckle as I rang off. I'd turn the stabilizer over to Hans. By 0600 tomorrow he'd know the length of the dick on the fucking machinist who'd made it.

On an impulse, I called my old pal Tony Mercaldi back at DIA. We couldn't say anything important on the open line, but I used enough innuendo, allusion, and body English to make it clear what I needed. Tony, ever the Air Force colonel, harrumphed and grumped and made nasty noises, but said he'd start checking things out for me soonest. I gave him Hansie's scrambler fax number so he could send me the goodies I needed.

The real work done, I dialed Major Geoff Lyondale. There was no answer, so I tried Sir Aubrey Davis's office at the Ministry of Defense. The phone bring-bringed three times, then a male voice answered, "Extension fifty-six."

He'd answered Sir Aubrey's phone just like the spooks back at Christians in Action at Langley answered theirs. What did they do, send 'em all to the same goddamn training sessions? I studied the stabilizer I'd humped back on the train as I sipped Bombay and explained who I was.

There was a pause. Then the voice came back on the line and told me that Sir Aubrey would be pleased to take dinner with me at the East India Club on St. James's Square at seven. That was an hour from now. "Sounds good to me."

"Sir Aubrey will meet you in the American barroom. If you arrive first, please feel free to order."

How genteel. How polite. I decided to be positively British. "Super. Smashing." *Fuuuck* you.

I was sipping my second pint of Yorkshire bitter, and munching on my sixth quail egg, when he ambled in. He started to call me "Commander," then halted, ratcheted his monocle into place, and counted my stripes. "*Captain* Marcinko, so pleased you could join me." He extended his hand. It was no warmer or hardier than the time I'd shaken it at former secretary of defense Grant Griffith's reception just about a year ago.

Sir Aubrey waved his hand vaguely in the barman's direction. I watched as he slipped away for a few seconds, then brought back a bottle of red wine, uncorked it, and decanted it carefully into a simple, round decanter. He poured a balloonful for Sir Aubrey and slid the glass deferentially across the bar. "There you go, sir, your usual."

"Thank you, Paulo." Sir Aubrey's hand went round the stem and he swirled the wine on the bartop. Then he picked the glass up and peered at it. His narrow nose went over the rim, he inhaled deeply, then sipped cautiously, swished the wine loudly in his mouth, then swallowed. "Ah." He smiled. "Good Old Boat."

"Old Boat?"

"Barca Velha—that's Portuguese for 'old boat,' old man. A great—and as yet largely undiscovered—wine made in the Douro region by an old friend of mine. I buy ten cases of each exceptional year at the vineyard. They store it for me here. I drink nothing else at this club, save for port or champagne. This"—he swirled the wine again—"is the 1975 vintage. Would you like to try some?"

I drained the ale and cleansed my palate with a quail egg. "Sure." Why not? So far as I am concerned, wine is wine. I keep boxes of blush Chablis in my fridge, and my red wine's served by unscrewing the top. I've had good wines, but frankly I don't go for all that sucking and swishing and "what an audacious vintage" talk.

A glass was put in front of me. I picked it up and took a mouthful. It was as if a claymore had gone off on my palate. I could sense flavor bursts of chocolate, currant, and at the back of my mouth, vanilla. It was wonderful. It was sensual. It was the best fucking wine I'd ever had. I drained the glass, savoring the aftertaste. "That is terrific stuff."

He peered down his nose at me, ratcheted his cheek muscles, and allowed the monocle to drop. It swung like a pendulum thrice, then stopped dead center on his chest like a glass bull's-eye. "Thank you, old man. Glad you approve."

We stood at the bar for ten minutes or so, talking about the sorry state of things—mainly commiserating about CNO, and the sorry state of affairs that had allowed the assassinations in the first place. He was a strange one. His neutral gray fish-eyes never gave a hint of what he was thinking—they just looked at me, blinking every once in a while, showing no emotion at all. Then, the bottle of Old Boat sitting empty on the well-worn bar, he took my arm and ushered me down the long, wood-paneled hallway toward the main dining room.

As we walked, he explained that he and CNO had enjoyed a rare working relationship. They'd met two decades ago, when CNO had been posted to CINCUSNAVEUR as a three-striper (that's a commander for those of you who don't read uniform jacket sleeves) aide, and Sir Aubrey was, as he put it, "a minor functionary at one of our security services."

He guided my elbow, steering me to the right. "We were two old Cold Warriors," he said. "Our professional lives were entirely purposive: we did battle against the Soviet Bear. We hunted him. We stalked him. Trying to discover his most private thoughts, endeavoring to uncover his most sensitive political and military machinations, gave our lives significance. We had a God-given mission."

He paused while a maître d' in black tie showed us to a lone table, separated from the others by two yards, that looked out on the square through huge, arched windows. We were seated. Sir Aubrey tucked a starched white napkin under his chin. A new bottle of Barca Velha was set on the table, uncorked, decanted, and poured. He tasted. He approved. He nodded at the sommelier to pour me a glass, then ordered him to leave the decanter on the table.

"Then," he continued, "the Soviet Bear disappeared. The Cold War evaporated. For someone like me who'd focused his entire career—in my case more than a half century, Captain—on the Cold War, the loss of my sole adversary in what amounted to no more than a blink of time, left me feeling a strange sense of emptiness, of ennui, of purposelessness." He stared out into the square. I followed his eyes.

He turned back to me. "It was Admiral Secrest—your CNO—and our Admiral of the Fleet, Sir Norman Elliott, who brought me round. They realized, perhaps before anyone else, that there was a new danger. This one perhaps even more critical than the Soviets. The Sovs, after all, were a single target. This new menace, they insisted, presented tremendous problems precisely because it was anonymous, faceless."

"Fundamentalist terror," I blurted. "That's the battle CNO and I have been fighting at home."

"Precisely." Sir Aubrey waited as a waiter approached to hand each of us a menu. He sipped his wine. "I'm planning to have the curry. It's quite acceptable. If not, I believe I'd take the entrecôte."

Frankly, food didn't matter very much right then. I had more important things to learn. "Sir Aubrey, why the hell did you ask Pinky Prescott to TAD me over to you?"

"Captain—may I call you Dick?"

"Of course."

"Dick, then. Dick—in the past six months, your CNO, our Admiral of the Fleet, and I have all noted with distress a new trend toward terrorism of a certain sort."

"You have?" I wanted to hear more, because CNO had indeed begun to see a new and particularly virulent form of terror. It had been one of the reasons behind my trip to Cairo.

Sir Aubrey nodded. "Yes. If you look at quantitative studies only, there's been nothing but the slow increase to which you probably refer. But if you overlay that material with political reporting, there seems to be an emerging pattern of global terrorism—transnational terrorism is what the admirals and I called it—that is unprecedented."

That was CNO's theory, too. But within the Pentagon, no one else had drawn similar conclusions. Why had that happened? The answer is simple: because no one ever overlays intelligence. Why? Because intelligence agencies, like virtually every command structure, are what can be called stovepipe commands.

In essence, that means DIA people report to DIA. CIA people report to CIA. The State Department has its own intel structure. Each has its own mission; each has its own objectives. DIA leans heavily toward TECHINT; CIA keeps its eye on eco-political developments; and State focuses on internal politics. Moreover, each agency guards its information jealously. Not for security reasons, but so as to preserve its budgetary sanctity.

Oh, sure, there's the National Security Council, which is supposed to provide intelligence policy for the president. But in reality, the NSC spends most of its time fighting a constant turf war with the Department of State. Then there are the President's Foreign Intelligence Advisory Board and the President's Intelligence Oversight Board. They're supposed to provide an independent view on the nation's overall intel priorities. In fact, both boards are filled with cabinet rejects, political cronies, and wanna-bes.

Finally, there's the Intelligence Community Staff, which sits at 1776 G Street, not a thousand feet from the Oval Office. ICS is run by a three-star—these days it was an Air Force lieutenant general. Allegedly, ICS coordinates the flow of intelligence. What it really does is referee turf battles between the various spook agencies.

Bottom line? Nowhere in the community was there a "big picture" outfit—somewhere that took nuggets from everyone and tried to make sense of them.

But CNO had. He'd done it by reading State Department cables (God knows how he'd laid his hands on them), DIA reports, and CIA position papers. He'd gathered NATO materials on Western Europe. He'd pieced together NSA intercepts from the Balkans and Southwest Asia. He'd snared Drug Enforcement Agency studies.

He, too, had often spoken of a new terrorism—terrorism without borders or specific nationality—whose one focus was the destruction of the West. It was an enlargement of the battle that had been going on for some years, directed against the West by mullahs, from Beni Saf in Algeria, to Kabul, Afghanistan. But this new wave was infinitely more dangerous. It was being waged by an army of mujahideen soldiers recruited from all over the Muslim world. They were being trained together at sites in northwest Afghanistan. Their funding was coming from Iran, and also by the burgeoning heroin traffic in Afghanistan. Their leadership was unknown.

CNO had mentioned all this to me shortly before I'd taken my Green Team squad to Egypt. He'd bitched that his fellow service chiefs hadn't reacted positively to his theory, but he was convinced that he was correct, and what's more, his old friend Admiral Sir Norman Elliott of the Royal Navy thought much the same way he did.

He believed that Mahmoud Azziz abu Yasin was a small but significant part of this new form of worldwide terror, which is why he'd gone to the mat so that I could snatch him. We'd agreed to explore things in detail when I returned. Now, CNO and Sir Norman were dead, but Sir Aubrey was covering the same ground.

"I believe the bombing at Portsmouth could be part of that pattern," he said.

I asked why he thought so.

"I'll get to that in good time." Sir Aubrey sipped his wine. "As I was saying, I know about your work—CNO was quite specific with me when it came to describing your capabilities."

"CNO and I thought alike when it came to counterterror."

He nodded. "I know. And you've been hard at work. Very commendable."

I saluted him with my glass. "Thank you."

He raised his glass as well, sipped, and replaced it on the napery. "Now, as to your question about the Portsmouth bombing. In the past week, there have been six seemingly unconnected terrorist acts." He sipped his wine. "Have you been informed about them?"

I told Sir Aubrey I'd been out of touch. He brushed a fleck of something from his chest. "Ah, of course. That would be Cairo. Mahmoud Azziz abu Yasin. Too bad about him. I would have liked to see his debrief."

I must have flushed. "I don't know what you're talking about."

"No matter." He shrugged. "I can tell you, Dick, that there is very little in the CT arena that I do not learn about." He paused to let that sink in. "Don't worry, I have no intention of passing the information on to your Admiral Prescott."

I guess the look on my face betrayed me. I shifted course. "Sounds like you have a wide net, Sir Aubrey."

He said nothing. The Cheshire-cat smile on his face told the whole story.

"You were talking about unconnected terrorist acts this past week."

"Ah, yes." He paused as the waiter bore down on us and slid two plates onto the table, then meticulously spooned clumps of brown substance from a large porcelain au gratin dish onto them. I guess it was curry, although it didn't look or smell like any curry I'd ever eaten. Two sauce boats of chutney were served, as well as relish dishes of shredded coconut and chopped peanuts.

I looked up. "Is there any hot sauce?"

The waiter appeared shocked. "The curry is Madras recipe, sir. It is already quite piquant."

I tasted. It was as spicy as glue. "May I have some hot sauce, please?"

"If you insist."

"I insist."

Sir Aubrey watched as I dumped half a bottle of red chili sauce on my plate and mixed it with the alleged curry.

"You were saying, Sir Aubrey?"

He put a forkful of curry in his mouth and chewed. "I find this curry quite spicy." He filled my wineglass, then his. "In the past six days, the main train station in Moscow was bombed. So was the Belgian diamond exchange in Antwerp, and the Italian stock-market building in Milan. There was an explosion at a French power plant that disrupted one quarter of the country's electric supply, while within hours, in Frankfurt, an explosion disabled the city's subway system for two days. More puzzling is the fact that no one credible has claimed credit for any of those actions."

"You said six—you listed only five."

"Ah—of course, there was the strike at Portsmouth."

I sipped my wine. "You believe they're all connected?"

"I do—as examples of this new, transnational terror."

"Most people would consider your premise a hard sell, Sir Aubrey, especially as there have been no sort of common demands —not even any messages from the perpetrators."

He looked at me with sadness. "I realize that. In fact, I tried to convince Admiral Prescott when he and I met yesterday, but he quite disagreed. He completely discounts a transnational pattern. His theory centers on the Iraqis, which is how his investigators are proceeding. It's all quite irrational, of course, but there was no dissuading him. He seems to be quite fixated."

"Pinky gets that way."

"Pity." Sir Aubrey wiped the corner of his mouth with the napkin. "But you don't consider it a 'hard sell'?"

"Not at all." The transnational theory had always made sense to me. I believed, for example, that Mahmoud Azziz was representative of this new trend. He was an Egyptian who had been trained by the CIA in Afghanistan to fight against the Soviets. Years later, he'd put that training to use again as a member of the Egyptian Mujahideen, a small fundamentalist group based in Cairo that uses terror tactics against the Egyptian government to force it to become a fundamentalist Islamic republic. The Egyptian Mujahideen, in turn, is part of the worldwide organization known as the Islamic Brotherhood, which channeled drug money from Afghanistan, and oil revenues from Iran, to groups like Azziz's, for the purpose of furthering Islamic fundamentalism by any means possible. So Azziz had been sent from Cairo to the United States to create chaos and terror. When we'd captured him, he was on his way to Pakistan, where he'd probably link up with more tangos and go who knows where to create further mayhem.

There were hundreds of thousands more like Azziz—and hundreds, if not thousands—of local fundamentalist groups scattered all over the globe. After all, the U.S. had spent billions equipping and funding mujahideen guerrillas during their fifteen-year war against the Soviets in Afghanistan. Among them were the more than twenty-five thousand Muslim volunteers engaged by the CIA. They were mostly poor, unschooled Arabs, recruited from mosques from Brooklyn to Baluchistan, by using a dozen different front organizations.

Now, I said to Sir Aubrey, it was common knowledge that many of those fighters, and much of the CIA's equipment, were being turned against the West. In the former Yugoslavia, Muslim veterans of the Afghanistan campaign were fighting alongside Bosnian Muslims. The same C-4 and Semtex explosive that had been humped by camel from Peshawar through the Khyber Pass a decade ago was now being used by mujahideen fighting sectarian guerrilla wars in Kashmir, Tajikistan, Azerbaijan, and Kurdistan. Stinger antiaircraft missiles used to bring down Soviet MiGs and MI-24 Hind gunship choppers on the outskirts of Kabul were reappearing from the Balkans to Somalia, where they were employed against Western aircraft.

There was also something I didn't tell him. I didn't add that I knew some of those lethal supplies had been smuggled into the U.S., where Mahmoud Azziz had used them to blow up half a dozen targets across the country. I also didn't tell him that when we'd snapped Mahmoud Azziz up in Cairo, he'd been carrying a passport with a Pakistani visa and fifty thousand English pounds.

I knew that a decade ago, it was from Peshawar in northern Pakistan that busloads of Muslim volunteers made their way to CIA-run training camps in northwest Afghanistan. Today, those buses were still filled with disaffected Muslims from Egypt, Algeria, the former Soviet Union, and even America. Members of scores of terror organizations—from huge ones like Hamas and Islamic Jihad to such tiny splinter groups as the South Yemen Liberation Army— traveled to mujahideen training camps in northwest Afghanistan, where they were taught how to seek revenge against the West.

And their motivation? It could be found every day in the newspapers. The fact that Israel was making peace with its Arab neighbors was bad enough—that, alone, was reason for a holy war. But there were other events as well. Muslims in the Balkans were slaughtered by both Croats and Serbs, and the West did nothing to stop the carnage. In the former Soviet Union, Azerbaijani Muslims were facing ethnic cleansing by Armenian Christians—and the

Russians just looked on. Throughout Western Europe, ultranationalists threw Molotov cocktails at boardinghouses and dormitories full of Muslim workers, and the police always seemed to have trouble arresting the guilty parties.

I said I'd learned from research that the sole element keeping hundreds of thousands of alienated, impoverished, disenfranchised Muslim fundamentalists from consolidating was a natural tendency toward tribalism. "The old philosophy—'My brother and I against my cousin; my cousin and I against the world'—is still the prevalent modus vivendi throughout most of the Muslim world," I said, watching as Sir Aubrey nodded in agreement.

I swallowed a fork of tasteless curry. "But, if the Muslim fundamentalists worldwide *could* be fused into a single camp with a single goal, they'd present a threat to the West even more dangerous than the Soviets. Because with the Soviets, the specter of massive retaliation kept them at arm's length. To a mujahideen warrior, Sir Aubrey, a bullet in the brain means a guaranteed trip to heaven."

"Precisely." He drained his glass and refilled it. "Now, let us suppose that the tribalism *is* being overcome—that all these incidents are actually being directed by a single source and focused against the West."

"That would make it the largest terrorist organization in the world."

"Indeed it would, Captain." He paused. "Have you ever read any history? Arab history?"

I had, and I said so.

"What do you know about Saladin?"

"That he was what—an eleventh- or twelfth-century Egyptian. A warrior. He took Jerusalem from the Crusaders. Built the wall that still surrounds the Old City."

"Very good. But there was something else about him, too. He was the first Pan-Arab. The first son of Islam to try to consolidate all Arab people under the green banner of the prophet Muhammad."

"He failed."

"Yes, he did. The times were not right. But for centuries thereafter, his Pan-Arab legacy lived on. A single, nontribal Islamic culture spread from Spain to the Indian Ocean, from the Urals to the equator. And ever since, there have been Arabs who dreamed the same dream as Saladin: to unite all of Islam under the green flag."

He had a point. I thought about it. "I can think of three recently: Assad of Syria, Muammar Qaddafi, and Saddam Hussein."

"Yes—of course, before them came Egypt's Gamal Abdel Nasser. He was able to unify Syria and Egypt back in the fifties." Sir Aubrey paused. "It was to be the first building block of a unified Arab nation encircling the Mediterranean."

"He failed. So did the others."

"Yes. For a number of reasons. Perhaps most significantly, because each of them was ultimately a nationalist, and each represented only a small segment of Islam. None, therefore, was able to win more than parochial support. Besides, what are men like Nasser, Assad, Saddam, and Qaddafi at their core? They're politicians. Islam will never be reunited by a mere politician.

"But what happens if a new Saladin appears on the scene? A visionary; an individual who represents no single nation, no specific segment of Araby; a man who exemplifies true Pan-Arabism, and who can unite Saudis and Sudanese, Yemenites, Moroccans, Syrians, Afghanistanis, Baluchistanis—the whole patchwork of Islam from Casablanca to Peshawar."

I pondered the possibilities. I didn't like what I came up with at all. "Isn't it highly unlikely that such an individual could exist, given the political situation today?"

"Unlikely?" Sir Aubrey's fish-eyes wandered toward the square. "Certainly, it is unlikely," he said, his voice distant and detached. "But, dear sir, it is not entirely impossible. CNO didn't think it impossible. Neither did Sir Norman. And neither do I. That is why I insisted to your Admiral Prescott that you and your unit be seconded to me for the immediate future."

Pinky hadn't told me that. He'd said only that I'd be working with Sir Aubrey's people. There's a big difference between "working with" and "commanded by," and I said so in unequivocal terms.

He poured the last of the wine equally into our glasses. "I understand." His voice took on a steely tone. "But you are on sovereign British soil, Captain, and I must insist on maintaining command and control. This is not Egypt, after all. Make no mistake—I need your help. Moreover, I want it. But you must work in concert with our assets, and under our direction. CNO said he had to keep you on a short leash, and he warned me to do the same, should our paths ever cross."

Tough as those words were to swallow, they sounded just like CNO to me. God, I missed the old warhorse.

Sir Aubrey must have seen something in my face. The tinge of a wistful smile crossed his own—a cloud's shadow moving across a meadow. "He used to call you his favorite junkyard dog, you know." It was the first trace of emotion he'd shown all evening.

"*Canis lupus* Marcinko—that's me."

"I'm sure of it." He drained the last of the wine. "And I know we will all work splendidly together." His expression brightened. "Despite the fact that no one has taken credit for the incident at Portsmouth, we obtained some good operational intelligence late today—intelligence that points the finger toward certain fundamentalist groups, and we want to exploit it to our benefit. There have been definite positive developments. As you can imagine, I do not want to speak of them now. But if you can come to my offices tomorrow morning at ten . . ."

Such gents, these Brits—making war by banker's hours. Well, it wasn't my style to wait around. "Pardon my French, but what the fuck, Sir Aubrey—let's move now. Why sit on it?"

"Because—"

"'Because'? Screw excuses. My CNO is dead. So is your goddamn Admiral of the friggin' Fleet. But all you seem to want to do is sit on your fat ass sucking down your fucking Old Boat, while there are tango assholes out there laughing at both of us." I stood up. "That ain't my style, Sir Aubrey. I'm not one of your newfangled C squared CO Navy types."

"What?"

"Can't Cunt Commanding Officers. Cockbreaths who only pay lip service to their mission orders. Lemme tell you, Sir Aubrey, I joined the fucking Navy at seventeen to fulfill my military obligation. I discovered I had a career when I joined the Teams. And when I was commissioned, when I became a SEAL—it became an obsession." I put my face up to his. "And I don't do my job by sitting on my butt and asking, 'May I?'"

His face flushed. "Nevertheless . . ."

"Look—like you say, this is your country. But it was my CNO

who got killed. I want a piece of the fucking action, and I want it now."

He looked at me in an infuriatingly unruffled manner. "Believe me, Captain, you will get your piece of, as you say, 'the fucking action.' But you will get it tomorrow. At ten. In my office."

He turned toward the window and stared out at St. James's Square. In the darkness outside I could distinguish the outline of an immense Bentley limousine as it glided from starboard to port to a stop in front of the club.

"Ah, I see my car has arrived." He rose, dropped his napkin on the table, brushed off the front of his bespoke suit, and started toward the dining-room doors. "Good night, Captain," he said without turning.

Chapter

5

I WAS LATE. FIRST, TONY MERCALDI CALLED ON THE SECURE PHONE IN Hans's cabin to pass on two nuggets of wisdom about the Foca, and to tell me that half a dozen faxes would be on their way within twenty-four hours. Then, Pinky got to me, jabbering about new intelligence, demanding to know what Sir Aubrey and I had talked about (fat fucking chance I'd tell him), and complaining that Randy Rayman couldn't find me anywhere. Finally, I stopped off at the Marriott, called Rogue Manor, and woke up Half Pint Harris. I told him to grab eight of Green Team's most experienced shooters, get their butts on a London-bound plane out of Dulles ASAP, and charge it all to my credit card. Pinky would piss and m-m-moan—after all, he'd denied my request for additional men. But there was no way I was going hunting without a virtual full platoon—and I *was* going hunting.

So, it was close to 1030 when I was finally ushered into the inner sanctum at the Ministry of Defense, just off Whitehall. I was carrying a huge, securely wrapped package containing the stabilizer fin I'd retrieved from Portsmouth harbor, and was followed by a hulking, suspicious MOD security man.

"Ah, finally." Sir Aubrey rose from behind the huge antique partner's desk that dwarfed him and waved Fearless Fosdick Yard off the case. "We'd been ready to declare you MIA, Captain," he said, extending a limp paw.

The two other men in the office also rose. He turned me toward the first. "Captain Dick Marcinko, this is Major Geoffrey Lyondale, Earl of Lockemont, commander of the Royal Marines Special Boat Squadron."

Instinct means a lot to me. And instinctively, I didn't like this guy at all. He looked like an ad from a men's fashion magazine. Tall, Eurotrash thin with prominent cheekbones, and sporting the kind of finely tailored, pinch-waisted, double-breasted, chalk-striped suit favored by people like Fred Astaire and the Duke of Edinburgh.

He wore his hair longish—the way the models in those Calvin Klein perfume ads wear theirs. A bright paisley handkerchief flopped foppishly over the breast pocket of his oxford, gray suit coat. His shirt was striped in green and purple, with a high, tight, white collar that made his head look like a ventriloquist's dummy. The white French cuffs were secured by small gold coins. His tie had huge white polka dots on a black background. But it was the tan suede wing-tip shoes that pushed the whole package over the edge. He looked down his aristocratic nose at me, thrust his hand vaguely in my direction, and sniffed (only Brits can sniff when they talk), "Chawmed. Cawl me Geoff, old man."

I took his hand, gave it a squeeze that made him wince, and answered in my best cockney imitation, "Geoff old man, call me Dick the prick, 'cause 'at's wot eye yam."

That brought a smile to the face of the other party. I turned toward him, extended my hand, and said, "Dick Marcinko."

"Lord Brookfield, Dick," he said, extending his own. "Call me Ishmael."

He had the brightest green eyes I have ever seen. They were the color of emeralds, and they bore into mine as if he were peering into my soul. He was as tall as I, and muscular in a thin, ascetic way. His short hair was coal black and straight, his skin tone the color of burnished copper by firelight. He wore dark trousers, and a multihued Harris Tweed coat over a gray cashmere turtleneck. His shoes were mahogany suede, and obviously bench-made. His hand was cool and his grip strong when it took mine. "I've heard a lot about you from Geoff."

"Have you?"

"Metter of feckt, he hes," Lyondale said.

That old phrase about mincing words took on a whole new meaning at this point.

I could see by the look on Sir Aubrey's face that things weren't going as smoothly as he would have liked. Well, Sir Aubrey was a big boy. He could handle it.

I figured it was time to get down to business. "I brought you something that might help us establish responsibility." I took the Emerson CQC6 from my pocket and slashed the wrapping, uncovering the stabilizer. "I found this yesterday."

"Where?" Sir Aubrey's eyes were wide as proverbial saucers.

"Portsmouth—in the harbor."

Geoff Lyondale's plucked eyebrows rose half an inch. "I had my lads search thoroughly. Where did you—"

"The far side of the chennel, old man—beyond the ferry route." I could tell by the look on Geoff's face that he'd never thought of having his men look there. "It's a stabilizer from a Foca minisub—a six-meter Foca. Crew of one. Holds up to six passengers, and half a ton of explosives. Made by MondoMare in La Spezia. It's the same kind of minisub used by Italian frogmen. It came off when the sub brushed a concrete piling that fell off a barge. That's how they came and went."

Lyondale looked critical. "How do you know it's a Foca?"

I knew because Tony Mercaldi told me. "Ran tests last night. Positive ID. Each piece of the Foca is numbered." I showed them where. "This one was delivered three years ago to the Yugoslav Navy base at Split."

Sir Aubrey fixed his monocle and examined the stabilizer, running his fingers over the metal. He flexed his cheek muscles and the silver-rimmed glass dropped back atop his waistcoat. "What's the range of this thing?"

"Three hundred fifty miles plus."

Brookfield scratched his chin. "So it could have launched from France—or the Channel Islands. Guernsey, perhaps."

"Sure. Or it could have been shit from a mothership to come a-calling."

Sir Aubrey coughed discreetly. "Very interesting, Captain."

I nodded. "Which, as I said last night, we should act on—now."

"Indeed," Sir Aubrey said. "That is precisely why I asked you here this morning."

I looked at Brookfield pointedly. "Isn't this a purely military matter?"

"You see, old man," Geoff Lyondale interjected, "I've hired Lord B as a consultant to SBS. He's been thoroughly vetted by Sir Aubrey. Top-secret clearance and all."

I turned toward Brookfield. "What's your operational background, sonny?"

Lyondale started to object, but Brookfield held up a manicured hand. "None at all, Captain. I'm what you operators call a thumb-sucker. Purely academic. I'm here because Geoff and I go back as far as Eton—we're a couple of Old Boys."

I didn't need this sort of thing so early in the day. "What is this crap? He's here because they took cold showers together when they were teenagers?" I looked at Sir Aubrey. "Goddammit, lives are at stake."

Brookfield continued unruffled. "In addition, I speak a modicum of Arabic. I've studied the Muslim world now and then. In fact, I've published three well-received little books on the subject."

"Lord B is being modest," said Sir Aubrey. "He took highest honors at Oxford. He speaks seventeen Arab dialects fluently, thirty others passably. His first published effort, *The Oriental Mind*, received the Prix Goncort. Two years ago, as he worked on the restoration of the Phoenician galley he himself discovered off Tyre, he was kidnapped by Hizballah terrorists. He was held for three months in the Bekáa Valley."

Captured by Hizballah was no way to spend time. "It must have been quite an experience. How did you survive?"

"I prayed a lot. I argued theology with my captors. I read the Koran." Lord Brookfield looked at me intensely. "I had an epiphany, chained to a radiator in Baalbek. I realized that, should I get through my crisis, should I survive, I had a sacred duty to help my friends here understand Islam; understand it so well that Hizballah, Hamas, Islamic Jihad, or any other group would have no reason to kidnap and kill Westerners anymore."

I was dubious about that. Like I said, perps are perps.

"He survived," Geoff Lyondale said proudly, interrupting my suspicions. "And he kept his promise—he came to me and offered his services. I jumped at the chance to bring him on board." He clapped Brookfield on the shoulder. "Lord Brookfield bridges both worlds. He can—and does—meet regularly with fundamentalist mullahs, Islamic radicals, moderate Egyptians—the whole spectrum of Muslim thought. And reports back to us on his findings. It's all very valuable."

I was dubious. But that's my nature.

Lyondale, however, seemed positively intoxicated by Brookfield's meetings with tango groups. "Besides," he bubbled enthusiastically, "Auntie was delighted, too."

"Auntie?" Who the hell was Auntie?

"Her Majesty," Sir Aubrey explained before I could ask. "Young Geoffrey is Prince Charles's second cousin. He is quite the Queen's favorite these days."

Just what I fucking needed—a Royal. I tried to smile. It didn't quite work.

Lord Brookfield caught my pained expression and brought the conversation back on track. "In any case, Captain, even you must admit that we thumb-suckers have merit from time to time."

I held up my hand. "I agree. In providing background. But not the sort of 'hot' intel my shooters need to score a hit."

"No? What about the current crisis? You say, for example, that the fin from the Foca came from Split, Bosnia."

"Right."

"And Split is in Serbian hands, isn't it?"

"I guess." I hadn't kept up with the current intel dumps on the Balkans.

"So that would make the perpetrators Bosnians, right?"

I shrugged. Maybe it would, maybe not. I wasn't assuming anything.

"Except, I heard from a source of mine—an imam in Turkey, who said he'd been told by a fellow imam in Macedonia—that a Muslim group calling itself the Sons of Gornji Vakuf hijacked a Foca forty-six days ago, and the Serb Navy covered up the theft because it didn't want to be seen as inept."

"Gornji Vakuf?"

Brookfield nodded. "The site of an appalling massacre in early 1994. Bosnian Serb fighters entered the village. They killed every Muslim they found—more than six hundred in all. They crucified the men, raped, tortured, then killed the women, and murdered the children. The scene was discovered by a unit of U.N. peacekeepers

—in this particular case British troops. Even those tough paras were overcome by the brutality of what they saw."

"So the attack at Portsmouth was what? Retribution for that massacre because the Brits got there too late? It doesn't make sense—first of all, they never took credit for the attack. Besides, wouldn't the Sons of Gornji whatever hit a Serb target?"

"It's not that simple. The Bosnian Muslims believe that the West has abandoned them. I've studied them—they always considered themselves Europeans. Now they're convinced that we here in Europe look at them in the same racist, anti-Arab way we look at the Algerians, Turks, or Yemenites who work in our kitchens—dirty Arabs. The Sons of Gornji Vakuf have vowed to make the West pay for its abandonment, and its anti-Muslim sentiments, by any means possible."

I looked at Sir Aubrey. "Have you heard anything about this?"

"Well," Sir Aubrey said, somewhat abashed, "as a matter of fact, not until Lord B informed me yesterday morning." He beat a tattoo with his fingertips on the fine inlaid wood surface of his antique desk. "But now, we're up to speed. The group exists. And the other elements of the story were verified. The sub disappeared from the former Yugo Navy base roughly six weeks ago. Now, you've provided hard evidence it was in Portsmouth harbor."

"Well, whoever did it—there's something else," I said.

"Yes, Captain?"

"I believe the terrorists came ashore in Britain."

Sir Aubrey's fingers went *thrummmp-thrummmp.* "Why?"

I slapped the fin with my hand. "Because of this. The sub lost a stabilizer. It could be steered left or right, but not up or down. That makes getting to a rendezvous next to impossible. I think the crew ditched it, then swam to shore."

"Excellent reasoning, Captain. We are convinced of the same thing—in fact, we believe they are still here, and that we even know where they are."

"Cheltenham picked up message traffic yesterday at about noon," Lyondale interjected. Cheltenham was the main British SIGINT—SIGnals INTelligence—listening post, operated in conjunction with the earwigs from No Such Agency. It was located in the quiet Gloucestershire countryside, about eighty-five miles west of London. Its eight square miles of antennas were like a huge vacuum cleaner, sucking signals out of the air. "We couldn't decipher the meaning, until we called Lord B to come in and listen."

"They were speaking in Bacovici, a seldom-heard dialect from a small Muslim district southwest of Sarajevo," Brookfield explained. "Quite parochial. Hard to interpret. Very much the same way you Yanks used Navajo Indian 'talkers' during World War Two to confuse the Germans and Japanese." He paused. "But *I* know Bacovici. Studied it at Oxford. Sun-dried brick, quasi-defunct languages, and all that rubbish, y'know. Musty, dusty libraries, et cetera, et cetera, et cetera." He smiled beneficently. "So you see, Captain, thumb-sucking has its advantages."

Perhaps it did. "What was the message?"

"The gist," Sir Aubrey said, "is that our quarry have gone to ground in Portsmouth—waiting until it gets quiet so they can strike again."

"Then let's go get the sons of bitches. Five of my shooters should be here by noon. We'll hit 'em tonight."

"Not so fast, Dick," Geoff Lyondale interrupted. "First of all, we're not prepared to go anywhere tonight. We have neither operational intelligence nor a coherent mission plan. Second, when we do choose to stage an attack, the *we*, in this case, will be SBS. Your SEALs will support our assault."

"Hey, Geoff, in case you missed the story on CNN, it was my CNO who got killed."

"In deference to which," he said, "Sir Aubrey has decided to allow your men to participate in the raid. But my commanding officer, too, was murdered. In any event, this is not a matter for debate. The bottom line, as you Yanks are so fond of saying, is that SEALs will remain in support, while SBS performs the assault. It makes sense. You, after all, are only five. We will send a full squadron."

"Five?" He was one man short.

"You said you have five men arriving today."

"That makes six of us." Plus the others from Rogue Manor he didn't know anything about.

"Surely, you'll be with me in the command center."

"No fucking way, Geoff. I don't sit on my ass while my men's lives are on the line."

"Command, Captain, is a sacred duty—but it doesn't require that you sacrifice yourself. Besides, this is all moot. Five or six men cannot do the job properly. We will need at least fifty. *We* have them and you don't."

He was right, damn him.

Thanks to Pinky da Turd, the lady may have spread her legs and given me the green light, but my dick was currently tied in a knot. Doom on me. "What's your plan?" I asked, thoroughly depressed.

Tommy and the boys were waiting in my suite when I got back. They'd already run up a hefty room-service tab, so to save the U.S. taxpayers further deficit spending, we adjourned to a pub two blocks away on Davies Street, occupied the secluded corner table, and took our Courage by the pint.

Tommy explained that our bundle must have had heart trouble, because he'd gone into shock by the time they'd put to sea and died shortly before the rendezvous.

"There was no sign of that in the cover documents."

"Nope," Tommy said. "He had a clean bill of health—no problems."

I shook my head. "Maybe it was the carbon monoxide. All that time in the trunk of Doc's car."

"Maybe. We dumped the body before the rendezvous."

That was good. No corpus delicti for Pinky—or anyone else—to find.

Then I brought everyone up to date as much as I could, sitting in that public place, not to mention the fact that we were probably being shadowed by one or two of Sir Aubrey's watchers. I described the players, explained the sorry hand of cards we'd been dealt, and hinted that reinforcements were arriving soon.

Our circumstances didn't make anybody happy. Still, the men surrounding me were the real nucleus of Green Team—shooters I knew I could depend on no matter what happened.

Stevie Wonder had put his career on the line for me dozens of times. I call him Stevie Wonder because he wears opaque, wraparound shooting glasses, and he swivels his head left-right-left, right-left-right, in a passable imitation of—you guessed it—Stevie Wonder. This goofy-looking, red-haired ex-Marine (in appearance he's somewhere between Howdy Doody and Ted Koppel) holds two classified Silver Stars for missions in North Vietnam back in the early seventies, so there's no doubt he knows how to shoot and loot. Stevie tried to go to BUD/S—Basic Underwater Demolition/

SEAL training—at the age of thirty-two. He lasted just under six weeks out of the twenty-six he needed before his USMC-issue feet gave out.

Even so, he was as tough and resilient as any SEAL in the world—and smarter than 99 percent of 'em when it came to operating in a hostile environment. Lots of operators can jump and dive and patrol when ordered. There are fewer and fewer these days who live to kill. Wonder is one of them—a true hunter. He's the kind of aggressive, driven, energetic asshole who looks for missions, instead of waiting to be told what to do. Indeed, Stevie'd killed more Japs than anyone at Green Team—except me.

Tommy T had volunteered to work with me even though he'd been the commanding officer of SEAL Team Eight and a trip to Green Team meant moving down the chain of command from CO to executive officer. Rank and standing didn't bother him in the least—what counted was the possibility of doing what he'd trained all his life to do, kill Japs. Tommy's my kind of warrior, too. Like me, he leads from the front—he doesn't ask anything of his men he won't do first.

One indicator of his success was that the current SpecWar commodore, a bald, bean-counting, squeaky-voiced twerp I'll call Captain Sphincter Twiddle Jr., tried to assign Tommy to a six-month tour aboard an aircraft carrier, while he was CO of Team Eight. Why? Because Tommy was spending too much money training his men for war, and not devoting enough time to the playing of football, baseball, and volleyball. To Commodore Twiddle, the Little Creek Amphibious Base intramural league was more important than SEAL Team Eight's ability to go to war—and because Tommy didn't see it that way, Twiddle wanted to get rid of him.

I was especially happy to have Tommy with me now because he'd served with SBS during a two-year exchange posting. He'd even kept in touch with some of the Royal Marine NCOs who'd sea-daddied him during the hazing process that SBS puts all newcomers through. I knew that with Tommy on the scene, we'd be able to circumvent Geoff Lyondale's restrictions.

Nasty Nicky Grundle downed his second pint and bellied up to the bar for another round. I'd selected Grundle for SEAL Team Six when he was but a 220-pound, twenty-year-old tadpole. A decade later, I'd discover what a deadly Frog he'd become when I was recalled to command Red Cell at CNO's behest. By then, Nicky

Grundle had been blooded in battle. He was one of the swim pair who blew up General Manuel Noriega's personal gunboat, the *Presidente Porras,* during Operation Just Cause. Nasty'd designed the C-4 explosive charges he and another SEAL carried half a mile. The recipe called for half a pound of C-4. Nicky, following my Spec-War dictums, had used two pounds of explosive—and blown the *Porras's* two three-ton diesel engines 150 yards down the harbor.

Howie Kaluha's broad shoulders blocked the view across the table from me. Howie's a master chief these days. I remember him as a boatswain's mate third class in Vietnam. He was a hunter who preferred two-man patrols that lasted five or six days in the boonies to the usual one-night, six-man shoot-and-loots. The day I met him he was wearing black pajamas, walking barefoot, and carried only a knife, and as many claymores, grenades, and M-60 detonators as he could pack in an oversize haversack. SEAL legend says that Howie had more hand-to-hand KIAs than any other single Frog in Vietnam. He himself takes credit for a mere one hundred Victor Charlies. His Navy Cross and three Silver Stars tell me he's a modest man.

Doc Tremblay having been left behind in Cairo, Duck Foot Dewey filled out the current detachment. Allen Dewey is a short, barrel-chested shooter from Maryland's flat-as-a-pancake Eastern Shore whose avocation is, obviously, mountain climbing. A veteran of SEAL Team Six and Red Cell, Duck Foot is the son of a WWII NCDU boatswain's mate—that's Naval Combat Demolition Unit, the precursors of all UDTs and SEALs—who landed on Omaha Beach on D day, and the older brother of a SEAL who's currently a PO2—that's Petty Officer Second Class—at SEAL Team Four. He's seen action in Grenada, Panama, and Somalia.

In Grenada, Duck Foot—a PO1 in those days—lost his temper when the operation turned into a total clusterfuck. Intel was nonexistent. Four of his platoon drowned when the senior SEAL commander—who led from behind, in this case from aboard a ship several miles away—had ordered Duck Foot's platoon to jump into eight-foot seas even though they carried more than one hundred pounds of equipment. Despite the losses, Duck Foot led the exhausted survivors to their objective—the Governor's Mansion. And when he ran into roughly 120 heavily armed Cubans up there, he stacked them like cordwood—he must have shot thirty single-handedly.

The Army would have rewarded Duck Foot's achievements with a Medal of Honor. I would have put him in for a Silver Star. But the CO of SEAL Team Six in those days was a guy I'll call Art Harris. Art, who never really wanted his men to kill anybody, made sure that Duck Foot's accomplishments got lost in the paperwork avalanche that customarily follows combat. None of the Barn Dance Cards—the after-action reports filed by unit commanders—mentioned Duck Foot's extraordinary achievements under fire.

We sat there for an hour or so, pondering the possibilities. None of them seemed very promising. Between Pinky da Turd and Sir Aubrey, I'd been boxed in quite neatly. Pinky was giving me no wriggle room, and Sir Aubrey had assigned me to work with a fucking fop. Quite a setup.

Well, I have always believed that when caught in an ambush, the only thing to do is to attack. Okay—Pinky Prescott, Sir Aubrey Davis, and Major Geoff Lyondale had fucking ambushed me. Good for them. Now it was going to be my turn.

I finished my third pint and set the glass down. "Listen up, assholes."

Tommy T took the first available train to Poole, the small port city on England's southeast coast where SBS had its headquarters. He still had friends down there, and I wanted an intel dump on Geoff Lyondale. Dump, hell—I wanted to know exactly how this asshole ran his unit.

Stevie Wonder wandered over to the Marine House, where the embassy's USMC guard contingent lived, to pump Uncle Sam's Misguided Children for information. Marines stay current when it comes to scuttlebutt. Nasty and Duck Foot worked the corridors at CINCUSNAVEUR. They oogled the secretaries, flexed their pecs, talked their way inside as many offices as they could, and gathered intelligence under the watchful eye of Hansie. The single place they couldn't infiltrate was CINCUSNAVEUR's sixth-floor comm center. There, behind barred windows, reinforced walls and ceilings, and safe-tight doors, eight rooms of state-of-the-art equipment gathered intel, sorted SIGINT reports, and sent encoded messages worldwide. Not even Hans could get up there without someone knowing.

Meanwhile, Howie Kaluha took the underground to London's East End where the city's largest Army & Navy store, Silverman's, is located. Howie was armed with all the petty cash I could lay my hands on, and a two-page handwritten shopping list.

And me? I paid a visit to an old girlfriend on the third floor of the American embassy over on the square. That's where our compatriots at Christians in Action maintain London station. My old flame's name is Nancy, and she still remembered me fondle-ly enough to let me borrow her secure computer terminal for a couple of hours and do some database searching about my new acquaintance, Call Me Ishmael, Lord Brookfield. While I typed and read, she massaged my neck and shoulders. When I'd printed up an armload of documents, we repaired to her flat in South Kensington where she massaged other parts of me.

He was, according to the printout, an only child, the son of Lord Louis Brookfield and a woman named Hagar, eldest daughter of a bedouin sheikh of the Awafi tribe. Lord Louis was a respected Arabist scholar from Oxford who'd volunteered—as had many of Britain's elite—as a commando during World War II. After training, Louis was assigned to Libya, where he served with the Polish brigade known as the Desert Rats. When the North African campaign ended, he'd been posted to Palestine, where he ran an intelligence network of bedouins against Axis agents.

Just after the war, so the story went, he'd had a mystical experience while climbing Mount Sinai to watch the sunrise from the Santa Katarina Monastery. A voice had told him to wander in the desert. He did so—for six months he forged himself on Sinai's cruel anvil, living an itinerant, mostly solitary existence. During his pilgrimage, he spent three weeks in an Awafi bedouin camp near Wadi Gebel. It was there he fell in love with the sheikh's daughter, Hagar. The two were married in a bedouin ceremony.

After the war, Lord Louis and his new wife returned to Laocoon's Gate, the five-hundred-acre Brookfield ancestral estate in Surrey. It was there that Hagar bore him the son they called (appropriately enough) Ishmael.

The youngster enjoyed all the advantages of his upper-class birthright. He'd excelled at everything in which he'd ever participated. He was a competition-grade skier and nationally ranked amateur tennis player. He'd been a member of Britain's 1992 Olympic shooting team. His income—estimated at more than £340 million annually—was derived from more than four and a half square miles of property he owned in the Mayfair, Knightsbridge, and Hampstead sections of London. He kept a thirteenth-century palazzo in Siena, a modernistic villa in Beaulieu-sur-Mer on the French Riviera, a chalet in Les Amants, high above Lac Léman, and a rustic beach house on the fashionable Caribbean island of Mustique (where a few other notable Brits, including Princess Margaret and Mick Jagger, also maintained million-pound getaways).

I read press clips from the 1992 Olympics and pored over a *National Geographic* that showed a young Lord Brookfield diving to recover Philistine artifacts off the Lebanese coast. The society pages of the London newspapers gave me a portrait of a self-assured but certainly not complacent young man. He was as obsessive about everything he did as I was—an overachiever who wouldn't ever quit or abandon a project half-finished.

Rested and massaged, we went back to the embassy, where I called my old friend Tony Mercaldi back at DIA on one of the CIA's secure lines. Tony said he'd wash Lord B's name through a Defense Intelligence Agency database, although he'd never heard the name before so he doubted there was anything of substance on file. Half an hour later he called back apologetically to report that Call Me Ishmael had his own dossier at DIA—and it was pretty thick, too.

What's in it? I asked.

Tony started with the biographical material, which jived with the CIA's notes so closely that the two agencies had probably used the same sources. Then he got to the current stuff. He said DIA believed Brookfield had been used by Whitehall as a diplomatic backchannel to several Arab leaders in the Gulf during Operation Desert Shield/Desert Storm. He had also been used to pass messages to two of the Iranian regimes that followed the Ayatollah Khomeini. He had what was described as "close personal relationships" with the Syrian president, the leader of Pakistan, and the Saudi royal family.

Because he'd been used to pass sensitive information, DIA had assigned its gumshoes to take a closer look at Lord B. Tony had scanned asset reports that chronicled Brookfield's activities on behalf of British intelligence, his detention in Lebanon, his friendship with Geoff Lyondale, even his personal security detail, which was headed by a former SBS first sergeant named Todd Stewart. He'd also been programmed into NSA's computers, which meant that overseas calls were scanned. The most recent notation in NSA's Brookfield file was a SIGINT report of a call last week from Cairo—no identification of the caller—to Lord B's Hampstead town house.

Merc's information dovetailed nicely with what the CIA databases had spit out. The most recent report from Langley—a psychological profile done less than three months ago—opined that the young Lord Brookfield might have suffered long-term Stockholm syndrome—that is, empathy for his captors—stemming from his three-month incarceration in Baalbek. The reason was that his political views—at least those expressed in the frequent newspaper op-ed articles he wrote for the *Times* and the *London Observer*—had become more sharply pro-Muslim after he'd suffered his hostage experience.

Four and a half hours later, my research completed, I walked back to the hotel. There, in the lobby, Lord Brookfield was waiting for me. He was sitting on an upholstered bench, perfectly creased trouser legs crossed at the ankles, reading the *London Times* through tortoiseshell half-glasses. Standing just in back of him, arms crossed, was six feet six or so of the most muscular, dangerous-looking black man I'd ever seen.

Brookfield saw me come through the revolving doors, slid the glasses into the breast pocket of his shooting jacket, and rose to greet me. His shadow moved as he did, watching me the way *Schutzhund* rottweilers watch their potential targets. "Captain," Brookfield said, extending his hand in greeting. "I was hoping I'd catch you."

I shook his. "Nice to see you, Lord B."

"I was thinking we'd go across the street to my club and chat a bit—perhaps you'd like to try the sherry. It's imported especially for us."

It sounded good to me. I looked up at the dark specter blocking all the light. "Who's Frankenstein's monster?"

"Ah—my companion and bodyguard, Todd Stewart, late of the Isle of Skye. Huge, isn't he?"

There was no denying it. Stewart was probably just shy of 250 pounds, although his body fat couldn't have been more than 1 percent. His round face, accented by a thin mustache, was expressionless. He had the cold cobra's eyes of a professional shooter. He was dressed in a fashionable double-breasted suit of muted plaid, but instead of shoes, he wore black cowboy boots made of—I took a second look to make sure—sharkskin. His hairstyle was almost a carbon copy of my own—pulled back into a single braid that ran down his back. Except that his was tied with several strands of Dress Stewart tartan, while mine was restrained by plebeian elastic.

"I've heard of black Irish, but you're the first black Scotsman I've ever met." I put out my hand. It was ignored.

"Please excuse Todd—he has an aversion to touching people, unless it's absolutely necessary."

"When does it become absolutely necessary?"

"When he kills them," Brookfield said matter-of-factly. "In the Falklands campaign, he was cited for extraordinary performance. He's a hand-to-hand specialist. A knife man. He'd penetrate the Argentine lines—and then, he'd penetrate the Argentines." A wry smile came over Brookfield's face. "You see, after I was kidnapped in Lebanon, I realized that I might present a more inviting target than I had imagined. So, Geoffrey found me Todd. He'd just left SBS after twenty years and was seeking employment. That was eighteen months ago—and we've been together ever since. He's managed to keep me safe and sound. It's a good arrangement, don't you think?

"Whatever works, Lord B."

We exited the hotel and walked back up Duke Street to Grosvenor Square, turned left, crossed Brook Street, and ambled half a block to an anonymous ivory doorway at Number 69. Brookfield opened the heavy door and motioned for me to precede him inside.

It wasn't fancy. In fact, it was shabby in the genteel way most of London's clubs are worn: threadbare, hundred-year-old Persian carpets on the floors, tattered leather chairs, and well-used tables. But the marble foyer was impressive, and there were Old Masters on the walls. Brookfield led me back through a reading room to a long bar that looked out on a disused courtyard.

An octogenarian bartender in a striped waistcoat brightened as we came into the room. "Afternoon, m'lord," he said, a wide smile on his face.

We sat facing each other in ancient leather wing chairs, a

half-bottle of Saville Club Fino and a liter of San Pellegrino on a silver salver between us. Todd remained standing in the doorway.

Brookfield, who was drinking the bottled water, toasted me. "Cheers."

I lifted my sherry glass in his direction. We sipped. His green eyes never left me. "You're deceptive, Captain."

"How so?"

"You play the part of knuckle-dragger quite well. And yet, you're quite sophisticated, aren't you?"

"You tell me."

"I know you came up through the ranks—a mustang, isn't that what the Americans call enlisted men who become officers?"

I nodded.

"And I know that you have advanced degrees, despite your propensity toward vulgarity, violence, and shock tactics."

"Unpredictability is an important—even crucial—element of special warfare. I find it useful." I watched him as he sipped. "So, Lord B—Ishmael—what the fuck? Why the invitation to this little tête-à-tête?"

He smiled at me. "I believe that you are underestimating the opposition. I want to make sure you don't."

"You mean your pal Geoff?"

The look on his face told me he hadn't liked my little joke. "Of course not—I'm talking about the forces who killed your CNO."

"They're terrorists. They'll die."

"It's not as simple as that."

"Why not?"

"Because those 'terrorists' you paint with such a broad brush are really decent souls, despite their actions. It's just that they've been pushed beyond the limit by your society. They are tired of the West's historic anti-Islamic racism—based on caricature, prejudice, and ignorance. They're tired of being poor and ill-educated and taken advantage of. They're tired of being killed by others while you—we—in the West just stand by."

"So they react by killing innocent people."

"You may not like their methods, but those methods are understandable, after so many hundreds of years of humiliation. It's their way of getting attention for their plight—of making the rest of the world wake up. But that's not the point. The point is that—"

91

"That's exactly the point. Don't ask me to empathize with a bunch of assholes who believe their ticket to heaven is a magic-carpet ride that begins when they detonate a car bomb or blow up an aircraft carrier. Don't ask me to feel sorry for scumbags who murder innocent people."

"Your view is parochial. It is the view of a typical, uneducated, Western military assassin. I give you more credit than that, Captain. So, just for a minute, look at things from another perspective. Take the Gulf War for example. In the West it was seen as a great alliance. To the disenfranchised Muslim it was seen as a modern Crusade— Christendom and its corrupt Arab allies versus the purity of Islam. That is the lesson preached in mosques from Fez to Kabul."

"But that view is wrong."

"Perhaps to a Westerner, to a non-Muslim. You must, Captain, walk the proverbial mile in our shoes. Look at recent events as they are seen from the Muslim point of view. The bombings all across the United States, for example—"

"You can't deny they were terrorist acts, can you?"

"I certainly can deny it—if, from my perspective, I am waging war against the West. In that case, I can define it as a series of small but significant battles won by my side."

"And the perpetrators?"

"Islam's soldiers in the great war against nonbelievers."

"If they are soldiers, then I will hunt them down and kill them."

"Hunting them will be impossible for you. You are an outsider. They have support and infrastructure. Did you know, Captain Marcinko, that the men you perceive as terrorists can go to virtually any Muslim neighborhood in England and receive help, because most of the Muslims who live here feel discriminated against by the West? So, they tend to see these, ah, lethal activists much the same way the peasants living around Nottingham once saw Robin Hood."

Lethal activists—quite a designation for people who killed innocents indiscriminately. How genteel. How politically correct. Obviously, the man had a way with words. I let it pass. "Robin Hood?"

"Yes. And not only in England. Algerians and Tunisians in France; Turks in Germany, Libyans in Italy, Palestinians and Lebanese in the United States—they, too, will give refuge to any who stand for Islam against the slanders, misrepresentations, and prejudices of the West. Moreover, it is my belief that all of them—no matter what country they come from—are just like the peasants of Sherwood—waiting for their Richard to return."

The argument didn't impress me. "They're going to have a long, long wait."

"Time is of no concern, Captain. Muslims, you see, have faith— unshakable faith. We have faith in the Koran; we have faith in ourselves; we have faith that we will persevere. We have to."

"Have to?"

"History and religion are the two great cornerstones of Islam. Each teaches us to have faith. So, Muslims are great students of history. Indeed, I have come to see Muslims as history's orphans— cast out, ridiculed, persecuted, and poor."

"What about all that oil money in the Gulf?"

"I meant poor in the spiritual sense. Riches mean nothing. They are but a means to an end—the restoration of multinational Islam. Our decline began, one might argue, when Boabdil, the last Muslim ruler of Spain, gave up the keys to the city of Granada in 1492—the same year, incidentally, Christopher Columbus sailed for the New World. That decline continues even today—the West's abandonment of the Muslims in what used to be Yugoslavia is evidence of it. If we truly mattered, if we were a power to be reckoned with, that genocide would not have been allowed."

He sipped his water. "You see us as caricatures, Captain Marcinko. We are not. You see us as 'fundamentalists,' who martyr ourselves on what you call 'a magic-carpet ride.' We are more than that."

I found it interesting that he was including himself and said as much.

"Yes, *we*." He looked at me in the same crazily beatific way that newly reborn religious zealots tend to look. "I converted to Islam during my time in Baalbek. It was my destiny."

That was news. That hadn't appeared in DIA's files. Still, it was also absolute confirmation of what had been hinted at in the CIA profiles I'd read back at the embassy. Stockholm syndrome, hell— the guy had gone all the way. "Destiny?"

"Yes," he said emphatically. "But it is also my destiny to use all of my knowledge, my power, and my resources to help the West understand Islam, and to help Islam deal with the West. I am unique, Captain. I am a man of both worlds—your Western world, and my Eastern one. You may find this hard to comprehend, but there is a whole society that believes the West is immoral, decadent, and corrupt. To those who follow Islam, which means 'submission,' there is but one way—the way of jihad."

"The Muslim word for holy war."

"That is one definition—and the most common one. It is apt that you, a Navy officer, would define jihad that way," Brookfield said, his eyes boring into my own. "But there is another translation. Jihad also means a total, supreme, unlimited, immeasurable, all-out effort."

"I can relate to that. It's what SEALs have to summon up during BUD/S."

"BUD/S?"

"Basic Underwater Demolition/SEAL training. Think of it as a six-month kick in the balls."

He looked at me as if I'd offered him something distasteful to eat. "The kind of effort the Afghanistanis summoned up to turn back the Soviet invasion and defeat the Red Army cannot be compared with any so-called basic training," he said derisively. "You must change your basis of reasoning, Captain."

"Must I?"

"Yes. To our way of thinking, in Afghanistan one of the world's two superpowers was defeated by intense faith."

I wasn't about to let him get away with that. "Not to mention seven billion dollars in aid from the United States."

His eyes shone with white-hot anger. "The money didn't matter. The most important statistic, Captain, was that there were three million martyrs in our holy war—and if jihad demands it, we are willing to provide three, four, five million more—any number to achieve the goal our jihad requires."

"Jihad again."

"Yes—jihad again. Total effort. It is *that* definition which leads me to warn you again: do not underestimate these people. It could be dangerous for you. After all, we defeated a superpower."

There it was again—"we," not "they." I studied him intently. The expression on his face was frightening. He was clearly over the edge.

Well, it was time to bring him back to reality. I finished my drink and slapped the glass back on the table with a loud *thwock*. "Lord Brookfield, there was a big difference between the Soviets and the

United States. Believe me—I spent more than thirty years working that particular battlefield, so I know what I'm talking about."

"But your goal was always to preserve your country—strategically, you and the Soviets relied on the theory of mutually assured destruction to ensure that neither of you fired first. Those who wage jihad are different. They, Captain, are willing to pay any price. Death means nothing. You nonbelievers cannot fathom the depths of our passion. Besides, your military is bound by too many rules and political decisions to make it an effective opponent these days. Your society is too big, too open, too naive, to win against a society willing to martyr itself in order to win."

I grinned at him. "Maybe. But then there's me."

"Ah, yes. You—America's Rogue Warrior." He looked at me in a way that was indescribable except to say that even I found it frightening. "You, Captain, are a challenge." His green eyes bore into my own. Suddenly, I understood where this was all going. This was to be between him and me—up close and personal. I liked that.

Now it was my turn. I stared him down until he looked away. "If you've ever read my books, Lord Brookfield, you'll know that SEALs are dangerous when we're provoked. In fact, we get absofuckinglutely lethal."

"Yes, I gathered that."

"Well, 'gather' this, cockbreath—because, like the old master chief says, you'll see the material again: when I wage jihad, I don't take prisoners."

Part
Two

BRAVO

Chapter

6

WE WERE SUMMONED DOWN TO POOLE AT 0600 FOR AN OPERATIONAL briefing. My eight shooters from Rogue Manor had arrived at Heathrow the previous morning—oops, I just clean forgot to tell P-P-P-Pinky about them—and so we left London at 0100 in a convoy of three battleship gray CINCUSNAVEUR Land Rovers. We lumbered our way through the lush green Surrey countryside past Woking, Farnham, and Alton just after midnight, worked our way around Winchester in the chill darkness, and lost our way at the Romsey crossroads at about 0410. We got back on track, passed through Ringwood at dawn's early light, and came up on Poole from Bournemouth, to the east, at 0440.

As we worked our way through the ancient streets, I realized I'd forgotten just how depressing the town was. Poole is a dreary, coastal working-class town to which had been added, during the Second World War, a Royal Marine barracks. Once a major port, Poole had been overshadowed by its newer neighbor Bournemouth, which gained prominence in the late nineteenth century as a Victorian seaside resort. Gradually, the smaller, poorer stepchild, Poole, had gone to seed.

Indeed, in many ways it reminded me of my own childhood

home. Lansford, Pennsylvania, like Poole, was a meager, confining sort of place where you lived, you worked, and you died. In Lansford, you lived in housing owned by the coal mine and got your groceries at Kanuch's, where Old Man Kanuch kept a ledger with how much you owed tallied up in thick pencil strokes. The only solace was offered by the Slovak bars where they served shots, beers, and pickled pigs' feet to generations of labor-toughened, rough-handed men who trudged in covered with coal dust, men like my grandfather Joe Pavlik.

Poole had its family grocery stores and neighborhood pubs, too—and its slums. But it also suffered the kind of distasteful, unplanned urban sprawl that includes minimalls, bowling alleys, and multiscreen cinemas, all done in plastic pseudo-Tudor.

It was raining steadily now, the kind of bone-soaking, arthritis-nurturing rain you get in Western Europe. I could feel it working on my hips and elbows. We worked our way through the town toward the Royal Marine barracks, which sat on the water, just opposite Brownsea Island. As Tommy T drove the narrow streets, I peered through the windscreen, half-mesmerized by the irregular, flamaque syncopation of the wipers. Things were much the same as I remembered from my SEAL Team Six days.

We identified ourselves and proceeded through the gate. The officers' mess was the same squat, morose structure I remembered. I was certain that the rations inside would be the same tasteless, gluey glop they'd fed me before, and that when I went to the crapper, the TP would be shiny on one side, sandpaper on the other, and have the cardboard consistency of mashed egg cartons. We drove past. The well-worn red brick and the cracked concrete pathways were coated with rain.

Tommy drove straight to HQ and parked our Land Rover in the visitor's spot. The others pulled up next to us, and I watched as my grungy bunch emerged and stretched, oblivious to the downpour. Tommy—always the fashion plate—wore a Burberry, a blazer, and his Royal Marines tie. Everyone else, me included, were in casual civvies—jeans, boots or running shoes (I was in my thong sandals), sweatshirts, and assorted Gore-Tex or leather jackets. We were met by a spit-and-polish lance corporal who gave Tommy a big smile, looked at the rest of us as if we'd materialized from another planet, then ushered us onto SBS's quarterdeck.

The news Tommy'd brought back to London after his trip down

here had been as gloomy as the weather was right now. Things were bad. Morale sucked. The reason could be summed up in precisely three words: Geoffrey fucking Lyondale.

It would seem, Tommy had learned, that the earl was more interested in pursuing the good life in London than he was in making sure that his shooters honed their fragile, frangible skills. So, training these days was slack.

Let me digress, gentle reader, to put this unhappy fact into context for you. When I was CO of SEAL Team Six, each man shot a minimum of three-thousand rounds a day during training cycles, and one thousand rounds a day between training cycles. I didn't care how they shot—one-handed, two-handed—shit, they could have used their cocks to squeeze the triggers for all I cared. My orders were simple and precise: to hit a three-by-five index card planted on a human-sized target every time they pulled the trigger.

For a shooter, that's the bottom line—hit your goddamn target every time you shoot. They had to hit the fucking target whether they were climbing an ice-coated oil rig, struggling up a slippery caving ladder to board a ship, dropping off a bouncing chopper, or coming out of the fucking surf. They had to hit it whether they were fresh or burnt out, sharp or hungover, well rested or shit-can tired.

I just love it when SpecWar commanders hold shooting competitions these days. They run them like conventional target shoots—complete with warm-ups and slow-fire events. And what do the participants do? They punch paper.

Well, combat is different from target shooting. Your adrenaline is pumping, your sphincter is tight, your mind's racing, and there are assholes out there who're shooting back at you. It's known as stress shooting—emphasis on the word *stress.* You go through the door and you ding yourself on walls or furniture. There's smoke and there's noise. You're hurt or confused. And you still gotta hit the tango and kill him. There's only one way to do it. The same way you get to Carnegie Hall—*practice.* Shoot hundreds of thousands of rounds, until shooting becomes as natural as breathing. At SEAL Team Six I used more ammo in a year than the entire U.S. Marine Corps did.

Now, here's the rub: if you miss even a few days of shooting practice, your edge disappears. Just like your muscles will start to deteriorate if you miss more than three days of PT, your shooting skills will erode if you don't shoot all the time. Not so much that anybody will necessarily notice—but a hair's width at a time. That infinitesimal erosion, however, is just enough to make you lose the edge in a one-on-one with a bad guy. So the answer is simple: you shoot. All the time. Every day. And thus will thou stay alive. End of sermon.

At Poole, they didn't shoot every day. Not anymore. Not since Geoffrey had taken over. He'd cut back on ammo to save money. He'd cut back to save wear and tear on the kill-house. He was probably related to most of the American SpecWar COs I knew— Can't Cunt Commanding Officers, who spend their time whining and explaining why they can't do this or can't do that.

There was more. The earl had also restricted SBS's ability to maintain what he called unauthorized—read backchannel— intelligence networks. Everything had been centralized, so that the earl and his old Eton buddy Call Me Ishmael controlled the flow and the scope of SBS's operational intelligence. There were no more forays into Britain's port areas to chat up the wharf rats, stevedores, crane operators, and tugboat hands. By curtailing the activity, Lockemont ran a neater organization. But in my opinion, he'd lost the ability to develop operational intelligence that would allow him to act quickly and effectively.

Geoff Lyondale, dressed in starched Royal Marine BDUs, greeted us just inside the doors. The look on his face told me he hadn't been told I'd arrived with more than five shooters. And he asked where Randy Rayman was. Damn, I said apologetically, we'd forgotten him again. I shook my head and suggested that perhaps he could catch a train later in the day.

I introduced my men to the SBS commander. He shook hands with each one formally but distantly. They didn't have the spit-and-polish look officers like Geoff mistake for military competence. No, *my* men look and act like dirtbags. If you read their fitreps, they were unruly scum—rogues who should be kept in cages between wars. But those fitreps were all too often written by professional staff officers like Pinky, or unproven youngsters like Randy Rayman, who had no firsthand knowledge of what qualities make a true warrior.

I, however, was happy with my long-haired, scurvy-looking crew. Tommy, Wonder, Nasty, Howie, and Duck Foot had acquitted themselves well in Cairo. And as for the newcomers, Half Pint

Harris had rostered himself and his old swim buddy, Piccolo Mead, to the contingent. Like my XO Tommy, Half Pint had once served a tour in Britain: a year and a half with the SAS. Rodent was another pint-size shooter. At the age of eighteen, he'd made seventeen kills during a six-month Vietnam tour. Warrant Officer Second Class Purdy Boy Floyd was a machine-gun specialist from Oklahoma whose second love was C-4 explosive. Chief Petty Officer Carlosito, like Duck Foot, was a SEAL Team Six survivor of the clusterfucked Grenada operation where he'd lost four of his closest buddies. He'd rejoined Green Team from a billet in Puerto Rico after I assumed command. Carlosito had worked for me at Red Cell. So had Rooster, Sergeant Snake, an airborne asshole turned SEAL, and Doctor Dan. They were all old-fashioned shoot-and-looters: each one of them was combat tested and battle proven, as the weapons ads are fond of saying.

Speaking of shooting and looting, I mentioned to Geoff that we were light on weapons. Oh, the eight guys from the Manor had come armed. They always travel with Mad Dog Frequent Flyer knives in their belts or boots. FFs are composite knives that do not show up on any X-ray or metal detector, but can still slice through a thick web belt—or a human neck—without any effort. They'd also smuggled H&K USP pistols in their checked luggage, as well as schlepped a suitcase full of my clothes and other personal goodies. But we had no submachine guns, and no ammo. I asked if it was possible to remedy the situation. Geoff's hemming and hawing told me that I'd better start scrounging. I flicked an eyebrow at Rodent, my SFC, or Scrounger First Class, who got the message loud and clear.

Lyondale asked whether he could speak to Tommy and me in private, while my shooters grabbed some breakfast in the enlisted mess with his men. "It's your show, Geoff."

Accompanied by Squadron Sergeant Harvey—the Royal Marine equivalent of a SEAL master chief—we quick-marched through a series of hallways into what appeared to be a nonsecure conference room. In the center, nevertheless, sat a table to which a huge sheet of paper had been taped. I recognized the outline of Portsmouth harbor, drawn in bold lines. A series of clear plastic overlays with red crayon markings on them designated several of what appeared to be dockside warehouses in the narrow strip of land between the west of the Navy base and the town proper.

Two officers in tunics, a captain and a lieutenant, waited table-side. They had the bookish look of intel squirrels.

Lyondale made introductions. Handshakes all around. He offered coffee. Tommy and I accepted. Squadron Sergeant Harvey poured. I know enlisted men. After all, I used to be one. And I've never forgotten the lessons I learned as an enlisted Team puke. Well, the look in Harvey's eyes was the same as the look in my old platoon chief Ev Barrett's eyes, when Barrett was faced with incompetent, idiotic, prissy young officers who believed the gold badges on their collars made them gods. It's a look that says, "Disregard following messages."

I gave Harvey a wink and a nod, then turned back to the table ready for business. The anxious intel weenies tallyho'd and began their formal show-and-tell.

Half an hour later, I knew no more than I'd known when we'd walked into the room, and I said as much to Geoff. He hadn't run any thermal tests on the warehouses. Nor had he done visual or sonic penetrations. What his operators had done was cruise up and down the warehouse area under his direction, looking for movement. Minute-by-minute reports of activity were transmitted back to HQ on secure scrambler radios, then analyzed on a huge grid. The results were predictable: zero.

"What about operational intelligence?"

Lyondale assured me that he'd obtained hard evidence.

Hard and operational are not necessarily the same thing. I asked how old the data was, and what kind of sources he'd used. He said he'd used satellite data.

"What?" I wondered how he'd managed to get an eye in the sky so quickly. Changing a satellite's course can take days.

He explained that there had been a SPOT satellite in the area, and it had been programmed to seek data on the Portsmouth area.

Great. SPOTs are commercial imaging satellites. French commercial imaging satellites to boot. And their resolution was a mere five meters—in other words, they could make out nothing that wasn't at least 16 feet in length.

How the hell that would help, I had no idea. I'm used to VELA graphics, which give me six-inch resolution from twenty-two thousand miles in space. And, I asked, what about tactical info? Like, how thick was the roof—would it support an assault force? What kind of doors led to the stairwells, and were the hinges on the inside or the outside? Could they be jimmied or did they have to be blown with shotguns or shaped charges?

Geoff didn't quite have the answers. Those problems would sort themselves out when the team hit, he assured me.

He explained that Lord Brookfield had helped develop the intelligence package, and he—just like Sir Aubrey, he emphasized —had complete faith in Lord B's abilities. I asked whether he'd determined if the Sons of Gornji Vakuf had additional missions planned. I asked if he knew how they were armed—with what— and what types of communications they were capable of.

He said that those sorts of details were secondary to the necessity of hitting the tangos immediately. He pointed at a rectangular outline on the map. The terrorists were in this warehouse, he said. He was sure of it. Accordingly, by using a superior force to overcome all obstacles, he had decided to stage a frontal assault tonight. Storm the warehouse, root out the tangos, and take at least one prisoner for intelligence purposes.

I couldn't believe what I was hearing. He didn't even know how many T's his men would face. This op had goatfuck written all over it.

"What about the locals? Any word about recent developments from the wharf rats?" Shit—I'd have sent my men out to work the pubs.

"Mere enlisted men conducting independent intelligence ops, Captain? Be serious," Lyondale snorted derisively. His intel wee-nies added they hadn't bothered to interview any of the locals because they didn't want to compromise operational security.

"You're probably already compromised, Geoff old man," I said.

Lyondale's eyebrows arched. "How, old chap? Our chatter was encoded."

"Sure, your transmissions were scrambled, but they use energy. You don't need million-dollar equipment to eavesdrop. Shit—I can use a fucking television as an early-warning system."

"Impossible."

"Listen, Geoff, old cock, whenever there's heavy radio chatter, TV sets develop interference. Flickering. Snow. You don't need to buy high-frequency scanners—one man watching a cheap TV'll do the same thing."

"I doubt that very much," Lyondale pronounced. "I've never heard of it."

The cockbreath was about to commit suicide. Except, *he* wasn't going to be the one cut into ribbons—it was his men who'd die, while he looked on and sipped his fucking cuppa.

Maybe there was some way to improve a bad situation. I asked if his decision to assault was irrevocable. It was, he said. Okay, I suggested, what about going from the top down, instead of the bottom up? It's easier and more effective and allows you to flush the bad guys into a prearranged ambush.

Lyondale thought about that for a while and finally agreed that a chopper assault via fastrope was not a bad idea. "Good video, too," he added.

"What?" He couldn't be serious.

He was serious. "Video. I'm planning to invite a CNN camera crew to join us. Of course we'll embargo the tape until it's all over. But we need the publicity—budget cuts and all that, y'know."

He was a bigger asshole than I'd imagined. I looked at Tommy, who rolled his eyes in disbelief. "Whatever you say, Geoff." Now, I was more than willing to accept Green Team's support role. I didn't want anything to do with this incipient debacle.

By midmorning I'd worn Geoff down enough so that he relented, passed out a dozen of his precious MP5s and three thousand rounds of ammo, and allowed me and my men to use the kill-house. We worked in seven-man squads, each squad paired with an equal number of SBS troopers, so we could learn how we all worked. When I commanded SEAL Team Six, I insisted that we cross-train with as many CT units as possible so that joint operations wouldn't deteriorate into joint clusterfucks.

SBS, for example, clears rooms in the classic British manner pioneered by SAS—which is, to throw a crash-bang grenade inside, then immediately enter the room with bullet and bayonet. The philosophy is that if you use enough bullets, bayonets won't be necessary. So the room clearers come in blasting, firing through doors into closets, cupboards, and other likely hiding places. They shoot into the ceilings and floors, too. It's effective, but it can be detrimental to ornamental architecture.

We work differently. We scope the area with thermal and audio imaging, then stack seven men outside the door in what's known as a train. To the right of the door is a point man and a breacher. To the left are the room clearers and rear security man.

When the team is ready, the last man in the stack—the rear security man—squeezes the shoulder of the man in front of him, which indicates that he's fully prepped and ready to shoot and loot. Each man in turn squeezes the shoulder of the man in front of him, so that by the time the number one man's shoulder is squeezed, he knows that everyone in the stack is locked, loaded, and ready to go.

The number one man then makes eye contact with the breacher and nods three times. The breacher then blows the door, and the two room clearers move in. Number one man goes left, number two man goes right. They sweep left-right and right-left until their fields of fire converge, but unlike the Brits, we do not shoot unless we make visual contact with the enemy. In this, our technique is closer to the German CT unit, *Grenzschutzgruppe*-9 (GSG-9), or Israel's General Staff Reconnaissance Unit 269, *Say'eret Maktal*, known colloquially as The Boys.

If you're operating jointly, you'd better know where the other guy's field of fire lies, because if you don't, you can easily kill each other. Believe me, there's enough of Mr. Murphy's Law to go around, and every little thing that can be done to frustrate him should be done.

In any case, I was glad to see that despite the lack of leadership, the SBS troopers were the same gung ho lot they'd always been. At lunch, we managed to sneak a few of the noncoms off the reservation long enough to enjoy a bull session and several dozen pints of Courage bitter at the Rose & Thistle, half a mile from the barracks gate.

Assholes like Geoff believe in the old-fashioned military caste system that separates the officers from enlisted men and noncoms. They lead from behind and treat their men as if they're idiots. I've always believed in unit integrity. And I create it from the top down. I eat, drink, piss, shit, and fuck with my men. I ask nothing of them that I haven't done first.

Story. My sea daddy, Lieutenant Commander Roy Boehm, the kick-ass ex-boatswain's mate godfather of all SEALs, commissioned SEAL Team Two on January 2, 1962. At that time the unit was so top secret that almost no one in the Navy knew of its existence, which had made its creation a virtually impossible task. Of course, to Roy, the word *impossible* never existed.

After he'd made his final selection, he assembled his new unit for its first briefing. The men were sworn to secrecy, too. They were

107

warned on pain of death—and Roy was patently capable of carrying out that threat only too well—not to explain who they were or what they did to anyone. Well, that very day, one of the SEAL Team Two plank owners, Jim Watson (who would later become my first point man in Vietnam), got himself tossed in jail for being . . . himself. He called Roy from the lockup. Roy came down and retrieved him.

From his cell, Watson could hear Roy talking to the cops. "Turn him over to me," Roy said. "I'm his commanding officer, and I'll fucking kill this young puke sailor." Watson listened as Roy explained how he'd rip him a new asshole. He'd kick his no-account dipshit pus-nutted butt so hard Watson would be licking the fucking toe of Roy's goddamn boondocker. He'd keelhaul the son of a bitch.

The cops turned Jim over, and Roy escorted him out of the station house by the scruff of the neck. Watson was scared shitless. "Come with me you worthless shit-for-brains asshole," said Boehm. Then, once they were outside, Roy told Jim, "Let's go grab a goddamn drink someplace."

"What about all those things you said inside?" Watson asked.

"Shit, son, that was an act so they'd release you into my custody. I can't get mad at you for doing the same things I've been doing for years. But I'll tell you something—if you ever try to do anything I haven't done first, I'll kick your ass into next fucking *year*."

After that, there was no place on the face of the earth—or anywhere else—that Jim Watson wouldn't have followed Roy Boehm.

Roy, God bless him, passed a lot of his wisdom on to me when I became a SEAL. I'd already realized that leading from the front was the only way to go. But Roy helped me hone my leadership capabilities in such areas as using alcohol as a tool. Yes, alcohol can become a tool. In fact, a CO can learn a lot by drinking with his men. You can see how they respond to outside stimuli, discover how they react to stress, even expose character flaws (for example, a guy who becomes easily provoked after a couple of drinks will not be a great undercover operator—he'll draw attention to himself and threaten the mission). Booze is also a leveler. It is one of the elements I use to create unit integrity.

And, in situations like the current one I was in, an hour or so of shared pints in a pub gave us SEALs a month's worth of guidance about Geoff that might have taken a week to pry from the normally closemouthed SBS noncoms under nonalcoholic conditions. In any case, at about 1400, suitably fortified by Courage and conversation against BS, the combined unit snuck back to the reservation for the formal briefings, which were conducted in the same nonsecure room as our early-morning session.

I wondered if the tangos had any ELINT—ELectronic INTelligence—capabilities. If they had, we were letting them in on all of our secrets.

Actually, it wouldn't have mattered very much. The briefings were drawn straight from the British Urban Warfare manual, which opines that occupying forces have everything on their side—cover, confusion, booby traps, fortified buildings—and the assault force has no choice except to expose itself.

I do not agree with that point of view. I have always believed that, with good intelligence, an aggressive and unconventional force can stage urban assaults with limited casualties to the assaulters, and heavy ones to the tangos.

But my point of view didn't count for horsepiss today. Here, I was a supporting player—just another spear carrier. Of course, given Geoffrey's bright idea of inviting the media to come along, I was frankly delighted to leave things that way.

The target Geoffrey had selected was a warehouse that had been converted to an office building. The revised scenario was almost reasonable. The place would be cleared by seven-man teams of SBS Marines. Some would drop from a pair of Puma choppers, fastrope onto the roof, and work their way down. Others would assault from the ground. Each team would commence work on a specific portion of the building, clearing the office and storage spaces one by one.

They would either kill the tangos on the spot or drive them down to the building's three exits, where forces that had slipped into the area prior to the assault—including my SEALs—would be waiting in ambush. If at all possible, we'd capture some of the tangos alive so we could interrogate them.

There was nothing basically wrong with the concept. It was the problems of execution that bothered me.

Let me explain. Basically, effective clearance—whether it is room, passageway, stairwell, or building clearance—depends on what Everett E. Barrett, chief gunner's mate/guns, UDT-21, used to call the Law of the Seven Ps. *Proper Previous Planning Prevents Piss-Poor Performance,* is how Ev put it.

When I commanded SEAL Team Six, we spent months and months perfecting our room-clearing technique. Basically, it is a choreographed exercise that combines unambiguous leadership from the front, thorough planning, efficient, decisive movement, and full use of concentrated fire and violence of action. There is also one paramount factor without which everything else is redundant: audacious fighting spirit.

Let me repeat that. Audacious fighting spirit.

According to the figures on my mental tote board, SBS was about to be ground into sausage. Sure, the unit had audacious fighting spirit and violence of action, but Earl Geoff wasn't about to allow them the sort of free rein that would unleash those lethal, noble qualities. He was the kind of officer who got queasy when he cut himself shaving.

- Unambiguous leadership from the front? Don't make me laugh.
- Thorough planning? Do the phrases *seat of the pants* and *off the cuff* mean anything to you? We had no structural photos—only the 5-meter SPOT images, which gave us only the building's most basic outlines.
- Efficient and decisive movement? Let me put it this way: there were no plans for the inside of the building. And no one seemed to know where to obtain them.

Obviously, Geoffrey Lyondale had never met Ev Barrett, because he violated the Law of the Seven Ps word by word.

We grabbed three hours of rest. Then, at 2100, we began our preassault checkout. There's more than meets the eye here. Radio frequencies have to be coordinated. Hand signals, too—you don't want someone getting killed because he thinks you're saying "drop" when you're actually signaling him to shoot the son of a bitch behind him. To add to our enjoyment, Lieutenant Commander Randy Rayman arrived in his dress blues, looking like a fucking recruiting poster.

I greeted him in blackface. We'd applied dark cammie cream to all exposed skin surfaces. And, thanks to a meeting of the minds between Squadron Sergeant Harvey and my SFC Rodent, we'd received assault kits—Nomex flight suits, assault vests, tactical web gear, and balaclavas. I'd also made sure that my men had enough lethal supplies to protect themselves.

I offered Randy my tube of war paint. "Want to suit up?"

He looked at me as if I were crazy. "I'm not here to play cowboys and Indians, Dick. I'm here to observe and report back to the admiral."

"Well, you can tell Pinky it's cold as a witch's tit, and I'm sore as hell and I'm wet, and if I don't kill somebody soon I'm gonna bust." I dabbed a blackened fingertip on the end of Randy's nose. "Now, maybe you better run along, cockbreath, before I start picking on *you.*"

0215. The choppers were scheduled to pick up the assault element at 0445, for a twenty-five-minute flight to Portsmouth. The rest of us—my shooters, Geoffrey, and his C³I—that's Command, Control, Communications, and Intelligence unit—would lorry in a convoy the fifty-two miles from Poole to Portsmouth.

Geoff had allocated one hour for our trip. "Isn't that cutting it kind of close?" I asked.

He explained that we'd have a police escort. Exactly what every surprise attack needs. Tommy shook his head. The goatfuck factor had now increased by another 100 percent.

Fortunately, I was able to secrete my shooters in one of the lorries by the time the CNN camera crew and correspondent arrived. I could hear them as they did a stand-up interview with Geoff and Randy Rayman.

Geoff extolled the competence of his men and explained how the mission was going to go off like clockwork. Randy prattled on about his experience in Special Operations and went on to express his total trust in SBS's ability to avenge the death of our CNO.

0315. On the road. The fucking wind and rain whistled through the ragged tarp that draped the lorry. After fifteen minutes or so we dropped off the bench seats and huddled together on the floor the better to keep ourselves warm and our weapons dry.

A bright light illuminated our lorry. I snuck a peek from under the tarp. It was the goddamn CNN crew, camera wrapped in a plastic garbage bag, shooting through the sunroof of their Mercedes, cruising past us. In-fucking-credible.

0344. The convoy got lost. We stopped dead in the water for twenty-five minutes. I could hear Geoff on the radio, berating the police driver for not having the right maps. He was screaming at him on an open channel, too—the better for everyone in the neighborhood to hear him rant and rave.

0409. Back on track, rumbling toward Portsmouth. We hunkered in silence, each man lost in his own thoughts. It was now that the uncertainties of what we were about to face began to sink in and gnaw at us. Indeed, this was always the hardest part—that long flight, seemingly endless boat trip, or whatever, before the final assault.

It is at that time you become one with every warrior who ever lived. Hunkered in the wetness of that hard truck bed, we were no different from Alexander's Macedonians, Caesar's legions, the Light Brigade, General Pickett's infantry at Gettysburg, the Marines in their landing craft pounding toward Tarawa, the Canadians about to land at Dieppe, the GIs assaulting Omaha Beach, or my SEALs from Eighth Platoon on a parakeet op in Vietnam.

We, like they, were about to commit ourselves totally, to put our lives on the line.

And the only way to do that is to give your body and soul completely to the God of War. I looked at my men. Their faces showed the kind of warrior's resolve that told me they were ready to fight and to kill.

0502. Portsmouth. We slowed to a crawl as we made our way through the darkened, slick streets. A heavy ground fog gave everything a surreal, almost theatrical quality. We reached a police roadblock and pulled through it. The lorry finally ground to a halt, and we piled out, illuminated by the flashing blue and yellow roadblock lights. I wondered whether the cops were using secure tactical frequencies or whether their chatter was open mike. Because police scanners are illegal in places like England, the cops often forget that bad guys don't care about the niceties of law and use 'em anyway.

The hair on the back of my neck was standing up. That was natural. Senses get so keen at times like this that every sound becomes amplified inside your head. It seemed to me, for example, that the lorry brakes had screeched loud enough to wake the entire city, the dropping tailgates could be heard for miles, and the pounding of our boots on the glistening pavement was telegraphing our position to the enemy like jungle drums.

And just as all of that was playing in my head, the fucking CNN crew decided to turn on its lights so the correspondent could do a fucking stand-up.

I nodded to Stevie Wonder, who carries wire cutters the way some folks carry American Express cards. Ten seconds later the problem was solved—to *my* satisfaction, at least.

The main assault was going to consist of two Puma choppers with fourteen SBS shooters in each bird, and three fourteen-man platoons on the ground. I checked my watch: 0512. By now the helos had left Poole and were heading our way. The ground-assault units were in place. I moved my SEALs to our assigned position, a listening post about two hundred and fifty yards to the northwest of the main entrance—Major Geoff had assigned us bleacher seats—and listened to the radio earpiece in my right ear.

I could hear Geoff, Randy Rayman, and the rest of the command staff chattering in the C³I lorry half a mile down the road, heedless of operational security. How he could "command" from the inside of a windowless van I didn't know. I'd always gone down the rope with my men. That way I knew what was really happening, what kind of support they needed, and, most important, I could cover up any operational flaws that might cause more administrative bullshit than was warranted when the Monday-morning quarterbacks showed up three days later with their twenty-twenty hindsight and three bags full of perfect scenarios.

I crawled ten yards past the corner of our position and peered through night-vision glasses at the warehouse facade. Now, the lack of on-site tactical intelligence became glaringly apparent. The SPOT pictures on the walls at Poole had indicated a long, rectangular building. Indeed, that's what the imaging satellite had photographed, and that's what Geoff's plan had assumed. But thou shalt never assume because, as Ev Barrett used to say, "it makes an *ass* of *u* and *me.*"

So, here in real life, the target building was not as advertised. It wasn't just another big rectangular warehouse, as Geoff had described it. Instead, there was a central structure flanked by two wings. The building's dominant structure was a cube six stories high and perhaps 150 feet square. That part had a small, flat roof.

Abutted to the cube were two two-story rectangular wings, giving the structure the look of a pregnant letter *I*. The ground level of the wings were windowless brick facade, so that the troopers hitting the sides of the warehouse would need assault ladders to take them up to the first-floor roof, where they could bust through the windows and enter the two wings.

That was going to complicate things immeasurably. It would mean coordinating three assault groups instead of just one. I listened as the SBS troopers queried Geoff about ladders. There was an embarrassing silence. It was obvious he hadn't thought of bringing any. He ordered the troopers without ladders to assist assault team three.

Three was the force that had been tasked with massing around the front door, where it would set up a gauntlet into which the tangos could be swept. But the entrance was a clusterfuck waiting to happen. At the front, fifty feet of mirrored glass looked out upon a semicircular driveway. If I'd been inside, I'd have tamped C-4 explosive behind the glass, making the whole front of the building into a deadly fragmentation device. I said as much to Geoffrey and was told to keep radio silence.

I shut up and listened. The ground assault team leader radioed Geoffrey that he'd discovered trip wires and disarmed two explosive devices as he and his men moved into position. "They expect us, Major. We've lost surprise."

Geoff was having none of it. "Carry on, Sergeant—move in and take the entry."

Asshole. If you lose surprise, you're gonna lose men. Better to pull back and go into a siege mode: cut all power to the target, insert listening devices, use thermal imaging. Shatter the windows inward with AT4 shoulder-fired rockets. Then, when you know where everyone is, assault using the cover of CS tear gas, flashbangs, and other devices to stun and overwhelm the enemy. Geoff was ordering his men on a suicide mission.

I heard the distant approach of choppers, their engine sounds muffled by the wet air. I trained my NVs on the warehouse roof. Two Pumas dropped out of the mist, their rotor blades creating vortexes of swirling air and rain. I could see the silhouettes of the Marines inside as they made ready to drop down the fifty feet of soft, reverse-woven cotton rope.

The choppers hovered but didn't come in. It became painfully obvious that both of them couldn't flare above the warehouse at once—there wasn't enough airspace. So the choppers circled while the pilots discussed the matter with Geoff. That was when someone on the roof fired a shoulder-held surface-to-air missile, and the Puma closest to the warehouse exploded in a flash of orange-blue light. Seconds later, the glass at the warehouse entrance burst outward, cutting the SBS assault teams into ribbons. The instant after that, the entire warehouse, which had been wired with high explosive, disappeared in a huge fireball and came down on itself.

I remember sitting in a bubble room known as a Special Classified Intelligence Facility, or SCIF, when the tragedy at Desert One took place. Over speakers carrying the secure satellite transmissions, I listened to the sounds of brave men burning up in one of the most colossally goatfucked SpecWar operations ever. Like many in that SCIF, I had tears in my eyes that night. I knew those who had died. I also vowed that never again, if I had the opportunity to command another SpecWar unit, would my warriors ever be sacrificed the way those brave Delta troopers had been.

Now, stunned at what I saw before me, I knew what had to be done. I turned on my heel and started back toward the C^{3}I lorry that sat five hundred yards away. Tommy and Nasty followed, jogging behind as I double-timed a steady cadence, murder in my heart and mayhem on my mind.

I opened the door of the van without knocking. Geoff Lyondale was sitting at the console, a look of disbelief on his face. Randy Rayman sat next to him, his head in his hands.

Geoff stared at me. "I say—"

I held up my hand like a traffic cop. "No, Geoff, old cockbreath, there's nothing to say." I pulled the asshole out of his seat by the scruff of his neck. He started to object. I broke his nose with the side of my hand. He struggled. I slammed him against the steel wall of the lorry a few times to loosen him up, then opened the door and drop-kicked him down the stairs onto the wet pavement.

I stared down at him. "You fucking coward. You deserve to die."

Terror in his eyes, he rolled away from me. In my peripheral vision I saw Randy Rayman start to come at me. Without looking, I backhanded him and he went down. "Stay the fuck out of this."

I was seeing nothing but red right now. I wanted blood. Geoff fucking Lyondale's blood. I dropped on top of his lordship and started beating his head into the pavement like a fucking soccer ball.

A couple of his perfect teeth came out. Too bad. He started to bleed from his ears and nose. Pity. I kneed him in the balls and he threw up all over me. No matter. I went about my work, screaming obscenities. This sucker was going to die for his sins.

Nasty and Tommy tried to pull me off him. I was having none of it, and I flailed at them between punches at Geoff's face. "Lemme the fuck alone." If I had to kill them to kill him, that was okay by me, too.

By the time Half Pint, Carlosito, Rooster, Sergeant Snake, and the others gang-tackled me, punched me out, and dragged me down the street by my legs, I guess old Geoff wasn't feeling much of anything. The last I saw of Geoff, Stevie Wonder was bending over him, with what looked like a Syrette of morphine in his hand. Then Tommy T must have either applied a helping of leather sap to the upside of my head or slipped me a choker hold, because suddenly everything went black.

Chapter

7

RANK HAS ITS PRIVILEGES. SO, I WASN'T THROWN IN THE BRIG AFTER MY unscheduled appearance (performing an unusual variation of the ballet *Assault With Intent to Commit Murder*) on CNN, although that's where his royal highness Pinckney Prescott III, VADM, USN, wanted me. There is a six-by-eight holding cell in the basement at CINCUSNAVEUR, and Pinky cut orders to the Marine guards to put me there until my men and I could be shipped back to the States—with me in chains.

But, as I said, rank—in this case, a combination of Her Majesty the Queen, and His Majesty, Command Master Chief Hans Weber —has its privileges. Buckingham Palace, filled with Royals who had their own problems, was both outraged at Geoff Lyondale's preposterous behavior and (more to the point) fearful that further unfavorable publicity surrounding "The Event," as it was being described in the tabloids, would place them in a worse light than the one they were already in.

So, a depth charge rolled out of Buckingham Palace and dropped on the Ministry of Defense, where it was shunted to the Embassy of the United States of America, where it was nudged over to North Audley Street, where it—and a gallon of Maalox, no doubt—was left on Pinky Prescott's desk. Hansie said they could hear his anguished screams two floors away.

There were, therefore, no manacles and chains, no six-by-eight holding cell, no keelhauling. But the old MACPOC made it clear I was about to be confined to quarters until things quieted down. But it would be Hans's choice of quarters, not Pinky's. He also scattered my men to the four winds—the better to keep them out of sight and mind—then he checked my luggage at the Marriott, handed me an overnight bag, and said he'd found me a room sans bath at the Special Forces Club, an out-of-the-way refuge for SpecWar operators visiting London. The club is in Knightsbridge, in an unassuming, unmarked town house located on Hans Crescent between Harrods and Sloane Street. Hansie ordered me to bunk there until he sounded the all clear—he figured he could handle things in the next two to three days.

He may have saved my behind, but he also reamed me a new asshole in the best Ev Barrett style, reminding me in demure master chief's fashion that one does not blankety-blanking cold-bleeping-cock the blanker-blanking commanding officer of a bleeping Royal Marine CT unit, on *his* turf, after twenty-three of *his* men have just been turned into hamburger.

He probably had a point, although in my own mind what I'd done was completely justified. In the United States Navy, when you assume command of a ship or a unit, you personally assume total responsibility, authority, and accountability for every element of your men's lives. This happens nowhere else in the military. I take the responsibilities of command seriously. I believe that my men come first. I believe that no matter what the consequences to me, my men must be protected. But I also believe in shared responsibilities. I believe that my men must look after one another—that we must always function as a collective unit, not a collection of individuals.

Shortly after I'd assumed command of SEAL Team Six, I told the men what I expected of them. I told them I'd promised CNO that I would not fail, and therefore *they* would not fail, either. I told them that henceforth their loyalties would be—in ascending order—to their partners, to their squads, to their platoons, and to the Team. "We will take care of each other," I insisted. "If you screw up and waste your swim buddy, I will waste you. You will be history."

Well, Geoff had screwed up. He had not assumed total control. He had operated without properly assessing his situation. He had not taken ultimate responsibility for his actions. He had also failed as a SpecWar leader by blindly accepting incomplete, flawed intelligence, then using it without questioning its reliability, despite a high probability of dire consequences to his men.

Worst of all, he had used the mission as something to further his career. Does that shock you? It shouldn't—after all, it's been done before. An example? You want an example? Okay—what about the asshole supervisors at the Bureau of Alcohol, Tobacco and Firearms who had ordered their men to raid the Branch Davidian compound in Waco even though the raid had been compromised. According to my pals at ATF, some of those supervisors had grandiose ideas about the raid's ending up on *Top Cops* or some other TV infotainment show, and their careers skyrocketing. Geoff Lyondale had gone ahead with his harebrained plan because he wanted to look like a hero on CNN.

And what had happened? Answer: his self-aggrandizing behavior had caused good troops to die. So far as I was concerned, that justified whatever I'd done to him—and more. I wish I'd killed the son of a bitch.

I grabbed the overnight bag, took the underground—that's subway in Brit—to Knightsbridge station, then walked down Hans Crescent just past Basil Street, where I knocked at the unmarked door of the SF Club. Hazel, who's been behind the reception desk for the last couple of centuries, answered my knock. As always, she remembered my pseudonym. How she does it, I don't know—but if you've stayed at the Club even once, she knows you by sight evermore.

"Captain Snerd. Nice to see you again, sir." She adjusted her size-16 dress and primped the bun in her gray, English hair. She looked like Mrs. Miniver's great-aunt. "Sign in, please. We have Number Six waiting for you. Second floor."

She knew better than to ask why I was in town. She followed me to the guest book and handed me an old-fashioned fountain pen. As I signed in—Capt. Herman Snerd, USMC (Ret.)—I perused the guest list.

Two majors with Arabic surnames, nationality Pakistani, were registered. They'd arrived two days ago. That was not unusual. While Saudis or other Gulf Arabs seldom stayed at the SF Club, preferring lush accommodations at the Ritz or the Intercontinental, many Pak officers, who liked to think of themselves as seasoned warriors, preferred the spartan rooms with shared bath down the hall.

I climbed two flights of squeaky stairs (in case you're wondering why my second-floor room was three stories up, in Europe, the ground floor is called the ground floor, what we in the U.S. call the second floor is called the first floor, and so on), hung my bag in the Victorian armoire of a small, slightly shabby room furnished with single bed, sink, ladder-back chair, and side table, and then descended to the first floor, where the bar is located.

Unlike most bars in London, they keep Bombay at the Special Forces Club. I ordered a quadruple Bombay on the rocks and received four one-sixth gill measures and two ice cubes. A gill is a quarter of a pint—four ounces. A sixth of a gill—the normal amount of liquor you get in a Brit shot measure—is two-thirds of an ounce, an anemic quantity of alcohol, if you ask me. Of course, nobody asked me.

I drank in solitary splendor for about a half hour. Then I heard voices on the stairs. Two brown, mustached faces poked into the barroom. I saluted them with the remains of my Bombay.

They turned out to be the Pak majors. I introduced myself as Captain Snerd—no need to let anyone know more than that. They said their names were Yusef and Haji. We were all probably lying. It didn't matter. We sat over Famous Grouse and Bombay and chatted about the best curry restaurants in Karachi, the sorry increase in opium traffic coming out of Afghanistan, and the wonderful time I'd had when I visited their country a couple of years back on a corporate assignment. They excused themselves after half an hour of Scotch, quail eggs, and potato crisps. I finished my Bombay, then decided to go upstairs and grab a combat nap.

Two hours later, refreshed, I padded down the hall and dropped myself into a huge, claw-footed bathtub where I soaked and steamed myself clean then toweled myself dry. Back in my room I slipped into a comfortable pair of slacks, a short-sleeve polo shirt sporting a SEAL Team Eight logo, an ancient pair of running shoes and an old tweed jacket, wandered out, and grabbed a snack and a couple of pints at a pub just off Knightsbridge.

On my way back, I window-shopped outside Harrods. The Christmas lights and decorations had recently gone up, and I— along with hundreds of other equally mesmerized passersby— peered through the thick glass at scenes from Charles Dickens's

Christmas Carol. As I turned the corner onto Hans Crescent, a trio of men came up the opposite side of the street, walking past the Harvey Nichols store toward the underground stop.

I stopped short and watched from behind a knot of tourists because I recognized them all. There was Major Yusef, all spiffed up, and Major Haji, in a suit, too. The third man sported jeans, cowboy boots, and a short, waxed cotton Barbour jacket. It was Todd Stewart, the huge, nasty-looking ex-SBS asshole who worked for my least favorite Eurotrash, Call Me Ishmael Lord Brookfield. There was a ruthless, hard edge to Todd the sod that made me want to have a word or two with him. Perhaps in a quiet, dark alley.

Well, maybe I'd get the opportunity someday. In the meanwhile, curiosity got the better of me. I crossed the street as they descended into the tube stop, watched as they bought tickets, went down the escalator, and grabbed an eastbound train. I followed, one coach behind, sneaking peeks through the glass door between the two. The trio changed at Leicester Square, transferring onto a Northern Line train, which they rode to Hampstead.

The huge black Scotsman in the lead, they walked up the exitway toward two big elevator doors. No way could I follow unnoticed. An arrow to my left pointed toward the stairway. A tourist sign told me that Hampstead Station was the deepest in London—192 feet below ground. Great—I hadn't done PT in a while. I galloped up the stairs two at a time. As I rounded the top, my lungs were bursting.

I waited, gasping for breath, until they'd handed their tickets to the tube man. I followed as they walked down a short hill—the street sign said Hampstead High Street—lined with upscale boutiques and trendy restaurants, and rounded a corner at Downshire Hill, just past a small French bistro.

It had started to rain. It had also gotten damn cold. They had coats. Me? I'd been out for a bite and a brew. My short-sleeve polo shirt was wet clear through because my tweed jacket soaked up water like a sponge. They marched in shoes—in Todd Stewart's case, ornate, ostrich cowboy boots. As usual, I wasn't even wearing socks, only my ancient sneakers, which currently resembled squeegees.

Okay, okay, okay—I'm a Frogman. I'm supposed to operate in maritime environments. Even so, I hoped they'd reach their destination soon, because it was getting maritimely uncomfortable.

I got my wish. Just past a small church, they turned right, walked through a waist-high wrought-iron gate and into an immaculately restored, ivory-colored, four-story, stucco Regency villa. An antique tile plate cemented into the stucco gate pillar read BROOKFIELD HOUSE. I ducked onto the church portico and watched, shivering.

Six minutes later, a familiar car the size of an admiral's barge eased down the street and stopped in front of the villa. Lord Brookfield himself emerged, immaculate as ever, and dodged the raindrops as he scampered up the stone walk to the ornate wooden door. The limo pulled away.

There I was, my hair soaking, water running down the back of my neck, my feet squishy-wet cold. Let me tell you—it didn't matter. It didn't matter because I was hit with the proverbial ton of fucking bricks.

Let me lead you down my convoluted—and I will admit completely unconventional—trail toward enlightenment.

- Item: CNO and Sir Norman Elliott were the two leading proponents in their respective countries of a revolutionary hypothesis about a new form of transnational, Islamic-based, fundamentalist-inspired terrorism emanating from Afghanistan.
- Item: Mahmoud Azziz had a Pakistani visa in his passport and fifty thousand British pounds in his pocket the night Green Team had snatched him. He was, logic said, on his way to Pakistan.
- Item: Pakistan—a nation riddled by corruption, ethnic strife, and growing Islamic fundamentalism itself—was, so it happened, next door to Afghanistan, where thousands of CIA-trained mujahideen fighters now mustered to fight a new fundamentalist *jihad*, a total effort directed against the West.
- Item: two Pakistani officers were now meeting with the man who had apparently convinced the entire British intelligence apparatus that CNO and the Admiral of the Fleet had been killed because the U.S. and Britain hadn't supported Bosnia against Serb aggression.

Why had the Brits swallowed that story? They swallowed it because it made sense. Besides, I'd had a hand in obtaining hard proof that the hit against CNO and Sir Norman had been staged by perps who'd stolen a minisub from the former Yugo Navy base at Split. Moreover, given the current world sitrep, the assumption just plain made sense.

But wasn't I the Slovak sphincter who was always saying, "Thou shalt never assume?"

In other words, what if our supposition about motive was based on what the KGB used to call *aktivnyye mery*—active measures—or what CIA officers refer to as black or *dis*information (gentle readers, take note: you will see this material again).

What if CNO and Sir Norman hadn't been murdered because the Western allies didn't support the Bosnian Muslims, but had been assassinated *because they'd been leading the fight to alert the West against this new transnational, fundamentalist wave of terror?*

What if all those supposedly "connected" acts of terror Sir Aubrey had spoken of were simply diversions—random attacks designed to distract Western intelligence from the real terrorist targets, CNO and Sir Norman Elliott. If that was the case, there had to be (as they'd say in Navyspeak) an unequivocal, guaranteed, indisputably defective component in the chain-of-command interface.

Let me put that in plain English for you. Somebody was a fucking traitor. And I was going to discover just who it was.

A message was waiting for me back at the SF Club. A Captain Owen had called and would meet me at the Guinea for dinner at twenty hundred hours.

That buoyed my soggy spirits. Mick was a shooter and a looter, a lead-from-the-front, kick-ass-take-names hell-raiser who'd served with 22 Regiment for more than a decade now. As a precocious junior officer he'd been part of the assault team that had gone into the Iranian embassy at 16 Princes Gate. Later in the decade he'd led the raid that blew up eleven Argentine aircraft on Pebble Island during the Falklands War.

During Operation Desert Shield/Desert Storm, he'd spent thirty-seven days behind Iraqi lines, destroying communications facilities, sniping at isolated pockets of Iraqi troops, and spotting mobile SCUD launchers before his platoon from D Squadron was discovered by two entire Republican Guard companies—more than three-hundred men against Mick's eight. A fierce firefight ensued, and Mick lost two of his men. The survivors then led the Iraqis on a merry chase across more than 130 miles of cold, rough terrain that claimed another of his platoon, a sergeant who died of hypothermia. Even so, before Mick's five survivors slipped across the Syrian border to safety, they'd managed to kill more than 220 of the Iraqis, destroy three tanks, four APCs, as well as half a dozen trucks and Land Rovers.

For his exploits in Iraq, Mick received the Distinguished Conduct Medal—one of only four to be awarded during the Gulf War. His men all received Military Medals. Not content to let things rest, he'd lately spent his time covertly hunting IRA tangos—there were still a few there despite the peace talks—in Northern Ireland. The score so far was Owen twelve, IRA nil.

At 1920 I pushed my way into the crowded bar at the Guinea, put my back up against a long-legged bird in boa and miniskirt, ordered myself a pint of Young's bitter, and made small talk with the bar manager, an engaging chap named Eric Wells, who'd served with the paras as a boy and loved the work. Finally, he got around to asking me what I did for a living.

"I shred."

"Shred what?"

"People, mostly."

A broad smile came over his face. "Sounds like you have fun."

"Beats working."

"What did you say you did?"

"I didn't."

"What's your name?"

I told him.

He looked at me again, and this time he really saw me. "You're the American SEAL they call the Rogue Warrior." He wagged his index finger at me. "You've been on the telly lately doing the nasty-nasty to the CO of SBS."

So he'd caught my performance on CNN. I asked him what he'd thought.

"Well, old Geoff Lyondale sounds like a real sorry bugger—"

"He is."

"Then I guess he deserved what he got."

I grinned. "How would you feel about writing a letter to a certain admiral I know saying just that? I need all the help I can get these days."

Eric guffawed. "What about another pint instead?"

Half an hour later, Mick's hefty frame filled the doorway. He's built like an NFL running back—five nine and 225 pounds, with twenty-four-inch thighs, a nineteen-inch neck, and a thirty-two-inch waist. He's a terrific amalgamation, combining the density of cinder blocks with the agility of a great broken-field runner and the quickness to do the hundred in less than ten seconds. He crushed my hand in his size-10 paws and bellowed up to the bar.

"Nurse!"

Eric took a peek and came a-running. "Mickey, you old sod." He stuck his thumb in my direction. "He with you?"

Mick nodded affirmatively.

"I shoulda known." He drew a pint of Young's and slid the glass in front of Mick. "Mick and me was squaddies in the Para Reg." Eric displayed the backs of his hands, which were crisscrossed with scar tissue. "Majored in fuckin' pub-brawling in those days. Wear our Class Twos out to the local and work ourselves into a lather takin' on all comers." The thought brought a smile to his face.

It made Mick throw back his head and laugh, too. "Hadn't thought of that in years," he roared. "Then there was Northern Ireland." He stuck his huge thumb in Eric's direction. "He was in my brick."

" 'Brick'?" I'd never heard the term.

"Brick. Patrol, you stupid bloody wanker," Mick explained with all the obscene patience of a chief.

The two of them looked at each other and grinned, sharing what had to be a secret, deadly memory—the kind of thing my old SEAL shipmate from Vietnam days Mike Regan and I share when we reminisce about hunting VC on our two-man, weeklong patrols along the Cambodian border.

Mick showed his big teeth. "Oh, Dickie—you woulda loved it in Ulster." He lifted his glass and inclined it in Eric's direction. "To the auld days, you murderous sod."

Eric drew himself a pint, returned the toast, and the two of them downed their brews without stopping.

"Have you done with the goddamn touchie-feelie shit already?" I nudged my empty glass across the bar in Eric's direction. "All this fucking sentiment is making me thirsty."

We ate real Black Angus steaks two inches thick and English-grown baked potatoes with the best Devonshire sour cream I've ever had, sharing two bottles of great French red that Eric and the Guinea's manager sent over. I'd thought the Guinea served only pub food, but hidden behind the pub is a first-class, full-service restaurant that has to be one of the ten best in London, so far as I'm concerned.

Mick and I caught up on SpecWar gossip, complained about the assholes to whom we reported, groused about imperfections in the chain of command, traded war stories, and then got down to the business of sharing information along with our wine. Like Toshiro Okinaga, my old friend with Kunika, the special police intelligence unit in Tokyo, who helped me recover the Navy's lost nuclear Tomahawk missiles, Mick Owen and I go back a long way.

And, like Tosho, Mick stayed in my corner when most of my so-called "friends" deserted me in droves because the Navy put pressure on them, and they succumbed. Mick hadn't. He'd written me in prison. He'd called after my release. And he'd lobbied his bosses in my behalf.

So, there's very little I won't talk about with Mick, although there wasn't a whole lot I was willing to say inside the restaurant. The tables were close together, and you never know who's there.

So, we finished with good cheese and vintage port. Then Mick had a double Remy and I had a quadruple Bombay Sapphire, we bid good night to our hosts, paid the bill, and walked out into the cold night air.

It had stopped raining and the black sky was studded with stars. We turned right, walked up Bruton Place to Berkeley Square, and turned right again, walking against the traffic flow.

Mick brought me up to date on operational intel in the matter of CNO's and Sir Norman's murders. SAS—unlike SBS under Geoff Lyondale—maintains a huge network of informal intelligence sources. Within hours of the assassinations, even though the unit had not been assigned to help solve the case, that net had been activated. Within forty-eight hours, Mick's people had quietly targeted a number of suspects—among whom were the same Bosnian Muslims from the Sons of Gornji Vakuf Geoff Lyondale had been tracking. But the SGVs weren't the only probables: SAS believed that while SGV may have done the actual operation, some sort of huge tango network was involved.

I agreed with that premise. The op that killed CNO was too big, too complicated, too professional, to have been pulled off by half a dozen fundamentalists acting alone. They needed support, money, gear, and training. After all, what they'd done was equivalent to a SEAL op I would have been proud to lead.

- They'd brought a minisub into a hostile harbor, either from a mothership or by sailing it across the Channel, and navigated it onto a bull's-eye a few hundred yards from their target.
- They'd breached Royal Navy security (okay—so it wasn't very good, but they'd done it anyway) and placed their mine directly below the gangway CNO and the Admiral of the Fleet would use.
- They'd made the hit, then exfiltrated cleanly.
- When attacked, they'd killed a large number of their enemies, created confusion, and sowed terror.

That sounded pretty fucking good to me. It also didn't sound like any goddamn terrorist op I'd ever heard about. No, this was a professional job. The people who did it were good. They had money. They had training. They had expertise. They were warriors. That made them very, very fucking dangerous.

What's more, SAS's CO had informed the permanent war council of top-level Ministry of Defense, Home Office, MI5, and MI6 officials of his intelligence-gathering activities. The group, called the Cabinet Office Briefing Room, was known as COBRA. Sir Aubrey Hanscomb Davis represented the MOD on COBRA, which meant he had known about the Sons of Gornji Vakuf at least twenty-four hours before my first meeting with Geoff and Lord B.

I could see the pulse in Mick's big neck pumping when I told him I believed that Monocle Man, which is what I called Sir Aubrey, had been holding back in a big way on operational intel.

Mick frowned. "It's almost as if he wanted Geoff's op to fail."

That was the way I saw things, too. I told Mick about my unscheduled tour of Hampstead earlier in the day and added I was planning to take a look inside Lord B's mansion.

"That could be hazardous to your career."

"Career? What career?"

"Okay, okay, I know you don't give a shit about—what the hell do you Americans call it? Career path?"

"'Career track.'"

"Career track. But a black-bag job—it's dicey. Even for us.

Especially for you." Mick's face was serious. "Besides, I wouldn't assume anything. You know how fucking devious spooks are. The meeting with those Paks could be anything." We walked a few dozen yards in silence.

"That's why I want to see what's there," I said. "It could be anything."

"Smart-ass." We'd gone completely around the square one and a half times, now. Mick edged me toward Berkeley Street. "I'll walk you back to the SF Club."

"Where are you staying?"

He winked lasciviously. "Belgravia. With a friend."

They hit us in the labyrinthine pedestrian underpass that runs beneath Hyde Park Corner. There are perhaps half a dozen of these in London. This one—one of the two biggest—runs almost a third of a mile from end to end. It has more than a dozen entrances and carries pedestrians under the endless stream of traffic from three of London's busiest thoroughfares, Grosvenor Place, Piccadilly, and Park Lane, where they run together at Hyde Park Corner.

During the day, buskers—street musicians—play guitars in the tile-walled, concrete tunnels that run like mazes for hundreds and hundreds of feet. Knots of people bustle through. Late at night the tunnels become eerily quiet, taking on a sinister, quasi-ominous patina. The traffic noise disappears once you're twenty feet below ground. Still, footfalls echo. Voices carry.

We'd walked down the ramp on Piccadilly, just past the Intercontinental Hotel and across from the Wellington Arch, when we realized we weren't alone. It's at times like these that the antennas go up. I didn't have to say anything to Mick. Like mine, his body had already changed its whole attitude. It was an imperceptible shift, but it was there. We'd suddenly become aggressive in body and spirit. We exuded deadliness.

Okay, okay, gentle reader, I know you're going to accuse me of using pseudo-macho psychobabble bullshit. Well, as Ev Barrett would say, "listen, and learn, boychik, because you'll see this material again."

Story: as a youth, the great Japanese warrior and swordsman Miyamoto Musashi visited a monastery where a particular martial technique was taught. Instead of being welcomed by the novices, from the moment Musashi entered the dojo he was instead confronted aggressively by them. Finally, one of the school's most advanced students challenged him to fight. Musashi killed him with a single blow of a wooden sword.

Why had this episode taken place? An old priest took Musashi aside and explained why his mere presence had incited such a negative reaction. "You must learn how to project qualities other than anger and blood," the priest told the ambitious young swordsman. "Right now, your aura is too fierce—it compels others to challenge you. But there will be times when you do not want to arouse, when you want to camouflage yourself, to go unnoticed."

Musashi thought long and hard about the old priest's advice—and ultimately he took it. The Way of the Warrior, he finally realized, was more complex than he had imagined. You can, he came to understand, create an intangible yet obvious aura about yourself. You can project nonaggression, or you can radiate deadliness.

What I'm talking about here has nothing to do with the kind of saloon bravado I see all too often—the brash, snotty braggadocio that too many guys mistake for manliness. No, this is different. This doesn't have anything to do with a combination of testosterone and alcohol.

It has to do with Warriorship—with the ability to control your aura, your ambience, at all times. So much of warfare is uncontrollable—the weather, the odds, the arrival of Mr. Murphy, for example—that Warriors should strive to influence as much of the situation as they can. You can manipulate the way you are perceived.

As we'd taken our after-dinner stroll, Mick and I had projected neutrality—two white guys, walking and talking. Our body language betrayed nothing about who we were or what we did. There was no aggressive tilt, no menacing slant to us. People didn't cross the street to stay out of our way. An elderly woman walking her Airedale had smiled at us as we passed her.

Now, that all had changed. I glanced at Mick. The whole way he carried himself projected mayhem, death, pestilence, and affliction. His body language told the world, "Do not fuck with this one."

We came to an intersection in the maze. The Brits, bless 'em, had built these things well. They put mugger mirrors at each intersection, so you can see if there's some coster waiting with his cosh. We could see it was all clear, so we rounded the corner. Now we'd come to the deepest part of the underpass—a passageway that ran for a hundred yards, uninterrupted, under Knightsbridge.

Our footfalls echoed in the tunnel. I glanced behind me. Four men dressed all in black were moving up behind us. They were masquerading as skinheads and punks—except that instead of the universal jackboots, which make noise on concrete, they were all wearing running shoes or ninja boots. Two of them carried short machetes. Another held an old bayonet. The fourth had a cudgel.

Ahead of us, two more skinheads came round the far corner, slapping heavy chrome tire chains.

I took the Emerson folder off my belt. "Mick, you carrying?"

"Not to worry, mate." He brought a collapsible, spring-loaded cudgel out of his jacket pocket and *spronggged* it open. "Let's do 'em."

You go into encounters like this accepting that you're probably going to get hurt. The idea, of course, is to hurt the other guys more than they hurt you—and to do it to them first. That's the other thing: these episodes, when they're carried out by professionals, tend to last only a few seconds—certainly less than a couple of minutes. Everything is concentrated and crystallized. Quick and dirty.

Remember when I talked about violence of action? That's what had to happen here.

So we didn't wait to get zapped. We didn't run the wagons into a circle or go waving our hands in that hoodoo-judo-karate bullshit you see in Hollywood movies.

We did what every SpecWarrior knows how to do best—we went on the offensive. Indeed, we knew all too well that a violent counterattack is the only acceptable solution to an ambush.

So, screaming at the top of our lungs, we wheeled and charged the quartet behind us, intent to commit murder written all over our faces. I brought down the pink-haired cudgel-man with my shoulder and sliced the back of the hand that held the club.

I slit vein as well as cartilage, so there was a lot of immediate blood flow. That is good, because when people bleed, they tend to become distracted.

This was what you might call a textbook case. The asshole looked down at his hand and screamed bloody murder, which gave me the opening I needed.

I thrust the Emerson into his neck horizontally and brought it out straight forward just above his Adam's apple, severing his carotid artery and windpipe, just like you'd slaughter a sheep.

He went down for good. But not before he'd covered my new blazer with warm blood.

That was one. Mick shouted, "Go right!" I rolled. A body came flying past me, flung face-first into the tile wall. That was two.

Rule One of the yet-to-be-written Marcinko street-fighting manual will be: Don't waste your time counting the bodies.

But I'd broken the rule. So I got tagged. One of the skinheads snuck up on my port side, reached around, and tagged me with the tire chain just below my right armpit. I thought I heard ribs crack. It felt like I'd been frigging shot. I dropped like a sack of shit and the Emerson dropped out of my hand.

It was doom on Dickie time.

He slashed again, the chain making sparks as it whapped the concrete inches from my head. I kicked out in the skinhead's direction, rolled away, and tried to scramble to my feet. Except, I was having a hard time getting off the deck. My legs were rubbery and my whole right side had caught fire. He came after me with the chain again. I caught it as it bounced off the wall, pulled him down on top of me, and rolled him over.

Now I got the chain around his neck, my legs locked around his waist, and twisted until I heard bones snap. He was dead meat.

Peripheral vision of orange hair. A machete came slicing toward my head. I ducked. The punkster swung again, slicing the shoulder pad of my blazer. Fuck—I unlocked my legs, rolled away, and put the fucking skinhead I'd just killed between me and the blade.

Whaaack! The blade sliced through the meat of his thigh and stuck in the bone. While machete man tried to extricate his weapon, I grabbed a handful of orange hair, pulled him close and head-butted his nose, broke it nicely, then twisted his head around and bit a chunk of his ear off. When that didn't appear to slow him down any, I gouged his eyes. *That* finally made him scream.

Mick pulled the machete man out of my hands—lifted him four feet off the ground and brought him down hard, headfirst. I heard the asshole's neck break.

I scrambled to my feet and put my back against the wall for protection, whipping the chain from side to side like the biker from hell. I looked around—there were only two assailants left standing. I limped toward one, flailing chain, but he turned and ran—

skedaddled around the corner to the underpass that led toward Piccadilly. The other turned and ran toward Knightsbridge.

I approached the intersection cautiously and glanced up at the mugger mirror. All clear.

It was time to collect intelligence—see who these assholes were, and who'd sent 'em. I started back and knelt over an inert form with orange hair and exceptionally bad BO. Gingerly, I went through its pockets. They were empty, except for small change and a five-pound note. I checked a second skinhead. He didn't have ID either. Was this a trend?

I was on my way to the third skinhead when Mick's huge hand turned me around and nudged me toward the Knightsbridge exit. "C'mon." He slid his arm around my shoulder. "Let's haul balls, Dick—before somebody shows up and discovers this mess and we get asked questions we don't want to answer."

I was hyperventilating. My rib cage hurt like hell, too. But there was no way I was going to leave. "Hey, hey, wait—my knife." Emerson CQC6s cost more than $600. I wasn't about to leave it behind so some fucking London bobby could have a souvenir complete with my fingerprints.

I went back, picked it off the ground, wiped the blade on an inert skinhead, and hobbled over to where Mick waited, big arms crossed. I looked at him.

There are times when you want to kick somebody in the balls—and this was one of 'em.

Why? Because the son of a bitch wasn't even breathing hard.

Well, he's four years younger than I am. And he hasn't been rode as hard and put away wet as often.

"Okay, Captain Owen, your grace," I groaned, "I've had the fucking dinner and I've had the fucking floor show. So what's next?"

Mick looked me up and down critically. "How about a visit to fucking hospital?"

I hate to admit it, but his suggestion actually sounded good.

Chapter

8

MICK PATCHED ME UP AT HIS GIRLFRIEND'S HOUSE. THERE WAS NO NEED to raise eyebrows at any emergency room. Besides, I may have been bruised, tender, and sore as hell, but nothing was broken.

Then we spent the rest of the night listening to the radio to see if our fracas had made the news (it did, described as a fight between skinhead factions, which made me wonder who was doing the covering up—the government or the bad guys), sipping Bombay Sapphire and analyzing our situation.

Who the hell had set those assholes on us? What was the motive?

Mick's first question brought a smile to my face. "Okay, Dick, who wants you dead?"

I laughed. "We *do* have all night, don't we?"

Three hours later, we hadn't reached any conclusions, but at least we'd made some decisions. Most important among them was that it was time to take the offensive. With Hansie's help I'd assemble my shooters quietly and slip them out of town before Pinky knew what was happening.

There was another element as well: Mick was concerned that since one attempt had been made on us, another would follow. We weren't sure whether it was me or Mick the skinheads had been after. Mick had left a long trail of IRA corpses in Ulster—in fact, the Provos had put a twenty-thousand-pound bounty on his scalp. So he solved that problem by taking us both out of circulation. We shifted our base of operations to an SAS urban-warfare training center outside London. He had six hundred acres of buildings, hangars, tunnels, roadways, and sewer lines, all contained on a secluded, classified site less than fifty-five miles from Piccadilly Circus.

The place was known as the FAMFUC (for FAMiliarization Facility/Urban Combat). It was where SAS's Special Projects teams developed and refined the scenarios they'd use to deal with hijacked planes or trains, formulate new ways to stop buses, cars, and trucks, and devise effective, lethal ways in which to deal with urban terror. The Queen's bodyguards trained there. So did the three-man SAS wet-affairs units that worked with SIS, snatching or neutralizing IRA tangos the same way we used to go out with Christians in Action in Vietnam to kidnap and kill VC cadres.

We used to call our assassination ops "taking out the garbage." SAS's current terminology isn't too far from ours. They're calling it "rubbish removal" these days.

Forty-eight hours later, we'd set up a joint command post at FAMFUC, far away from Sir Aubrey's watchers, and Pinky's whining. Now da Turd was probably doubly pissed at me—first, I'd managed to escape his arrest order without so much as a by-your-leave. Second, the commander of SAS's most elite counterterror team had just requested that my men and I be TAD'd to his unit.

Pinky's immediate reaction was to deny the request. He fired a salvo of cables back to the Pentagon. He argued that I was an American officer and as such should not be subordinate to a Brit (it hadn't bothered him a whit when he'd assigned me as Geoff Lyondale's subordinate, but that was then and this was now). He maintained that, since I had violated my orders by trashing poor old Geoff, I should be removed from command. He hinted that I was drunk most of the time and therefore unfit for command in the first place.

But Mick knew how to play the game, too. He had his old comrade-in-arms, SAS's most decorated former commanding officer, General Sir Peter de la Billiere, phone his old friend, a four-star Army rat I'll call Cash Harris.

These days, Cash runs the Special Operations Command back in the U.S. He has a thick book with a lot of markers in it, too. So Cash called one of them in. He phoned his old friend, Tom Crocker, a four-star who just happens to be deputy chairman of the Joint Chiefs of Staff. When Cash played quarterback at West Point, Tom Crocker was his favorite wide receiver.

General Crocker did what he did best: he ran with the ball. He loped down the sidelines, sidestepped the defense by cutting through a private door with cipher lock, and headed straight into the hideaway office of the chairman of the Joint Chiefs of Staff, a Marine general named Barrett, who also wears four stars. Let's do the math on this. Four plus four plus four equals twelve. Pinky— you remember him—wears a mere three stars. That was nine too few to do anything about Mick's bumper-pool politics.

So, with Pinky shut out for the time being, we set up housekeeping at FAMFUC. It was the perfect situation: not only had we been officially seconded to SAS, but neither Pinky nor anyone else had any idea where we were.

I played stay-at-home the first few days, raising my Safety Net back in the States on a secure telephone. I called my old pals Tony Mercaldi back at DIA and Irish Kernan at No Such Agency. I wheeled, dealed, cajoled, and threatened until they promised to perform enough sleight of hand to get a couple of VELA or Lacross satellite tracks shifted for a few weeks. Stevie Wonder got on the horn to his pals at Vint Hill Station and convinced them to play with their switches and dials, too. Mick, bless him, worked his wiles on the boys at Cheltenham, where Britain's Big Ears were housed. When he was in London, he made a point of chatting up his contacts at MI5 and MI6 to find out what the bad boys were up to.

In seventy-two hours, we'd developed half a dozen leads. Concrete? No. Possible? *Certainement.*

I told Mick that no matter how many leads we developed or suspects emerged, we still had to run a break-and-enter at Lord B's villa in Hampstead.

Mick was chary about a black-bag job at Brookfield House. Too much risk, he argued. Not enough evidence, he said.

I ticked off the arguments in my favor. It all came down to one indisputable fact: it had been Lord B who'd pointed the finger at the Sons of Gornji Vakuf as the perps, shifting the entire direction of the British response to the assassinations.

Yeah, Mick said, that's true. "But the more we investigate, the more it appears as if the SGVs actually did the job."

"Sure, they may have done the killings. But not for the reasons we've been told." I ticked off my disinformation theory for Mick. I added that since the Sons of Gornji Vakuf had conveniently blown themselves up, there was no one to interrogate about motive. Besides, I added, my instincts were seldom wrong in cases such as these. "Unless we take a look for ourselves, we won't know for sure. There are too many fucking mazes and mirrors here."

Mick sighed. He rolled his eyes. But in the end he agreed that there was too much at stake for us *not* to go in. If we discovered Lord B was pure as the driven snow, fine and dandy—then the suspicion could be shifted to Sir Aubrey, or even Geoff Lyondale. But if we found out Brookfield was dirty, then we'd know how to deal with him.

Mick and I snuck down to London and began a recon of Hampstead. Meanwhile, we put our men on an eighteen-hour schedule of concentrated shooting and looting. We drew weapons and supplies from SAS's quartermaster—MP5 submachine guns, black Nomex coveralls with Kevlar-reinforced elbows and knees (does it seem to you that ever since Vietnam I can't get away from working in black pajamas of some sort? Seems that way to me), antiflash hoods (commonly called balaclavas), body armor, gas masks complete with secure radios, and side arms. SAS prefers the old-fashioned, single-action Browning Hi-Power. For us Americans, Mick provided Glocks in nine millimeter. Once we were armed and dangerous, we drew fifty thousand rounds of ammo and went to work, rehoning our skills, shooting against SAS's best for pints of IPA bitter.

Why all the ammo? Why all the practice? The answer is simple. In CT work, you have one goal and one goal only: hit the bad guy first and make damn sure he/she/it can't get back up. You have to be able to shoot without thinking—pure reflex. That's the reason behind all the weapons training.

See, for a Green Team shooter, the hardest part of the job is getting to the target. The easy part is killing the son of a bitch. Remember when I told you that stress shooting and hostage-rescue tactics are a perishable skill that can be lost in days? Okay—now here's the rest of the equation. Think about pulling the trigger and double-tapping your target—in training it's a three-by-five index card; in real life it's an armed and dangerous tango—after you've just (please select one or all of the following):

- Humped it on a two-mile swim in forty-eight-degree water.
- Spent the last two hours beating your kidneys into Jell-O riding a small boat in the open ocean on ten-foot swells, then climbed a slippery caving ladder to storm a ship, the same way we did in *Red Cell.*
- Sailed into town on a "foil" parachute after dropping twelve thousand feet free fall sans benefit of oxygen and skidding thirteen miles from where you dropped out of the plane.

What I'm trying to say is that you've already extended yourself physically more than 99.99 percent of the world's population ever will, and only now *(Now!)* do you get the chance to settle down, be cool, shoot the bad guy first, and save the hostage.

In the movies it looks easy. Of course, in the movies, it isn't really Arnold Schwarzenegger or Charlie Sheen or Sylvester Stallone dropping out of the sky, coming up out of the water, or down the fast rope. It's some stuntman (probably an ex-SEAL).

Besides, in real life, it doesn't happen like that. In real life you're so hyper, so absolutely juiced from your freefall/swim/boatride/climb/fastrope, that you're absofuckinglutely ready to fucking kill the first fucking thing you fucking see. Am I fucking making myself clear through ironic repetitive use of the F-word?

In real life, to real SEALs, killing becomes a form of emotional and physical release—it's the reward for having survived the ordeal of getting to the target in the first place. In fact—and I've been there—all you really want is to get the job over with. You want to kill the motherfuckers and be done with it, so you can go off somewhere with a cold beer and a hot piece of ass and release the pressure.

Did you ever wonder why SEALs train so hard? Have you ever thought about the rationale behind hell week back at BUD/S, when SEAL pup trainees—the 10 percent or less who survive hell week—are formed on an anvil of unbelievable pain, hurt, and stress. The answer is that during hell week they get their first taste of what it will be like when they're called on—maybe it'll be only once in their lives—to hit their man or fulfill their mission no matter how juiced, how cold, how wet, how tired, how dinged, or how fucking scared they are.

So we went back to the basics, too. Sight-acquire-fire. Hit the goddamn three-by-five like it's a no-brainer. That's what I taught SEAL Team Six when I created it. And that's what we did at FAMFUC. Sight-acquire-fire. Sight-acquire-fire. Do it until you get it right. Then do it under stress—after climbing ten flights of stairs at breakneck speed. Or fastroping fifty feet from a flared chopper. Or abseiling off a roof and slamming through a window. Or—well, you get the idea.

Now, as to our gear, conventional wisdom states that the better gear you have, the easier the job is. So far as I'm concerned, however, Kevlar-reinforced clothes, state-of-the-art MP5s, night-sighted Glocks, and other, more exotic Star Wars equipment isn't the answer. It's part of the solution, but not the whole solution. Equipment is a tool. It's the man using it that makes the real difference.

Indeed, I've always maintained that the right man is the ultimate weapon; that the right man makes the best fighting machine. Bottom line? All the tech toys in the world aren't worth a shit if you don't have a warrior's heart.

It's like the asshole who takes years of judo, karate, kendo, et cetera. Then, on the one day he's finally called to task on the street, the stupid numb-nuts doesn't know how to function because there's no one holding a score card, and nobody to call "time out" when it starts to get rough. That's not what a Warrior's about.

Being a Warrior is to be about death; to be about killing. In my line of work you have to be able to hate. You must have the instinct to go for the kill—to look your opponent in the eye and to murder him without thinking—or you'll be the one who's killed.

So, as far as I'm concerned, it's fine to have all those nice toys to play with, and all those nice costumes to wear. But it's the animal underneath that counts. Please try to remember this material, because you'll see it again and there's going to be a quiz. End of sermon.

Meanwhile, the clock was ticking. Now, Mick and I stayed at FAMFUC working the phones, while I sent Wonder into Hampstead for sneaking and peeking. After all, he was a Force Recon Marine and didn't mind long trips behind enemy lines. Three days later, he came back to report that Brookfield House was empty—Lord B and Todd Stewart, along with four suitcases—had taken a cab to Terminal Four at Heathrow, where they'd climbed on an Air France flight to Nice.

That was good news and bad news. Good news: the place was ripe for plucking. And I was obviously the mean motherplucker to do the job right. Bad news: Lord B had flown. Why had he gone to France? What was he up to?

I formed the troops. I told them that Tommy and I were going to break into Brookfield House as soon as it got dark, and that Mick was coming along to make sure the proprieties were observed. I explained my reasons. I asked if anyone had any questions or suggestions.

Nasty Nicky Grundle, self-appointed enlisted SEAL ombudsman and shop steward, had a few: "C'mon, Skipper—how come you fucking officers get to have all the fun?"

Then he suggested there'd be a job action if the platoon wasn't included. When that didn't work, he hinted about mutiny. I was having none of it. Then he threatened to hide my Bombay.

I relented. After all, I'm a reasonable guy.

Chapter

9

BREAKING AND ENTERING HAS NEVER BEEN ONE OF MY STRONG POINTS. I've always been a blow-the-fucking-door-off-its-hinges-and-storm-the-place kind of guy. But once in a while during a mission, slightly more finesse may be necessary. That's why as the FIG—Frog In Command—of SEAL Team Six I sent a dozen or so of my more feloniously inclined tadpoles to locksmith school, where—aside from picklock 101—they learned the basic intricacies of deciphering cipher locks, tumbling safe tumblers, and unbolting dead bolts.

At Red Cell, where our mission included breaking into the nation's most sensitive installations, I took my men's unconventional talents a step further, having the rudiments of bypassing electronic burglar-alarm systems inculcated in them by a guy Stevie Wonder went to junior high with back in Jackson Heights. The DIQ's—that's Dude In Question's—name is—well, I'll just call him Eddie the Burglar.

Eddie is a five-foot-five Irishman sporting the same kind of shiny black pompadour Desi Arnaz used to wear. He weighs in somewhere just below 120 pounds—in fact, if he wanted to, he could buy his clothes in the boys' department of most stores. Eddie works only twenty-five days a year. For twenty-four of them he plans to steal things—truckloads of furs and cases of unset diamonds are his most common targets. On the twenty-fifth, he pulls it off. He's always worked alone—which means he's never been caught, never been fingered, and never had to split the take. Over the past seventeen years, he's cleared roughly a quarter mil a year, tax free, which has bought him a lovely place in Bimini, a fifty-three-foot Hatteras, and a devoted Italian Catholic wife eleven years younger than he, who has no idea what he does for a living.

The minute Wonder told me about his friend, I knew I wanted to hire him. He'd be the perfect guy to teach Red Cell how to evade sophisticated electronic alarm systems—like the ones at nuclear-weapons stowage facilities that use infrared and sonar, the laser-based systems aboard boomer-class nuclear subs, or the passive magnet or movement-sensitive devices used by most defense contractors.

We met in a bar out on Long Island. I offered him $15,000 of your tax dollars to give us a one-week course on breaking and entering.

Eddie turned me down cold. "Fifteen grand? Whaddya, whaddya?" He popped his chewing gum and sucked on a Camel. "Whaddya? Crazy?"

I didn't think so.

He did. "Whaddya? Offering me friggin' money? Whaddya, whaddya? It's my friggin' patriotic duty."

As we worked our way around Brookfield House for a preliminary recon, I said a silent prayer of gratitude to Eddie the Burglar. Wonder's diagrams indicated three overt security arrangements. There was a narrow, almost undiscernible strip of foil tape around the perimeter of the ornate ground-floor casement windows—break the current by shattering a window and an alarm goes off. The window frames were also alarmed with magnets. Open the window and you set off the alarm. Ditto the first floor. The second-floor windows, twenty-five feet off the ground and six feet below the roof ridge, had neither tape nor magnets.

The service-entrance door was reinforced by a heavy steel-grate security gate. The windows of the kitchen, pantry, and servants quarters were covered by stout bars set into the window frames. All of Brookfield House's doors probably had either electronic contacts —open them and the alarm goes off—or pressure plates next to the hinges.

We drove to London, put the cars in an anonymous garage near

Victoria Station, and took the underground to Belsize, where we checked into an anonymous-looking motel. Then we walked up to Hampstead, watching each other's backs. There were eight of us in all. Tommy, Mick, Wonder, and me to commit the felonies; Nasty, Duck Foot, Carlosito, and Rodent to provide perimeter security while we did.

We'd traveled light. Wonder brought his prized set of Bay Ridge lockpicks. I'd handed out eight minitransceivers—secure, scrambled radio sets no bigger than Walkmans. They attach to your belt. You wear a receiver in your ear and speak over a wire mike. The batteries last for just over six hours, and the whole apparatus weighs less than half a pound. We also carried mini flashlights, a Minox camera, surgical gloves, two twenty-foot lengths of nylon climbing rope, and appropriate weapons. The entry team each had a rucksack in case anybody wanted to take souvenirs. I guess we looked like your everyday tourists—if your everyday tourists resemble a rugby team.

Mick, Wonder, and I were the first to arrive on-scene. We'd picked the Freemasons, an old pub less than a hundred yards from Brookfield House, as our rendezvous. We found seats by the bay windows and sipped pints of Guinness until everyone else arrived.

Eddie's philosophy of burglary was very much like my SpecWar doctrine. He Kept It Simple, Stupid. And he almost always went in through the "back door." "Go where they least expect you," he preached, sounding a lot like a good SEAL master chief.

Eddie had a willing congregation, so far as I was concerned. When, as a green ensign, I took Bravo Squad down the My Tho River to Ilo-Ilo Island in Vietnam, we didn't hit Mr. Charlie by walking up the canal from the west—the way he expected us to come a-calling.

Instead, we came in through the eastern "back door": a tortuous long haul through hip-deep mud, complete with bramble bushes as sharp as any barbed wire, poisonous snakes, booby traps, and other miscellaneous deadly obstacles. But, when we hit Mr. Victor Charlie, he was looking the other way, which meant we were able to kill lots of him before he realized what was happening. At the time, my little day trip to Ilo-Ilo was called the most successful SEAL operation in the Mekong Delta—ever.

Well, Eddie the Burglar, like any good unconventional warrior, also made a habit of hitting where he was least expected, even though it could mean more work initially. On buildings, he explained, that meant coming in through the roof.

The roof may be difficult to get to, but it is commonly the least protected element of a structure. You can cut a roof and not set off an alarm. Moreover, it's harder for a security guard to see someone working six or eight stories off the ground. After all, as Eddie told us, most people never look above eye level.

So up we went. You know what's wonderful about English housing? The drainpipes. Brits build their houses using solid, well-wrought, securely fastened cast-iron drainpipes that are as easy to climb as a stepladder. Brookfield House, which was a semidetached structure, had one four-inch, cast-iron drainpipe running up the front, and another running up the rear.

I posted my sentries. Duck Foot by the Freemasons, Carlos under the eaves of St. John's Church, Nasty close by the police station up at the corner of Hampstead High Street, and Rodent in the rear of Brookfield House to cover our six.

No sense in attracting attention to ourselves. We cut round the back and scampered up like monkeys after bananas, rolling over the ornate cresting. The canted, slate roof afforded us moderate cover. I crept over to the chimney and checked to see whether it was hot. It wasn't—which suggested to me heat had been turned down inside. We donned our surgical gloves.

There was no way to go down from the roof without cutting through it. But six feet below the crest was a single window. Mick and I each took one of Wonder's feet, and we suspended him upside down while he double-checked to make sure it hadn't been alarmed.

"Nah. This one's nonsecure." He opened it and pulled himself inside. "C'mon down—the water's fine."

Tommy tied two of the lines together, secured them to the chimney, and dropped them off the roof. Then, one by one, we clambered down and pulled ourselves inside.

"We're in," I whispered to my sentries. It was easy—almost too easy. But I've always been willing to take yes for an answer.

"Check," said Carlos. "It's quiet out here."

"Good." We were inside what must have been a servant's room. It was small—not more than eight by ten. It had a narrow iron-framed bed whose mattress sagged noticcably, a bedside table, a rocking chair, and a small dresser. A small, threadbare prayer rug sat atop old linoleum at the foot of the bed.

I cracked the door. "Let's move."

We made our way down a steep, creaky stairway. I didn't like the noise we were making at all. We passed the second floor and made our way down the worn, wood steps. At the first-floor landing, I stopped in front of a small butler's table. Atop it sat a tray holding several glasses. I wiped one with a finger, leaving a swath in the dust.

"No one's been here for a while."

I opened the door in front of me. Remember the old TV show *Upstairs, Downstairs?* Well, we'd been downstairs. Now it was time to see how the other half lived. We came out into an ornately painted drawing room. The furniture was Regency. The rugs were Aubusson. The walls were painted rich red, trimmed in white and gold. From one, a Gobelin tapestry looked down on the room. Another held a huge Old Master hunt scene. There was Venetian glass and Tuscan brass. A huge pair of candelabra flanked a striped sofa.

But it was the chest of drawers below the Gobelin that blew me away. Eight feet long, six feet high, and entirely covered in mother-of-pearl inlay, the intricate pattern set into dark wood.

Tommy's jaw dropped in awe. "That's an antique Syrian wedding chest," he said reverently. "Must be three hundred years old. The only time I've ever seen one similar, I was in a museum in Damascus—and this one's nicer."

The other public rooms were as richly and ornately decorated as the one in which we stood. But we hadn't come as sight-seers. There was work to be done.

Tommy took living room, drawing room, and library. Wonder slipped down to the basement to recon the kitchen, pantry, and wine cellar. Mike and I worked Brookfield's private study, hidden behind a trompe l'oeil doorway on the second floor, just off his bedroom.

It's hard to search when you don't know what you're looking for. I examined the books on Lord B's bedside table. There was a Koran and a King James Version Bible. The only other books were *Rogue Warrior* and *Rogue Warrior: Red Cell*. I flipped through them. He'd highlighted some passages and underlined others. Probably trying to get a better grip on who I was. Know thy enemy and all that crap. I slid my hand between his mattresses to see if he'd left any papers there. Nope.

"Wonder?" I'd sent Wonder to locate and double-check the security system. We didn't want any pressure plates or motion detectors going off.

"Yo." His voice was loud and clear in my earpiece.

"Anything?"

"All clear. This is a nuts-and-bolts system. Lord B was probably trying to save a few pennies when he put it in. On the other hand, if I knew anything about wine, I think I'd be impressed. You ever hear of anything called Château Pétrus?"

"Nope."

"Me neither. But this guy's got hundreds of bottles of it. Old stuff, too—1955, 1961, 1966."

"Tommy—"

"All clear here, Skipper. Nothing suspicious." There was a pause. "Hey, Wonder—"

"Yeah?"

"Did you say Château Pétrus?"

"Yup."

"Well, it costs up to about a grand a bottle, depending on the year."

Wonder, normally unflappable, was flapped. "You're shitting me."

We didn't need chatter right now. We needed results. "Hey, assholes—back to work." I flipped the antique silk carpets to see if he had a cache beneath them. Nothing.

I eased pictures away from the walls to see if he had a safe. Nada.

I turned to watch Mick searching the bookcase. "Find anything?"

He shook his head in frustration. "Nah—it's all clean so far."

"There's got to be something here."

"Why are you so sure?"

"Because."

"That's no reason, Dick."

"Listen—the guy's dirty. I know he's dirty. I feel it."

"Feelings don't prove anything."

I shook my head in frustration. "I know—I know."

145

We finished the bedroom and began a systematic search of Brookfield's study. I photographed his ornate, tooled leather address book, page by page. Maybe something would turn up. I picked the lock on the sole drawer of his eighteenth-century writing table. It was empty. I started to close it, then remembered my own commandment: Thou shalt never assume. I slid the drawer out and turned it over—sometimes people tape documents to the bottom of drawers. Brookfield was not one of them. Then I ran my hand all the way inside the empty space. Wedged way back between the dust panel and drawer was what felt like a business card. I extracted it between my fingers and examined it. It was indeed a business card—a triple-weight chip of vellum from a travel agency on Bruton Street, in Mayfair. The engraved script read Doreen Sims. The card went into my pocket.

Nasty's voice in my ear. "Security wagon turned off High Street."

"Lights out." We extinguished our flashlights. "Keep away from the windows."

Carlos whispered, "They're cruising past the church. All quiet." There was a pause. "They've stopped in front of the house."

Inside, we held our collective breath. My sphincter tightened.

"Checking the door."

We waited.

"Walking to the rear."

No one moved.

Now Rodent's voice came into my brain. "Back-door check." Christ—the guy must have walked right over Rodent, who'd concealed himself in the bushes next to the servants' entrance.

Carlos's voice: "Second man out."

Christ, what the hell was going on. "Sitrep?" I whispered.

"Cigarette break," Carlos answered. "Leaning up against the van like James Dean."

I stopped sweating.

"First man's clear," said Rodent, obvious relief in his voice.

"They're both leaning against the van smoking."

"C-o-o-o-l." That was Grundle's voice. "Are they making smoke rings?"

"Shut the fuck up."

We waited in the half-light. Finally, Carlos gave us an all clear.

Rodent sighed loudly. "The SOB walked across my left hand."

"Lucky you—since you jerk off rightie," Duck Foot chortled.

"Fuck you."

"Hey, hey, hey—this is serious, guys. Let's maintain op sec."

Duck Foot's voice was five by five in my earpiece. "Anything you say, Skipper." Then he laughed like crazy.

We were out and clear half an hour later, back in the Freemasons, quaffing pints. Duck Foot was six up on us—and feeling no pain—by the time we arrived.

Other than the address book and the business card, the house had been squeaky-clean. At least *we* hadn't discovered anything. I had three quadruple gins in quick succession, but even they didn't improve my mood. I was disappointed. Frustrated. Perplexed. Indeed, I'd hoped for results. We'd achieved nothing other than discovering Lord B lived in a spotless home, had bought both my books, and used a Mayfair travel agency.

Given the fact that I believed Lord B to be a terrorist, or at least a terrorist sympathizer, that was unusual. Tangos and those around them tend to leave paperwork around. From the days of Mao's Long March to Fidel's sojourn in the Sierra Maestra to Che Guevara's campaign in Bolivia, everybody kept diaries, journals, notebooks, and other written records. In El Salvador, the FMLN guerrillas walked around with tons of records in their knapsacks. As Ed Corr, one of our better U.S. ambassadors in San Salvador, used to say about them, "When they're not fighting, they're writing."

So the bareness of Lord B's house was disappointing. And we'd been thorough. Tommy knows all about antiques. He can find a secret compartment if it exists. There was none, anywhere. Stevie had worked all the walls, looking for hidden passageways, document caches, and safes. There were none. Mick checked the floors, the ceilings—even the wiring. He found nothing out of the ordinary.

This total lack of evidence spoke eloquently in favor of noninvolvement on Brookfield's part, an opinion Mick wasn't hesitant about expressing. But something was missing from the picture. Why? Because my gut told me he was dirty. And my gut is seldom wrong.

Then it hit me. The house was clean, because *it was supposed to be clean.* We'd broken in with no trouble because Brookfield wanted me to break in easily. He wanted me to scour the place top to bottom and come up empty. He even wanted me to be able to operate without Mr. Murphy along for the ride.

Of course. Brookfield House was squeaky-clean because Lord B knew I'd come visiting.

That was my style. How did he know it was my style? Because, gentle reader, he'd read *Rogue Warrior;* he'd read *Rogue Warrior: Red Cell.* He knew I made a habit of breaking into places.

So he'd left me only what he'd wanted me to see. The address book. The business card was probably the single piece of real intelligence I'd gleaned—and even that was now suspect because it was the only thing I'd "accidentally" discovered.

Now, I wasn't about to violate op sec and share any thoughts about my epiphany.

Mick drained his bitter. "I assume you lot can find your way back to the Holiday Inn?"

"Us highly fucking trained individuals?" I said. "Remember, you dip-dunk, no-load Brit asshole, we're elite U.S. Naval Special Warfare commandos—we can find our asses with either hand in total darkness."

"Without rehearsing," said Stevie Wonder.

"And chew gum at the same time," said Nasty.

"A thousand pardons, kind sirs," Mick said, bowing low. He slipped three five-pound notes on the bar. "A round for my delightful, if learning-disabled, children," he told the bartender. "And pay them no mind if they get a bit silly after a couple of pints—they're Americans, and they don't handle our good, strong British ale very well."

The next morning we split up, arranging a 1900 rendezvous at the downtown garage where we'd left our cars. Carlos, Rodent, Tommy, and Wonder decided that since their work was finished, they'd wander around Hampstead, trolling for birds—the kind that wear skirts. Nasty and I walked to Finchley Road and took the train to Bond Street, three or four blocks from CINCUSNAVEUR. I wanted to check in with Hansie, and he wanted some Copenhagen snuff, which was available at the North Audley commissary. I had a second mission, too: dropping in on the Bruton Street travel agency whose card was in my pocket, to talk to one Doreen Sims.

I left Grundle at the tube stop and made my way down South

Moulton Street past a gauntlet of fashionable boutiques and restaurants, then window-shopped the antique dealers on New Bond Street. I turned left on Bruton Street and walked about fifty paces until I came to a small alley. There was a wedge-shaped pub on the corner, and a small eighteenth-century town house behind it. To the left of the door were three doorbells, and three brass placards. Engraved on the top two-by-four-inch brass rectangle was the inscription BRUTON TRAVEL, FIRST FLOOR, PLEASE RING.

I rang.

A voice said, "Yes?"

"Snerd, Herman Snerd," I said by way of introduction. I asked if I could come up.

Of course I could. I walked up a narrow flight of stairs and rapped at the door. It was answered by a statuesque woman in a tweed suit, ankle-length skirt, and high boots. "Yes?"

"Are you Doreen Sims?"

"Yes, I am."

I smiled. "I was given your card by a friend, who says you're a terrific travel agent."

"Really." She paused and looked me over. She looked at my B&E clothes—ragged jeans, old sneakers, and my faithful $65 Pakistani leather jacket. I could see her doing mental calculations about the safety of admitting me. Finally, she said, "Do come in."

I followed her inside. It was a simple but elegant office—the kind of understated, posh milieu favored by people with huge trust funds. On the walls, dozens of inscribed photographs of movie stars, rock-and-roll musicians, and politicians hung like so many pop icons. I picked out Geoff Lyondale's smiling countenance— and the Duchess of Wales's. Obviously, Doreen Sims had somehow garnered most of London's celebrity business.

She sat down primly behind a low roll-top desk and indicated I should take the leather armchair opposite. "So—Mr. Snerd, isn't it?—what can I do for you?"

"I'm a friend of Lord B's."

"Lord Brookfield?" The look she gave me indicated that she wasn't giving my story a lot of credence. Still, I slid the card onto her desk. "He gave me your name last week. Told me you were a super travel agent—you could get me anywhere, anytime, on a moment's notice."

"That was kind of him." She picked up the card and examined it in an offhand sort of way. Then she looked at me quizzically. "Have you known Lord B long?"

"No. We were introduced recently by a mutual friend. I'm here on business. But I travel a lot."

"I see." She handed the card back, then gave me a warm smile. "Well, that was kind of him. I've only booked for him twice, y'know—the Italian trip two months ago, and now to Nice."

"He likes his vacations, doesn't he?"

"Oh, I don't think it was a vacation in Italy. He took Mr. Stewart and five other associates."

I nodded. "Right. Of course. And they went . . ."

"To Abruzzi. To Pescara, actually, on the Adriatic coast." She pointed at a huge, framed antique world map on the wall behind her desk.

I looked up, focusing on Italy. If the country looks like a boot, you find Abruzzi midway up the calf. I looked again—and actually saw something this time: the city of Pescara. It was directly opposite the Yugoslavian town of Split.

Split, in Croatia, was one of the major bases for the old Yugo Navy. More to the point, it was the location from where— according to the intelligence developed by Lord B's sources—the Sons of Gornji Vakuf stole the Foca minisub and used it to bomb the HMS *Mountbatten* and murder CNO.

That is, if they, in point of fact, had done the deed.

Whoa, you say. Where the hell is Dickie coming from now? Why is he all of a sudden wondering whether or not the Sons of Gornji Vakuf had actually killed CNO, when there'd been so much proof positive offered up?

Since you asked, I'll tell you.

- Item: I was the one who'd confirmed that the Foca whose stabilizer fin I found had, in fact, been delivered to the Yugo Navy three years ago.

    Murphy factor: It was Lord B who'd said it had been stolen by the Sons of Gornji Vakuf. Until then, not even Sir Aubrey, whose networks were pretty damn good, had known about that specific splinter group of Bosnian tangos.
- Item: Both Sir Aubrey and Mick Owen had confirmed the group's existence.

Murphy factor: But neither Sir Aubrey nor SAS could say whether the SGV had actually stolen the Foca. All we knew for certain was that a fin from the stolen sub ended up in the main channel of Portsmouth harbor.

That left me with a lot of questions unanswered, and a lot of potential for bad assumptions.

I know I'm being oblique. But follow me and you'll see where I'm coming from.

One of the most important elements both to spookery and special operations is deception. In the Gulf War, for example, a mere platoon of SEALs managed to convince two Iraqi divisions that they were in fact a huge Marine amphibious landing force. Their deception, which took the form of marking a beach as if it were being prepared for a landing, blowing up obstacles, and engaging in other forms of harassment, kept the Iraqi divisions in the Kuwait City region—miles and miles from the location where the real invasion would take place.

In the spook world, which the great old spymaster James Jesus Angleton used to call "a wilderness of mirrors," deception is more subtle than a platoon of SEALs and one hundred pounds of plastic explosive.

The objective is to create a series of events or facts that convince your opponent you are planning to do one thing, when in truth, you are preparing to do absolutely the opposite.

To accomplish this, you allow your adversaries a certain amount of real intelligence information—after all, they'd know if everything was fake. But within the real stuff, you slip in what's called in the trade black information—disinformation (see—I told you you'd be seeing this black-info material again).

Anyway, the percentage may be 95 percent truth and only 5 percent falsehood—but it is often enough to (a) convince your adversary that he has in fact uncovered something genuine, and (b) cause him to act on that information, and when it causes him to fail, not ever realize that he's been had. If you are successful, it is kind of like the old movie *The Sting*, in which the bad guy, played by Robert Shaw, goes off without ever realizing that Paul Newman and Robert Redford have, in fact, goatfucked him.

In the case at hand, Lord B told us about a new terrorist group, the Sons of Gornji Vakuf. The SGV were, in fact, genuine tangos. So far, so good. But what if he then injected a sliver of disinformation —that they'd stolen the Foca minisub from the former Yugo base at Split—into the story.

By doing so, he could lead us astray, causing us to assume, falsely, that these lethal, desperate Muslims had stolen a specific Foca, sailed it into Portsmouth harbor, and used it as a platform from which they attacked the HMS *Mountbatten* and murdered Admiral Sir Norman Elliott and CNO.

But that wasn't the only way to kill CNO. The SGV—or any other tangos—could, for example, infiltrate the Navy base at Portsmouth (it hadn't been very hard for me to do just that), swim out to the *Mountbatten*, plant their limpet mines or bombs or whatever, and then swim back to shore the very same way I had, without being observed.

In other words, you wouldn't necessarily need a sub to make the hit.

But what about the fin? you ask. Hadn't I cemented Lord B's theory when I found the Foca's stabilizer fin, traced it back, and discovered where it had come from.

Nope. I simply confirmed that the fin had come from a sub delivered to the Yugo Navy. Sir Aubrey confirmed only that it had been stolen six weeks before the *Mountbatten* was attacked. But the information about who had stolen the minisub had come from Lord B. It was Sir Aubrey—and I—who put two and two together. And now I realized we'd come up with five, not four.

Because, so far as I was concerned, it was altogether possible to steal the minisub, break off a stabilizer fin, and drop it slam-bang in the middle of Portsmouth harbor for someone enterprising like me to discover.

Am I sounding paranoid? Well, to be honest, I've been accused of being paranoid in the past, and it has kept me and my men alive.

My reverie was interrupted by Doreen, who was telling me something about Lord B's traveling to Nice. I knew that. But maybe she could tell me why. "Nice? You say he's in Nice these days. That means he'll be staying at his cottage in Beaulieu-sur-Mer?"

Doreen smiled at me. Obviously, I knew Lord B well enough to know he had a house on the Riviera. "That's right—he's at *l'Oasis bleue*, with Mr. Haji and Mr. Yusef. If you're going to visit them, I'd suggest a lovely inn, La Résidence, nearby. Or you could stay in town at the Negresco."

She paused and uncapped a $500 gold Montblanc fountain pen, which she held poised over a sheet of ivory writing paper. "Can I make you a reservation now, Mr. Snerd?"

So he'd gone to southern France with Mr. Haji and Mr. Yusef, the ubiquitous Pakistani majors. That factoid certainly gave one pause. "Not at the moment, Doreen—I'll get back to you." I had things to do. People to see. I wanted to get to North Audley Street, hit the fifth floor—that's where CINCUSNAVEUR's operations staff keeps its files—and see what the hell was in Nice.

I walked up Brook Street toward Grosvenor Square in a fog, my eyes on the pavement, my mind racing. Lord B was a diver—there were pictures of him in *National Geographic* raising his Phoenician galley or whatever. He was a crack shot. He'd been on the British Olympic team. He'd converted to Islam—so he said—during the time he'd been held hostage in Lebanon.

But what if he hadn't really been held hostage? What if he'd staged his own kidnapping and gone off to Afghanistan to take Tango 401? What if he'd been tutored by one of the thousands of ex-Spetsnaz, or former GRU and KGB paramilitary experts who, unlike me, didn't have a pension and hadn't written two best-selling books? He could afford to hire a brigade of 'em if he wanted to.

A lot of questions were on my mind, and very few answers.

Now Brookfield was in France. What in the hell could he be doing there, when there'd just been a bad terrorist incident right here in Goode Olde Britain? It didn't make sense.

I mean, here he was, an important consultant to the Brits, and he still goes off to France when he should be scouring his alleged network of sources to help Sir Aubrey.

Something in the equation didn't compute. I decided to list the possibilities.

One was that he could be taking a long-anticipated vacation. Nah—it wasn't his style. Lord B was not the type to abandon a project, especially one as important as his government consulting, to lie in the sun. He—like me—was obsessive about his work. I'd learned that when I'd researched about him. So he'd gone to Nice because it was important for him to be there. Why? That was the proverbial million-dollar question.

As I crossed Duke Street into Grosvenor Square, I stopped in my tracks. This sort of thing has happened to me before—and it's saved my life. Once, in Vietnam, I pulled up short, my foot holding just above the ground on a dike just south of Khe Sach. Why I didn't take that last step I'll never know—I can only describe it as some kind of primordial alarm system. Anyway, my foot frozen in space, I looked down carefully at the ground. There, embedded carefully in the clay dike, was the nipple of a "dragon's tooth." Dragon's teeth were what we called Soviet-made mini-mines. They didn't kill you, just maimed you. When you stepped on them, they blew your foot off.

I can't explain why I didn't take that step. But I didn't. And I can't tell you why I stopped short of walking into Grosvenor Square either. But my early-warning system went off, and just as I didn't drop my foot on the DT, I didn't continue into the square.

Instead, I stepped into a doorway and began to pay attention, treating the area as if it were hostile territory. And the more I looked, the more I realized that that's exactly what it was.

I counted sixteen Marines in their civvy gray blazers and dark trousers positioned around the CINCUSNAVEUR building. Judging from the bulges on their hips, they were carrying side arms.

That was truly extraordinary. Whenever the CINC was in residence, a pair of Uncle Sam's Misguided Children would normally be posted outside, walking an informal beat up and down the sidewalk in front of the old wrought-iron spike fence. But they'd be unarmed. Indeed, the Brits absolutely forbade any weapons outside the building, so all they carried were radio transceivers. That way, in a crisis, they could talk bad guys to death.

But as we all knew, the admiral was not in residence—he was back at Bethesda, having gallbladder surgery. Yet here was a full fucking platoon of Marines, all of them carrying heat, positioned outside the HQ building. Who were they expecting, the fucking president? Had they suddenly been scrambled to Threatcon Delta because Abu Nidal and the entire Baader-Meinhoff gang were about to gang-bang CINCUSNAVEUR?

Or was the terrorist they were seeking even more dangerous than any and all of the above—at least so far as one Pinckney Prescott III, VADM, USN, was concerned. The TIQ: that hop-and-popping, shoot-and-looting, hairy-assed Frogman known as Demo Dick Marcinko, Sharkman of the Delta—in a single word, *moi.*

From cover, I recced the area. Within the square itself, one, two, three, four, five pairs of men wandered aimlessly. Their bodies semaphored they were trying not to call attention to themselves—which made them all the more obvious to me. At the far end, in front of the embassy, two battleship gray USN cars sat idling. Six other vehicles—I could make out U.S. diplomatic plates—waited in no-parking zones close to each intersection at the embassy end of the square. They were positioned to cut off traffic, creating road-blocks that would make the entire square into a cordon sanitaire.

I squinted. Even from two hundred yards, the silhouettes inside seemed all too familiar: they had the bloodless look of NIS Terminators—the top-secret Naval Investigative Service Command Gestapo unit that targets four-stripers and above.

Grosvenor Square was no place for me today—not if I valued my freedom. So, instead of crossing into the square and heading blithely toward North Audley Street, I reversed course and headed back toward Bond Street, head down, face averted. One block away, I turned into the small lobby of Claridge's Hotel, straight-arming the liveried doorman who tried to stop me. Once inside, I found a phone booth, squeezed inside, dialed up the phone on Hans Weber's desk, and dropped the requisite 10P coin when I heard the sound of his voice.

"Command Master Chief Weber."

"It's me. What's all the fucking commotion at your place?"

"Jeezus—" There was real anxiety in Hansie's voice. He sounded absolutely panicked. "No names, son—the phones ain't secure."

"Roger that, Master Chief. Sitrep?"

"TARFU. Somebody told the admiral something that sent him over the edge. He wants your ass keelhauled in the worst way. Called up the whole goddamn cavalry to do it, too."

Damn. Nasty Nicky Grundle had been on his way to the commissary. Had they grabbed him? I started to ask Hans, but he was prescient.

"Your boy was snapped up the minute he walked in here. He's locked in the basement—Pinky's using him as bait to get to you."

"Can we talk?"

"Not now."

"When? Where?"

"We can't. I'll leave a message at the place we usually meet."

Usually meet? Where the hell was he talking about? My mind was blank. Before I could say anything else, he hung up.

Shit. Fuck. Doom on Dickie. I sat in the booth, sweating bullets. I had no idea what Hansie'd meant. Then the sound of sirens told me I'd better move—right now.

I bolted across the lobby, charged through the double doors to the dining room, crashed the kitchen, and went out the service entrance of the hotel just as I heard cars screeching to a halt at the front entrance. I cut down a mews, worked my way up an alley, and ran against traffic up a series of one-way streets, until I reached South Audley Street. I pushed open the front door of a church and caught my breath safely inside the vestibule.

What the hell was going on? I had no idea. All I knew was that I had to figure out what the hell Hansie had been talking about, then get to the garage behind Victoria.

Three minutes later I worked my way back to Berkeley Square, out of breath, frantic, and painfully aware that at least one gray car of Terminators was gaining on me, its insistent, American-style siren getting louder and louder.

I tried the front door of an office building. It was locked. I tried the town house next door. It, too, was locked. They were getting closer. I cut across the square, unmindful of KEEP OFF THE GRASS signs, and sprinted up Bruton Place to the Guinea, praying it wasn't closed. I pulled open the door and heaved myself inside, breathing hard.

"We're shut." Eric was washing pint glasses. Then he recognized me, waved me to the bar, and drew me a Young's without asking. "You look fuckin' dreadful," he said by way of greeting. "What's happened?"

I drained the pint. "Fuck you very much, too," I wheezed.

He'd started to pour me another when he was interrupted by the sound of a car screeching to a halt outside, and my exclaiming, "Oh, *shit!*"

I went wild-eyed. "Eric—"

God bless the paras. He didn't have to be told anything. "Kitchen," he growled, pointing toward the rear of the pub with one hand while he swept my glass off the bar with the other. "Left-hand door. Move!"

I hauled ass and hunkered down behind the fridge, heart *ka-bump-ka-bumping.* As the pulse pounded in my head, I realized all of a sudden what Hansie had meant on the phone. We'd always meet at the Goat—the old pub on Stafford Street where they served bratwurst as well as bangers.

From somewhere outside the kitchen door came the sounds of muffled voices. Then it went all quiet. Eric retrieved me three minutes later. A fresh pint of Young's was waiting for me, and I downed it fast.

Eric stood there with his arms crossed. "So, who the hell did you kill?"

I had no idea what he was talking about. But I knew I'd fucking find out soon enough—when I got to the Goat.

Chapter

10

DEPARTMENT OF THE NAVY
OFFICE OF THE CHIEF OF NAVAL OPERATIONS
WASHINGTON, DC 20350-2000

Secret

SER 0392/6N30864
19 November

FROM: ASSISTANT/VICE CHIEF OF NAVAL OPERATIONS (OPO9B)

TO: COMMANDER, NAVAL CRIMINAL INVESTIGATIVE COMMAND (O909N)

SUBJ: CAPT. RICHARD (NMN) MARCINKO, USN 156-93-083/1130: (APPREHENSION OF)

REF: (a) 11 USC 214.07
(b) 42 USC 688.32 (e)
(c) NAVCRICINST 0240.661

1. Subject to be apprehended and charged with the murder of Mahmoud Azziz abu Yasin, an Egyptian national.

2. Subject is to be considered armed, dangerous, and irrational.

3. Full interagency cooperation is deemed essential.

4. OPO9B will brook no foreign-government interference in this internal USN matter.

5. OPO9B to be advised daily on this matter through Elder Brother channel.

6. (Signed): Pinckney Prescott III
Vice Admiral, U.S. Navy
Assistant/Vice Chief of Naval Operations

Secret

Part
Three

CHARLIE

Chapter

11

ONE OF THE MOST SIGNIFICANT TRAINING EXERCISES I'D DEVISED AS THE CO of SEAL Team Six was an E&E in which I took away everybody's documents—their passports, driver's licenses, military IDs, AMEX or VISA cards, and so on, then assigned them to go from point A to point B within a defined time frame. My old friend Charlie Beckwith had developed much the same thing for Delta Force—but his exercises were almost always played out in CONUS —the CONtinental U.S. Mine were nearly all held overseas. I'd turn my guys loose in Brussels with $20 worth of Belgian francs and tell them to meet me ninety-six hours later at a trattoria in Rome's Piazza Navona. I'd dump them out of a truck just outside Frankfurt, give them one hundred deutsche marks and a slip of paper with a London address. I'd land 'em on the beach twenty miles from Alexandria with a handful of Egyptian pounds and directions to a villa in Cyprus. I'd toss 'em out of a plane over Guatemala and tell them to meet me at a bar in San Salvador's *zona rosa*.

Not everybody was equally successful at the game. All SEALs can chase pussy, drink beer, pump iron, swim for miles, throw themselves out of planes, and navigate underwater. Some SEALs can kill. I needed men whose unconventional talents—in addition to those listed above—also included role-playing and sweet-talking in various foreign languages. I wanted con men who'd be able to survive in any kind of environment, without the benefit of the military support system—in fact, without *any* support system. I needed individualists who wouldn't feel threatened if they were left behind after a mission to make their own way to safety. Those who did the best at my little unguided tours of Europe, the Middle East, and South America I kept; those who didn't were jettisoned.

I didn't create the E&Es from whim, either: during the Iran rescue mission back in 1980, two SEALS—let's call them Kline and Joey—went to Tehran under civilian cover to help Delta Force. After the mission aborted, Kline made his way across more than six hundred miles of hostile territory to safety in Turkey. Joey pulled off an exfil right under the Iranian mullahs' noses in Tehran. I learned from their experience.

Now, looking at the single sheet of CNO letterhead Hansie had left for me at the Goat, I realized that my men and I were in as much jeopardy as Kline and Joey had been back in 1980—except the enemy wasn't a bunch of Shiite tangos, it was the U.S. Navy. I was under indictment for murder. The Green Team squad I'd taken to Cairo would be charged as accessories. Nasty Nicky Grundle was sitting in the basement of 7 North Audley Street behind two inches of steel door.

Not to mention the fact that somewhere near Nice, in southern France, Lord B and his Paki friends were probably sipping champagne and making plans. We had to figure out what they were planning and stop him.

I took inventory. Actually, things could have been a lot worse. My Cairo team had its Freddie the Forger documents—which no one knew about, as the guys had entered the U.K. using the real names on their military IDs. That gave us passports and driver's licenses—most of 'em British Commonwealth, or EC. We had Azziz's fifty thousand pounds in cash, three of Freddie's best credit cards, and the clothes on our backs.

Oh, sure, on the one hand, we had no weapons, equipment, logistical support, or intelligence. But we could obtain all of those easily. And on the other hand, we had the most crucial elements for victory: raw energy, guts, determination, and the absolute will to succeed.

Obviously, then, we could not fail.

* * *

I sat the guys down and gave them a no-shitter. The fact that Pinky knew about Azziz's death meant he'd been handed the information. He'd not been need-to-know about our mission—in fact, CNO didn't trust him at all.

Okay, who knew about Cairo? Well, CNO, of course, but he was dead. The president did, too—but he and Pinky weren't on speaking terms. That pretty much ended the information chain.

Except . . . one other person knew about Cairo, too. Sir Aubrey Davis knew. He'd intimated as much to me over dinner at his fancy club on St. James's Square. My list of suspects, therefore, was pretty short.

When detectives want to narrow their lists of suspects, they use three criteria to search out the guilty party. Those are means, motive, and opportunity.

- Means: Sir Aubrey knew about my mission in Cairo. He'd probably dropped a tidbit to Pinky da Turd. Pinky, of course, went batshit—and issued an arrest order.
- Motive: Sir Aubrey had been the one to request my services, then tie my hands by insisting that I work with the incompetent Geoff Lyondale. It had been Lyondale who'd brought Lord B on board as a consultant. The answer, then, was obvious: Sir Aubrey had been bought and paid for. Lord Brookfield—estimated annual income £340 million a year—was probably paying Monocle Man a truckload of cash to sell out his country.
- Opportunity: with the Admiral of the Fleet, CNO, and me out of the way, and the traitorous Sir Aubrey in charge of Britain's CT operations, a world-class clusterfuck situation could be created by Lord B and his tango compatriots. Talk about transnational terrorism.

Except, there was a frog in the ointment, and its name was Marcinko.

I'd come a-calling, planting my size 11E's where they shouldn't have been. So the situation had to be remedied. First, they tried to elbow me out of the way by foisting Geoff on me. When that didn't work, they tried to wax my ass in the underground passage. And when that fell through, somebody leaked word about Azziz's untimely demise to Pinky da Turd, who didn't need much urging to issue an arrest warrant with my name on it.

So, there was no doubt about the fact that we had been double-crossed. I held the evidence for that in my scarred hand. The bottom line, no matter who had betrayed whom, was that I—and, by extension, my men—were all outlaws now. That meant no contact with our normal information sources at DIA and No Such Agency—they'd simply turn us in. Nor could I ask support from my Safety Net of chiefs scattered across the globe—helping me would put their careers in jeopardy, and there was no way I'd ask them to do that. No—we were on our own. We'd have to live off the land—rape, pillage, loot, and burn as we went.

"Sounds like your everyday SOP to me, Dickhead," Wonder said.

"Yeah, what's your point—*sir?*" asked Duck Foot, spelling it with a *c* and a *u.*

I'm blessed to have men who know me well enough to be properly respectful.

Their reaction buoyed my spirits immensely. Okay—it was time to act. Our first objective would be to get Nasty out of jail. After that, we'd scatter. The Cairo squad—Tommy, Nasty, Howie, Wonder, and Duck Foot—would make its way to Germany, then go south, through France, to Nice.

I drew up my duty roster and listed the men's assignments. In a flash of inspiration, I decided to take Rodent with me—much to his obvious delight. He was a scrounger in the tradition of James "Hoot" Andrews, the chief storekeeper whom Roy Boehm shanghaied from under Admiral Hyman Rickover's nose (Hoot was serving on the Polaris missile sub USS *George Washington* at the time), when Roy needed a world-class "expediter" to equip SEAL Team 2. Hoot may have worked for Rickover, but he'd served at UDT-21 for six years, and once you're a Frogman, you're always a Frogman—the Teams come before anything else. So Hoot went to work for Roy, and Roy got his new command equipped in record time.

Besides being an able thief, Rodent wasn't on anybody's wanted list. That meant he could use his ID to get inside Patch Barracks, the European HQ for the Special Operations Command that sits on a hillside overlooking Stuttgart. Once he was through the gate, he could "borrow" equipment, purloin intelligence, and filch whatever else he thought we might need. And if we didn't find what we wanted at Patch Barracks, we could utilize one or two of the POMCUS caches in southern Germany.

POMCUS (Prepositioned Outside Military Custody of the U.S.) stores include weapons, ammo, fuel, trucks, radios—all the crucial resupplies that NATO forces would have needed for the first thirty days of a Soviet land invasion of Western Europe. Some of the goods were on NATO military bases. Some were in municipal storage facilities. Others were hidden away in secret bunkers— bunkers I knew the locations of.

So, while Pinky might think we were outmanned, outgunned fugitives, it wasn't going to be like that at all. In fact, when we finally went nose to nose with Lord B, we'd be as prepared as we would have been if we'd come straight from Dam Neck. Doom on you, Pinky.

Moreover, while me and my merry band of renegades toured Europe, the rest of Green Team would knuckle-drag around Britain, leaving obvious trails for Pinky and Sir Aubrey to follow. Hopefully, Sergeant Snake, Rooster, Carlos, and the rest of the team would lead them and their bloodhounds far enough off the scent so that we could do our work, neutralize the tangos, and come back with enough scalps on our belts to clear ourselves—or at least make it too embarrassing to prosecute.

By the time we got back to the FAMFUC, Mick Owen had heard the bells, whistles, and sirens, too. He figured we had about two hours before the roof fell in.

"I wish I could help fix this, Dick—but it's way above my pay grade. Special Branch and MI5 have been brought in. MI6, too. Every fuckin' spook in the world is probably gonna be looking for you. Shit—I probably had an easier time getting out of Iraq than you're gonna have leaving the U.K."

He might not have been able to grease the skids anymore, but he was still able to slip us a few goodies. He gave me two Magellan GPS trailblazers—battery-operated, handheld Global Positioning System computers that use a network of satellites to provide precise data on your location. They're smaller than this book in your hands, but they're powerful. You punch data into the Magellan using its twenty-four-key system, and presto: your precise position in latitude and longitude appears on a small screen.

We could also use the Magellan to chart our course. You punch your destination in, and the computer gives you a series of readouts showing where you are relative to the target—very, very helpful if you're looking for a tango camp out in the desert. Mick also gave me a waterproof, thermal range-finder, seven Glock-19 pistols with Trijicon night sights, twenty-eight sixteen-round magazines, and five hundred rounds of his best hollowpoint ammo.

Best of all, he let me have two of SAS's secure SATCOM burst transceivers. So long as the British military's secure telecom system was running, and I could recharge the batteries once a day or so, I'd be able to talk to Mick and communicate with my men. Mick and I devised an eight-digit KISS cipher system so I could report where I was and what we were up to. Because my old Safety Net wasn't going to be much help anymore—not for a while—Mick was going to be my single point of contact while we were on the run. I gave him a general outline of what I planned to do—omitting several specifics. I didn't, for example, tell him about my plan to liberate the POMCUS goodies, or my final destination in France. It wasn't that I didn't trust Mick, but just in case MI5 decided to slip him 75 mgs of IV sodium pentabarbitol or any of the new designer drugs, I didn't want him talking in his sleep.

We left the FAMFUC singly and in pairs, slipping over the fence at half a dozen points just in case the gate was being observed. Our rendezvous point would be the Guinea, four blocks from CINCUSNAVEUR—from which we had to extricate Nasty Nicky Grundle. Mick had already called Eric Wells from a pay phone. The former para said he'd be happy to find us a foxhole to crawl into for a couple of nights. After that, though, we'd be on our own—blind jumping into space.

I was last out. I hugged Mick. "Fuck you, asshole."

"Sod you, you sorry wanker. If you need me, either burst me or contact me through Eric. I'll make sure he knows where I am."

"Roger that, Mick. But make sure you check your six—they're gonna pull your short-and-curlies to get at me."

CINCUSNAVEUR is a hundred-year-old, seven-story building with two basement levels. Hey, hey, out there—no skipping forward to the next action sequence. Come on, pay attention: you will see this material again. Anyway, as I was saying, on the ground floor and first basement level are many of the command's creature features—the barbershop, medical unit, bank, cafeteria, gift shop, and so on. The second floor is filled with VIP offices—the CINC's cabin, for example, is on two—and the unit's ornate conference room, which is located right where Dwight D. Eisenhower had the office from which he planned D day. Next door to the conference room lives the State Department POLAD—the resident POLitical ADviser who makes sure CINC doesn't say or do anything impolitic.

The first, third, and fourth floors hold CINCUSNAVEUR's apparatchiki—hundreds of three- and four-striped middle managers, who justify their existence by turning out reams and reams of memos, treatises, reports, assessments, and briefs. How anybody can call something seventy-six fucking pages long a "brief," I'll never know.

During my UDT Replacement Class 26 training, we incipient Frogmen wore WWII-vintage kapok life vests as part of our training gear. The vests weighed six pounds dry and twenty-six pounds wet—and the instructors managed to keep them wet all the time. In the water, the vests became cumbersome sea anchors, weighing us down and keeping us from swimming efficiently. On land, coated with sand, they got even heavier. Like those kapok vests, CINCUSNAVEUR's blue-uniformed bureaucrats manage to keep the Navy from decisive action through the sheer weight of their redundantly overwhelming, cumbersome paperwork.

Please, sir, your exalted paperpushership, the IRA has just tossed a grenade through the window of the British Admiralty. May I humbly request that we buy a set of antigrenade screens for our own windows so we won't be vulnerable? Intelligence tells us that the Paddies are gearing up to make an example of us next week.

Of course you can, my beamish boy. Just fill out this requisition, sign these few dozen forms, and we'll have your antigrenade screens in twelve to eighteen months.

But your exalted penmanship, our need is immediate. The threat is real, and imminent.

Imminent? Why didn't you say so, lad. No problem. Just put your John Hancock on this additional sheaf of papers, write me five or six memos outlining the reasons why and how screens stop grenades, and we'll have those little suckers to you in a mere nine months. Of course, moving that fast means you'll need the permission of my superiors, who've just left on a three-month TAD to Washington. As soon as they get back, I'm sure we can accommodate you. In the meanwhile, bub, it's time for my scheduled coffee break, so buzz off.

The top two floors—five and six—are where most of the

command's classified materials are located. On the North Wing of Five, protected by cameras, cipher-locked doors, and an impressive array of passive detection devices, is the NAVOPS—NAVy OPerationS—center, where all of NATO's war plans for Europe are contained inside six massive fireproof safes. Five others hold all of the Navy's unilateral tactical and strategic plans for the defense of Western Europe. There are SpecWar scenarios and fleet deployments, aircraft-refueling logistics, sea-lift capabilities—in essence, most of the Navy's current classified, sensitive, and top-secret documents for every destination between the Washington Navy Yard and the Seychelles can be found on the computer disks, microfiche negatives, or hard-copy files on the fifth floor.

On the sixth floor, behind barred, sealed windows, lies CINCUSNAVEUR's massive communications center. The climate up there is strictly controlled by four massive air-conditioning and filtering units that sit on the building's roof. Shielded UHF, VHF, microwave, and satellite antennas are connected by bug-proof fiber-optic lines to the NSA-built transmitters and receivers. From top to bottom and wall to wall, the place is filled with billions of dollars of communications gear. There are satellite transceivers that bounce scrambled signals 22,000 miles in the sky. There are microwave radios, cellular phones, analog and digital devices—you name it, they got it.

Then there's the countermeasures stuff. Since every bit of message traffic received by the U.S. Navy in the Atlantic or Mediterranean is CC'd here to CINCUSNAVEUR, there are tons of antieavesdropping equipment in play. And since the Pentagon knows all too well that diplomats love to read other people's mail, the sixth floor is used by DIA as its E-mail hub for Western Europe, with messages coming direct from Arlington, or through the Naval Imaging Command at Anacostia Naval Station for dissemination to France, Germany, and Italy. DIA has its own set of antitheft devices in place.

Now you might think that, given all of the above, CINCUSNAVEUR is an impregnable, hardened target.

Guess again. I'd done the equivalent of a preliminary recon during my few recent visits to the place—habit, y'know. There is a technical term for the security capabilities I'd noted. That term is *clusterfucked*.

The entrance is manned by a quartet of Marines, who're sequestered behind a six-by-eight-foot cage built of seven-eighths-inch bulletproof glass. They look like fish in a barrel, which is exactly what they'd become if I came bursting through the two glass front doors and pulled a sawed-off twelve-gauge filled with six Kevlar-tipped sabot rounds followed up by two CS gas shells. There's no fallback position for them; no way to seek cover and return fire. There's also no way they can blockade the front of the building—no defendable chokepoint.

Entry is a turnstile—you insert your ID card in a slot, the gizmo reads the magnetic strip on the back just like a credit card, the turnstile turns, and you're in. To exit, you do the same thing. Nobody checks the picture, nobody compares your name with a list of approved occupants.

Once you're inside, you simply clip your ID card to your lapel or your belt, and you're free to wander the halls as you please. Only on the fifth and sixth floors do they ratchet the security a notch or two—and even so, the ratcheting is really more rat shitting than anything else. On five, there are real locks on the doors. Real locks take more than thirty seconds to get through. And on six, there are Marines who actually glance at your ID card before they let you in the comm center.

Oh, yeah, sure, there are cameras in the hallways—but most of them don't move. Of course there are cipher locks on the doorways—but there's always someone coming or going, and all you have to do is wait just out of camera range and slip in just as Lieutenant Blivet Sphincter, USN, heads to the head. "Oh, gee, thanks, Lieutenant . . ."

Unbelievable, you say. Incredible, you exclaim. You mean to tell us taxpayers that the hub, the locus, the fucking nerve center of all the U.S. Navy's European operations is lying with its legs wide open and ready for a real case of hurt-me, hurt-me screwing?

Yes, that's absofuckinglutely what I'm telling you. Moreover, I was the perfect size-twelve Big Dick to do the deed.

But you shouldn't fuck without foreplay. So first, we'd need two uniforms. One for Nasty, and one for Wonder. I had Nasty's—the dress blue officer's uniform Hansie had slipped to me would fit him easily. Wonder's was another matter. We decided to make him a Marine, since he'd been one as a child.

That's right—as a seventeen-year-old cannon fodder Force Recon Marine back in the early seventies, he won two Silver Stars for half a dozen classified missions in North Vietnam and Laos. On the second of them—ninety-two days behind enemy lines—he got blown off a mountaintop just outside Hanoi. He still has fragments of his neckbone coming loose from that roguish op. Last year, one of the smaller ones worked its way due west, coming out through the bottom of his left eye. At first, Wonder thought he had another bad hangover. That should give you some idea about his lifestyle.

Anyway, the asshole still speaks fluent Jarhead. So Duck Foot took his measurements, then scaled the drainpipe of the Marine House, which sits on Lees Place, a lightly traveled, narrow street about five hundred feet from CINCUSNAVEUR HQ. He popped through an open second-floor window and walked the halls. It's amazing—even though the place has two video cameras outside, and Duck Foot made his approach in broad daylight, no one paid him any mind. Once he was inside, no one questioned his being there, even though he talked to half a dozen people.

Inconceivable, you say. No, it's not. Security is the last thing anybody thinks about, because it interferes with creature comforts. Inspections or security checks are tiresome. Gates and bars make it hard for people to come and go. The last thing most base commanders want is a kick-ass security officer who's always nagging about OpSec or perimeter control. So they let things slide.

Security details, for example, are most often made up of newcomers who don't have assignments, or people about to transfer out. They don't know—or care—what the routines are, or who should (or shouldn't) be on post. At the Marine House, there may have been two cameras deployed. But they were pointed at the doorway, not the outside gate—so no one saw Duck Foot approach the building and scamper up the drainpipe. There were bars on the ground-floor windows, but the first- and second-floor windows were left wide open.

That sort of thinking used to make it easy for Red Cell—and it made stealing a uniform effortless for Duck Foot. So he walked the halls for three-quarters of an hour, browsing the goods. When he was satisfied, he picked out a 44-regular Alpha uniform—belted green jacket, khaki shirt and tie, thirty-two-inch-waist green pants (inseam thirty-four), black shoes, and barracks cover (size 7⅛, if you please)—from three first sergeants' lockers.

In one of the double-rack bunks he discovered an ID card under a pillow. From the way things were packed up around the bedside, its owner was apparently on leave. How convenient. In another room, he boosted a pair of crossed-pistols badges—the ones worn by provost-marshal Marines—and pinned them on the lapels of the Alpha blouse. Now, Wonder worked for the judge advocate general.

While Duck Foot was shopping, Wonder betook himself to a barber where his Howdy Doody hair got trimmed down to a top buzz and whitewalls. I can tell you he wasn't happy about that.

Bright and early the next morning, First Sergeant Stephen Noel Wonder sauntered into CINCUSNAVEUR HQ. The Marines in the fishbowl never gave him a second glance. His card worked the turnstile. He reconned the first-floor hallways, noting the positions of all the security cameras. He noted that my jacket photo from *Rogue Warrior: Red Cell* was posted at the visitors' security desk, inside the Marine checkpoint, and over the doorway.

Wonder picked up a copy of the current command newsletter— the NAVEURACTCOMREP (NAVy EURope ACTivities COMmunication REPort), which thoughtfully provided a list of offices and phone extensions, as well as a report on all the command's current extracurricular activities—trips and excursions, bus schedules to the joint base commissary down in Surrey, and a list of goods for sale. Every terrorist should have one. He took the elevator to the basement. He had a cup of coffee on the first-level cafeteria and read the newsletter.

Then he walked down the fire stairs on the north wing of the building to second level, where Nasty was being held. The subterranean cellar, built of hundred-year-old, painted brickwork, had the low arched ceilings and narrow, tunnel-like passageways common to Victorian architecture. Indeed, the basement was the oldest element of the building, comprising its original foundation. The tunnel between the two wings had been enlarged and reinforced during World War II to provide an air-raid shelter for Ike and his staff.

The holding cell in which Nasty was being held had been added after the war. It was a steel box measuring six by nine, with a sink and toilet built at the far end, and a narrow slab bunk down one side. There wasn't even a lock—the door was secured by a simple latch arrangement.

The problem was, three Marines were on guard outside, and as a former member of the Corps, Wonder had qualms about killing them. "I don't do Marines," he said when he returned to the Guinea to brief me. "Maim, maybe. Kill—no way."

I told him he was getting soft in his old age.

He told me, "Eat shit and bark at the moon, sir." I was glad to see that he spelled it c-u-r. I like consistency.

Wonder ran the probs and stats and we sat around head-shedding them.

- Getting in—no problem.
- Getting out—problem. Stat? Wonder's card would get him in the front door. But to get Nasty out of the building, we'd need another card so he could go through the turnstile. Solution? Steal another card.
- Marine guards—problem. Stat? Since killing them was not an option, the only thing to do was set up a diversion. Solution? Setting off the fire alarm was the most obvious. In buildings such as CINCUSNAVEUR, everyone has an assignment. You do not sit and twiddle your toes when the bell goes off.

But there might be other things we could do as well. To see what they were, I bundled my hair up inside a po' boy cap, borrowed a big duffel coat from Eric, took a cab to the Marriott, which backed up against CINCUSNAVEUR, and walked the perimeter of the building to see what I could see. I may have been on Pinky's 10 Most Wanted list (I may have been his entire 10 Most Wanted List), but the watchers I'd seen a day and a half ago were now gone.

Guess what: it is expensive to maintain full-court-press surveillance. Terrorists know this. That's why they take their damn time so often. They can afford to wait us out.

Anyway, my preliminary target assessment led me to be optimistic. The roof of the building and all its sensitive antennas, cables, and air-purification devices were completely unprotected. Moreover, it could be reached by entering the Marriott next door, taking the elevator to the top floor, breaking onto the hotel roof, and traversing from one building to the other—Infiltration 101 for my Red Cell veterans. There were no sensors or trip wires. There were TV cameras mounted at each corner, but they were pointed down at the street, not up at the roof surface.

I could fuck with the antennas easily—really screw up communications—but that wouldn't draw the Marines from Nasty's cell. Still, it would help draw attention away from the basement. The other thing I noted on the roof were the locations of the plumbing vents. I duly tallied them and made a mental note to buy some Saran Wrap.

At ground level, a huge sewer-pipe excavation was next to the northeast wall. The company doing the digging was aptly named the Murphy Co. The excavation itself was unprotected—it was covered with loose timbers and ran right up against the CINCUSNAVEUR foundation. All the better to leave a couple of bricks of Semtex or C-4 plastique. If I tamped it right, I could bring the whole fucking building down on itself using less than fifty pounds of explosive.

The possibilities for screwing with North Audley were endless. But it wasn't my job to pull a Red Cell exercise—it was my job to get Nasty out of jail. So in the end, we kept it simple, stupid, because we discovered CINCUSNAVEUR's Achilles' heel—and we used it.

Behind the excavation, on the north side of the building, was a single, anonymous-looking white wood door. It was never locked. There were no TV cameras covering it. And guess what—it opened onto the main corridor of the HQ building. Walk inside, and you ended up in front of the elevators, safely past all the security turnstiles and checkpoints. And yet no one had checked you out.

What's going on here? Why does the Navy's most important facility in Europe have a completely insecure doorway?

Why? Because it's the smokers' door, that's why.

Let me explain. New government health regulations state that all USG—that's U.S. Government—buildings (with the exception of the houses of Congress and their office buildings) must now be smoke-free environments. So, what do all the newly ostracized smokers do? They find a convenient place to indulge their habit. In Washington, you can see them standing outside the main entrances of their departments, puffing away. Some departments have even installed huge, outdoor ashtrays for them.

In proper olde London, however, the CINC had decreed the main entrance to 7 North Audley off limits to smokers. His reason? He believed they didn't look genteel standing there, puffing away. Not dignified and all that.

So, at CINCUSNAVEUR, smokers congregated in the alley just

behind the HQ building. To accommodate these nicotine addicts, the alley door was always left open. Day and night. Twenty-four hours a day. Seven days a week.

You think I'm writing fiction here. You're sitting there saying, "They can't be that dumb."

Well, my friends, they are that dumb. This is for real—as insane and absurd as it may appear to be.

Okay, thanks to CINCUSNAVEUR's suck-and-puffers, we now had a way to smuggle ourselves inside—Nasty back out—without going through the turnstile. I spent another half hour perusing the target, watching people come and go, noting the traffic flow and the pedestrians on the street. I concluded that our best chance of success lay in staging our op in broad daylight, using the hustle-bustle of rush-hour London to our advantage.

Half an hour later, I was back at the Guinea, drawing diagrams on big sheets of butcher paper and making assignments. Then Wonder slipped into his uniform, and he and Rodent marched up to North Audley Street, lighted up, then slipped inside the smokers' door. Sixteen minutes later, they brought Nasty Nicky upstairs and walked him outside so he could enjoy the good Cuban cigar they'd brought for him. I watched from across the street, happy to see the relief on Nasty's face.

Of course, two hours later, as Nasty was chugging his fifth pint of Young's bitter at the Guinea, he complained that we'd taken too fucking long to come and get him. Wonder shut him up by offering to put him back.

Chapter

12

THE BEST MED CRUISE I EVER TOOK WAS AS A MEMBER OF EV BARRETT'S Second Platoon (we called it the Second-to-None Platoon) of UDT-22. We sailed aboard the USS *Rushmore,* a WWII-vintage LSD, or Landing Ship/Dock, that had originally been built for the Royal Navy. We visited Naples, where I'd served as a radioman. We visited Greece. We visited Turkey. And we spent a memorable two weeks on the French Riviera.

Most of the team stayed in Marseilles, eating bouillabaisse and rouille, and playing musical bordellos. I went east—I took the train to Cannes, and Nice, where I saw my first topless French beaches and got my first taste of the Gallic version of la dolce vita, played out at sidewalk cafés set on the wide seaside boulevards—Canne's Croisette, or the Promenade des Anglais in Nice. I drank café au lait from the big, deep, bowl-like cups sans handles the French used to use and fell in ninety-six-hour lust with someone named Simone— or was it Nicole—who kept me up for all four days. Literally. Ah, youth.

Then, as CO of SEAL Team Two, I got to visit the Riviera once again. It was after Charles de Gaulle had pulled the French out of NATO. The ultranationalistic—some of us might say xenophobic—

French were reluctant to share any information about their nuclear capabilities with their former allies. So SEAL Two, whose responsibilities in those days included Western Europe, was tasked with keeping tabs on our former NATO allies. That made perfect sense to me—send Frogs to check up on frogs.

Since I spoke both fluent French and fluent Frog, I volunteered myself to lead the mission. I took six men with me—one squad. We flew to Paris on different airlines, rendezvoused, spent a day getting our bearings, then took the overnight train to Nice. There, we rented two cars and posed as tourists. We ate well, drank well, fucked great, and had a terrific time driving around. We even saved the government money by bivouacking in one of the dozens of campgrounds that lie all along the southern coast.

We spent six days prowling and growling around a sizable nuclear power plant—Installation Number 12 was its formal designation—that sat on a small peninsula just west of Nice, on the far side of the city's small airport. That sounds simple, but to actually take the pictures we had to penetrate the fence line, the power facility, and—most important—the nuclear-waste storage area.

We had two missions to accomplish: one tactical, one strategic. The tactical mission was the simpler of the two. It was to develop a plan to destroy the installation in the event of a Soviet attack. The contingency planners at NATO, who knew all too well the sorry history of French collaboration with the Nazis in World War II, did not want any French nuclear plants falling into Soviet hands.

The strategic mission, which was much more difficult, was to discover whether Number 12 was simply a generating plant—that is, used its fissionable material exclusively to produce electricity— or whether its reactor was actually creating more fissionable material than it used.

If it was, then the frogs had built what is called a breeder reactor. Breeder reactors create materials—such as plutonium and heavy water—that can be used to build nuclear weapons. Since we'd already been committed to sneaking and peeking anyway, Christians in Action had asked the Pentagon to have us answer that question for them while we were on-site.

Now, there are no more Soviets to worry about, but the ultranationalistic French still refuse to share any of their nuclear information with the rest of the world. *Plus ça change, plus c'est la même chose*—or, as we Yogi Berra Yankees say, it's déjà vu all over again.

We'd had an easy exit from Britain. There was a cursory passport check, no customs, and no waiting as we filed through embarkation with the rest of the day-trippers heading for the cheap wines and farmhouse cheeses of the French port towns. Tommy, Duck Foot, Howie, and Wonder took the hovercraft to Calais, the boat train to Paris, and then headed east to Germany, to a POMCUS depot near Marburg where they'd do their shopping. Nasty, Rodent, and I hovercrafted across the Channel to Boulogne, then trained through Paris to Bonn. There, after the wurst lunch we'd had in days, I tried to contact my old comrade-in-arms (I used to call him the hotsy-totsy-fuck-you Nazi when we trained together), Herr General Ricky Wegener, who had led the top German CT unit, GSG-9, when I was CO of SEAL Team Six. But Ricky was nowhere to be found—he was probably consulting for one of the oil-rich sheikhdoms in the Gulf for his customary $2,500 a day plus expenses.

I used to charge fees like that and travel first-class, too. I got recalled—Ricky didn't. Now, I'm a fugitive, and he's still eating caviar. Well, more power to Herr General Ricky.

After twelve hours and meager results, we took the train to Karlsruhe. Rodent rented a car and flew down the autobahn to Stuttgart, where he pried a few goodies loose from Patch Barracks. Meanwhile, since Azziz's cash was burning a hole in my pocket, I bought us three old but fast BMW bikes, three sets of leathers, and the biggest saddlebags I could lay my hands on. Then, like the cast of *The Wild Ones*, we *vroom–vroomed* south, carefree tourists in search of regional cuisine. We hit Strasbourg (white wine, bread, sausage, and pâté), Dijon (red wine, bread, sausage, mustard, and pâté), Lyon (rose wine, bread, sausage, and pâté—do you sense a certain culinary repetition here?), then shot straight down the Rhône River, turned left at Châteauneuf-du-Pape (red wine, bread, sausage), and sped southeast onto the Riviera (topless bathers, topless bathers, topless bathers).

The team linked up in Nice sixty hours later in a park facing the Promenade des Anglais, just across from the old Negresco Hotel. I was pleased to see that Wonder was driving a huge Mercedes sedan. Yes, they hide cars in some of the POMCUS caches, too. Thoughtful, isn't it?

We HQ'd at a no-star hotel just off the beach road, a klick and a half east of Beaulieu. The place was bare essentials—two racks per room, one sink, one bidet, a single ladder-back chair, and a dresser. But we didn't mind, because Maman Soleil, who ran it, cooked herself silly in the postage-stamp-sized kitchen. The dining room was narrow and reeked of Gauloises and garlic, old cooking oil, and onions. The wine was stored in barrels. It all made my mouth water.

I grew up on food like this, eating at Old Man Gussi's kitchen table above the Italian restaurant where I worked. Big plates of family-style food—and don't hold anything back. So we checked in, I peeled off six of Azziz's fifty-pound notes, pressed them into Maman's *mains,* and told her, *"Nous avons les faims des loups, Maman*—we gotta eat, Mama."

It didn't take us long to discover where he was, because Beaulieu is a very small town, and Lord B had obviously established a routine. In the mornings he swam on his private beach—which told me that he had discipline, because the water was cold. In the afternoons he sunned, lying next to his heated pool, and in the evenings he and Todd drove to Monte Carlo in a bright red Ferrari, and he spent the night gamboling at one of the discos.

The game was to remain low-profile. So we didn't infiltrate and plant monitoring devices or passive audio sensors—Lord B had guard dogs, and taking a guard dog out tends to attract attention. Instead, we did things the old-fashioned way: we staked out his villa using three-man, radio-equipped teams that worked six-hour shifts, and the trio of BMWs I'd bought in Germany. One man watched from across the road, one from the east, and the last from the west. We discovered almost immediately that Lord B had houseguests. I drove over in the Mercedes, wandered onto the beach, and peered through binoculars. Guess what? I'd seen the guests before: Major Haji and Major Yusef, the Peter Piper proper pair of pickled Paks from the SF Club who'd met with Brookfield at his house in Hampstead. Two and two was adding up to four.

It was easy surveillance. Thanks to Rodent and the POMCUS caches, we had night-vision devices and long-range glasses. Thanks to Mahmoud Azziz's fat envelope of fifty-pound notes, we had Beemers. Even the location worked in our favor. Lord B's place sat right on the beach. It had a long, narrow driveway of crushed stone, and an electronic gate. We discovered four closed-circuit cameras sweeping the grounds. Those posed no problem so far as we were concerned. The real security system was composed of three massive rottweilers, who roamed the grounds at will. The perimeter of *l'Oasis bleue* was a ten-foot wall whose top was encrusted with jagged shards of broken glass. There was a vacant lot to his east, and a villa full of Eurotrash to his west.

We also kept a low social profile—although that was rough on my normally exuberant and perpetually pussy-crazed boychiks. But we managed. We did the majority of our eating and drinking at Chez Soleil—no hardship duty, believe me. We stayed away from *cherchering les femmes* at the discos and clubs. We paid attention to the job.

And we even came across the unexpected. The second night, Duck Foot came back from tracking Lord B to Monte Carlo all excited. "Skipper—"

I hoisted myself halfway out of my threadbare blanket. "This better be good, asshole—I was in the middle of a very erotic dream."

"The guy from Cairo—the Nubian."

"Huh?"

"Remember I told you I saw an African guy with Azziz—a big asshole in robes? I trailed him to the Meridien, then he changed clothes and left for the airport?"

If I didn't remember, I did now.

"Well, he's Brookfield's bodyguard. It's gotta be the same guy."

That sat me straight up. Over my thirty or so years of shooting, looting, hopping, popping, prowling, growling, and other miscellaneous lethal activities, I have concluded that there are few coincidences in my professional life. The fact that Lord B and Mahmoud Azziz abu Yasin were connected only served to reinforce that judgment. I was glad the son of a bitch was dead.

And now that I knew for sure Lord B was dirty, I wrote out his death warrant in my mind, too.

On the fourth day of surveillance, Lord B deviated from his routine. Just after noon, he and one of his Pak houseguests drove into Nice with Todd at the wheel of a huge Jaguar saloon. They parked near the Negresco, then ambled down to the seaside, where they wandered aimlessly for half an hour along the Quai des Etats-Unis, and up into the shopping district. Except they weren't wandering aimlessly. They were engaging in tradecraft to make sure they weren't being shadowed. They doubled back on themselves, they hooked around corners, they peered in store windows to check reflections. They did all the things that experienced gumshoes do to make sure that they aren't being followed.

Then, after they'd checked, double-checked, and triple-checked, they walked up into the old section of the city, behind the Avenue Marshal Foch, and into a obscure couscous restaurant on a bustling side street.

Inside, they were met by a tall, mustachioed man in a brown suede jacket worn over a loud-print sport shirt, impeccably pressed tan slacks, and woven Gucci loafers. He put his arm around Lord B's shoulder and led him to a table. The trio ordered lunch, talking animatedly, as Todd stood in the doorway playing watchdog.

I know all of this because Tommy and Howie had shadowed them into town, and Tommy, whose French was fluent, followed them into the restaurant. Lunch took an hour and a half. Tommy said that the couscous was as good as he'd ever eaten, and the carafe of *vin du Provence* was probably Châteauneuf-du-Pape. I didn't give a shit about the food—what were they talking about, goddammit? That, said Tommy, he didn't know. They all spoke in Arabic. But there was news: after lunch, Howie tracked Lord B back to his villa. Tommy stayed with the new guy. And guess where he went? He took the airport road and drove through the gate of the same goddamn *Installation Nucléaire Numéro Douze* where I'd played hide-and-seek when I was but a Froglet.

That opened up a lot of possibilities—none of them very agreeable. For example, I knew from my SEAL Two foray on behalf of the CIA that Number 12 was indeed a breeder reactor that made weapons-grade plutonium.

Oops. That's probably still highly classified information. Please write a statement in the margin of this page that you won't divulge Christians in Action's little secret, sign your name at the bottom, then tear it out and sent it direct to: CIA, Post Office Box 12627, Rosslyn Station, Arlington, VA 22209.

Okay, okay. I know that—just like my literate and proverbially skeptical editor—you're asking why was I so suspicious. After all, all Lord B had actually done was have lunch with some Arab at a great couscous restaurant, after which, said Arab went back to work at the neighborhood breeder reactor.

Well, gentle reader and skeptical editor, my suspicions were founded on a number of confluent elements. First, no one engages in the kind of antisurveillance tradecraft Lord B had just engaged in without good reason. Second, he was traveling with a pair of Paks. Well, Pakistan is one of those Islamic nations currently in the final stages of developing a nuclear-weapons program. Third, all of the current crop of terrorist experts agree that the two major areas of concern when it comes to weapons proliferation amongst terrorist groups are (1) nuclear, and (2) chemical/biological.

So a number of scenarios began to play in my head. None of them was very pleasant. For example, was Lord B about to bootleg a small but deadly amount of enriched uranium or plutonium so he could make his own nuke using Pakistan's facilities? Perhaps he was planning to facilitate a transfer of verboten plutonium to the Paks and collect a tidy finder's fee. Or maybe, being a tango at heart, he was about to plant enough explosives in *Numéro Douze*'s reactor to vaporize the coastline from Nice to Monte Carlo. The only way to find out what he was up to was to slip inside the plant, see what they had there, and then come up with a plan to neutralize whatever it was.

I racked my mind to remember details about the reactor from SEAL Two's mission, but to be honest, specifics were pretty fuzzy. All I remembered was that we'd approached from the water by swimming around the airport and infiltrated through a poorly protected fence line. No other details came to mind. Time does that, I guess—or Bombay. Maybe when I saw it again, I'd start remembering.

What worked in my favor was the fact that no matter what part of the world they're in, nuclear plants are all laid out with basically the same physical arrangement. There's a perimeter fence. There's an access facility—a gatehouse. There's an administration building. There's a storage facility. There's a tank farm, where they keep fuel for the emergency cooling system and auxiliary power units. There's a shielded waste facility, and there is the reactor building—a huge power block consisting of the containment building, where the reactor is located, the turbine building, where the turbines transform nuclear energy into electricity, an auxiliary building, where many of the backup cooling systems are located, and a huge cooling tower, where the superheated water is cooled down before it's recirculated back through the reactor core's steam generator.

Moreover, since I'd been penetrating these types of military facilities around the world since I was an E-5 and Ev Barrett was putting his size-10 boondocker up my ass on a daily basis just to keep my mind sharp, I knew all about the security measures we'd be going up against—and they didn't worry me in the least. Security—what there was of it—would be concentrated around the power block, the storage facility, and other operational areas. The rest of the grounds would basically be mine.

In fact, the security around nuclear power plants—whether they're in France, the U.S., or anywhere else—is not so very different from the security around most Fortune 500 corporate complexes, or government installations. Whether it's General Motors, Texaco, Coca-Cola, Three Mile Island—or the White House—security concerns can be broken down into nine universal primary spheres of vulnerability.

They are the perimeter, the communications system, the security detail, the command-and-control structure, the daily patterns of activity, the access and egress, the system of nomenclature (do you call the main entrance the Main Entrance or the Jones Street Gate—that's important when you're responding to an emergency), the amount of integration (or lack thereof) with the local authorities, and the mind-set of the CEO.

All other vulnerability factors revolve around such variables as geography, the local laws, and the products involved, and these can be custom-tailored to exploit the situation in your favor.

You're asking what the hell I'm talking about. Okay, here's a specific example—the nuclear power plant we wanted to infiltrate. I know about the nine universal areas of concern—and how to overcome them. So let's now look at the attribute that makes this particular plant most vulnerable, and how to exploit it.

The unique feature I'm talking about is the fact that this installation makes electricity using nuclear energy.

What does that mean? It means that nuclear power facilities such as this one tend to design their security measures around a response-oriented defensive security strategy whose single objective is to deter radiological sabotage. The components include tall fences and locked gates, electronic sensors to guard against intrusion, cameras to observe the compound, and roving patrols.

Defensive security is commonly fashioned around a five-part tactical plan:

1. Detect and assess a penetration of the compound.
2. Delay the attack.
3. Respond with a counterattack.
4. Clear the site of infiltrators.
5. Secure operations.

That may all look good on paper, but I can tell you from experience that in real life, the security master plan generally turns into a clusterfuck when it gets put to the test. Why? First, because the folks who run nuclear power plants don't train their security details in proactive forms of response often enough. It's expensive to do so. A truly thorough security op means securing the power block areas. Let me put that in English: shutting down the reactor becomes a real possibility. Just ask any power-company vice president if losing half a million bucks in revenue is something he likes to do on a regular basis.

Moreover, because of what managers like to call safety considerations, they almost never allow their security teams to engage in live-fire exercises against moving targets. Somebody might get hurt and slap a lawsuit on the facility. Indeed, most security employees are never trained in aggressive tactics because of the possibility that if they were, say, to shoot some tango dead, the tango's family would sue—and probably win.

Last, most of the folks who walk the beat at nuclear plants make minimum wage or damn close to it. Why? Because aggressive, effective security of the human kind is labor intensive—and expensive. It demands that you manage well, motivate successfully, and bestow rewards for keeping your environment safe. Those things cost money—which often does not sit well with bureaucrats, managers, and boards of directors.

So you end up with an absurd situation in which industry pays millions for sophisticated sensor devices, television monitors, electrified fences, and computer-operated gates, but only pennies to the rent-a-cops, high-school dropouts, and other assorted idiots hired to run those million-dollar goodies.

(Airports are the same, incidentally—remember the fun I had at Narita in *Rogue Warrior: Red Cell?* The people who throw your baggage into the hold make two or three times as much as the folks who scan that luggage for explosives. You figure it out.)

I satcommed back to Mick Owen, letting him know where I was, and giving him a brief dump on what I'd found. I requested a status report on my condition.

Mick's answer came back six hours later. It wasn't optimistic. He had been told to shut down whatever was left of our joint tango-searching operation. The chain of command had informed him there was no immediate problem, and he was ordered to return to Hereford posthaste. He had no reason not to comply, so he was heading back. The SEALs I'd left behind in Britain were being sent back stateside. Nothing, however, would dim his commitment to me. He'd stay in touch and try to help as much as he could.

As for my situation, the search had been widened now—Interpol had been asked to join the manhunt. So had the immigration authorities of all NATO countries. The name Marcinko was now enough to cause immediate arrest and detention in any of the NATO countries when it came up on a passport-control computer screen.

The entire text could be summed up in three words: doom on me.

Well, it wasn't the first time *that* had happened. And I knew all too well there was only one answer to the problem: go on the offensive. Kick ass and take names.

Chapter

13

WE SAT DOWN AT MAMAN'S LONG TABLE. WHILE WE HEAD-SHEDDED, *on a bu nos bouillabaisses à grand bruit* and ate our baguettes and quaffed our *vin du table comme les tous.* The problem was to change our MO without altering the efficiency. Under normal circumstances, we would have hit Number 12 the same way Red Call had gone into all the other installations we'd ever attacked—creating a diversion (or diversions) and then infiltrating the areas where we wanted to leave our improvised explosive devices. But in this case, we had to get in and out without attracting any attention.

We had to distract the security force's attention, but do it in a way that wouldn't let them know they were being hit. We had to get in, see what we had to see, and slip away leaving no evidence behind.

That made for headaches. Believe it or not, it's easier to shoot and loot than it is to sneak and peek. Just ask Duck Foot Dewey. During Operation Desert Shield/Desert Storm, Duck Foot made twenty-nine one-man forays into Kuwait City to deliver communications supplies, explosives, and other lethal goodies to the Kuwaiti resistance, and to plant listening devices close enough to Iraqi headquarters so that allied intelligence was able to monitor many important conversations. He holds the Exalted Order of the Eastern Star, the highest honor the Kuwaitis can bestow. It was, in fact, pinned on his chest by Emir al-Sabah himself. Duck Foot's mission was to get in and out without the Iraqis knowing he was ever there. That meant no killing the sentry who discovered him by accident, because he wasn't supposed to be discovered at all. It meant leaving no evidence of any kind—physical, electronic, whatever. It was tough work, believe me. It takes longer to accomplish. And it puts a lot more pressure on the operator.

Here, too, the job was going to be made more difficult because we couldn't do any damage or leave any tracks. Frankly, that ain't my style. See, I think of myself as a reverse engineer. You look at a nuclear plant, and you see a nuclear plant. Me, I look at a nuclear plant and I see the hundreds of ways I can destroy it. Turbines, condensate pumps, the radwaste system, the cooling network— they all exist solely so they can be demolished, annihilated, decimated, pulverized, by yours truly, Demo Dick Marcinko, Shark Man of the Delta.

There was also the matter of Lord B. If we made a lot of noise, we'd let him know we were on the scent, which would make it harder to catch him red-handed. And, boy, did I ever want to catch this motherfucking cocksucking pus-nutted pencil-dicked tango red-handed.

And, as if all of the above weren't enough, I was operating under a severe manpower constraint. We were seven men. I couldn't keep an eye on Lord B and still get inside the nuclear plant. So I made an executive decision: it was more important to see what was there than it was to surveil Call Me Ishmael. We'd check up on him—but irregularly.

We did a quick inventory. Rodent had picked up a few toys at Patch Barracks that would help us out immeasurably by blanking out the plant's communications network. The only problem is that as soon as they were activated, they'd leave a signature that No Such Agency would immediately identify.

Why is that? It is because every piece of secure communications equipment, every frequency jammer, every burst transmitter, every sensor and monitor that is purchased by the government, has to be vetted by NSA. The reason is that NSA doesn't want anybody using scramblers that they can't unscramble, jammers they can't override, or burst transmitters they can't decipher. So every single piece of comm gear, from the CIA's SATCOM transceivers to DIA's secure cellular phones, to the field radios used by USAF FACs—that's Air

Farce Forward Air Controllers in SEALspeak—has been outfitted with an NSA-designed computer chip known as DREC—Digitally Reconnoiterable Electronic Component. DREC allows No Such Agency to unscramble signals, tell where it's coming from.

The reasoning behind this lunacy, so the head of NSA testified during a closed session of the Senate Select Committee on Intelligence some years back, is that if the Soviets captured a bunch of U.S. equipment and started to send bad information, we'd know it because we could see that they were sending from a position that wasn't on any of our maps.

In reality, it was done because NSA wants to be able to open everybody's mail. It gives them political clout within the intelligence community. It guarantees their budget.

Fuck the politics—all that concerned me was that the minute we started jamming, NSA would read our signals. A little light would pop up on a map out at Ft. Meade, and the intel squirrels would start deciphering pigeon entrails, and after a few minutes of hocus-pocus, they'd begin jumping up and down like organ-grinder monkeys because they'd see there was a jamming unit operating where no jamming unit was supposed to be operating. At which point they'd send out the cavalry, and the ass of yours truly would turn to grass.

So when we switched our jamming toy on, we'd better be ready to haul balls out of France. Because there'd be a posse coming after us toot sweet. To jimmy the odds in our favor, both on the scene and at NSA, I decided to set the time of attack for 0300 Sunday—107 hours hence. Reason? Given the six-hour time difference, it would be 2100 at Ft. Meade, and as everybody knows, unless there's a war going on, nobody pays much attention to switches and dials on Saturday night. And the French? The crew at Number 12 basically shut things down as much as they could on Friday evenings. Personnel was at just over 50 percent until Monday morning. That meant we'd have them at a numerical disadvantage. *Quel dommage* —what a pity.

We did a preliminary target acquisition. Things had changed since I'd led SEAL Team Two's mission. Number 12 still sat on a mile-and-a-half-long, half-mile-wide peninsula, its back to the sea, its eastern flank adjacent to the airport. But the tiny, one-runway airport I remembered had been replaced by a two-runway, huge, international facility that took up almost three square miles. The mouth of the Var River had been moved a full kilometer to the east, and the old waterway had been drained and land-filled to provide land for the jumbo jets that brought the millions of tourists to Nice every year. As CO of SEAL Team Two, I'd had an easy fifteen-minute swim to Number 12. This time, we'd be forced to swim for just over an hour through rough current and undertow.

What hadn't changed was the basic layout. Number 12's main gate was still on the west, with a five-hundred-yard-long macadam road parallel to the water, running from the triple-gate ACF, or Access Control Facility, to the two-lane highway that meandered along the coast from Cannes to Menton, on the Italian border. Directly east of the plant—the airport side—lay one hundred yards of sparsely vegetated sand dunes. The seaward end of the peninsula behind the plant was mostly marshland that looked like a wildlife refuge.

I tend to be either biblical or evolutionary when it comes to ops. Sometimes I am both—the better to confound my enemies.

In the beginning, for example, was the word. And in my book, the word is that man must evolve. He must learn to crawl before he can walk. And thus, on the evening and the morning of the first day, we began by crawling on our bellies like snakes, making slow and thorough progress through the brambles and thorns of the sand dunes in order to discover the weaknesses of the target that lay before us.

Then came the evening and the morning of the second day— which in actuality took place at the exact same time as the evening and the morning of the first day. And yea, Duck Foot and Howie swam around the point and came in from the sea—amphibians who made the transition from water to land and thus were able to explore the half mile of salt flat between the shoreline and the plant itself.

And night followed day, and day followed night (I'm not being literal here, gentle reader. Remember—we had a mere 107 hours to do all of this), and we tracked the employees as they came and they went, and we walked among them and lifted their wallets, and verily we stole their ID cards and driver's licenses, the better to assume their identities should it become necessary. We shadowed Lord B's mole, André Marcel Dall'au, known to us as Marcel Mustache. He was the superintendent of the power-block control room, a position that gave him access to the entire facility. He lived well—far above the standard a man of his position should enjoy. His colleagues drove old Renaults and Peugeots. André careened around Nice in an Alfa-Romeo roadster. They brown-bagged their lunches. He ate at fashionable restaurants. They lived lives of quiet desperation. He maintained two mistresses. Marcel Mustache, we learned, explained his opulence by hinting that his wife's family had money. We knew better.

Why did we know better? Because Tommy T and Stevie Wonder tossed André's two-bedroom flat when the wife and kid were out for a stroll. It was there we discovered that old André wasn't a frog—he was a Arab. Tunisian, in fact, according to his passport. And when Tommy broke into the IBM computer sitting in the living room, he discovered by reading the Quicken for Windows program that André had been salting money away for the past nine months. Lots of money.

On Thursday at 0400 we tested Number 12's perimeter defenses. Wonder and I swam across two hundred yards of water to the east of the plant, crawled through the brambles, went over the periphery fence, and camouflaged ourselves twenty-five yards from the pair of chain-link, ten-foot-high, barbed-wire-topped fences that sat directly behind the BURT.

What's a BURT? you ask. It's a Big Ugly Round Thing, asshole. You know—the huge concrete structure common to all nuclear power stations? Okay—if you're a dip-dunk nuclear dweeb no-load engineer who uses only proper nomenclature, you refer to the BURT as a "containment building." Everybody else calls them BURTs or CANs, as in "I'm going to the can." (If you get caught in the CAN during a nuclear "incident," you get . . . crapped up!) Anyway, the fences—there were two of them, ten yards apart, were separated by a series of microwave sensors.

I thought we were shivering enough to set the sensors off—you get goddamn cold when you come out of the water and lie completely still for fifteen minutes or so. But obviously, our vibes weren't carrying that far. So we tossed a few rocks at the sensors. There was no response. We tossed a few more. After a quarter hour or so, a lone ranger appeared, carrying a flashlight. He wandered along the inside fence, checking the cordon sanitaire between the fence lines for fresh tracks. When he discovered none, he turned his flashlight off and wandered back to his guard post to get himself a fresh cup of coffee.

We waited another quarter hour, then resumed tossing rocks. The sequence repeated itself: our security man trudged back again to see what was making the system go off. He discovered nothing. He went back to his shed.

We threw more rocks. He came out again. Wonder and I repeated the routine half a dozen more times. Finally, we got no response. Obviously, our security man had finally realized that his million-franc system was on the blink, and there was no need to inspect the fence line every time it went off.

That left the TV monitors to defeat. Guess what—an aggressor can float right through a fence line if he knows how to do it—even though there are TV monitors trained on him. How is it done? Well, in most cases—like this one, the security planners sell the powers that be on a double strand of chain-link fences. It sounds good, right? Then they sell them cameras, which are aimed at the fences, so that anyone coming over will be picked up.

But guess what? Unless chain-link fences are aligned absolutely exactly, the basket-weave pattern they create on a TV screen looks like tweed. A perpetrator who moves very slowly will not show up on the screen, unless the guard assigned to watch the monitors is paying very, very strict attention. And, just in case you didn't know it, most guards don't pay strict attention to the screens in front of them. Because if they did, they'd experience retinal burnout in less than a week.

By 0540 we'd exfiltrated and were warming up with a couple of cafés au lait. I was happy because it hadn't taken long to come up with an effective assault plan. I was unhappy (life is like that, y'know) because I would have liked to recon the target once or twice more before we hit. The more information you collect, the more intelligence you can gather, the less chance Mr. Murphy has of sneaking up behind you, holding you by the shoulders, and whispering "BOHICA" in your ear. BOHICA? Yeah—Bend Over, Here It Comes Again.

I would have liked a lot of things, but as is almost always the case, my desires were overtaken by real-life events. Rodent returned from SOG duty to report that Lord B had driven the Ferrari to Nice International, where he'd rented a Gulfstream III. Rodent, God bless him, had wheedled and deedled the *jeune fille* behind the desk and gotten a peek at the flight plan. Today was Friday. Lord B was leaving Sunday at zero nine hundred. That's nine A.M. to you civilians out there. Destination—Karachi. That gave us tonight and only tonight to take a peek inside Number 12 and see whatever there was to see.

Ready or not, here we come. At least I'd preselected an escape route. We'd go east, across the border just north of Ventimiglia, and autostrada south to La Spezia, where I still had a hairy-assed Incursari Frogman friend or two I could count on not to turn us in. Ah, La Spezia—the fresh fish was incredible. The linguine and razor-clam sauce was world-class.

Even if the whole world was on our tails, we'd eat well while we figured out what to do next. And to be honest, I was running out of options. It was only a matter of time before one of Pinky's rockets would score a hit and we'd be snapped up by some bureaucrat/cop. You can't hide in Europe the way you used to be able to. There are too many databases, too many computer terminals. Too much shared information.

Then there was Lord B, on his way to Pakistan, gateway to Afghanistan and the terrorist training camps. Fortunately, I knew the territory. I'd been there a few years back, on assignment for GlobalTec International, a Fortune 500 oil-drilling company. Three of their top-level people had been kidnapped in a series of Katzenjammer Kidz hijackings. GTI had hired me to Katrina fix. I was broke in those days, between alimony, child support, and the cost of a defense attorney for the two trials the Navy put me through. So I signed on, got the judge's permission to leave the country for three weeks, and played Shark Man of the Delta in backstreets and alleys from Karachi to Peshawar.

I got GTI's boys back, too. And it didn't cost 'em an arm and a leg, either—at least not any of GTI's arms or legs. As for the bad guys—a group of no-goodnik desperadoes under the command of a wild-haired, bearded asshole (doesn't *that* sound familiar?) who called himself Commando Sheikh—well, there are nine less of them around these days than there were before my visit. It was a very, very satisfying trip, all things considered. I got to—let me find a polite way of saying this—vent my frustrations in a physical manner, GTI was happy, and my lawyer got paid his pound of flesh.

I thumbed through the pocket-size address book I always carry in my wallet. Yeah—Iqbal's phone number was there. Iqbal Shah was a retired inspector of police in Karachi. As a government official, he'd made $30 a month in salary, and $500 in bribes. Now he made

$25,000 a year bribing his old colleagues on behalf of GTI. He'd been my initial POC—Point of Contact—when I'd arrived in Karachi.

We went back to Chez Soleil and began our load-out. Once we left the hotel tonight, it was *au revoir, Maman*—although we wouldn't bother saying good-bye formally. No need to let her (or anyone else) know we were about to hit and run. No matter—we'd paid for another week three days ago.

Even though the checklist was five by five, I had a nagging sensation that I'd omitted something, and that if I didn't remember what the hell it was, this op was going to turn FUBAR on us.

I decided that perhaps a good meal would jar my mind and said as much to the troops.

"Cooool." Nasty Nicky Grundle made the sign of the cross. "What are we about to eat, Skipper—the last supper?"

We left Chez Soleil at about 1600 and drove into Juan-les-Pins, parked across from the Palais des Congrès, and wandered through the tiny *pinède*—the pine grove for which the town is named—to La Petite Source, a *bifteck/frites* restaurant, commandeered a table, and ordered.

Tommy T's eagle eyes spotted it first. He looked up from his steak. "Hey—Skipper, look across the street."

I peered through the window. Two long-haired, guitar-carrying, ragged-jeans-sporting teenagers were opening the door to a storefront. The banner above the doorway proclaimed FOUTEZ LES NUKES!

Now, I realized all of a sudden what I'd forgotten: camouflage. I broke into a wide grin.

Chapter

14

0100. IT WAS TIME TO GO HUNTING. THE OP WAS TRADITIONAL Marcinko—Keep It Simple, Stupid. We six SEALs in the assault team would go into the water at a point roughly 1,800 yards from the peninsula on which the plant was located. We'd swim as a group. That way there was less chance of someone getting lost. Besides, if you've ever had to swim at night across a mile or so of open, rough, choppy water, you understand that it's easier to lose your bearings swimming alone than roped to a swim buddy. Anyway, we'd go together, then split up just off the shoreline.

Tommy, Nasty, Duck Foot, and Howie would come up the ass end by swimming around the point and make their way through the wildlife preserve. The fence line at the rear was the least protected, and their access would be relatively easy. Tommy and Nasty would work their way around to the administration building and go through it with the proverbial fine-tooth comb. Duck Foot and Howie would prowl and growl through the storage facility.

Wonder and I assigned ourselves a repeat performance at the sensor field. No problems there. We'd play havoc with the microwaves, then "float" across the fence, moving slowly, and wham-bam-thank-you-ma'am, we'd be inside the compound. Our targets were the power-block building and the radwaste facility. After all, Wonder was always bragging that he knew all about nuclear reactors since he'd served on Boomer-class subs. This would give him the opportunity to prove it.

The swim would be problematic, but not an insurmountable problem. It was uncharacteristically warm on the Riviera this winter. Temperatures were in the low sixties during the day, falling to just over forty degrees at night. The water temperature was about sixty-three. That's chilly for most folks, but even though we weren't wearing wet suits, it was still warm enough for us SEALs—if we kept moving.

From my long experience in cold-water operations, I know that once you're swimming in water that's colder than sixty-three degrees, the energy you expend and the muscle "burn" keep you all right for about an hour and a half. After that, you start to lose both energy and body heat. After two hours or so, things get uncomfortable. Uncomfortable, in this case, means hypothermia, followed shortly by unconsciousness, followed promptly by death.

I also knew that it would be bad if we crawled ashore and had to lie around all wet for more than a few minutes, especially after an hour-long swim. So I followed Ev Barrett's law of the seven P's—Proper Previous Planning Prevents Piss-Poor Performance— and distributed a pair of waterproof bags to each swim-buddy team. Towed behind, the bags would contain dry, warm clothes and footwear, a radio for each swim team, as well as a bunch of antinuke bumper decals we'd bought at the "Fuck the Nuke" store.

That was our camouflage. We'd leave copious evidence that the plant had been infiltrated by a bunch of "Save the Whales" activists. I hoped to further convince the authorities of my deceit by leaving behind a few small booby traps. Nasty and Rodent had spent the afternoon building half a dozen IEDs—Improvised Explosive Devices. They were real KISS explosives, the kind of basic bang-bang that amateur tangos tend to use. Oh, damage would be real—but very, very limited.

Finally, there was Rodent—my rat in the grass. Since I pronounced him too small to swim and too mean to drown, we positioned him in the Mercedes across the highway, opposite the plant access road. The car was hidden behind a thicket, facing east, ready for the getaway. Rodent was in perfect position to keep us posted on what was, or wasn't, coming in our direction. He was also in charge of the jamming equipment, which he'd powered up by jury-rigging a power line to the Mercedes's generator.

It was my hope that we'd come and go with such efficiency that Rodent wouldn't need to hit the jammer's ON switch. Still, there was no taking too many precautions. If the folks in the control room decided to call 911, I wanted to be able to squelch them. And, I rationalized, even if the jug-ears at NSA read our jamming signals, we might convince them and everyone else that we weren't a bunch of rogue SEALs, but your friendly, everyday animal-loving Greenpeacers, who'd stolen USG equipment and tried to blow up a nuclear power plant with it.

Such thefts have happened in the past. In fact—let me digress here for just a minute—trading in military goods (everything from automatic rifles to top-secret radio equipment) is a burgeoning industry back in the U.S. National Guard armories are being pilfered regularly these days. Even active-duty bases are being ripped off. Not six months ago, some asshole stole six Colt 633HB submachine guns from SEAL Team One in Coronado. And at the most recent administrative inspection over at NAVSPECWARGRU 2—an admin inspection is when a team goes over every nut and bolt in the inventory—it was discovered that a Mark VII MOD 2 SDV, or Swimmer Delivery Vehicle, was missing.

Of course, things started to go wrong almost immediately. (The nasty little voice in my head said to me, "Of course you're being goatfucked, you asshole—that's how you know this is for real.")

GF Factor One: both the air and water were colder than I'd anticipated, and it got colder still as we swam farther out. By the time we lined up with the seaward point of the peninsula, the water was no more than sixty or sixty-one degrees. The air was fifteen degrees cooler, and there was a wind as well. We were going to fucking freeze out there.

GF Factor Two: there was a wicked undertow, and the current—which I estimated at about a knot and a half—was running against us. No matter how hard we swam, we were basically doing little more than treading water.

GF Factor Three: Stevie Wonder is not a Frogman. Which means that swimming more than a mile is a real chore, so far as he's concerned.

How cold were we? Well, at BUD/S—Basic Underwater

Demolition/SEAL training—they figure that the stinking trainees, as they're called, can last in sixty-five- to seventy-degree water for about twenty minutes, sitting down or dead-man floating. If the water is between sixty and sixty-five, the instructors are allowed to keep the class immersed for only fifteen minutes. Even so, you get so cold, the shivering drives you almost insane. You clench your fists. You bite through your lips. You piss on yourself—or your swim buddy—in futile efforts to stop the cold.

As I just said, tonight the water was probably somewhere around sixty-one. That is c-o-l-d, which is spelled a-b-s-o-f-u-c-k-i-n-g-l-u-t-e-l-y f-r-e-e-z-i-n-g. B-b-believe me. And were we miserable? I was so goddamn cold I thought I was back in hell week.

The only way to stay warm was to swim my heart out—a steady side-stroke rhythm that kept the muscles burning, the heart pumping, and the cold almost manageable.

That was fine until we'd been in the water about thirty-nine minutes and Wonder's Achilles tendon seized up like an engine whose oil has just drained out. He went dead in the water and started to sink.

I heard his bitching cut off by a mouthful of Mediterranean. Simultaneously, the twelve-foot swim-buddy line attached to my waist tugged. I swam back to him, brought him to the surface just in time to get hit in the face by another wave, slapped the water out of his mouth, spat water myself, and asked, "What's up?"

His lips were whitewashed. In fact, there wasn't a whole lot of color left in his face. But he put on his usual brave front. "Goddamn cramp."

"Where?"

He told me. "It's nothing. Don't worry 'bout me—I'll make it just fine."

"Sure you will, asshole. Now fuck you—just relax. Float, breathe, and let me try to massage it out."

"Don't waste your time." But he did as he was told. I worked his lower leg. "How's that?"

"It hurts like a motherfucker."

"How would you know?"

He wasn't in the mood for banter. "Cut me loose, Dick—you go ahead. I'll catch up."

"No way, asshole." I knew that to abandon him meant death by hypothermia. Without moving, or with reduced motion, Wonder had only half an hour or so until his body temperature started to drop precipitously. Normal body temperature is 98.6 degrees. Lose six of those degrees, and your speech starts to slur. Lose seven, and you start forgetting things. Lose eight, and you don't give a shit what's happening to you. Lose nine, and your eyes start to glaze over. Lose more than ten, and you begin a long, often irreversible slide to coma and brain death.

Of course, in Wonder's case, he'd been dead from the neck up for so many years, it would be hard to tell when he actually became comatose. But I knew I'd miss the son of a bitch if he kicked off on me. Who would I pick on? Where would I ever find another Ted Koppel/Howdy Doody look-alike? Besides, Wonder had killed more people in and out of combat than anyone except me, and I liked the thought of keeping him around as an example to others. So I told him to lie back and enjoy the ride.

So I huffed and I puffed, and we were both more dead than alive when we finally struggled ashore after an hour and thirty-eight minutes in the water. I grabbed the radio from the bag and signaled to let everybody know we hadn't drowned and that we'd go on "hold" until I was ready. Then I dragged him up the shoreline well back into the dunes, where the strong seaward wind would be broken by thick sea grass and thistle. Damn—he didn't look good.

I checked his eyes. They'd rolled back into his head. I slapped his face until he came to, sort of. I dried him off as best I could, rolled him onto his stomach, smacked the water out of him, got him into dry clothes, then lay on top of him to warm him up.

After fifteen minutes he started to come around. He groaned, moaned, coughed up another pint of seawater, then passed out again. We lay there for another quarter hour. I could begin to feel the warmth coming back to his body. Finally, he began to move.

"Stay where the fuck you are," I told him, snuggling closer. "This feels good. In fact, if you had tits on your back, I'd marry you tomorrow."

"Eat shit and bark at the moon."

It was good to know he was recovering. I rolled him over, rubbed him down, and we began to unpack the waterproof bags. Shit— time was a-wasting, and there was work to be done.

0419. We were now more than an hour behind schedule. But we were all back in business. Wonder and I crawled up to the perimeter fence line. We went up and over, sans problems. Now it was on to barrier number two. We began lobbing rocks into the sensor field. Right on cue, the sleepy security man stumbled out of his shed and began searching the path between the two fence lines. Obviously, he found nothing. We made him repeat his performance three more times. When he didn't show on our last effort, we began to move slowly, deliberately, to the fence line.

I went over first, moving inch by inch up the chain links, over the three strands of barbed wire, and down the other side, until I was positioned six inches off the ground in a spread-eagle stance that made me look like Spider Man. Then it was Wonder's turn. He made the same deliberate moves up and over.

0432. I began moving toward the second fence, erasing my tracks with a branch as I walked backward. Slowly, deliberately, I crossed the sensor field inches at a time. Despite the temperature—it was in the low fifties—I was sweating heavily. Now, up the opposing fence. Wonder followed me, a step at a time, twenty-five yards away.

0436. We were both up and over. I radioed that we were inside and got a signal from my two other teams that they, too, had made it without incident.

Wonder and I cut behind the tank farm and headed toward the cooling tower and the back of the BURT, pausing to slap three or four FOUTEZ LES NUKES stickers on the sides of the white, round one-hundred-thousand-liter fuel tanks. The perimeter fence line at Number 12 encircled more than six hundred acres. We were concerned, however, with no more than fifteen of them—the part of the facility with controlled access, where Marcel Mustache could do Lord Brookfield some good.

Just behind the tank farm was the huge, poured-concrete cooling tower, where the spent steam was chilled back into water, so it could be pumped back into the system and recirculated. We hopped a ledge and peered at the ass end of the power-block control facility.

Wonder's right hand went to nine o'clock. I followed his gesture. There were two cameras at the block-house/cooling-tower juncture. I gave him a thumbs-up. We could circle to the right and they'd never see us.

I moved down the ledge. Wonder shadowed me. As we came up on the BURT, I saw a shadow move amongst the shadows. I came to a full stop and silent-signaled Wonder to do the same. He'd already done so. That was another reason for not letting the asshole drown. We'd been operating together for so long now that we virtually never had to talk, or even signal. We read each other's body language—every nuance, every twitch, blink, and heartbeat.

Today, every FNG—that's Fucking New Guy—lieutenant coming into SEAL Team Six is so pumped up and full of himself he thinks he's got to teach his squad how to do everything all over again. Well, they're usually full of something, believe me. Fact is, most of the chiefs at Six have been on the job for more than a decade. A couple have been there since the beginning.

What new lieutenants should be doing is S^2—Shutting the fuck up and Sitting the fuck down, and hoping their platoon chief takes pity on them and teaches them a thing or two. That way, they won't break right when they should be breaking left; they won't angle into the wrong field of fire and kill their own men; and they won't wreck the unit integrity that the platoon chief has spent all his fucking time building.

Maybe, after two or so years of operating with the same eight or sixteen men, the FNG officer will get the picture and actually become part of the team. Now here's the rub—the chances of that actually happening run from slim to none.

Why? Because in these days of downsizing and reduced budgets, Naval Special Warfare has become a primo place to serve. There are lines of Annapolis grads waiting to get into BUD/S. In fact, there's such a glut of SEAL officers these days (there are more than one hundred-and-ten men for every one hundred slots), that FNG lieutenants don't spend more than fourteen months with a platoon. Then they're rotated out so a new FNG officer can come aboard. Bottom line? No-shitter truth? The platoon may achieve unit integrity, but most of its young officers won't ever do the same, because they simply aren't around long enough to learn how to operate at the same level as the men they are allegedly supposed to command.

And the men know it. So, do you think they listen to what FNG lieutenants say? Fuck, no. They know the officers are cannon fodder anyway, because their operational skills are nowhere near the level of the enlisted men's.

When I commanded SIX, I stole my FNG ensigns and lieutenants right from Organized Chicken Shit—which is how I refer to Officer Candidate School. I told 'em they were FNGs—bottom of the fucking barrel cannon fodder. I told 'em they were lower than whale shit, that they didn't deserve to lick the sweat off a Team master chief's balls.

"But here's the fucking deal," I told them. "*If* you don't flunk fucking lunch, and *if* you learn how to lead from the front, and *if* you never ask your men to do anything you don't fucking do first, and *if* you're fucking committed to the goddamn Team before anything else, then welcome aboard—you're gonna be an integral part of a unit with unit fucking integrity. If you don't want to play by those rules, then fuck you very much, and good-bye."

And guess what—when I commanded SEAL Team Six, the FNG ensigns and lieutenants were part of the solution, not part of the problem. Today, those FNGs have gone on to command SEAL Teams of their own. And—doom on you, Navy—they're my own fifth column of guerrilla SpecWarriors, teaching their men the way I taught them, fighting the system, preaching unit integrity, allowing their junior officers to learn, learn, learn the ways of killing and of making war. Endeth the lesson.

A roving patrol came around the corner of the BURT. Two rent-a-cops from the look of 'em, although since this was France, they were probably fucking government bureaucrats, because these plants were all RDF—*République de France*—property. They didn't even have radios. Over their shoulders hung the six-inch-in-diameter, leather-cased punch clocks that bargain-basement watchmen all over the world seem to carry. You've seen 'em—you make your rounds, and at each post there's a key, which you insert in the bottom of your punch clock and turn. It imprints the station number on a circular disk, so your supervisor knows you hit station X at X o'clock. Whether or not you saw anything amiss is not part of the equation. You were there, that's the important thing. The check has been made on the list. One of the rent-a-cops carried an ANPDR-56 rad meter—a basic indicator for alpha radiation.

My instinct was to TTS—Tap 'em, Tie 'em, and Stash 'em. I slid the sap out of my sock and silently edged forward. Wonder caught my eye. He shook his head and gave me a vigorous thumbs-down.

What the fuck. Why was he denying me my fun? I shook my head at him as if to say, "Negatory." Then, all of a sudden, I realized what he'd gestured. Four more security types strolled round the corner. He'd seen them coming from his vantage point.

Okay—we'd wait 'em out. I dropped flat on top of my waterproof bag. Stevie was already pancaked. We waited while the frogs passed out cigarettes—Gitanes, from the horse-manure smell of them—and lighted up.

They smoked and gossiped, field-stripped their cigarettes, then moved on. Wonder and I moved on, too. We circled the BURT. No way we could get in there. The place is sealed tight from the inside—no doors, no vents, no nothing. It's built out of six feet of solid concrete, lined with five inches of solid steel. To get inside the reactor compartment, you first have to slip into specially made protective coveralls, which you pull on inside a secure "mud room" that sits next to the control room. Then you pin a dosimeter on, to make sure you won't get too many REMs. A REM, for those of you who never took Nuclear Physics 101, is an acronym for Roentgen Equivalent in Man—the quantity of ionizing radiation whose biological effect is equal to that produced by one roentgen of X rays.

Anyway, once you've been checked out, you pass through three separate remote-controlled, airtight steel doors to the reactor. You can carry nothing larger than a fountain pen inside, and you can bring nothing out. Not even Marcel Mustache could hide something in there without twenty-five people watching him do it.

Which left the radwaste facility as the most likely spot. We made our way behind the BURT, skirting the floodlit back side of the power block, and crossed under a series of huge pipes to the long waste storage area.

The building was built in two sections. The first was a huge, open-fronted shedlike affair that held the detritus common to all industrial sites. There were empty tanks that had held nitrogen, oxygen, and acetylene. There were pyramids of rusting fifty-five-gallon drums that had once contained solvents, cleaning agents, and lubricants. There was old machinery and scrapped equipment.

The other section was a secure warehouse that held all the radioactive waste generated by the plant. Inside would be fifty-five-gallon drums of heavy water, as well as shielded containers holding the reactor's spent fuel rods. These would all be stored under water, in a fifty-yard-by-twenty-five-yard pool.

It occurred to me that the radwaste facility would be the perfect spot to cache something you didn't want found and still have it in plain sight. People tend to stay away from radiation waste facilities because the chance of contamination is so much higher there than in any other portion of the installation. In fact, to make sure that radioactivity is not seeping out through the ground or the air, the installation is ringed by ARMS—an Area Radiation Monitoring System of active gamma-ray detectors that trigger 135-decibel Klaxon horns if they sense a dangerous level of radiation.

Wonder and I probed the shed. We discovered nothing out of the ordinary—in fact, judging from the dust and cobwebs, no one had been around for quite a while. So we moved on. The radwaste building beckoned.

Wonder reached in his back pocket for his trusty lockpicks. "Damn, Holmes, this makes me nervous. I don't wanna glow in the dark."

"We won't be inside more than a few minutes. We'll be perfectly all right."

"I'd feel a lot better if we had coveralls and booties."

Well, I would have, too. But we didn't have any, and I wasn't about to go looking for some right now. "Listen—if you're lucky, you'll grow a third ball in about a month."

"Maybe I'll grow a second cock, too."

"Sure you will—right in the middle of your fucking forehead. Just think, Wonder—you'll be able to provide a whole new definition to the phrase *giving head.*"

"Fuck you." It didn't take him more than twenty seconds to open the door. We slid inside.

It was like walking into a tropical climate. The place was dimly lit with greenish fluorescent lights that hung high above the storage pool. The walls were bare, except for a series of freshwater hoses set fifteen yards apart, provided so that if workers got drenched with radioactive material or water from the storage area, the hoses could be used to wash them off until they could be more thoroughly decontaminated. From the water, heated to over a hundred degrees by the canisters of spent fuel rods, steam rose. It was as if we'd walked into a hothouse.

I took one side, Wonder took the other. We explored the drums and containers on the concrete skirt. All were marked with the bright yellow nuclear-materials symbol. Nothing seemed out of the ordinary. As we moved to the center of the warehouse, I could see the lethal radioactive containers at the bottom of the pool. The luminescence of the water made it shimmer, giving it an ethereal, otherworldly quality.

We came full circle. Nothing. I dropped the waterproof bag I'd carried slung over my shoulder and scratched my beard. My instincts are very good. Seldom am I mistaken. But here, just like at Brookfield House in London, we were coming up dry.

"Let's go round again."

Stevie's face showed that he didn't want to stay here any longer than he had to. But he gritted his teeth, and we worked our way around the concrete one more time.

I spotted it two-thirds of the way around the pool. There was a rectangular box colored so similar to the pool floor that it was almost invisible. You had to really look to see it. The container was five feet long, two feet wide, and about a foot high, with what looked like about twelve separate compartments built into it. It looked like a giant egg carton with handles on each end.

I peered down. The damn thing had Cyrillic writing on it—or that's how it looked from where I stood. Maybe it was Arabic. Maybe it was French. Who could tell.

I pointed. "Wonder—"

Stevie came over for a look. "Damn. That sure ain't no heavy water."

"Or fuel rods either." I looked around. "Let's find something to snag it—bring it out of the water and take a look."

"Sounds good to me."

We poked around. There were some short timbers, and a broken pallet at the far end of the warehouse. But that was it. "Lemme check outside."

Wonder slipped through the door. An eternity later—actually, two minutes or so—the door opened, and he came through holding what looked like a twelve-foot length of one-inch water pipe with a ninety-degree joint at the end of it.

"Let's try this."

We slid the pipe into the water. By stretching, we were able to reach far enough to snag the handle on the near side of the container. "Great. Okay—"

We pulled gently. The box didn't budge. We tried harder. Nothing. Then we really put our backs into it. "Heave," I grunted.

The damn thing moved about an inch. Then the fucking joint separated, and we tumbled ass backward onto the concrete. I landed hard on my tailbone, which didn't appreciate the wallop.

"So much for plan A." Stevie brushed himself off. "What's next, Dickhead?"

I responded by pulling off my shoes, socks, trousers, and shirt. "Time for a little swim."

"What are you, fucking crazy?"

I ignored Wonder long enough to pull the dive mask out of the waterproof bag and clip the Emerson onto my Skivvies. I know—I know, Frogmen don't wear Skivvies. But I was working undercover. "What's your point?"

"That's goddamn radioactive water. You'll fucking contaminate. Don't even think about it."

Actually, I had thought about it—for years. As a member of UDT-21, I'd been selected as one of the Team's Alpha Squad divers. ASDs were given advanced cold-water and deep-water dive training and were schooled in nuclear-weapons retrieval. Whenever a B-52 went down over the ocean, or in a swamp, we were rousted and scrambled to retrieve the bomb. It was all very top secret.

As part of our training, we worked out a series of dive tables that gave us a rough idea of how long we could stay alive when exposed to various degrees of radiation. Of course, those were the days when the military exposed thousands of personnel to lethal doses of radiation and didn't give a rusty fuck. But we were more careful than most, and although the water killed six Alpha divers, we never lost a man to radiation.

Later, as a SEAL officer, I participated in what we called NPUs—Nuke Pack Units. We were given an assignment to land in a hostile area—swim into Petropavlovsk harbor, say—carrying a small tactical nuclear weapon that could be carried by one man. We practiced our infiltrations during NATO exercises, playing the part of Soviet Spetsnaz special-forces naval commandos—and we always planted our suitcase-sized charges exactly where we'd been told. (The brass said we'd have twelve hours after planting a real nuclear device in which to exfiltrate. It was always my private feeling, however, that the fuses had zero-time detonators. What the hell—we were cannon fodder anyway.) As a part of this top-secret unit, I was thoroughly schooled in the rads and REMs of complicated radiation-exposure tables. I knew how much a man could take before he cooked himself.

Finally, as CO of Red Cell, I'd worked with nuclear scientists. It was part of our covert, real-world assignment, designated OP-06 Delta slash Tango Romeo Alpha Papa, code name Waterfall Weatherman. Under the OP-06 Delta designation of Red Cell we roamed the world doing security exercises at naval bases. Under Waterfall Weatherman, we operated in two-man teams, neutralizing targets that had been designated by the National Command Authority of the president and the secretary of defense. As part of the program, we'd had to disable a nuclear power plant in the Middle East. I'd spent three days working at a plant in South Florida, learning about REMs and rads and other nitnoy bullshit that would keep me and my men alive.

So I had a pretty good idea what I was doing, and the risk I was taking. First, I guesstimated I wouldn't be in the water for more than a couple of minutes. Then, the heavy water—the water closest to where the spent fuel rods were stored—was indeed lethal. But, being heavy water, it stayed at the bottom of the pool. The water where the container lay was not heavily contaminated. So, if I stayed only a few minutes, and if I didn't stir the pool too much, and if I didn't swallow anything, and if I hosed myself off thoroughly . . . well, you get the idea.

"Get one of those decontamination hoses ready," I ordered Wonder. "And when I come out, wash me off good."

"You're fucking out of your fucking gourd."

"Like I said, what's your point?"

"Ahh—" He threw his hands up in disgust. "What the hell."

I knew better than to dive. I sat on the edge of the concrete apron and slid myself down the incline. The water was only about one hundred or so—cooler than I keep the indoor Jacuzzi back at Rogue Manor. Still, the warmth was palpable. I'd look like a lobster if I took too long. Like a glow-in-the-dark lobster, that is. "Don't worry—this is why they invented Dr. Bombay." I adjusted my mask and slipped under the surface.

I swam to the container and looked it over quickly, trying to figure the best way to move it. I tried lifting one end. The goddamn thing weighed a ton. I ran a fingernail over the surface. Lead. I tried to open the top. It didn't move. I reached under the lip with the blade of my Emerson and pried. Nothing—it appeared to be sealed solid. Okay—I'd drag the fucking thing up, no matter how much it weighed. I grabbed the handle, set my feet, and heaved.

It only moved about an inch. But it *moved*. I dug my heels and tugged again, straining every fucking muscle in my legs and back judging from the series of pops I heard from those regions. It moved another inch.

Now I knew I wanted this motherfucker bad. And it was going to be mine, too. I surfaced long enough to grab a breath, then went back to work. I heard Wonder saying something, but I wasn't paying attention, so I dove again.

I was real surprised when Wonder joined me underwater.

What's up? I asked by shrugging.

Enemy seen, Wonder responded by clenching his fist and pointing his thumb toward the bottom of the pool.

How many? I asked.

He held up two fingers.

Direction?

He pointed toward the near end of the building. The fucking security guards were probably making their rounds. Now I tried to remember whether their punch-clock stations were inside or outside. If they punched the clocks inside the radwaste building, we were gonna be dead men—toasted.

We waited. Seconds ticked off in my head. We were fucking cooking in this water. I turtled. I looked around. No security guards. We'd lucked out.

Wonder sputtered to the surface, shook off as much water as he could, and breathed deeply. "Fuck me." He started moving for the apron.

"C'mon, let's go to work, asshole—now that you got wet, you might as well stay."

With the two of us heaving, we had the crate out of the water in about thirty seconds. Hell—it only weighed 250 pounds or so. I ran for the wall and turned the spigot. I hosed Wonder down good, then stood still while he worked me over, then directed the nozzle at the crate.

We dragged it behind a pile of drums where we couldn't be seen and examined it. I looked at the writing. It was indeed Cyrillic. Soviet military issue. Banded with steel tape. I worked at the band with my Emerson. Finally, I was able to get some leverage and snap it. Wonder and I pulled the cover off.

There were spaces for twelve "eggs" in this egg container. Six of the spaces were empty. The others contained wet olive-drab cans about the size of a quart of paint—obviously, the crate hadn't been sealed very well. The cans all bore the BW—Biological Warfare—materials sign.

Well, at least I knew it wasn't botulism. Botulism has to be refrigerated—and this stuff had been cooked but good in the hundred-degree water. So what we had here could be virulent *E. coli*, anthrax, salmonella-C, or any of half a dozen other lethal agents that thrive in hot temperatures. I hefted a can. It weighed about two pounds. I took three and handed them to Wonder. "Here—you may need 'em."

"Yeah—if I ever wanted to cause World War Three." He put them in his watertight bag. "Do you know how much damage you could do with this shit?"

I knew all too well. And Lord B was a cunning son of a bitch to hide it where he had. Who'd ever think of looking for biological agents in a goddamn nuclear plant. "We could take out the whole east coast of the United States. Or all of Britain or France. Slip it in the Paris water supply tonight and kill two million people tomorrow. Or dump it in a reservoir. You're the New Yorker. What's the main one for the New York City water system?"

"Croton."

"Yeah—Croton. That would make the World Trade Center bombing into child's play."

"This is baaad shit, Dickhead."

I dropped my three cans in my waterproof bag and zipped it closed. "It's bad news, too—Lord B got here ahead of us. Half the fucking crate's empty."

Chapter

15

THERE ARE TIMES WHEN, DESPITE ALL THE PLANS YOU MAKE, AND regardless of your mission parameters, something turns you into a killing machine. It happened to me in Vietnam after Clarence Risher, the only SEAL I've ever lost in combat, was killed at Chau Doc up on the Cambodian border during the 1968 Tet Offensive. In the months after Risher's death, I showed Mr. Charlie no mercy. I went hunting nightly. I always brought back scalps. And I learned how to terrify my enemy—truly spook them. I began booby-trapping the bodies of those I'd killed, and the hooches where they lived. I brought back VC ammo, doctored it, and returned it to their caches so that when it was fired, it would explode in the chambers of their weapons. I used the VC's symbology against them. For example, one night I left a sextet of VC corpses sitting in front of their hooch. They sat in a row, like Buddhist priests, their legs crossed. In their laps, they held their heads. Into each skull, I'd stuck a smoking joss stick. That must have been a sight when mama-san came home.

Brutal, you say? Yup. Unpleasant? True. War is not a meticulous, polite, proper event, played out by gentlemen on a chessboard. War is horrific, chaotic, messy, and nasty. It is frenzied, inhuman, brutal, and terribly violent. There is a lot of death—none of it pretty. There is endless carnage—none of it nice. There is copious blood—none of it neat. There is cruelty and wanton killing. There is death by friend and by foe alike.

War is ferocity and violence of action. A lot of the liberal, pantywaist press got all upset when, as part of the great sweeping motion that flanked the Iraqis, U.S. forces used bulldozers to bury Iraqi troops alive in their trenches. I remember questions in the Pentagon briefing having to do with whether or not our forces were "fair" or not.

What bullshit naïveté. What numb-nutted ignorance of the real world. What the Americans did saved American lives. More Iraqis died than we did. That's the point of war in the first place—kill more of the enemy than he kills of you. But from the way it was written up, we should have gone in and asked the Iraqis if they'd like to, perhaps, maybe, come on out of their trenches and join us for some milk and cookies, or taken 'em on one by one.

Indeed, sometimes I think we've become too conditioned by war as seen on TV in old cowboy movies. You know the kind—where John Wayne tosses aside his six-gun when the bad guy runs out of ammo? The kind where the good guy fights six desperadoes in a bar and his white hat never comes off his head?

Hey, friend, that's not the way it happens. You get mad at your enemy when you're in combat. You want to kill him—any way you can. I have always taught my men that the act of killing my enemy is an act of respect toward him. Why? Because by killing him I deem him lethal—which is his duty toward me. I have also discovered over my more than thirty-year career that it is a cleansing act to kill your enemy—to kill him with violence and terror in the Old Testament style.

War, after all, horrific as it is, purifies the Warrior's soul. It gives him a reason to live.

But sometimes, as I said, the Warrior's soul turns to blackness and absolute wrath.

It happened after Chau Doc. It happened here and now, too.

The discovery of the BW agents brought me to a white heat of fury. It enraged me because these weapons were intended to be used against civilian targets by tango assholes whose motives could be summed up in two words: wholesale murder. When I formed SEAL Team Six, the Navy wanted me to create a counterterrorism unit—a hostage-rescue team. The goal I set was more ambitious. It was to put together a unit that could go anywhere, could do anything it had to, in order to kill terrorists *before* they killed innocent civilians. We called it antiterror, a proactive term, as opposed to the more conventional counterterror, which is a reactive way of dealing with the problem after the fact.

To achieve my goal, I did whatever I believed was necessary. Threats, blackmail, intimidation—I used them all against the Navy system because the end was worth the means. The unit's creation was worth the hits I took. The fact that SEAL Team Six was the most capable and lethal antiterror unit ever created made the scars I wore from combat with the Navy brass my badges of honor. The fact that they trained under combat conditions with the world's best equipment made it bearable when the Navy pronounced me an unpredictable rogue who couldn't function as part of the system.

But, ultimately, that system prevailed. I was removed from command. I was replaced with a series of by-the-book commanders who turned one of the greatest shoot-and-loot units ever created into a huge, cumbersome, top-heavy bureaucracy. When I created SEAL Team Six, I chose seventy-two shooters. Repeat: shooters. Now, there are more than five hundred slots—most of them support troops, including women. Training fatalities have been cut to zero. There's a great SEAL Team Six touch-football team. But the number of real hunters—Warriors who are capable of operating clandestinely anywhere in the world to hunt and seek and destroy no matter what the odds—has, like the days of September, dwindled down to a precious few.

Thanks to CNO, I had been given what few commanders are ever given—a second chance. When he gave me Green Team, it was as if I'd been given my life back again. Once again, I'd been given the chance to lead a lean, mean fighting machine whose job was to kill tangos by any means possible—to do it to them before they did it to us.

But now, with CNO dead and the apparatchiki firmly in command again, I was once again the uncontrollable rogue who had to be stopped—and Pinky intended to stop me by having me arrested for murder. Murder in this case being the death of a tango who was tied into a worldwide, transnational conspiracy. Just as CNO had said, the threat today was greater than it had ever been. The evidence in our waterproof bags also proved that the opposition was planning murder on a scale that hadn't been achieved before.

Well, I could ratchet things up, too. I took the SAS burst transmitter from the bag and sent Mick Owen a quick message telling him I'd discovered BW materials. I let him know I'd contact him again in two hours with specifics. I sent the rest of the team a quick message ordering them to clear out. Then Wonder and I set to work.

We rigged an IED with some muscle. I took a golf-ball-sized chunk of C-4 explosive and stuck a detonator set for ten minutes into the middle of the plastic. I rolled a condom over the whole thing to keep it waterproof, then tied the rubber off. While I made my IED, Wonder was making another. Why two IEDs? Because that's the way Ev Barrett taught me to do it with satchel charges twenty-five years ago. "You stupid blankety blanker," he'd growl, "what the hell are you gonna do when you're fifty feet underwater and you've only brought one motherblanking igniter? Answer that, you no-load geek asshole."

We tossed the two explosives into the deepest part of the pool and watched them sink among the drums of spent plutonium. With any luck, we'd have a mini-Nagasaki in less than a quarter hour.

Time to move. We slung the waterproof bags over our shoulders and, after making sure that all was clear, went out the door.

I stayed close to the building. Wonder was tight behind me. I used hand signals. We'd cross the compound, cut around the power block, and exfil by going over the fence due north of the administration, where there was only one chain-link fence. He nodded and gave me a thumbs-up.

I was looking at Wonder, so I didn't see Marcel Mustache himself coming around the corner of the open storage shed. I actually walked right into the son of a bitch.

"*Excusez—*" He actually started to apologize, until he realized we hadn't been properly introduced. Maybe he thought I was one of the night watchmen.

I didn't hesitate. I said, "*Pardonnez-moi,*" then I sucker punched him. He went down, the surprised look on his face classic in its Gallic incertitude.

I rolled him over and frisked him quickly, took his wallet and every piece of paper he was carrying as well. I handed my waterproof bag to Wonder and threw Marcel over my shoulder. There were questions I wanted to ask him, but this was neither the time nor the place.

"Come on." I wasn't in the mood to wait around because it was going to get highly radioactive in a very few minutes.

Wonder and I sprinted back the way we'd come, along the low ledge that ran behind the containment building, Marcel's limp body jouncing on my shoulder. I thought we were doing great. That was when the area radiation monitors went off.

Talk about your fucking bells and whistles—there were Klaxons and sirens and all the goddamn lights in the entire plant seemed to come on at once.

"What the fuck?"

I didn't know what the fuck either. All I could think of was that we hadn't hosed off enough from the radwaste pool, so we'd tripped one of the fucking ARMS antiradiation sensors. Either that or they'd been on to us and they were springing their trap now.

I radioed for a sitrep. Bottom line: Wonder and I were the only ones left inside the perimeter. Actually, that was good news. We just had to worry about us. We worked our way alongside the containment building, crossed a small patch of grass behind the power block, and made our way cautiously alongside the glass walls of the modernistic control center.

I dropped Marcel's body and crouched alongside it as a white-smocked, four-eyed dweeb came out the side door, leaned up against the wall, and lit a cigarette not two feet from where I lay in the only shadow in fifteen feet. Shit—didn't he know that smoking was hazardous to my health? I stood up. He turned toward me, his jaw dropped, and he started to say something.

But he didn't: Stevie came up behind him, dropped him with a choker hold, and laid him gently on the grass. Then we sprinted for the administration building. Wonder vaulted the fence first, then helped me bring Marcel over the razor wire. It tore him up a bit, and he landed on his head—but so what. We worked hurriedly, mindless of sensors, cameras, or any other intrusion devices. Once we were clear, we hauled balls for the rendezvous point.

We pulled off the road near Ventimiglia to do a quick stat check and a field interrogation. Marcel Mustache's wallet held two thousand English pounds, and a reservation slip in his name at a hotel somewhere in Dorsetshire, made through Bruton Travel, for three nights next week. The other papers included an agreement for the charter of a Lear jet, and a pocket diary handwritten in Arabic.

I was intrigued. I had a real need to know what Marcel was planning in Britain. Rodent popped the trunk. I pulled Marcel out and tried to stand him up. He wouldn't comply. Nasty, who's had medical training, checked him over and discovered why.

"He's gone, Skipper. Neck's broke."

It occurred to me that I was two for two in dead-prisoner statistics. First, I'd lost Azziz in Cairo. Now Marcel.

We worked quickly, burying the body in the railroad right-of-way just off the highway, while Duck Foot tried to make head and tail of the Arabic scrawls in the diary.

We finished our work before he finished his. But he got the gist of things for me. "Bottom line, Skipper, is that Marcel handed off six—I can't make it out—somethings to Brookfield yesterday."

Bingo. Lord B was on the move to Pakistan with six cans of BW agent. We pulled back onto the highway and headed east, while I tried to figure out what the hell to do. The radio was buzzing about the explosion at *Numéro Douze*. From what the announcer said, we'd done considerable damage: the plant would be off-line for about six weeks. In another positive note, the frogs, it seemed, were blaming everything on antinukers, so it looked as if we were going to be in the clear—at least for the immediate future.

I took the time to burst Mick Owen, too. Even though we were working on SAS's secure comms, which NSA can't read, you don't want to crowd the satellite, especially when there are people looking for you. So I kept my message short. I told him exactly what was on the cans Wonder and I had taken and asked for instructions. I added that six cans were already with Lord B, on their way to Pakistan. I let him know about Marcel Mustache's reservations in Dorsetshire, suggesting he send someone down there to register under the right name, to wait and see what turned up.

Mick must have been sitting in front of the fucking SATCOM, because I got a fast answer back. He signaled that my canister query was being processed ASAP and he'd have results within the hour. He said he'd check on the hotel in Dorsetshire. He asked what about our plans.

I responded. Said we'd be going east—following Brookfield—and could he help us, as my cash was running low. I couldn't use the bogus credit cards in Europe. In fact, I couldn't use 'em anywhere they had computers, because once the store or airline ticket desk enters the account numbers, it takes about ten seconds until they realize the plastic's fake. Then they call the cops and arrest you on the spot. That would be bad juju.

Mick bursted me the name of a contact at La Spezia—a *colonnello* who'd advance me twenty thousand pounds, give us whatever equipment we'd need, and take the lethal cans off our hands so they could be forwarded covertly to him back in Britain for analysis. And he took the liberty of suggesting that we go through Brindisi, to Corfu by ferry, take a second boat to the Albanian mainland, grab a bus to Tirana, and fly out of there.

I transmitted: "We must be married." I'd been thinking roughly the same thing. It made perfect sense. Albania was the poorest country in the region. They needed hard currency. They wouldn't ask too many questions. And best of all, there were no computers in Albania to help track us down. I could buy our tickets to Pakistan with impunity: it would be a week before they realized we'd used forged cards, by which time we'd be long gone. I gave Mick a Bravo Zulu for his job well done. I noted that I'd be using the name Snerd when I called his Italian pal, just in case Marcinko was on anybody's computer.

We waited another half hour, until Mick signaled an analysis of our booty. He'd run it past his top BW people and they'd gotten very upset, because, he said, they'd told him he wasn't supposed to know about this stuff. It was a lethal and—most disturbing— virtually indestructible combination of anthrax and plague that had been developed by the Russians only last year. It was known as BA-PP3/I.

That was worrisome. Worrisome, shit—it was downright frightening. I knew about inhalation anthrax. As the CO of SEAL Team Six, I'd been told about Soviet experiments in biological warfare. In 1979, more than sixty people died when a canister of anthrax broke open at a military research facility at Sverdlovsk, just east of the Urals in the central USSR. BA-PP3/I was the latest and most deadly variation of that research.

It combined the almost-always fatal qualities of inhalation anthrax with the deadliest configuration of plague, known as pneumonic plague. The combination is 100 percent fatal if it's not diagnosed and treated within a few hours of infection—which is virtually impossible when it infects a bunch of victims during a terrorist incident.

Let's pause here for a short course in biological warfare etiology, courtesy of Dr. J. D. Robinson, M.D., a Washington D.C.-based physician who taught this stuff to me when I ran SEAL Team Six. And don't skip the following few paragraphs, either. As the wise, old chiefs at Officer Candidate School used to tell us, "You will see this material again."

Inhalation anthrax—*Bacillus anthracis,* or *B. anthracis* in the textbooks—is an airborne bacillus, or rod-shaped bacteria. The spores have a natural resistance to both heat and cold that can be intensified by scientific development. In other words, you can develop a strain of *B. anthracis* that is virtually indestructible.

How does it work? Well, gentle reader, let me take you through a cycle. Let's say a terrorist detonates a biological-warfare bomb in a crowded location. Victoria Station. Los Angeles International Airport. The World Series.

Hundreds are killed or wounded by the explosion. That's to be expected. There's confusion. There's chaos. Mr. Murphy is hard at work. And no one realizes that the bomb spewed BA-PP3/I over a sixteen-square-mile area (that's right, friends—the range of one of these little canisters is four miles by four miles) because no one was looking for biological evidence—the authorities send only EOD personnel—the bomb squad.

But inside that explosive Trojan horse hides the real killer. We already know that BA-PP3/I is impervious to heat. It is, therefore, perfectly camouflaged by high explosive. C-4. Semtex. Generic plastique—*Ka-boom!* And thus, out into the air go billions of invisible, pestilent, *B. anthracis* spores released by the explosion.

Who breathes them? Anybody within those sixteen square miles, or even a few more, depending on the wind conditions. But, since these soon-to-be-dead folks weren't injured in the blast, they go home and consider themselves lucky.

Doom on them. After one to five days of incubation, the victims begin to experience general malaise, which is Dr. Robinson's polite way of saying that they feel like shit. They don't sleep right. They wake up fatigued. They get myalgia—a $20 word that means their muscles hurt. They cough and their joints ache. Maybe they call their doctors because they feel as if they're coming down with a cold.

By now, they're already as good as dead. But they don't know it. In fact, all of a sudden, many victims now begin to feel improved. Maybe there was the hint of a fever—but now it's disappeared. So they go back to work, telling their colleagues they thought they were getting the current croup or flu or whatever this season's "it" (as in "it's going around") may be. Terrific—they've now infected their workplace.

And suddenly, twelve hours later, they get hit with a fucking ton of bricks. First there's severe respiratory distress—they can't breathe, and when they do, they sound like goddamn gasping, wheezing bronchitic smokers. They sweat pints—losing vital body fluid. Their skin goes white—then blue. Their temperature soars. They go into shock and lose consciousness. Then they die. Total time from initial breathing of the BA-PP3/I bacillus: 190–240 hours.

Let's move on to pneumonic plague. It comes from *Yersinia pestis*, a plump, polymorphic bacillus. Under normal lab conditions, *Y. pestis* are susceptible to sudden temperature fluctuations. But the strain developed by the pesky Russkies was somehow able to withstand extremes both of heat and cold, making it a perfect "coupler" to the anthrax.

Plague's initial symptoms are similar to those of anthrax—the same sort of severe malaise, headache, intermittent fever and chills—except they are often accompanied by a swelling of the lymph glands under the arms or in the groin area. The initial stage lasts forty-eight to seventy-two hours. Then shit really happens. Pneumonic plague victims feel constantly nauseated. Sometimes they vomit uncontrollably. Most also suffer from bloody diarrhea. The lungs are affected, too, causing victims to cough blood. It's not a pleasant disease, believe me. But it doesn't last long—seventy-two hours at most. Then comes death. Total time from inception: five to eight days. I don't want to use a bunch of technical language on you, but sometimes you just gotta. Here it is: BA-PP3/I is some mean, motherfucking shit.

Okay, okay. I can see a few of you out there holding up your hands and saying, "Whoa, there, Demo Dick—what's going on?" You're surprised. You're asking me how come the Russkies, our new pals and virtual allies, are still developing biological weapons of mass destruction, then giving them to tango organizations, when they can't pay their own bills at home and they're begging for Americanski aid.

Let me explain something. The death of the Soviet Union was simply another step in a continuing battle. Some of our exalted leaders fail to grasp this obvious fact, which is why they're shocked when they discover—horror on horror's head—that the Russians are still recruiting American intelligence officers to spy for them.

My friends, get real. We won the Cold War by driving the old Soviet Union into bankruptcy; by making them spend 74 percent of every ruble on defense until they crumbled from within. Now, however, the Cold War revisionists—a bunch of 'em are currently running the State Department, not to mention the do-nothing can't cunt dip-dunk thumb-sucking hind-tit asshole dweebs who control most of the country's think tanks and universities—have decreed that it wasn't military intimidation and defense policy that kept the Soviets off edge, but the politically correct policy of gentle restraint (more accurately called whimpering appeasement) that led to the end of the Cold War and the dismantling of the Soviet Union.

Excuse me, but that's a pile of horse pucky. Of course, I'm not here to argue history. I'm here to talk about terrorism-based biological warfare. Fact: Lord B and was on his way to Pakistan, home of a growing fundamentalist Muslim population bent on mayhem. Fact: Pakistan sits next door to Afghanistan, a country with more terrorist training camps per square mile than anywhere else on earth, no government, and the world's most plentiful supply of opium poppies. Fact: the bad guys were packing six canisters of BA-PP3/I, which made them DFTs—Dangerous Fucking Tangos —in anybody's book.

Ultimate fact: I had to stop them before they passed the canisters on to their final destination and a whole bunch of innocent people got hurt.

We made the journey to La Spezia with no problems. I used my Brit pounds and U.K. passport when I changed money in San Remo—we still had just over one hundred of the fifty-pound notes I'd taken from Azziz in Cairo. I gave each of the men five hundred pounds in cash, kept fifteen hundred myself, and turned the rest into lira, which made me a millionaire, so far as Italian money was concerned. Because we hadn't used the jamming equipment, I was reasonably certain that NSA hadn't sent the cavalry after us. Still, there was no need to take any chances. We'd pay cash for everything.

We stopped in Genoa for lunch, staying out of the chaos of the port area and heading instead for a rustic little *taverna* I know on the

Via della Libertà on the eastern edge of the city. Then it was on through Rapallo, Chiavari, and Borghetto di Vara moving at a steady 120 kilometers per hour, until we pulled into La Spezia just before cocktail time. Nasty, Tommy, and Duck Foot, who had arrived first on their bikes, had already begun to make a dent in the beer supply at the Jolly Hotel.

I dialed the number Mick had provided and waited as the phone *bring-bringed* half a dozen times.

"Pronto."

"Colonel Angelotti?"

"*Sì.*"

"My name is Snerd. I'm a friend of your friend in London."

There was a momentary pause. "*Sì, sì.* Of course. I'm so glad you are in town."

"So am I. Can we meet?"

"Of course we can. I have been looking forward to it. But not at my office, please. Let's have dinner, instead, so I can show you a taste of our Ligurian cuisine."

That sounded good to me and I told him so. "I have a few fellow tourists with me."

"That will be no problem. I gather from our mutual acquaintance that you have some friends who live here in town, too."

He was asking whether or not I knew a lot of the Italian Frogmen—*Incursari*—and whether or not they knew me, too. Good point.

"I do—I know a lot of them."

"Then we should meet at a wonderful little trattoria outside La Spezia itself, so we can keep things private. Take the old road south out of town to Portovénere. There is a little restaurant there called Gambero, and I will see you there at twenty thirty. You cannot miss the restaurant. There is also a hotel close by where you might want to stay."

"*Mille grazie, Colonnello.*"

"It is nothing, *signore.*" The phone went dead.

His suggestions sounded good. But just to make sure we weren't being set up, we drove down to the port immediately and surveilled the restaurant and streets around it. Paranoid? Maybe—but I didn't want any surprises.

We set up a countersurveillance at 1830. By 2015 I decided that things were kosher. We assembled, walked into the restaurant, and ordered six carafes of the *vino di tavola*. The place overlooked the harbor, and we took a big window table. The only other patron was a tubby little guy in the corner who bore a curious resemblance to Porky Pig. He was dressed in an incongruous, loud plaid sport coat wore his hair slicked, and sported a pencil mustache. He was working on a platter of deep-fried squid and a liter of white wine.

We sipped and watched as Porky finished two plates of squid and a second carafe of wine. He caught me gawking and smiled at me. I felt stupid. We ordered a second round of *vino* and some antipasti as well. After all, it was past 2100 and the colonel hadn't showed yet. By 2130 I was beginning to get upset. Then Porky arose and waddled over to our table.

"You must be Signore Snerd. *Buona sera.* I am Luciano Angelotti." He smiled. "Please, Signore Snerd, take your chin off the floor."

"You're Colonnello Angelotti?"

"Sì."

"But—"

"Ah, you assumed since I am a friend of your friend Mick Owen, I would be—how do you say?—specialized forces, sì?"

"Sì."

"To the contrary. I have known Mick for years. We became good friends when I was in support of—how do you say it?—a joint activity, yes? In Sardinia. I needed something. He provided. He could have gotten in great trouble for doing so—maybe it would have finished his career. But still he went the extra for me. I was very, very grateful."

"Mick's like that."

The Italian nodded. "Yes, Mick's like that. Anyway, since then we have been a—what do you say?—mutual aid society."

"Were you ever in Special Forces?"

Angelotti roared with laughter and patted his ample midsection. "Never, *signore,*" he said with a flourish of mock anger. "I don't swim, I never earned parachute wings—to be honest, I haven't even fired a rifle since basic training."

"Then what do you do?"

He smiled beneficently, appropriated a chair from the adjacent table, plunked himself down at ours, and poured himself a huge glass of wine. He peered through thick, wire-framed glasses at my shooters, then downed the glass of wine. "First, on behalf of the Italian armed forces—although I'll never tell them about your visit—let me welcome you to Italy."

"*Mille grazie, Colonnello,*" Tommy T said. "We are honored to be here with you."

Angelotti poured himself another glass and drank it as if it were water. "He is a polite boy," he said, indicating Tommy. "You have trained them well, Captain."

"Thank you."

"It is nothing." He drank another glass of wine, tore the heel off the loaf of bread on the table, and used it to mop up some olive oil that remained in one of the antipasti dishes. This guy was unbelievable. "Now—you ask my assignment. Simple. I am the regional supply officer for all Italian Naval Specialized Forces."

I filled my own glass, touched the rim of his with mine, and drained the wine in a single gulp. "It is my very great and profound pleasure to meet you, too, Colonel," I said, meaning each and every syllable.

We left La Spezia thirty-two hours later with seven duffel bags stuffed with goodies, twenty-thousand pounds in fifty-pound notes, and seven world-class cases of heartburn. That man could *eat.* Not to mention the fact that he could soak up the grappa like a *spugna.*

To play things safe we skirted the big cities and ran along the Adriatic coast through Ancona, Pescara, and Bari. Things went so smoothly I was beginning to worry. I shouldn't have: Mr. Murphy caught up with us just as we reached Brindisi. We missed the ferry to Corfu by three-quarters of an hour. Since it was off-season, there wouldn't be another for a day and a half. So we hunkered down at a one-star hotel and kept things low-key until we could make it through the cursory customs check, watch as our passports were stamped, then climb aboard and settle down on wood-slat benches for the seventeen-hour ferry ride to Kérkira. We left the Mercedes outside the hotel, but took the BMW bikes with us. I could probably barter them in exchange for a fishing-boat ride from Kassiópi or Nimfai to Albania, so we wouldn't have to dogleg through Greece and go through another border check.

I stood on the stern and watched the Italian coast fade in the mist behind the ferry's wake. The diesels, running at a throaty growl, made the deck shudder slightly. It was gray, windy, and cold. A constant, soaking drizzle cut through to the bone.

In the past half hour I had developed the same queasy feeling in my gut I do whenever I make a nighttime insertion into dangerous, unknown territory. God, I hate jumping blind.

Part
Four

DELTA

Chapter

16

WE ARRIVED AT KARACHI INTERNATIONAL WITHOUT INCIDENT AND took a couple of cabs the ten or so miles into the city for less than $2 each. Customs and immigration was a breeze. Hell—you could bring a nuclear-equipped Tomahawk missile into Pakistan and not disturb the customs officials, just as long as you had enough cash in hand for appropriate baksheesh. So, it was easy for seven men with mere combat packs, semiautomatic pistols, and five-hundred rounds of hollowpoint ammunition. Of course, we were the good guys!

It was good to see Pakistan again. My favorite land of hot food, cold beer, and warm weather would be a terrific spot for a holiday. Except, of course—please don't sweat the minor details—for the daily diet of car bombs, kidnappings, thugs, and thieves. Actually, it's exactly the sort of place I like to go to have a good time. Some people like to go hunting wild boar in Arkansas, or Rocky Mountain sheep in Montana or Idaho. I prefer the kind of two-legged big game you can find in places like Sind Province or Karachi.

We settled ourselves at the Karachi Sheraton, the spacious four-star where I'd stayed when I'd visited on behalf of GTI to retrieve their kidnapped engineers. It made an ideal temporary base of operations. The communications are better than many Paki

225

government offices had. There is a big swimming pool so the boys could exercise their muscles. There are four restaurants, and even a jogging trail that meanders through a huge walled garden.

While the men played tourist, I called Iqbal's number. A *dhaba-deli* voice singsonged, "GlobalTec International, may I helping you please?" at me, and I asked for him.

"Whom may I say is making the inquiry?"

"An old friend."

There was a pause. Then Iqbal's throaty growl came onto the line: "Retired inspector Shah."

"I know who the fuck you are, you miserable cockbreath porkchop-eating Muslim asshole," I said by way of greeting. "The question is, do you know who I am?"

He started to reply.

"Don't use names," I warned. "Remember, the phones have ears."

"You are the one I used to call 'uncircumcised vermin,'" he said without pausing. "He who uses his right hand both to eat his *pappudom* bread and to wipe his unworthy bottom-crack."

"The very same."

Iqbal roared with laughter. "Welcome, Vermin-Pasha to my homeland once again."

"I thank you for your graciousness, my camel-humping lard-lipped former-government-servant friend. But to be serious for a moment—do you remember where we shared our wonderful first lunch?"

"'Come on, ice cream,' is what you said," Iqbal chortled. "How could I ever forget?"

That went for me, too. Not six hours after I'd first touched down in Karachi on behalf of GTI, Iqbal, who'd been assigned to me as a "minder," had taken me to a local curry house as a form of immersion indoctrination to his culture. See, just as Mexicans like to strut their machismo by eating bowls of jalapeño peppers like candy and asking their unsuspecting *yanqui* guests to do the same, or Yemenites foist spoonfuls of *harif* on naive *Anglit*-speakers, the Pakis intimidate their newly arrived visitors by taking them to restaurants where the curry is so hot that the sauces have been known to eat through the aluminum bowls in which they're served.

The former policeman had taken me to just such a place—a hole-in-the-wall just off the Chundrigar Road. The curry had come in steaming bowls. It was hot—so hot my arms were bathed in sweat when I started spooning it up. But I knew something about my culinary history Iqbal did not. There is nothing I will not eat. When I served in Phnom Penh as the U.S. naval attaché in the midseventies, I was taken to a number of Cambodian cobra feasts by my Khmer kolleagues. A cobra feast is a five-course tasting menu built around cobra—the perfect meal for a Navy snake-eater. You start with cobra-skin salad, go on to cobra kabobs, cobra eggs, cobra blood, and then come to the pièce de résistance, *le venin:* the poison sac of the cobra itself, which has been preserved in cognac.

But cobra is only one of the exotic dishes I've enjoyed over the past three-plus decades of First, Second, Third, and Fourth World cuisine. Roast ox penis? Delicious. Braised chicken beaks? Ate 'em by the bowl. Dog? Let me put it this way: the phrase *How much is that doggie in the window?* takes on a whole new meaning when it's a restaurant you're peering into. Raw monkey brains? Yup. Crocodile tail? I've ordered it roasted, baked, steamed, and salted. Fish eyes—they're best fried, like sheep testicles.

So Iqbal's little mind game was no problem. As a matter of fact, he'd made it easy. First, he'd brought me to a world-class curry place. Second, there was nothing in the bowl I couldn't identify. Not only did I finish two bowls, but I asked for extra chilies on the side and finished them, too.

Iqbal had been impressed. I was the first gringo to have made it past a quarter of a bowl, and he told me as much.

"I'm honored not to have flunked lunch," I said after we'd finished, "but is there anyplace we can go for ice cream now?"

"Why?" he asked.

"That way, tomorrow morning, I can sit on the throne and scream, 'Come on, ice cream.'"

"Throne? Come on, ice cream?" He thought about what I'd said, his round, brown face all screwed up in contemplation. Then he broke out into a big, broad smile and laughed and laughed. "I get it—I get it," he'd said proudly. "That was bathroom humor. Very British, too."

There was still laughter in his voice as he hit the punch line again. "Of course I remember."

"I'm glad you do, Iqbal. I can be there in fifteen minutes."

"I will be there in ten, waiting for you."

* * *

I drank beer, Iqbal drank tea. It was good to see him again. He'd aged. The mustache and beard, once luxuriously black, were now salt-and-pepper. His hands and feet were wrinkled like weathered leather in the hot climate. But he still had his bright smile, white teeth, and quick wit. And there was probably no one in the country who could expedite things as quickly and as well.

Over vegetable curry hotter than I remembered it, I wiped perspiration from my face as I gave Iqbal the background for my visit. Well, as I've always believed, if you're not sweating, you're not eating. I didn't tell him everything, of course. But I outlined the basic facts: we were in pursuit of someone named Ishmael, a Lord Brookfield from London, who had arrived three to five days ago, flying to Karachi in a private jet. I wanted to be able to find our target and shadow him without arousing suspicion. I wanted to be able to go anywhere he went. I needed housing, transportation, weapons, and intelligence. Iqbal nodded, his expression serious, as I told him what I wanted to do, and how.

"It is possible, of course," he said. "But it will cost money."

I extracted a precounted wad of fifty notes from the nylon bag I carried around my neck. "This should do for a start."

He felt the money between the first two fingers of his right hand. "Nine hundred English pounds."

"You haven't lost the knack, have you? Close enough. It's eight hundred fifty."

"That will open a lot of doors."

"Good. Now—we'll need cars."

"That is no problem. I can lay my hands on two old Land Rovers."

I nodded. "Terrific. What about an airplane?"

Iqbal wiped up the last of his curry with a wedge of flat Afghani bread. "I know of one. We use it sometimes. It is flown by an American."

"No way." Most of the expats in this part of the world either worked for Christians in Action or were CIA alumni.

"This American is different. He is an ex-Marine. GTI brought him in from California a year and a half ago to fly their engineers up to the coastal drilling sites. He was supposed to stay only six months. Then he met a local girl—a cousin of the Bhuttos—and he married. Now he lives in a big villa just behind police headquarters, owns his own plane, and flies only when he wants to."

"What's his name?"

"Campbell. Richard Campbell."

"I'll talk to him." I wasn't excited about the prospect of bringing an outsider into my merry band of marauders, or staging a mission in an airplane that was probably older than I. But I have an open mind in these matters. Besides, Campbell didn't have to know what we were up to—he just had to fly the fucking plane where I wanted him to fly it. And if he had a problem with that, I wasn't above tossing him out the hatch at fifteen-thousand feet. After all, Howie Kaluha could fly most anything that had propellers, and Tommy T was more than halfway to his pilot's license.

"What about weapons?"

I knew the answer to that one already. Weapons weren't going to be a problem, either. Not in Pakistan, the Land of the Rising Gun. After all, the CIA had spent hundreds of millions of dollars here in the eighties, arming the mujahideen to fight the Soviets across the border in Afghanistan. Those weapons were now filtering back into general circulation—everything from AKs the Israelis had captured in Lebanon back in '82 and traded to the Agency in return for sophisticated missile-guidance systems, to three-hundred Stinger missiles that the Afghanis had "lost" somewhere between Kabul and Peshawar.

And if I wasn't interested in surplus, I could buy new. Twenty miles south of Peshawar, which sits thirty miles east of the mouth of the Khyber Pass, is the small town of Darra. There are six thousand people in Darra—half of them are weapon makers. All you can hear when you walk down the quarter-mile main drag is the sound of hammers hand-tooling guns, and the *craaack* of test-firing out in back of the hooches. I always think of Darra fondly because the whole place smells like cordite twenty-four hours a day. Visit there, and all you want to do is go to war.

There are just under one hundred shops, and they'll build you anything you want, from a working replica of an eighteenth-century dueling pistol to an M60 machine gun. RPGs, mortars, even cannons, can be found on Darra's muddy streets. And the quality is good. Not as good as the SEAL Six armorers at DEVGRP, maybe—but better than most anything I'd ever seen in the Third World. So if we wanted AKs, M-16s, or anything in between, they could be had.

Besides, I knew that Iqbal had his own private arsenal here in Karachi. We wouldn't need SMGs—submachine guns—here. After all, we had our SAS Glocks, and I was interested in keeping our profile as low as possible. Still, Iqbal kept a small arsenal for visiting firemen. The ex-policeman had a huge gun safe at GTI headquarters. Inside were half a dozen aging Remington 870 Wingmaster pump-action shotguns, some old Chinese-contract Inglis High Powers, and a few Vietnam-era SKS automatic rifles. They'd be more than adequate for our immediate needs.

Let me say a word or two about firearms and ammo here. I'm not one of those bulletheads who memorizes every fact about every fucking piece of equipment I carry. I really don't give much of a rat's ass what the fps of each goddamn load is, or what the fucking muzzle-energy batshit widget-foot-pound speed of a bullet may be. That's important if you're a sniper, or a hand-loader. I am neither.

Doc Tremblay, for example, can recite loading tables, muzzle speeds, and foot-pounds the way priests say Mass, or sports-radio hosts reel off 1960s batting averages. He has to know those facts because he spends so much of his time squinting through a telescopic sight.

Also—to be perfectly frank—I was never one of those sports dweebs who spent his adolescent hours memorizing the stats for the 1956 Dodgers, or the 1963 Baltimore Colts. I was too busy chasing pussy back then. My personality hasn't changed in the ensuing years, either. For me, the bottom line is that I consider weapons the tools of my trade—not some fancy accoutrements to be fondled, collected, worshiped from afar.

For example, I like my Emerson CQC6 folder because it, better than any other folding knife, does the jobs I want it to do. But that doesn't mean it's not a tool. Sure, I can cut myself out of a tight spot with it, but I have no problem using it to skewer a piece of meat over the fire, open my mail, or tighten a screw if there's nothing else around to use. I prefer Heckler & Koch USPs, or, if they're not available, Glocks, because those two are the most dependable off-the-shelf pistols one can buy. Screw all the space-age technology that went into R&D—I like 'em because I can bury 'em for a month, dig 'em up, rinse 'em off, and they'll still shoot straight even though the action is caked with mud. That's the same reason I use HK MP5s, while most of the SEAL teams have gone back to the CAR-15. The MP5 is the most reliable SMG made these days.

But if I can't get my hands on a Glock or an HK, then I'll use whatever I can find—*anything* I can find. Same thing goes for ammo. If I can't find the custom-made stuff I'm used to, then I'll take Winchester or Federal off the shelf or buy reloads or find thirty-year-old government surplus, or whatever

Because the bottom line with weapons is that it doesn't fucking matter what weapon you use—Glock, HK, Browning, or zip gun. And the ammo can be anything from Hydra-Shok, Black Talon, or Silvertip, to generic round-nose lead reloads. The bottom line is that you have to be able to hit the fucking target. And no gun is gonna do it for you. That's *your* job. The gun is simply a tool. Thus endeth the lesson.

Okay—transportation and weapons were easy. Intelligence, however, was going to be the most difficult element to achieve. Frankly, I wasn't sure whether or not I'd be able to track Lord Brookfield here. It's one thing to operate in Europe, where you look like most of the natives. Even places like Egypt, Jordan, Indonesia, or Vietnam are no problem—there are enough European tourists so that it's possible to blend in easily.

But here in Pakistan, which is basically a country under siege, my men and I stuck out. This is not a tourist center. You don't come here to see the sights. It's dangerous.

You think I'm engaging in hyperbole? Let me quote to you from a recent Top Secret DIA Country Survey:

A tidal wave of indiscriminate lawlessness and political violence is crashing across Pakistan, imperiling Pakistani and foreigner alike. . . . Only essential, seasoned personnel should reside in Pakistan, and they must keep security concerns in the forefront of their consciousness. The following areas are to be considered off-limits to all personnel: working-class areas of Karachi, the interiors of Sind, Baluchistan, and the entire North-West Frontier Province, Peshawar, where bombings are a daily occurrence, and Pakistani Kashmir.

Now, so far as I was concerned, there wasn't anyplace I wasn't able to go. When I let my hair down and wore Pakistani clothing and thong sandals, I could go native—walk the alleys and market-places without attracting undue attention. But here, even though I could walk the streets without attracting attention, I couldn't make conversation. Once I opened my mouth, my disguise was worthless. I can't speak Urdu, Punjabi, Sindhi, or Pashto. As for the rest of us—we all looked like gringos with the exception of Howie Kaluha. But like me he, too, would be compromised the minute he opened his mouth.

So sneaking and peeking would be difficult. Moreover, we'd be competing with thousands of informers, spies, agents, and just plain snitches who lived by selling snippets of information to each other on a daily, sometimes hourly basis. The Pakistani secret police have to deal with terrorism by Kashmiri separatists, Sikh militants, and WAD, the Afghanistani Intelligence Service. In Sind Province, dacoits—descendants of the original Thugees (from which we get the word *thug*)—kidnap and murder virtually at will. In the south, Shiite Muslims battle Sunni Muslims, and they all fight against the government, which is seen as too progressive and unfundamentally Islamic.

That's just the domestic scene. As for foreign intelligence, the Agency still maintains one station in the capital, Islamabad, one here in Karachi, and a third in Peshawar. Christians in Action beefed up its Pak presence when it was building the Afghan resistance movement. They maintain it today because Pakistan and Afghanistan share more than a thousand miles of border with Iran, the hub of Islamic fundamentalism. MI6, too, works Pakistan, because the Brits still consider it part of their sphere of influence. So does the former KGB, now metamorphosed as Russia's State Intelligence Service, or SIS.

Each of these organizations ran networks of agents, informers, and lookouts. Each, I knew, would soon hear about the arrival of seven healthy, athletic American males. Cables would be sent, and cables received. The only thing that would keep us from becoming dead meat was the happy fact that intelligence agencies are lard-slow bureaucracies. By the time they'd learned of our arrival, we'd be long gone—or at least out of sight.

I asked Iqbal about housing. That, he said, was the least worrisome of our problems. GTI had three vacant villas. We could use one of them, which would get us out of the Sheraton, where more than half the employees were police informers or worked for one of the competing intelligence nets.

"Well," I said, "then why the hell are we still sitting around here scorching our stomach linings when we could be working?"

Iqbal installed us in a GlobalTec villa on the eastern outskirts of the city, in a neighborhood I remembered from my previous visit. The house was perfect. It had a dusty courtyard big enough to turn a semi around in—all the better to lay out our chutes and repack them. There were ten-foot walls and a huge, tracked gate. I remembered the place: it was one of the half dozen on which I'd done a security survey, and I was gratified to discover that the company had actually followed my suggestions. So, there were grilles and antigrenade screens on the windows, a stout front door, and a house within a house—a fortified wing that could be entered only through a two-inch thick steel door that would take a pound of C-4 to open. Nobody was going to surprise us here.

The neighborhood was also ideal. It was quiet, secluded, and filled with nondiplomatic transients, Aussie, Brit, and Norwegian oil-drilling engineers, Canadian bankers, and a team of French computer dweebs. Speaking of computers, we even had access to the GTI mainframe, and to all of the company's other resources as well.

Using Iqbal's contacts (and my English-pound notes), we began to develop intelligence. But first, we hired one of the best local "fixers." Let me explain. In many Third and Fourth World countries, when you arrive at Cairo or Beirut International, it is a good idea—read mandatory—to have a man waiting for you. He takes your passport and immigration forms, slips the requisite bribe into the documents, and clears you through the officials in no time.

You can, of course, enter without a fixer. Sometimes, you breeze right through. On occasion, however, it may take a few hours: you wait while the secret police go through your wallet, the customs officials finger everything in your suitcase, the immigration man examines your passport stamp by stamp and visa by visa. If someone doesn't like what they see, they may decide to strip-search you—an altogether unique and colorful experience in countries where rubber gloves are not ever used. Six hours later you emerge sore as hell (both literally and figuratively) from the terminal having missed the bus to your hotel, leaving you at the mercy of a taxi driver who'll charge you three times the normal fee.

Iqbal sent our fixer, Nazim, off to the airport, to retrieve the list of private aircraft arriving over the past week. He was armed with $100 in Paki rupees, and we told him we wanted lots of change when he returned.

Six hours later, we had copies of documents showing us Lord B had arrived seventy-two hours before we had. Further, Nazim was able to report that Lord B had been met at the airport by the Iraqi consul general and whisked off in a motorcade to the consulate. According to Nazim's best sources in the Pak secret police, Brookfield hadn't left the consulate since he'd arrived.

Lord B's destination made sense. The Paks had backed Iraq in the Gulf War and still had close relations with Baghdad. During the Gulf War, the Karachi consulate had been used as a transshipment point for weapons and explosives that were targeted against allied diplomats in Pakistan, Indonesia, and Hong Kong.

My immediate reaction was to set up a surveillance. Iqbal shrugged. "It is not wise."

"Why not?"

"The Iraqis are already under scrutiny."

"But not by me."

"Yes. But you see—"

That was the problem. I didn't see. I wanted to make my own evaluation. Take my own target assessment. Then I'd know what to do. My eyes narrowed. Was Iqbal trying to hide something from us? Was someone else paying him baksheesh? There was only one way to find out what was going on: see for myself. "I want to take a look."

Iqbal smiled ingratiatingly. "I implore you, Pasha Vermin—"

"Don't fuck with me, Iqbal."

His face went impassive. He shrugged. "As you wish, Pasha Vermin. It is your decision."

I let my hair down, slipped into my sandals and marketplace clothes, and we drove into town. Iqbal parked the Land Rover by an apartment block close to the racetrack, and we walked south along the Khaliq-uz-Zaman Road, then turned right. We proceeded down a narrow street, made a series of right-hand turns, and came up on the consulate from the south side. As we approached, I saw why Iqbal had not jumped at my surveillance idea.

The place was crawling with spooks. There was literally a line of cars with pairs of "watchers" parked along the curb where the consulate wall ran parallel to the street. As we came up on the corner, I made another pack of vehicles, sitting with their motors running, outside the front gate. If we'd wanted to set up a surveillance, we'd have had to take a goddamn number.

I realized I was now screwed, fucked, and gang-banged. If Iqbal and I stopped and reversed our course, we'd attract the attention of every fucking pair of eyes on the street. If we continued on our merry way, we'd come under the scrutiny of the Iraqi countersurveillance teams, which I knew would be watching the watchers.

I looked over at Iqbal, who had "I told you so" written all over his face. "Okay, okay—you were right, and I'm an asshole," I said through clenched teeth.

There was nothing to do but brazen it out. We crossed over to the opposite side of the street and swung around the corner. The consulate building had its own surveillance system in play, too. I counted eight remote-controlled TV cameras. Two sat at each corner of the building, just under the eaves, sweeping in counterpoint to one another. Four others, on tall poles high above the razor-wire-topped wall, swept the street and roadway.

One of them panned with Iqbal and me as we walked, following our movement.

I cursed at myself. I was a worthless shit-for-brains pus-nuts pencil-dicked asshole geek. It had been a stupid fucking idea to come out here. Guess what. I was now a guest star on *Candid Camera*. My face was on videotape. Lord B would know goddamn well that I'd followed him. In a one-hundred-yard walk along a fucking Karachi street, we'd lost the element of surprise. Doom on me.

When I gave it some second thought back at the villa, I decided that I wasn't in as bad shape as I'd first believed. In fact, I decided that my blunder might actually work in our favor: if Brookfield knew I was lurking in the neighborhood, maybe it would spur him to come after me before he was ready.

The more I thought about it, the more I realized that goading him to act before he was ready was the perfect strategy. The great Chinese warrior-philosopher Sun Tsu had said as much in his book *The Art of War*, more than two thousand years ago. "Use deception," the Chinese general told his disciples. Like all the truly great soldiers, Sun Tsu was an unconventional warrior—a man after my own heart.

He kept it simple, stupid: "When they are strong," he wrote, "avoid them. When they are weak, destroy them. Make them think you intend one thing, then do the other. Provoke them to act precipitously."

For the past weeks, I'd been reacting to Lord B. That was no way to win. To win, you take the initiative. You instigate the action. You make the opponent react to you. I'd forgotten one of my own basic tenets—something Roy Boehm, the marvelous maverick mustang misfit godfather of all SEALs, had beaten into me so many years ago, in his own inimitable two-fisted style.

"Don't wait for them to come to fuck you," he'd said. "You go out and fuck the fucking fuckers first."

His words ringing in my head, I called a head shed. First priority: intelligence. To secure that, we'd need a prisoner. I assigned Wonder and Howie Kaluha that mission. I told them, "I don't want to hear from you until you bring me back a good story. What you do with the evidence is up to you."

We needed to get our equipment ready to go. That would be Nasty and Rodent's job. I told Iqbal we'd need 21 Glock magazines, plus five hundred rounds of the hottest jacketed 9mm hollowpoint ammo he could lay his hands on. We'd also have to send someone up to Darra ASAP to buy us seven AK-47s, 3,500 rounds of 7.62x39 ammunition, and seventy AK magazines. Iqbal had made inquiries, and he'd advised against showing our faces up there—there were too many spooks, tangos, and other unsavory characters out and about. I agreed—why complicate our lives right now. They were full enough.

We used the villa's courtyard to repack the chutes Luciano Angelotti had given us in La Spezia. You never jump a chute you haven't packed yourself. Moreover, these were *Incursari* chutes, which means they'd been used in water jumps. That makes a difference: seawater decomposes parachute silk after ten or twelve immersions if the chutes aren't thoroughly washed immediately after use. The salt water weakens the fabric, which can disintegrate on opening shock, sending the man wearing it to his death.

I knew we'd be HAHOing these chutes—that's High Altitude, High Opening in case you didn't remember—and I wanted to make absolutely sure that we hadn't been given seven rotting chutes. No need to find that out at twenty-thousand feet. So we unrolled them, examined them inch by inch, then packed 'em up again. They were old, and they'd been well used, but I believed they had at least one more jump in them. At least I hoped so. If not—well, *inshallah*.

While we checked our equipment, Iqbal hired watchers at the airport so we'd know if Lord B was going to move. Simultaneously, I sent Tommy, Duck Foot, Nasty, and Rodent out to parade past the Iraqi embassy at irregular intervals. I knew their hard bodies and gringo features on the TV screens would stir the pot.

While they marched past the cameras, Iqbal and I went to visit Dick Campbell, the Marine lieutenant colonel who'd retired, then married up. He had a big villa out between the stadium and the airport, in the Naval Staff Colony, a new development where, as Iqbal put it, "most of Karachi's who's and who's lives, Pasha Vermin."

Said Jarhead was batching it these days, said Iqbal, who explained that Campbell's wife was on one of her semiannual shopping trips to Paris. Iqbal had also said the Campbells lived in a unique house. As we pulled up, I realized it hadn't been hyperbole.

The compound was huge—more than two acres from the look of it. The house sat behind a twelve-foot wall. At each corner was a manned guardhouse built out of steel plate and bulletproof glass. The emplacements had gun ports and secure doors.

The only way in and out of the villa was a thick steel gate that ran on tracks. Half a dozen uniformed guards were standing outside, and I saw shotgun-toting gatekeepers behind the wall as we pulled over the gate track. Clusters of halogen security lamps pointed (correctly) away from the house so as to create a lighted killing zone, and four TV cameras swept the dusty brick courtyard. The courtyard itself had concrete planters strategically placed so as to provide cover for the security force, and a barricade to prevent someone in a truck from driving through the front door of the villa. Obviously, Dick Campbell was a man who appreciated good security.

He met us at the front door, a glass of something clear and on the rocks in his hand. He was obviously feeling no pain. He waved us through the ornately carved door with a friendly, "Come on in, you fungus-crotched dipshit geek no-load pencil-dicked pus-nutted asshole."

I looked at him strangely. Then I saw copies of *Rogue Warrior* and *Rogue Warrior: Red Cell* on the foyer table and realized what he was up to. My suspicions were confirmed when he asked, "Anybody want a Bombay on the rocks?"

I knew instinctively I was going to like him. "Fuck you, too," I said by way of friendly greeting. "Then eat shit and bark at the moon."

It turned out that even though he was older than I by some years, we'd served in Vietnam at roughly the same time. He'd flown F-4 Phantoms out of Da Nang, while I was prowling and growling in the Mekong on my first tour. Then he'd gone on to chop Charlie into bite-sized pieces during more than a thousand close air-support missions piloting Fart Carts—which is what Marines fondly called their A-4 Skyhawks.

Now in his late fifties, Campbell was as trim as when he'd flown "Zoom and Dooms"—F-8 Crusaders—off carriers in the sixties and his beloved A-4s in the seventies. He was the size of a small wide receiver: five eleven, about 175 pounds. He had playful gray eyes, a firm, cool handshake, and a Marine-clean shaven face and head. Yeah—the guy was Telly Savalas bald. "What's your radio handle?" I asked. "Eight Ball?"

He grinned. "Not quite. It's Rocky."

"Why, 'cause you look like a fucking raccoon? Or is it that you keep coming back for more punishment because you're too stupid to quit?"

Campbell gestured with the Bombay glass. "You're being too kind. You probably want a favor that could get me killed. Nah—remember the scene in *Rocky* where Stallone's training in the cooler, pounding away at a slab of beef?"

"Yeah."

He laughed. "Well, I had my share of long cruises, and there used to be times when I'd beat my meat, too."

"I always wondered what gave you carrier pilots such hairy palms." That brought a big smile to his face.

You had to like the guy. He had the right priorities, even though he'd gone native. Yeah—like me, he wore Paki clothes. Only his were white, clean, and ironed. That's what money will do.

While Iqbal took himself out to the kitchen, we settled down on overstuffed leather furniture that sat atop the antique rugs that covered the marble floor. I toasted him with my Bombay. It was the first I'd had in more than a week.

"No prob." He sipped his own martini. "Iqbal mentioned you may need transportation."

I outlined a probable scenario.

He shook his head. "No prob with that at all. As a matter of fact, it sounds like more fun than I've had in years."

We settled on a fee. It was, I thought, ridiculously low. But Campbell shook his head. "Frankly, I'd do this for free, except the fuel's so goddamn expensive these days."

I added that I also needed someone to make a milk run to Darra ASAP. That brought a smile to his face, too. "I've been looking for an excuse to get up there. There's an incredible HK-93 system knockoff I saw the last time I was there—and I've been kicking myself for not buying it. All I needed was an excuse. I'll fly up tomorrow morning."

"Great." I handed Rocky a small roll of English pounds and a handwritten shopping list.

He took a pair of wire-rim half-frames from his pocket and glanced at it. "No plastic? No M60 detonators? No RPGs?" A look of mock disappointment came over his face. "I thought you SEALs were serious about your business."

"We're already carrying the good stuff," I told him.

Chapter

17

WONDER BROUGHT ME MY INFORMATION AT 0720 THE NEXT MORNING. Lord B would move on to Afghanistan in thirty-six hours. He had meetings at a camp near Asadabad, the capital of Kunar Province in northeastern Afghanistan. Wonder obtained this nugget from an embassy driver—an Iraqi—who doubled as a member of the consulate security staff. The man was in a position to know Lord B's plans because he'd been assigned to help facilitate them. I asked which of the camps in the area Brookfield was going to. Wonder and Howie told me that was a fact the driver hadn't known. And they were convinced they'd squeezed the truth out of him. "He talked, boss," is what Howie said. "And he told us what he knew. Everything he knew."

And after they'd finished with him? Well, this particular DIQ— Driver In Question—would go into Iraq's MIA books. He'd left the consulate sixteen hours ago. He would never return.

You think that's heavy-handed, don't you? Snatch a guy, make him talk, then wax him. The fact is, it happens all the time in war. We did it to the VC in Vietnam—and they did it to us, too. There are hundreds, maybe thousands, of MIAs buried in unmarked graves in Vietnam. They were snatched from their foxholes or hooches or

240

tents by Mr. Victor Charlie. They were tortured. They were interrogated. Then they were killed.

That is how war is fought. Oh, we didn't talk about it a lot—still don't. It wouldn't be fashionable or nice or polite. And we Americans have habitually been led by people who for some reason want to wage fashionable, nice, polite wars.

You want an example? Okay—how about Warren Christopher, who was deputy secretary of state when he asked Delta Force's CO, Charlie Beckwith, to shoot the Iranian terrorists holding American hostages in Tehran in the shoulder, so *they* wouldn't get hurt during our 1980 rescue mission.

This is the same Warren Christopher who ran the State Department in 1993, when our boys got chewed up in Somalia because the rules of engagement drawn up by Christopher's staff and the White House Whiz Kidz didn't allow any kicking of ass or taking of names because "innocent" Somalis might get hurt.

Hmmmm. Do you see a pattern here?

Well, folks, it don't work like that. Despite what the striped suits of the world like Warren Christopher may think, war—as General William Tecumseh Sherman once said—is hell.

You don't believe it? Remember, if you will, the photographs of Marines at the Chosin Reservoir. Or the thousand-yard stares of grunts in Vietnam. Or the look of pure, absolute terror on the face of Mike Durant, the chief warrant officer whose Blackhawk chopper was shot down in Mogadishu. Well, Durant was well trained. He'd been told what would happen to him if he got captured, and I believe he was ready to die. But that didn't change the expression on his face. And—because he was caught on TV—the whole world got to see the hell he was in. His face was the real face of war. The face of terror and pain.

War isn't pretty—it's not the way you see it in the movies, where Sly, Steven, Chuck, Jean-Claude, Arnold, or some other asshole manages to take down 150 VC with a thirty-round mag while flexing his pecs and grimacing for the camera. But it's real—and it can hurt you bad. Believe me, war is hell.

The great Marine sniper and a true American hero, Gunnery Sergeant Carlos N. Hathcock, who had ninety-three confirmed kills in Vietnam, tells a story about a VC bitch he named Apache, whose habit was to skin Marines alive as she interrogated them. She sent one back to Hathcock's unit still alive—the kid died as he crossed the outer perimeter wire.

Apache had worked him over pretty good. Among the nasty things she'd done to him was cut off his eyelids. Cutting off a prisoner's eyelids was her trademark.

Hathcock hunted Apache. It took a while, but he finally sniped her. He says he had to kill her—because she'd murdered and tortured kids he'd known. But he didn't kill her just to get even. That would have been enough, given her history. But Hathcock had a higher goal: he killed her in order to save Marine lives.

Now, the powers that were, back then, didn't much care for Carlos Hathcock, or for sniping in general. They felt that sniping was too nasty, too spooky, too dirty. It wasn't gentlemanly—as if war is a gentlemen's game.

But Carlos knew better. He knew that every VC he killed saved between five and ten American lives. That's five to ten Marines who went back to their families—to their wives, their kids, and their parents. He sniped ninety-three (and had another four hundred probables), so at the very least, two thousand four hundred Marines who wouldn't have gone home alive made it back.

So far as I'm concerned, we Americans owe Gunny Hathcock a debt that we can never repay.

What it all comes down to is that we must wage war to win, not to lose or to draw. We must wage war to save the lives of our men and the lives of our civilians at home—in this particular case, the tens of thousands of potential victims of Lord B's biological warfare—while taking the lives of our enemies.

So I'm not above snatching a prisoner and then killing him. Unfair, you say. No problem. I can live with that. Unprincipled, you charge. I disagree. My primary principle is to keep my men alive any way I can, while fulfilling my mission completely.

Okay, you say, what about the Geneva Convention?

Well, gentle reader, the Geneva Convention doesn't apply much these days anyway. Did it apply in Lebanon in 1982, where shot-down Israeli pilots were tied behind cars and dragged through the streets? Did it apply in El Salvador, Honduras, or Nicaragua, where tens of thousands of innocent victims died? Did it apply in Somalia, where the bodies of American soldiers were desecrated by mobs? Or in Iraq, where a captured SAS sergeant was ordered to wipe the excrement from a latrine with his bare hands, then forced to lick his fingers clean? Face it: nobody pays attention to the Geneva rules anymore if it isn't convenient to do so. And for most of the Second and Third World, it's just plain inconvenient.

If I ever fight the Swiss, then I'll abide by the Geneva accords. Until then, I'll do to tangos what they want to do to me—but I'll do it to them first. With maximum prejudice and love of violence.

Endeth the sermon.

I bursted Mick Owen with the results of our interrogation and a request for intel. I needed to know what the hell was happening near Asadabad. I called Dick Campbell and—guardedly—let him know that we were about ready to move. He said he'd be ready when we were.

I got a return transmission from Mick half an hour later. According to the latest satellite snapshots, there were six camps within fifteen miles of each other, to the east and north of the provincial capital. All of them were active—that meant there were tangos in residence.

I knew about Asadabad. It was the nerve center for the Party of Islam, one of the four dozen or so splinter groups that was currently training Islamic fundamentalist foot soldiers to wage jihad against governments from Algeria to Egypt, from Bosnia to Bangladesh, from Yemen to the United States.

The entire jihad movement, built with seed money from Iran, was currently financed by Afghanistan's flourishing opium business. The country where the CIA had spent more than $6 billion to fight the Soviets was now the world's leading exporter of heroin to the United States.

You could argue that the fundamentalists had already won their holy war against the Great Satan. They were, after all, pumping hundreds of metric tons of heroin into our country every year without our being able to stop them. Those drugs were killing us from within—ruining our cities, destroying our infrastructure, sapping our economy.

I was happy to have the camp locations, which I punched into our Magellans. Problem was, they were scattered over three hundred square miles of rural Afghanistan, and I hadn't the vaguest idea which one Brookfield was going to. It could be any of them. There was also the possibility that he wasn't heading for a training camp.

He could be traveling to Asadabad to visit the province governor or to pay a courtesy call on the mullahs running the Party of Islam. He could be visiting the poppy fields and opium-processing facilities that dotted the inhospitable countryside. There was absolutely no way of knowing. I was goatfucked.

I thought about trying to plant a beacon, but it couldn't be done—first of all, we didn't have any beacons. Second, planting one would have meant getting inside the Iraqi consulate. I wasn't about to lose a man trying to do that. The only other way to track Lord B would be for Mick to have the spooks at Cheltenham's Division U play with their switches and dials and reroute one of the FORTE birds I knew they had flying overhead to track Pakistan's nuclear weapons program.

We'd quietly sold the U.K. five FORTE—for Fast On-board Recording of Transient Experiments—satellites in the last days of the Bush administration. The president had completed the transaction by signing an emergency National Security Finding, so that the birds could be delivered without having a congressional debate on the subject. That way, the Brits would gain a tactical advantage, and FORTE's capabilities would remain more or less secure.

The precursors of FORTE satellites, known as INDIGOs, BYEMANs, and Lacrosses, were first put up by the National Reconnaissance Office, or NRO, in 1983. The first generation were equipped with cameras and simple sensors—enough to give the West a technological advantage during the Cold War, but generations behind today's sophisticated, miniaturized imaging capabilities. The second generation added computer-based imaging. After BYEMANs and INDIGOs came Lacrosses, which are still in use by the NRO. Lacrosse satellites use radar and infrared imaging systems, and laser-based target acquisition. The latest versions, flown just before the Gulf War, were equipped with CW/BW (Chemical Warfare/Biological Warfare) sensors. They had a .23-meter resolution. That means they could see things as small as eight inches from their 155-mile orbit track. Using the computer enhancement equipment that's readily available, you can literally read a license plate from 155 miles in space.

An interesting sidelight about the names of these birds: all these satellites were originally developed under the administrative ticket of BYEMAN. When that was compromised by the Walker spy ring, they became known as INDIGOs. When Jonathan Pollard leaked both the INDIGO technology and its ultrasecret code word to the Israelis, they became Lacrosse. In 1992, the Lacrosse designation was augmented with a new code word: FORTE. Who knows what they'll become now that you know about FORTE.

The reason for the augmentation was a generational increase in intelligence-gathering capacity. FORTEs have all the capabilities of Lacrosse, which means they can produce photographic images (currently they have a .15 meter resolution), as well as use radar and infrared to peer through heavy cloud cover. But that's where the similarities end. FORTEs have tremendously advanced nuclear-warfare-sensing features. The version we gave the Brits uses a highly sophisticated sensor—its formal designation is the DS21 Multi Spectral Thermal Imager—that can spot anything from chemical residue released during plutonium reprocessing to the distinctive heat signature of a nuclear weapon on ready alert. FORTE's sensors can detect heat fluctuation from reactor cooling towers and even identify the sort of characteristic vegetation damage that normally occurs at weapons-grade radwaste sites.

Mick answered my request with a hearty "Fuck you." But I knew he'd be busting his butt to convince the computer dweebs to help us out. In all honesty, it wouldn't be much of a job—the difference of perhaps a couple of hundred miles in the bird's sweep area would cover us.

In the meantime, God helps those who help themselves. So we helped ourselves to as many of the supplies Dick Campbell had brought back from Darra as we could cram into battle bags, rechecked our chutes, loaded magazines, stripped, oiled, and reassembled our weapons, fused ten hand grenades per man (five frags, two white-phosphorus willy peters, three concussions), and divided twenty-two pounds of Semtex plastic explosive, 20 M60 detonators, ten time fuses, and twenty igniters between us. If somebody didn't make it, I didn't want us to lack for firepower.

Iqbal was late. The SOB was supposed to drive me to the gold market, where I wanted to exchange two thousand pounds for gold coins. Believe me, it's easier to trade gold than it is to ask some AK-47-toting guerrilla if he has change for a fifty-pound note. Now

245

I was an hour and a half behind schedule, which was an unacceptable margin even in Karachi, where split-second timing is measured in ten-minute intervals. Well, fuck him—I'd go anyway.

I slid into one of the Land Rovers. Tommy T jumped in, too. "Where to, Skipper?"

I told him.

"Great. I'll come along for the ride."

I waved at the guard standing next to the villa gate. He lifted the bar, swung the gate, and we nosed into the street. We turned left, then worked our way through the streets, heading southeast, toward the jeweler's market just north of the river. In the distance, I heard a car bomb go off. That was business as usual—there was at least one a day in Karachi. It kept the cops busy and made parking a game. Yeah—a game. Russian roulette. A second bomb exploded. This one was larger, and closer—we could sense the concussion. I found an alley close by our destination and stashed the wagon. We walked the last five-hundred yards, completed our business with a minimum of haggling, and headed home. As we drove, we heard two more car bombs. They sounded as if they were coming from the south—Faisal Colony maybe, or Sadat Colony. The cops were gonna be real busy today. So were the hospitals.

We were just pulling through the gate when some asshole rear-ended the Land Rover, pushing us clear through the gate. I was about to say something nasty when the son of a bitch interrupted me by shooting our gatekeepers and firing through our rear window.

I ducked, but not before I saw two pickup trucks pull up and disgorge a dozen nasty-looking assholes dressed like mujahideen. Where was the old Muslim hospitality? Obviously, these guys bore us no goodwill at all. I guess I realized that because they were carrying automatic rifles and ammo bandoliers.

I may be slow, but I'm not stupid. "Shit, Tommy—" We rolled out of the Land Rover and took cover behind the hood. I pulled the Glock out of my belt and dropped the asshole closest to me with three rapid shots that walked up his torso as he charged—damn, I was heeling. Well, he dropped anyway.

Tommy's pistol was already in use. Of course, he's younger and faster than I am. He double-tapped a tango carrying an RPG. Fucking show-off.

"House," he yelled at me. "You go, I'll cover."

I didn't have to be told twice. I dodged and rolled left, zigzagged right-left-right, then hauled balls for the doorway. Bullets kicked up dirt all around me. A round went through the heel of my boot and knocked me over. I flipped, tucked, rolled, saw somebody move to my starboard, picked him up in my front sight, and came up shooting.

I was lucky and the sumbitch went down. No, I wasn't lucky—I was practiced in stress shooting. I told my men that we had to be able to get it right the first time. I hammered them again and again. There'd be no warm-ups, no target practice, when we went to war. No matter how tired, how sore, how fucked up we were, we had to be able to kill the bad guy right out of the gate.

But it worked. We started with the basics, at a Virginia Beach shooting range. We dry-fired, using the old sight-acquire-fire technique. Then we worked with live ammo. Then we went outdoors. Rain, sleet, snow—we shot in them all. We combined target work with real-life situations. I called it stress shooting, because I induced stress, then we shot.

It works. I know, because here I was, under stress, and I was dropping these tangos.

I rolled against the door. It cracked. Wonder's face emerged. So did his AK. "Whatever you're selling, we don't want any."

"Fuck you."

He laughed. He rolled out and sprayed the trucks across the courtyard to keep the tangos' heads down. "Yo—Tommy . . ."

Tommy got the hint. He sprinted, rounds kicking around his heels. Tommy and I dove inside.

Wonder had things organized for defense inside the villa. But I wanted to take 'em on outside—I didn't want to fight a holding battle. Car bombs or not, the cops would be here soon, and I didn't need to explain myself to them. We were packed and ready to move out anyway—so we'd go early. We could hole up at Dick Campbell's until he got the plane ready and I had word from Mick about our target site.

I made the assignments in less than half a minute. We'd KISS and kill. Rodent and Howie would go out the back door and flank to starboard, Duck Foot and Tommy would do the same and go portside, and Nasty, Wonder, and I would go hi-diddle-diddle, straight down the middle. We'd come back for the bags as soon as we'd straightened out the matter of these assholes.

I led the way out the front door. The tangos had massed, using their trucks for cover. Terrific. I lobbed a willy peter just behind the lead truck. I heard the screams as it exploded.

"Go."

Nasty took point. On the run, he brought down a charging tango with a double-tap. Now I came through the door, charged ahead, firing as I went. Stevie had the AK burning—he actually cut one asshole in two. We set up a deadly field of fire, which got the bad guys' attention fast. We charged toward the Land Rovers in the center of the courtyard, rolled behind them, and used them as cover. It was like target practice: a tango would pop up, we'd pop him.

So far so good. The firing at us was both sporadic and unfocused. Par for the course. I've learned that tangos don't practice a lot of fire discipline. They like to shoot whole mags every time they pull the trigger. We shoot three-round bursts—but we hit what we aim at.

The bad guys were trying to withdraw. I guess they hadn't expected such a violent reaction coming at them head-on. Well, doom on them, because they weren't gonna get off that easy. The pincer was about to close.

Rodent and Howie had gone out the back, jumped the wall, and come around behind the tangos. I could hear them firing from the right. Then I heard three-shot bursts from the left side—Tommy and Duck Foot had arrived, too.

I winked at Nasty, who winked back. The big squeeze was on, and we were about to have some fun. He pushed forward, firing his AK from the hip.

It was all over in a matter of seconds. Which was good because I heard sirens and horns in the distance. That was the stage manager's cue to exeunt left. Translation: it was time to get the hell out of there.

I backed the Land Rover against the truck that had rear-ended me and pushed it out of the way. Tommy got behind the wheel of the other LR and swung around. The rest of the guys hit the door and grabbed luggage. We were clear in less than two minutes. I wheelied in the courtyard, floored the accelerator, and came out of the gate, churning gravel as I threaded the needle between the tango pickups and swung into the street. Tommy was right behind me. We hadn't gone three blocks when we saw two fire trucks and three police cars heading toward the villa, lights flashing and Klaxons blaring. Good—*they* could pick up the pieces.

We checked each other over for dings, bumps, and bruises over cold beer at Dick Campbell's palace. He played mother hen, clucking over us and wagging his finger under my nose. "There goes your fucking OpSec, Marcinko."

He had a point, although I was upset that Brookfield hadn't taken the bait and come after me sooner. No, he'd waited me out, dammit. And they'd probably grabbed Iqbal to find out what we were up to. At least that's the way I had to look at things.

I ran a mental list of what Iqbal knew and didn't know. He knew I'd discovered Lord B was going to Afghanistan. He knew that Dick Campbell had volunteered to fly us wherever we wanted to go. But he hadn't any idea how we planned to hit Lord B or when or how we'd extract. Those elements of our plan we'd fortunately kept to ourselves.

I bursted Mick Owen requesting an update and got back some good news. The FORTE he'd requested was being shifted. Now, it was simply a matter of fixing Lord B's position. And how did I propose to do that?

Good question. You can't track a plane with a satellite. The satellite moves on a fixed orbit, passing over a location every four to five hours. It has no more than a few minutes of picture capability. The bird can be programmed to look for specific things—terrain or buildings or vehicles. But it can't track them, unless they move very slowly (you can track a ship, for example, as I did in *Rogue Warrior: Red Cell*). So I had to tell Mick what to program the FORTE to look for.

Except I had no idea what to say.

I discussed the problem with Wonder, whose knowledge about these sorts of things far exceeds my own. Wonder played with his Howdy Doody hair and pondered the problem.

"What's he got that could give him away?"

I shrugged. I had no idea how he was traveling. The only thing about which I was reasonably certain was that he had six canisters of BA-PP3/I that he'd removed from *Numéro Douze*. But they were sealed—no way to sniff them out. Besides, FORTE wasn't built to sniff BW/CW material.

Wonder wasn't necessarily convinced. "Maybe—maybe not."

"What are you thinking?"

"Remember when we hauled balls out of the radwaste facility?"

"What's your point?"

"We set off the ARMS."

That was true. "Well, we'd been swimming in all that heavy-water shit. We probably looked like Cyalume in the dark."

"Yeah. Or Day-Glo." He scratched his nose. "But maybe it was the canisters."

"They were packed in lead. Besides, we washed them off."

"Maybe we didn't wash 'em off completely, Dickhead."

I thought about that.

"But remember," Wonder continued, "the outside shell leaked. The canisters were wet when you opened the carton."

No, I hadn't remembered. But Wonder had. He has a mind for details like that, which is why I'm happy I hadn't let him drown back there.

"FORTE can smell radiation," he said. "If it's the only radiation around. I learned that in Iraq."

He was right, of course. In the years after the Gulf War we'd used FORTE satellites to spot the locations where Saddam Hussein had stashed radioactive elements of his nuclear weapons program. Wonder had gone along on a couple of the inspection trips, masquerading as a U.N. weapons inspector. The thought of Wonder trying to be diplomatic brought a wry smile to my face.

I queried Mick Owen, who answered that they'd play with the switches and dials and get back to me. I wondered how he was getting them to move a pair of birds—he certainly couldn't say it was for me, because I was a persona non grata. Well, frankly I didn't give a shit how he was getting it all done—just so that it was getting done.

Dick Campbell brought out his charts and went over the flight plan he'd devised. We'd take off to the southeast and fly out over the Indus delta about fifty miles, as if we were heading toward one of the GTI drilling sites near the Indian border. Then we'd bank east, staying well away from the Pak missile sites at Dati and Badin, and work our way to the oasis at Cachro, where we'd make visual contact, then turn northwest, flying a basic straight line to Sukkur. From there, we'd follow the Indus River as it meandered north-northeast, taking a visual sighting on Dera Ismail Khan, then threading the needle through the mountain passes just to the west of Peshawar. Then we had two choices: we could breach the Afghan border by going over the Safed Mountains, or we could skirt Peshawar flying to the east, cross the border north of Asadabad, and hit the targets from the north side.

It sounded good to me. But flying wasn't my job. I had other variables to worry about. Like wind speed and direction and weight and oxygen (or lack thereof). My plan was to HAHO in. That meant we had to leave the plane at a minimum of twenty-eight thousand feet—perhaps more, depending on the altitude of the target.

See, with 28K of altitude, you can get a twenty-mile glide, *if* the weather's right and *if* the winds are with you. We learned that back in the Arizona desert, where we jumped out of 727s and C-141s from as high as thirty-five thousand feet. How high is that? Have you ever flown cross-country? The normal civilian flight path is thirty-seven thousand feet. You can't see a 727 from the ground at that altitude. We jumped from a mere two thousand feet lower— and you couldn't see us, either.

Anyway, if you're jumping from 28K and your target is at 150 feet above sea level, you can glide X miles. But if the target is in a high-mountain plateau and sits 6,700 feet above the ground, you need an extra 6,700 feet or so to make the same jump. Actually, you need more. Because the air is thinner on the ground—if that ground sits one-plus miles above sea level. And thin air supports a parachute less well than "fat" air. Which means that we'd be moving faster and descending quicker than if we were jumping over Phoenix or Tucson.

And there'd be the usual Murphy factors as well—headwinds, updrafts, and thermals, not to mention hypoxia (that's oxygen deprivation in the bloodstream for you nonmedical types out there), freezing cold, and the altogether possible malfunctioning of our well-used Italian chutes.

It was time to talk about happier things. "What are we flying?" I asked. I was hoping for a stable platform.

I wasn't going to get one. "A Provider—C-123," Rocky replied, a regulation USMC shit-eating grin on his face.

"What's the matter, couldn't you find a C-47?" Jeezus. I hated

C-123s. They were first flown in the midfifties, powered by a pair of big radial piston engines. We used 'em in Vietnam. Back then, they'd added a couple of jet engines to assist during takeoffs because the plane was noticeably underpowered, and there'd been a number of crashes during crosswind conditions.

After Vietnam, C-123s could be seen in various Third World air forces, or flying on a number of Christians in Action assignments. They are not good aircraft. Despite that fact, Richard Secord, a retired Air Farce general, bought one of the old rattletraps for Marine Lieutenant Colonel-turned-politician Ollie North's covert contra resupply effort. It lacked the proper navigation gear and was seldom airworthy. Even so, the pilots managed to fly dozens of supply missions until the Sandinistas shot it down with a Soviet-supplied SAM-7 missile on October 5, 1986, and thus began the scandal we have come to know as the Iran-contra affair.

The one positive thing about a C-123 is that it, like the C-130 Hercules, has an aft ramp, which can be lowered during flight. That makes a mass jump easier, because we could all go out at the same time if we wanted to.

"Don't sweat it," Campbell said. "This is GTI's plane. We take good care of it."

I hoped so. Some of the C-123s I'd seen were so beat-up that the foam that lined the tanks had come loose, which allowed chunks of plastic to work their way into the fuel lines—doom on whoever flew those rattletraps. In others, there was so much rust and fuselage deterioration that pieces of the plane had actually fallen off during flights.

"Any other good news?"

"Yeah—the weather report for your AO is good. No rain or snow or other distractions."

That *was* good news. "What about cloud cover?"

"Clear as crystal for the next seventy-two hours."

"Great." Actually, I hate getting good news—it simply means something else will go wrong. I prefer the situation to be completely FUBAR—Fucked Up Beyond All Repair. When you're really goatfucked, things can do nothing but improve.

Chapter

18

Mick Owen came through. "We have signal" is what he bursted me. That meant we were officially (by which I mean covertly) in business.

Brookfield moved six hours later. We let him go. The satellites would do their jobs. I received tracking information from Mick, punched the coordinates into the Magellan GPS, and drew corresponding lines on Rocky's air navigation charts. Two and a half hours after he took off, Brookfield's plane, which had feinted west toward Iran, turned north, and flown over Baluchistan, landed in Jalalabad, Afghanistan. The next TECHINT report told us he was heading north on the main highway toward Asadabad.

He stopped well south of the city, and the readings were constant for an hour. Once again, I punched the numbers into the Magellan, and we compared them with the topographical navigation chart on Dick Campbell's desk. Lord B was about halfway between Sarkani and Khas Konar, which put him in the foothills of the Kashmund mountain range. As the crow flies, that's less than twenty-five miles from the Paki border. But crows—not to mention C-123s—would have a hard time flying straight over those mountains.

Once again, it was time to move.

I couldn't risk a night jump because we didn't have the necessary equipment to allow us to see one another. So we'd go at dusk— enough light to make it reasonable, but dark enough to keep the bad guys from seeing us easily.

I was worried about hypoxia. The chute rigs had O_2 bottles. But I had no way of knowing whether they were full, half-full, or empty, or whether the oxygen had been in there for so long it had become contaminated.

As we packed out, Dick Campbell handed me a waterproof packet. I opened it. There were twelve gold coins inside.

"What's this?"

"Extra get-out-of-jail money for Afghanistan. Just in case."

I slammed him on the shoulder. "Damn, Rocky—"

"Hey, don't sweat it. I'll put it on the tab. You're already into me for so much fucking Bombay you'll never earn it out. Just do me one favor."

"Sure."

"Sign my books." He handed me his copies of *Rogue Warrior* and *Rogue Warrior: Red Cell.* I inscribed them with the appropriate four-letter words. "Fuck you very much, Bro—"

"No problem. Now let's get the hell out of here. Time's a-wasting, and we'll need a half-hour preflight check before we can go wheels up."

We took off, went into our preplanned evasion sweep southward, then flipped northwest. No one seemed to care who we were or where we were going. Rocky kept the plane between 10 and 12K in altitude. That was high enough so we could see where the hell we were going, but low enough so we didn't have to pressurize and deal with the C-123's O_2 supply.

There was no way I was going to play with a C-123's O_2 supply. I'd learned that unhappy lesson as an enlisted Frogman. I was an RM2 (that's a Radioman Second Class, whose theme song is "Clickity-clack, clickity-clack, here come the girls from the radio shack") doing my time in Ev Barrett's Second-to-None Platoon at UDT-22.

I was also a parachute rigger, and in that guise I was assigned to act as jumpmaster for a series of UDT-21 night-jump exercises out of Suffolk, Virginia, about thirty miles southeast of what I still think of as the pussy-filled resort town of Vagina Beach. Suffolk's municipal airport, which was leased by the Navy, sat next to a big hog farm. That way, we Frogmen could jump out of planes and get happy as the proverbial (and in this case literal, if we drifted too far off course) pigs in you-know-what.

We were flying a C-123 nicknamed the Rusty Scumbucket, the only aircraft available that evening. It was my first time in a 123. It was also my first up-close-and-personal encounter with the young officer in charge that night, a young ensign from UDT-22 named— well, let's call him Eddie Emu, because he looked like a big, scrawny, bug-eyed bird who can't fly.

(A real-life digression. Just about two years ago, as Vice Admiral G. Edward Emu, deputy chief of staff of the Special Operations Command, Eddie tried to flip me the bird by getting my SEAL Team Six mementos chucked out of the UDT/SEAL Museum because he viewed—and still views—me with considerable disdain. Well, the feeling's mutual—I don't respect SEAL admirals who try to talk like warriors but have never actually killed anything on two legs. The toadies-cum-Frogmen who run the museum tended to agree with Eddie the Bird. But luckily for me, my sea daddies Roy Boehm and Ev Barrett, as well as a bunch of other fleet-sailor old-time Frogs, were around to show up at the membership meeting when Eddie's chuck-out-Demo-Dickie-or-you-won't-receive-any-support-from-the-Navy-anymore proposal was being debated. They derailed the good admiral's plans. Which means you can still see the engraved pistol and a replica of the sterling-silver SEAL Six belt buckle my men gave me when you visit the UDT/SEAL Museum at Ft. Pierce, Florida.)

Okay—back to the story. So I'd spent the night as jumpmaster, putting UDT-21 jumpers out the 123's side hatch, watching long-ingly as they disappeared into the darkness, emergency flares trailing after them. I wanted to jump, too. But Ensign Emu categorically denied me the pleasure. The evening's activities had been scheduled by UDT-21, and without the proper manifests, releases, and other rat-shit paperwork, and—well, let's put this sentence in his words: "No UDT-22 personnel can exit the god-damn plane unless it's parked on the goddamn runway—and that specifically means you, Radioman Second Class Mar*chinko.*"

I saluted and said, "Aye, aye, sir." In truth I guess I have to add that I spelled it with a *c* and a *u*, and that my fingers were crossed behind my back. So, as soon as the final jumper cleared, I looked around and discovered that the only personnel on board were the flight crew and me. My immediate conclusion? I deduced that the manifest had somehow been changed, and the plane had been, mirabile dictu, assigned to carry me—*ich, yo, moi, ani*—up for a UDT-22 night free-fall jump. I asked the pilot if that sounded okay to him. He said he had no problem—in fact, he gave me a double thumbs-up. So I strapped on a chute and a boot-flare and stood in the door while he banked back toward the target area for one last pass.

Of course, to suit up properly I had to remove my oxygen mask, then replug it when I'd finished. Well, the 123's O_2 hookup was TARFU, and so when I plugged back in, I got no O—just nice, thin air. And since we were flying at twelve thousand feet, I got more than a little dizzy and blurry eyed while waiting for the pilot to fly over my exit point. In fact, by the time I finally went out the hatch, I was barely semiconscious. But what the hell—one of the basic rules of being a hairy-assed Frogman is Never Lose a Good Free Fall. (We used to consider losing a good free fall about as nasty a thing to lose as a good hard-on.) So, I just went out the door woozy, dropping in a long HALO fall, the red-flaming flare trailing from my boot, and the wind up my spaghetti-sucking nostrils waking me up just as I fell through five-thousand feet. I finally pulled at nineteen hundred and dropped right onto the top point of the A-shaped runway—a perfect bull's-eye.

Eddie—he was always quick on the uptake—realized what perfidy I'd perpetrated when we both showed up in the UDT compound at about the same time. He knew I was supposed to be in a plane, not heading toward the rigger's loft with a balled-up parachute under my arm. One plus one equaled two, and he started in on me, trying to ream me a new asshole.

Of course I denied everything. But Eddie had spotted the chute, and then he saw the flare holder on my boot. He snagged them as exhibits one and two for the prosecution. He brought me up on charges of reckless endangerment or some similar bullshit and tried to have me court-martialed. Luckily, UDT-22's CO at the time, a Reserve lieutenant commander I'll call Dick Swanson, didn't see things the way Eddie did, and the charges were never filed.

Okay, I know what you're about to say. That I could have blacked out after I exited the plane and burned straight in, turning myself to jam on the runway. But I didn't burn in. I flew the edge of the envelope. And I learned a couple of valuable lessons. First, that the oxygen supply on a C-123 is unreliable. And second, that when you're in a bad situation, you have to trust in your ability to make it better yourself—without anybody else to hold your hand (or in this case, pull your rip cord).

Segue to the present. Both of the lessons I'd learned back then applied right now. I knew that because of the need to get these bastards, I'd probably do something just as dumb and/or reckless tonight. And if shit happened? Well, it's how you manage to fight your way through that counts, not the shit or the happening. Mr. Murphy will always be around. You have to ignore him when you can and work around him when you can't.

So we'd push the envelope tonight—maybe push it beyond where we'd ever gone before. I never want to lose a man, but if I do, I want it to mean something—to him as well as to me.

Everyone knows my position on this. I tell my men that safety has its place in SpecWar: during basic training. Safety is not something I factor in during real operations or final training workups. If you're going to go to war, you must train for war—not for peace or safety. You're supposed to be a professional who knows how to function *in* and during *extremis.* The sorry fact is that shooters don't get authorization to do that very often these days. Today's C²COs don't want to have their records blemished with something as foolhardy as a training accident.

So, the current crop of SEALs don't get the chance to hear real bullets whistle by their heads very often—which hurts them when the real thing comes along, because they're not ready for it. To be a warrior, you have to be willing to die. I know that sounds like so much fucking machismo bullshit, but that's the way it is. That's real life. You have to be ready for death. In training, that means taking things to the point where you could actually get killed—otherwise your men will never know what to expect or how they'll react. Now, this doesn't mean that I'm looking for ways in which to kill my men. I have always preached that while I'm ready to die, I'd rather kill the other guy before he kills me. Or, as Roy Boehm, who's killed his own fair share of bad guys, puts it, "Don't get mad, don't get even—get ahead."

We made the second and third checkpoints without problems. There was no extraneous radio traffic, and no other visible planes. I bursted Mick every ten minutes—without avail. That was a problem looming large. We couldn't circle above Pakistan endlessly without attracting attention, and we certainly weren't about to cross the border, where they had hundreds of Stinger missiles, until we knew precisely where the fuck we were going.

Welcome to Murphyville. I went up to the cockpit and plunked myself into the naviguesser's chair behind Howie Kaluha, who was flying copilot. "How's the fuel sit?"

Rocky Campbell shrugged in his harness and tapped the dials above his head. "We have another hour or so—maybe a little more."

Terrific—if the intel birds didn't pick up on the canisters' location in time, we'd run out of fuel. I considered a kamikaze attack. Nah.

We had about forty-nine minutes of fuel left when Mick Owen bursted a set of coordinates to the transceiver I held in my sweaty paw. I punched the numbers into the Magellan, ran forward to the cockpit, then entered our present position.

Rocky looked at the readout and nodded. "No prob." He played with switches and dials, then turned toward me. "You go out the door in seventeen minutes, which gives me half an hour to make Peshawar airport. I'll be burning fumes at that point, but what the fuck. Life ain't fun unless you got a few problems, right?"

How could I argue with the man?

He put the plane in a gentle climb now. As we crossed twenty-thousand feet, I said a silent prayer, plugged into our O_2, then dropped the ramp and popped the side hatch. I breathed—and the oxygen flowed. One more hurdle out of the way. I checked the Magellan. We were roughly seventy-five miles from the target and fifty-five miles from the drop now. The air coming into the fuselage was positively arctic. There was frost on my jump goggles. I could feel the cold through my gloves. This was going to be a bitch.

The plane banked right, then left, as we climbed through twenty-five thousand feet. Our insertion would be through the back door—flying from the north, parallel to (but southeast of) Afghanistan's Kashmund range. That way, we wouldn't have to retrace our steps on the exfil. It is bad juju to walk where you've been—especially if a mean bunch of motherfuckers are hot on your tail, which was a distinct possibility.

As visible as the ground was—the topography clearly delineated; the details absolutely visible—it amazed me to know that no one standing on the ground could see us. We were invisible to the naked eye. Only radar would find us up here. That gave us the advantage.

I stood in the door and watched the setting sun turn the mountain range to purple and gold. It was absolutely serene. The world below looked totally peaceful. It would be so easy to forget why we were here, so easy to sit back and enjoy the ride.

But there are things you do not do at times like this, and that was one of them. You cannot stop and smell the roses. You cannot think about the battles to come. You cannot think about the lethal, devastating effects your weapons will have on the enemy. You cannot ponder the philosophical/moral/psychological consequences of your actions. Because if you do, you will lose your edge. That's one of the things about war movies that has always disturbed me—and one of the reasons I stay away from them. All that endless talk about war that goes on—the pseudometaphysical psychobabble that filmmakers insert—is something I don't allow in my units. I have never been reflective about making war, when I'm making war. The time for reflection is after you have achieved your mission; when the enemy is dead. Until then, you don't suck your thumb or wring your hands or do anything else that will detract from the efficacy of your mission.

The plane banked again and the horizon shifted. I could see more than fifty miles out. Being able to see that much of the world gave us an edge. And believe me, we were going to need every particle of edge that could be found.

Rocky let me know that we were at twenty-seven thousand feet, and on our way to 29.5. I gave the proper hand signals. We stood in a line and checked each other out: helmets, goggles, gloves, rigs, harnesses, O_2 bottles. We worked the straps of our rucksacks. No need to have all the ammo we were carrying pop out when we were jerked by the slipstream as we jumped, or the opening shock when we pulled the rip cord.

Less than two minutes to go. There was ice inside the plane now. I worked my way forward and stood behind Dick Campbell as he leveled off at our jump altitude. He turned and gave me a thumbs-up. I threw him the bird. I hoped he'd make it back to Peshawar—he was a good fucking egg, and he deserved to make it.

Forty-five seconds to exit point. I know, you're asking how we knew it was *the* exit point, when we hadn't thrown out any wind streamers to check the prevailing winds so we'd know how we'd parasail, or called down to the drop zone to pop a smoke in order to give us an idea what the surface winds were like to make our landing easier, or radioed the weather service for their computer readout for the region to see if there were any wind shears to pound us into the ground or thermals to carry us up and away to Tibet.

Well, when it comes to real-world HAHO parachute jumps, gentle reader, all that safety backup and assistance goes out the window. In the real world you fly by the seat of your pants. Your decisions are instinctive—based on audacity and experience, mixed (you hope) with a sprinkling of luck, and seasoned heavily with the kind of kick-ass determination that will let you grind it out and win even if everything turns into a clusterfuck.

I stood in the door, my heart pounding, probs and stats racing through my mind. I tapped the instrument package on my chest. Everything appeared functional. I'd taped the Magellan to my right arm. I could punch figures into it as we glided—an improvised homing device. If it worked, this would become the first SEAL instrument-guided insertion. If it didn't, they'd find our desiccated, broken bones somewhere high in the Kashmund mountain range in a year or two. Maybe.

I peered at my men. Looking into the eyes of these six marvelous creatures, I saw they were prepared for anything. Their expressions were a combination of resolve and anticipation. Nasty saluted me with his middle finger. Wonder did the same. Tommy gave me a double. Howie and Duck Foot did, too. Despite their helmets, O_2 masks, goggles, and the weight of their combat packs, they moved with incredible resilience toward the ramp. There was bounce in their step. The playfulness in their body language gave them an offbeat, zany appearance—something somewhere between a leprechaun and a Tasmanian devil.

It is at moments like this I know there is a God. I know there is, because He has put me on this earth so I can lead men like these into battle.

The Magellan GPS told me it was time to go. I checked the straps on my oxygen mask, gave everyone a thumbs-up (followed by the normal finger wave), then ran down the ramp and threw myself out the door.

Whaap! The ice-cold slipstream hit my body like a sucker punch and I twisted in the turbulence. I fought the current to roll faceup so I could see the C-123's ramp as it slipped away in the darkening sky above me. That way I could count as my men jumped. Yeah—one-two-three-four-five-six bodies away.

I rolled again and threw a hump; the plane disappeared over my left shoulder. I pulled the rip cord. Opening shock—there are few things so appropriately named—caught me by surprise. The harness trapped my left nut dead center in my crotch and put such a squeeze on it I thought I was being fondled by a feminist blacksmith. Oh, but it was a good hurt. If you're wondering how a hurt like that can be good, you have to look at things from my perspective: you see, if it hurt, my canopy must have opened.

Speaking of which, I looked up quickly to check my canopy. There were no cuts or tears—so much for worrywarting about seawater-rotted silk. That had been an unquestionable concern. See, if a shroud is improperly washed after a saltwater jump, residual salt crystals are left in the parachute silk. The problem: salt crystals are sharp enough to cut through parachute silk when the fabric is stressed to the max by opening shock. The result is that the chute develops hairline lacerations, which quickly develop into major fissures, which promptly turns into a major clusterfuck, because the chute disintegrates on you and you break into little pieces when you hit the ground.

But my chute was A-OK—she'd done her job. I double-checked my status—there's no being too sure in situations like this. Two cells on the right-hand side were a little slow in filling, but the rest of them were taut as an eighteen-year-old's nipple.

The huge dial of the altimeter on my left arm told me I was at 27,600 feet. That was close enough to where I wanted to be to make me relax for an instant or so. I took a quick look around me to count the other chutes. One-two-three-four-five canopies.

Shit.

I counted again and came up with the same number. Double shit.

I looked down. I could see a speck three or four thousand feet below me, trailing what looked like a long streamer. I cursed and screamed into my oxygen mask and told the stupid son of a bitch to cut away and pull his fucking reserve. Then I looked again and saw that he had cut away—and what was streaming behind him was his reserve. He was a goner.

One man down and we hadn't even begun. This was not a good omen. But I had no time for grief—I had to go to work. I pulled to the right and started to circle, so that the rest of the troops could form up. I wanted to start things off in an orderly manner. After all, we had no lights and it would be almost dark by the time we hit the ground. On training flights, we'd worn strobe lights on our helmets and harnesses so we'd be visible to each other. You can't do that in combat because you'll give your position away.

We formed up, I checked the compass, got a Magellan reading, and headed northwest. I could hear the throaty ruffling of canopies as I watched the men jockey into position. We were probably doing about eighty miles per hour. That may seem fast to you, but we were actually bucking headwinds. Once, in Arizona, when we were jumping out of Marana, the CIA's clandestine airfield outside Tucson, twenty-four SEAL Team Six HAHO jumpers were picked up on Tucson airport's radar as we glided in formation at twenty-six thousand feet. The air traffic controllers mistook us for a flight of A-10 Thunderbolts, the slow-flying Warthog tank killers of Gulf War fame. That—ha ha—should give you some idea of the speed you travel when you HAHO.

I turned into the wind and felt a bit of updraft. That was bad. One of the problems you face during a HAHO jump is weight distribution. We'd all jumped at the same time. But Tommy and Rodent weigh 75 pounds less than I do. My rate of fall, about seventeen feet per second, is more than theirs, about sixteen feet per second. The bottom line is that I have to fight for altitude, while they fight for descent.

The problem's compounded when you hit an updraft. When that happened, my weight would carry me through it, while Tommy and Rodent would get sucked upward. To compensate, they'd have to "dump" their canopies—a dangerous maneuver in which they'd pull down on their right-hand toggles, which would put them into a tight right turn. With a "flat" chute, all the air that's trapped in the cells then goes out the back, the chute goes almost vertical, and you lose altitude fast. The problem is that if you lose too much air, the cells will rub together, you'll develop a friction fissure, and it's au revoir, sayonara, doom on you—then *splaat*.

These sorts of vagaries are why I always trained in saturation blocks of at least fifty parachute jumps per ten-day training cycle. These jump marathons served two purposes. First, the men flew together enough to build the kind of unit integrity that allowed them to know instinctively what each was doing and react to it. Second, the sheer number of jumps built confidence for those shooters—like Stevie Wonder and Howie Kaluha—who have always believed there is no good reason to throw themselves out of a perfectly good aircraft.

I eyeballed the altimeter. We were at sixteen thousand feet now—ten to eleven thousand feet above the Kashmund peaks below, and a little more above the valleys and high plateau. That gave me a glide time of ten to thirteen minutes if I could stretch things. I punched the Magellan's computer. We were twenty-three kilometers from target—just over fourteen miles. From experience, I knew that unless I caught an updraft, we'd come down in nine or ten miles, which meant a long walk in the dark.

I hung in the harness, depressed, and thought of all the other things that could go wrong. The list was very, very long. Finally, after what seemed like a half an hour but was probably about four minutes, the flutter of the canopy went up an octave or so in tone. Simultaneously, the pressure on my sore left ball told me there was a little additional lift in my harness. I checked the altimeter, then started my stopwatch. I was actually climbing. Climbing ever so slowly, but climbing nonetheless.

Had the rest of my crew caught the change and compensated? I craned my neck to see. I glimpsed three other canopies keeping pace with me. Good. A quick peek at the digital stopwatch told me I'd climbed roughly one hundred feet in two minutes. That translated to fifty feet per minute, versus my previous seventeen-foot-per-second fall rate, an altogether fair exchange.

Under normal circumstances I would have sat back and enjoyed the ride. But here there was too much to think about—specifically, who had burned in. Was it Wonder? He hated jumping, but he was a careful jumper. Nasty had once taken a Humpty-Dumpty fall during a HAHO exercise. And it took all of the king's horses and all of the king's men (not to mention his best neurosurgeons) to put him together again. Tommy T was a great jumper—a natural who loved throwing himself out of planes. So was Duck Foot. Howie Kaluha had made more than one hundred jumps from 25K plus. And Rodent had been on the Navy's parachute team. Of course, none of those quals meant shit during combat jumps. But it gave everybody an edge—or it should. Of course, there's always Mr. Murphy around to play havoc with events. Not to mention the Eighth Commandment of SpecWar: Thou shalt never assume. Damn it.

My reverie was interrupted by the sound of my canopy, which ruffled, popped, and broke into a steady whistle. To anyone who's spent any time jumping, those sounds translate as "the elevator's going *dowwwwn*, Señor Marcinko."

The altimeter had me at 9,800 feet. But we'd crested the mountain ridge, we were over rock-strewn foothills—and we were headed in the right direction. With a little more luck we'd wring three more miles out of this ride. I scanned the horizon and saw intermittent flickering out there. Were they villages or camps? Who knew. We'd find out soon enough.

Landing was as balls-to-the-wall as takeoff. I didn't flare, went straight in, and was dragged face first across one hundred yards of Afghanistani desert. My altimeter was mangled, my nose scraped raw, and the AK I'd carefully slung across my chest butt-stroked me on the right knee—hard. Other than that, my landing was picture perfect. The way I look at it, any jump you walk away from is a good jump.

I watched as the others came down. Nasty flew in next—flaring nicely and touching down as evenly as if he'd been riding an elevator. Then Wonder landed, teeth clenched. He was sweating. Then Rodent. He dumped air at fifteen hundred feet, circled twice hard right, then flew straight, flared, pulled up, cut away at two feet, and let his chute land by itself. Fucking show-off. Two more to go. They landed a football field away. I went puffing to see who'd made it and found Tommy and Duck Foot balling their canopies.

It had been Howie Kaluha who'd burned in. The big Hawaiian had now been added to the list of SEALs standing their eternal watch in heaven, waiting for the recall to muster for the ultimate war.

We buried out chutes expeditiously—enough to hide them but not as deep or completely as we might have. My feeling was that even if they were discovered, we'd be long gone. No one knew what had happened to Howie. It could have been the chute—sea-rotted silk—or tangled risers. It could have been a fissure. It could have been contaminated oxygen in his O_2 bottle. Fuck—it could have been anything. There was no time to dwell on it—we had to push on. We took inventory. We were missing Howie's load: half a pound of plastic, three grenades, ten AK magazines, two detonators, and a pair of Dick Campbell's gold coins. We'd have to live without them—and Howie, too.

We sorted our clothes and changed into lighter gear. It was cold in these foothills—high thirties from the feel of it—but we'd be moving and sweating under the weight of our combat packs, so we unlayered ourselves. We were each carrying close to one hundred pounds. AK ammo is almost twice as heavy as M16 ammo—but we each humped ten of the forty-round magazines. Then there were our sixteen-round Glocks—plus three extra mags apiece. We also carried three canteens of water each. You can go almost a week without food, but not more than a day without water, especially when you're sweating. I knew we'd find water in the tango camp, but I wasn't about to take any chances. I also had a pair of pocket waterproof binoculars, as well as extra batteries for the Magellan and the burst transmitters—there were no drugstores out here.

We carried no rations. I learned in Vietnam it's easier to live off the land, and we'd do so here, too. But we had our grenades, plastic explosives, and other lethal goodies. Each man had somehow managed to bring a piece or two of his own personal kit as well. Nasty and Duck Foot had their Field Fighter knives—fifteen inches of deadly steel designed by master knife fighter and survivalist expert Bob Spear of Leavenworth, Kansas. Wonder carried his keep-it-simple-stupid Ka-Bar. Rodent had his lucky U.S. Divers knife. Tommy carried a leather-covered sap in his sock, and a Mad Dog SWAT knife in his boot. And me? I was happy my Emerson CQC6 folder hadn't gotten lost yet.

The Magellan had also survived my sloppy landing, and I squinted to read the screen. The little green numbers told me we were just over five klicks southeast of our target. The good news was that the march would be to the west—downhill. The bad news was that once we staged our hit, we'd be climbing back up the fucking mountain range to scramble eastward, ho, across the border back into the relative safety—and let me stress the word *relative*—of Pakistan.

I jotted down the compass headings, then put Nasty and Wonder on point. Nasty was the pathfinder; Wonder held the thermal-imaging range finder Mick Owen had given me. Just behind him, Tommy carried the Magellan—he'd keep Nasty and Wonder pointed in the right direction. Duck Foot was rear security. Rodent and I took port and starboard watch. Weapons locked and loaded, we moved out.

We walked silently, each man intent on carrying out his assignment. Howie Kaluha was not part of the equation anymore. That may sound callous to you. It's not meant to be. He would have understood—in fact, he would have performed in the same way, if it had been one of us who'd taken the twenty-nine-thousand-foot plunge. It's not that we didn't care about Howie. We did. But when you're in combat, you can't brood about what's happened. You must remain sharp, focused, obsessive about your mission, otherwise you will fail. I knew that Howie's death would always stay with me. Later, there would be time to mourn him. Now, the best way to avenge his death was to succeed in taking down Lord B and his tangos.

It was past twenty hundred now, and dark. I made my way forward past Wonder and asked Nasty if he wanted to be relieved.

His eyes never stopped examining the ground ahead. "Nope."

"Just let me know."

"Roger that, Skipper."

I knew he'd never willingly be relieved. Nasty's the kind of shooter who gets bored if he's not being challenged. Put him in the back of the pack and he stumbles over his size 13s. Set him on point, and he's a walking bundle of nerve endings. Nothing gets past him.

I let him edge ahead and slipped back into the middle of the group. Six minutes later, Nasty's hand went up. I went forward to see what he wanted.

Nasty looked like a good hunting dog—his ears were back, the hair on his neck was standing straight up, and his right index finger was indicating a spot on the ground some two yards in front of him. I peered intently. The news was not good. How the fuck he'd seen it was beyond me. But that's what makes the great point men great—their ability to concentrate, to lock out everything but the ground ahead of them. There it was—the nasty top of a Soviet dragon-tooth land mine. These are similar to our BLU-43B antipersonnel mines or British Elsies. The Soviets had seeded hundreds of thousands of these and other various mines all over Afghanistan. They were sown indiscriminately—fired from projectors on helicopters and armored vehicles, shot out of howitzers, and dropped from planes. There were so many of them scattered that the Soviets often hadn't even bothered to conceal them—they knew the inhospitable terrain would take care of that after a couple of months.

I watched as Nasty made his way up to the mine and dug around it with his Field Fighter. He uncovered the little bugger and then retreated carefully the way he'd come. These were particularly nasty explosive devices. They were irregularly shaped and slightly bigger than golf balls—just nasty enough to take off a foot at the ankle. Shit. I didn't need this kind of problem tonight.

We'd have to make a detour—although I had no idea how far the fucking minefield extended. I wasn't even sure whether or not we'd already strayed into the goddamn minefield. The only thing to do was backtrack at least one klick, then work our way around in a big arc—adding perhaps five to ten miles to our trek. The schedule I'd carefully calculated was now OBE—in other words, Overtaken By Events—and we were clusterfucked.

I backed off, gave hand signals to tell the men what had happened, and we all retreated very, very carefully, retracing our footsteps as best we could. Six hundred yards back, I bursted Mick Owen to make sure the BA-PP3/I hadn't been shifted on us—I didn't need more bad news. We waited until he came back on line to tell me the canisters hadn't been moved. Then I took the Magellan and punched new coordinates into the keyboard, noted the changes, and showed them to Nasty. He gave me a thumbs-up, then set out moving to the north.

We moved even more slowly than we had because everyone was now paranoid about mines. Moreover, visibility was hampered because there was no moon. At least *that* dark cloud had a silver lining: the landscape we were walking over was positively lunar, completely lacking in cover. There was no vegetation, no rock formations, absolutely nothing to give us shelter. If we'd been patrolling by moonlight, we'd have resembled the human silhouette targets I'd used when training SEAL Team Six for night missions. We might as well have had big bull's-eyes painted on our black coveralls.

I looked at my watch: 0125. I checked Magellan. We were miles off course and hours behind schedule. Situation normal—all fucked up.

Chapter

19

It was 0420 when an exhausted Stevie Wonder finally silent-signaled me forward with the arm pump that translated as "enemy ahead."

I crept to his position and peered through the range finder. There they were—250 yards away, according to the digital readout. I'd expected tents—you know, like bedouins in Arabia. What I got was houses—you know, like Muslims in Afghanistan. It was a real kick in the balls reality check and a reminder of what happens to you when you're not on the receiving end of good intel (or, as was the case here, any intel).

Village was an overstatement. What we had here was the remains of a small village—a warren of perhaps a dozen sun-dried brick huts, some of them visibly decimated by gunfire, others shuttered and boarded up with scrap lumber and other detritus. It looked like any other poor Fourth World village from Asayut to Islamkot—the houses stood cheek by jowl along a single rutted street. There was a small square at the head of the street. On the square stood the twenty-foot minaret of a one-story mosque. The tower had been cut in half by a shell, and the mosque's roof had pancaked in. No one was going to kneel in prayer there anymore.

Behind and slightly below the houses lay a slender, winding

stream that probably served as the town's drinking water, outdoor laundry, and main sewer. The stub of a burnt-out tree was silhouetted incongruously in front of the closest house—maybe that had been the village chief's home. Six utility vehicles were parked randomly in the dirt—whether they were Toyotas or Land Rovers I couldn't tell in the darkness. But I was buoyed by their presence—at least we'd have some way to haul our butts out of this place when we'd finished our work here.

About fifty yards past the village was the rusting skeleton of a T-72 Soviet battle tank, minus turret and gun. I could make out two other hulks in the darkness. Obviously, there had been a battle here once. Whether it had been versus the Soviets or the current Afghan government was impossible to tell.

I cursed Mr. Murphy silently. Doom on Dickie for narrow thinking. I'd assumed we'd be going against tents. Tents are simple. You run a thermal imager over 'em, see which ones are occupied, then hit quick and dirty.

Huts are hard. Thermal doesn't penetrate six or eight inches of sun-dried brick. So you have to go door-to-door like a fucking vacuum-cleaner salesman. *Knock knock. Anybody home? Yes, you say? Okay—then die, motherfucker.*

We had to work fast. It would be light in less than two hours. When I'd planned this little jaunt, I'd timed our assault for 0400, the best time because that's when people are sleeping deepest. But because of the minefield and our consequential circumnavigation (now there are a couple of $20 words), it was 0430, and the earliest we'd be able to hit these tangos would be in the 0500 range—which is when light sleepers (like me) tend to get up for their predawn piss.

And we couldn't just go shooting and looting by the seats of our pants, blasting away at everything in sight. There are certain formalities that would have to be observed first.

Like what? you ask. Like reconnaissance, I say. After all, without reconnaissance, we'd be going in blind—and shooting holes in canisters of BA-PP3/I is something I didn't need right now.

In fact, to give you some idea why I have a few strands of gray in my hair and beard, let me lead you through a few of the scores of questions running through my mind at 0432 as I stared through my range finder at the huts 250 yards away.

- There were a dozen-plus houses in the village. Were they all occupied? Yes? No? If not, which ones were? How many tangos were there, anyway?
- Where were Lord B and Todd Stewart? Could we take them alive?
- Where were the six containers of anthrax/plague we'd come for? Were they being guarded?
- What kind of weapons were we going up against? Was there a sniper post in the tank shell?
- Had the bad guys scattered land mines or put out any other sort of perimeter defenses?

Are you getting the picture yet? You are? Good.

Questions like the ones above are why recon is so basic even the Bible teaches it. So, just as Joshua—a greatly underappreciated SpecWarrior, I might add—had done before he fit de battle of Jericho, I, too, sent out two spies secretly and said, "Go view the land and give me a sitrep."

And verily, Tommy and Duck Foot sneakethed and peekethed inside the village and returnethed safely unto my bosom to give me a status report. (Unfortunately for them, they didn't find anything similar to the harlot Rahab's house here in good old Afghanistan. Well, that's fundamental Islam for you—very little sense of humor, no Bombay, and distinct lack of pussy. And you ask why the motherfuckers *deserve* eradication.)

Anyway, when they came back to tell me what they'd discovered, they said they'd swept around back and come up the stream, moving through the village like the proverbial shit through the proverbial goose.

Sitrep? They'd found a pile of opium in the biggest of the huts—scores of burlap bags filled with brown stuff waiting for pickup. That made sense—opium is how much of this jihad was being financed.

They'd discovered the vehicles were gassed up and ready to go—auxiliary tanks filled to the brim and strapped down, and jerry cans of water stowed behind the rear seats. Conclusion: now that the tangos had their biological warfare goodies, they were going to move out.

They'd found an improvised shooting range beyond the stream, directly behind the flattened mosque—silhouette targets lying around and lots of 9mm and 7.62 shell casings on the ground. Weapons we'd be facing, then, included AKs and 9mm submachine guns and semiauto pistols. No probs there.

Occupied houses? At least four—maybe six, according to Duck Foot. They hadn't wanted to risk compromise by going inside. But from the scuff marks in doorways and general signs of foot traffic, they'd guesstimated four to six houses.

Numbers inside? No way of telling. Twenty to thirty from the tracks.

And Lord B? Todd Stewart? "No can say, boss."

It occurred to me that neither might be in the village. But what about the satellite—it had tracked the canisters here. Well, I'd assumed (assuming is bad juju, Marcinko) that Lord B would travel with the canisters.

Yeah? Well, who wrote those rules? Certainly not *moi.* The consolation was that we knew the BA-PP3/I, which I'd renamed BWR (pronounced beware, and standing for Biological Warfare Rat-shit), was somewhere in the village.

Also on the positive side, Tommy was happy to report that there were no sentries, booby traps, land mines, barbed wire, or other defensive elements set out. "The place is wide open, Skipper."

That made sense. This place was so far inside enemy territory, so out of the way and obviously inaccessible, that very little thought had been given to defense. Remember the Brooklyn cop? "A poip is a poip is a poip." It had been like this in Libya, too. Muammar baby had been so sure of himself that he'd set up many of his tango training camps with virtually no security measures at all. He was convinced, for example, that no military force could make it unobserved four hundred miles south of the Sidra Gulf to the camp twenty klicks outside Bi'r al Ma'ruf where IRA snipers trained alongside renegade Israelis, CIA turncoats, North Koreans, and Lebanese.

Of course, Muammar baby didn't know about Red Cell. It only took six of us. In December 1985, we went off the back steps of an Egyptair 727 at thirty-five thousand feet, parasailed thirty miles, walked another ten, then made hamburger out of sixteen of his best-paid assassins as they slept in their beddy-byes. We exfiltrated in the tangos' Libyan Army vehicles, running due east 342 miles in eight hours, right across the Egyptian border, before Tripoli had any idea something was amiss. Well, there were six of us tonight, too.

Three—Wonder, Rodent, and me—were veterans of the Libyan action.

0509. Time to go. The best way to do this deed was quick and dirty, keep-it-simple-stupid direct. Thus, the scenario was writ as follows: we'd move in, then we'd kill as many as we could before they realized what was happening. With luck, we wouldn't blow up the canisters of BA-PP3/I while blowing up the malefactors. That way, we'd stay alive and healthy.

I scratched the basic blueprint for the assault in the dirt and made assignments. We'd hit the houses Tommy and Duck Foot had marked as probables first, then work our way through the rest of them. We'd move in pairs, each with responsibility for a fire field of roughly sixty degrees. That was important. I didn't want us shooting at each other in the darkness, and because we weren't carrying walkie-talkies, we'd actually have very little idea where we were from second to second.

And we'd have to be quick. That's another Murphy factor. You want an ambush like this to be finished in a span of minutes. No prolonged firefights, no drawn-out assaults, no barricade situations. It's got to be wham, bam, slam—and it's over. Because if it isn't, you're in trouble because you're probably already outflanked, outgunned, and outnumbered.

We had another basic problem here. Four to six huts with probables, three pairs of swim buddies. That meant each pair got 1.33 huts at a minimum. Right.

Three of the probables sat next to each other at the head of the dirt street. They'd been hit by previous gunfire and lacked windows and doors. One of 'em had a gaping shell hole in the middle of the wall. All had been peppered with small-arms fire. The fourth hovel was slightly separated from the others. It had shutters and a door. I gave myself the dirty job of taking it on alone.

Wonder volunteered for the one at the foot of the street. That was fine by me. Wonder's always preferred to work solo. I asked him why once. He smiled that goofy Howdy Doody smile of his from behind his mirrored-lens shooting glasses and said slyly, "No witnesses."

The remaining two pairs of huts would be covered by Tommy and Duck Foot, and Nasty and Rodent, who would sweep through one then hit the other. Then we'd leapfrog house to house. The clearing method would be the same: toss a grenade in, then follow. I knew

the men wouldn't waste ammo, either. First, they had fire discipline. Second, as I tactfully explained, you never want to get caught
holding your dick in your hand in a village full of hostiles.

The morning's strategics and mathematics solved, we started our
wrist timers, split up, and crept toward our targets. I crabbed slowly,
finding what cover I could as I advanced. It's always the final 25
yards or so that are the most difficult. You're moving so deliberately,
so painstakingly, that it feels as if you're moving mere inches at a
time—which is exactly what you are doing. Moreover, you feel
totally exposed. It's a sensation of complete vulnerability—as if
spotlights were bathing you in brightness. Every sound is magnified
tenfold. Every scratch of boot on gravel, every breath, every
heartbeat, is amplified in your mind to boom-box proportions.

I wormed my way the last fifteen yards and settled myself under a
window over which a battered wood shutter was attached by what
looked like baling wire. I lay on my side, stuffed my ears with a pair
of disposable foam plugs, adjusted my goggles, then reached up
onto my vest and extracted a flash-bang device the size of a 16-oz.
beer can. I pulled the pin but held the spoon securely. These
flash-bangs had four-second fuses. I checked the countdown readout on my digital watch. We'd all set our timers at four minutes
before moving out—and there were fifty-two seconds remaining.

As the timer read eight, seven, six, I let the spoon fly over my
shoulder. At five I yanked at the shutter so I could heave the
grenade inside. The shutter was attached solidly. I yanked again.
Nothing. The goddamn thing was bolted in place, and the flash
bang was about to flash and bang in a big way.

I threw the fucking thing back the way I'd just come. It went off in
midair fifteen yards away. Even though I'd hunkered, the two
million candlepower flash still worked its magic on my retinas.

Spots before my eyes, I rushed the door. I was so goddamn mad
now that even if the fucking thing had been secured by steel bars, I
would have gone through it. I hit it with my foot and the wood
splintered.

I was inside—there was movement to my left. Two of them. It
was time for target acquisition—which meant getting the one with
the pistol pointed vaguely in my direction first. Except I couldn't
really see him—I was still seeing spots. I squeezed a burst and cut
him in half. Lucky me. The AK's muzzle rose, dammit—fucking
AKs always go up and right—and I had to force it down and left to

273

RICHARD MARCINKO and JOHN WEISMAN

hose tango two. At least I had peripheral vision—I sensed someone to my right. Another tango—he had an AK. Sick and tired of ducking my own ricochets, I kneeled and fired. The impact caught him in the chest and he staggered backward, into the room from which he'd come.

I followed, firing into the doorway to keep him away. Into the room. The tango was on his back and I put a burst into him to keep him that way. Two rounds went into his body—and then I heard an ominous click.

The sound of the firing pin falling on an empty chamber after the coup de grâce told me I was out of ammo. Doom on me—because tango number four over there on the far side of the room was leisurely reaching for his own weapon while I fumbled with my magazine release, groped for a full mag, and tried to shove it up into the housing, then ratchet the charging handle back and chamber a round—all in the space of a second or two.

He was just sitting on the edge of his bed as if he hadn't got a fucking care in the world—a huge man with curly blond hair wearing a bright blue thermal sweatshirt and ski underwear. Looked like a fucking Kraut, he did. Whoever he was, he was a pro. The expression on his face told me he knew exactly what was happening. His eyes never left me as I floundered with the AK. He reached up toward his weapon, a submachine gun, hanging from a peg by his cot, a slight smile on his thin lips.

It was all happening in slow motion. The muzzle was pointed at the ceiling. Ev Barrett's voice was in my ears. *Do not be a fumblefingers, Seaman Marcinko, you shit-for-brains geek asshole.*

His long, muscular left arm reached up. His hand grasped the pistol stock. *Take the fucking magazine and shove it into the fucking receiver.*

I was not ready. *You are not listening to my instructions, Seaman Marcinko. Your clumsy fingers are not working properly because you cannot control them if you persist in hyperventilating. Your weapon is empty and therefore worthless.*

The gun came down, down, down. Its muzzle swung toward me as he fired one-handed. *Seaman Marcinko, you had best seek an alternative method to do this cocksucker in, or you will soon be dead meat.*

The first shots of the burst hosed the wall six feet from my head, spraying me with brick fragments. He paused long enough to bring his right hand onto the gun to steady it.

Fuck. Talk about dogs that won't hunt—this AK wasn't gonna load. What did I need, a fucking memo from the chief of staff to tell me that? I dropped the assault rifle and rolled to my right, away from the sweep of his gun and the deadly swath of rounds.

I ripped the Glock out of its holster with my right hand and came up shooting. Talk about bad form—I hit him in the toe, the knee, the groin, the right elbow, and the neck. But he went down, still squeezing the trigger as he did, cutting a chewy pattern into the ceiling tile.

I know, I know—where's all that bull's-eye stress shooting you're always talking about? you ask.

Listen, bub—the object is to shoot 'em dead. Form and neatness don't count here. The motherfucker was *down*. I put a round into his head to make sure he stayed where he was. I checked myself for bumps and bruises—the back of my neck had been cut by something sharp—retrieved the AK, and shoved another magazine into it (without, of course, so much as a whisper of a problem), checked the hut to make sure I'd finished them all, then moved on.

I hauled ass fifty feet down the street and linked up with Wonder, who reported that he'd taken out six tangos with no problem. Of course, *his* fucking flash-bang had gone where he'd tossed it. We moved slowly back up 150 feet of mud street, keeping close to the buildings in the early-morning half-light, our weapons ready.

A sense of déjà vu came over me. I was back in Chau Doc on the first morning of the Tet Offensive with Eighth Platoon from SEAL Team Two, rooting VC out of the city, street-to-street and door-to-door with my asshole buddy Mike Regan protecting my six.

Stevie slid in front of me and took point. A shadow moved. He fired from the hip, bringing it down. Bullets sprayed the wall behind us. I saw muzzle flash from the burnt-out T-72 and sprayed the tank skeleton. Wonder pulled the pin on a willy peter. I watched the spoon *spronng,* and then he tossed it—a great baseball pitch that went fifty yards smack-dab on target just behind the tank.

It exploded in a huge white fireball. There were simultaneous screams. A burning figure silhouetted against the sky, then collapsed. Another tango down. I gave Wonder's shoulder a slam, and we advanced cautiously.

Something ahead of me moved. I squeezed the AK's trigger and brought it down. The whole village was in complete chaos now—explosions, smoke, flames, and choppy bursts of automatic-weapons fire were everywhere. It was like being back in Vietnam, before the days of lip mikes, earpieces, and miniradios. We'd worked out the areas of responsibility and the fields of fire. So whatever crossed our sights was going to be presumed hostile. If it moved, we'd obliterate it.

That's the way it has to be when you go in at four- or five- or six-to-one odds. As that great American patriot and balls-to-the-wall warrior Colonel Charlie Beckwith put it about the time he led Delta Force on the Tehran rescue mission, "You kill them all and let God sort it out."

Within minutes, it was over. Quickly, we went back over the bodies, making sure that none of the tangos were playing possum. Each got a bullet in the head—that was *our* insurance.

We formed up sweaty, dirty, and bloody in front of the ruined mosque and hunkered on the ground, totally exhausted. Frankly, we'd come away better than I'd expected. Tommy'd been nicked in the thigh. Bullet went clean through without hitting bone, but he was going to be one sore puppy if he tried to run any marathons in the next few days. He'd already popped himself with morphine and penicillin and was feeling neither pain nor gain. Nasty's left earlobe had been shot away. No more earrings for him. He was bleeding like a motherfucker, though—worse than Tommy T. By the time we got the blood stopped, his ear was wrapped in so many layers of bandage it looked like a small cauliflower.

Aside from those two, we were in good shape—if you didn't count the stress, dehydration, bumps, lumps, contusions, battle deafness (you think firing all those rounds doesn't affect your hearing? Huh, huh, huh—what are you saying?), and other normal wear-and-tear items.

I bursted Mick to let him know we'd hit our target, and I'd report on what we found ASAP. Then we went through the camp with the proverbial fine-tooth comb, sorting things out.

The thorough search of the village brought me to the conclusion that Lord Brookfield and Todd Stewart were not among the bodies, nor were they hiding anywhere. Well, at least the world was now home to thirty-two fewer tangos than it had been a few short minutes ago. They weren't all Islamic fundamentalists, either. We confirmed our suspicions when we examined the collection of papers, passports, and other documents we gathered from the huts and corpses. Most of those we'd killed were from Islamic countries.

There were five Egyptians, four Moroccans, four Algerians, one Saudi, even a Yemenite (you know what they say about *them*— every day a holiday, every night a Yemenite).

But there was unmistakable evidence of CNO's transnational-terrorism theory, too. We'd slam-dunked four Germans, a pair of Frenchmen, half a dozen Russians, a trio of Italians, and—most unsettling to me—a pair of Americans whose New Jersey driver's licenses showed Newark addresses. I made a mental note to pass their names on to Tony Mercaldi at DIA—when, that is, I could talk to Merc without getting myself arrested. Detailed inspections of the quarters where the Americans had been housed and the garbage dump revealed further bad news: evidence of three or four other Americans.

Why did I think they were Americans? Well, friends, when you use toiletries that have been made in the good old you ess of A, and you leave behind house-brand double-A batteries that come from a supermarket chain headquartered just outside Washington, D.C., and your empty prescription vial lists a pharmacy in Gaithersburg, Maryland, then I say you're either an American or you're living in America or you're leaving a very well thought-out false trail. If I'd discovered everything in the hooch, I'd have gone for the false-trail theory. But because the garbage was buried and layered, just as archaeologists discover garbage from ancient Rome or Greece, I tended to believe that it was real, and that a quartet of Americans had recently departed the camp—probably with Brookfield.

Something else had departed the camp as well: there were only five canisters of BWR. One had already started on its deadly odyssey. But where? With the Americans? With Brookfield? There was no way to know.

I went through the camp again. It was like all the other tango training camps I'd seen in Libya, Lebanon, and Sudan—bare essentials and a lot of ammunition, all tucked away in a remote, inhospitable location. Given Lord B's resources, why the hell couldn't he have found a better place? The answer, of course, was because out here in the middle of the Afghan wilderness, no one would bother him and his men as they trained. Here, he was protected by the mullahs.

I hunkered down outside one of the huts and fingered a few of the documents we'd captured. We'd been lucky to have hit them when we had. All the tangos had air tickets and travel documents.

Obviously, they'd been waiting for Lord B and his six deadly care packages to arrive. Then—according to the paperwork we'd found —each team would head in a different direction.

The Germans had been on their way to Bonn within hours. In their baggage were detailed maps of government buildings, with the security positions marked in red pencil, as well as stakeout studies, showing the schedules of guards and police patrols. They even carried a small notebook in which had been written their list of demands. Tommy translated. Among other things, they were going to call for the creation of a fundamentalist Muslim enclave in Germany. I checked the Egyptians' papers. They were from Cairo. Their passports had Pakistani visas, just as Mahmoud Azziz's had.

Was this the very camp Azziz had been heading for when we'd snatched him in Cairo? God, the Cairo op seemed years ago—in reality it had been mere weeks. Could the world have changed that much since? It was altogether possible. The world, after all, is strange. The world, after all, is fucked up.

The Egyptians were packing a hand-drawn map. Their notes were in Arabic, but the target they were after was obviously a big government complex somewhere in Cairo. They, too, had written demands, which Duck Foot was able to read—the resignation of the Egyptian president and the creation of a fundamentalist republic. I continued checking papers. Everybody was carrying maps, diagrams, and demands. The Russians were off to Moscow. The Moroccans were heading for Fez. The Frenchies and Italians were on their way to Geneva—they were carrying maps of the U.N. complex.

You may consider all this concrete, written evidence foolish on the tangos' part—a mere fictional device we're using to keep the plot working. Well, friends, I've been there, and I can tell you in no uncertain terms that terrorists tend to keep very complete records of what they do.

Why did the anarchist who threw the bomb that killed Archduke Ferdinand in Sarajevo back in 1914 keep a diary? Why did Mao Zedong keep notes and journals on his Long March more than half a century ago? Why did the PLO have more than two tons of paperwork—memos, phone messages, receipts, even doodles— detailing terrorist actions stored safely in bunkers in West Beirut back in 1982?

Why? Who knows why. All I can say is that, from the FMLN in El

Salvador to the Tamil Tigers, from the Democratic Front for the Liberation of Palestine to the Red Brigades, tangos write down everything they do.

Maybe it provides them a feeling of immortality. Maybe it validates their actions. I'm no psychiatrist, so I can't say.

What I do know is that because they put things on paper, my own work becomes easier. I can learn what tangos are thinking. I can peer inside their hearts and minds to find a pattern that I can use against them.

I contacted Mick just after 0750, to transmit a list of names off the passports we'd gathered, as well as other information that confirmed my initial suspicions about the camp's purpose. I told him we'd captured five canisters of BWR, but one was still at large, as was Lord B.

Brookfield, Mick radioed, was back in the U.K. He'd arrived a few hours ago, with five companions.

I did a little mental calculating. Lord B was flying a Gulfstream IIIA with auxiliary gas tanks. That gave it a 5,800-mile range. I knew that from firsthand experience. After all, Red Cell had flown Matsuko Machine's Gulfstream back to the States after we'd taken out Hideo Ikigami and recovered the Navy's stolen Tomahawk missiles, all of which you should remember from *Rogue Warrior: Red Cell.*

I punched numbers into the Magellan keyboard and watched as the display came up. The Gulfstream IIIA cruises at 550 miles per hour. According to Magellan, the air routing from Kabul to London was a mere 4,352 miles. Even my slow Slovak mind could do the mental calculation: seven and a half hours flying time—let's say eight and a half in case of headwinds.

It was 0825 now. We'd been on the ground since 1945 last night—more than twelve hours. Shit—that gave Brookfield more than enough time to fly home. It wasn't inconceivable that he'd been tucked in his beddy-bye in Hampstead while we'd been conducting our recon of this godforsaken place at 0-dark-hundred.

That brought me up short. Then Brookfield's plan became clear—he'd taken the missing Americans with him, and they were planning to attack the U.S. embassy in London. Evidence in hand? None. Gut instinct? Absolute. Had to be. I bursted Mick. I told him that Brookfield was planning to attack the American embassy and that Mick had to get the word out and take preventive action immediately. I could almost hear the "gulp" on the other end when I finished my transmission. But he gave me a "Roger, roger," and then the radio went dead.

He'd be a busy bugger over the next few hours—but then, so would I.

My plans made, I set Rodent, Duck Foot, and Wonder to work. We rigged the bodies with explosives and grenades, setting a series of ingenious booby traps and IEDs just in case anyone got nosy.

When those were done, the six of us dug a fifteen-by-twenty foot pit, nine feet deep. We used whatever scrap we could find to line the sides and bottom. We carefully laid the canisters of BA-PP3/I right in the center. Then we schlepped bags of opium from their hut and piled them atop the BWR. We found a beat-up pallet and used it to tamp the whole thing as best we could.

While they dug, I formed all the remaining plastique into one huge piece of putty, which I crammed inside a 110mm shell casing I found near the T-72, thus making what we old Frogs in the Teams used to call a shaped charge. See, by shaping the charge, the explosive force of the C-4 becomes very, very focused. In fact, according to a completely unclassified portion of the current U.S. Navy operations manual, what I was doing would give the C-4 a 60 percent "kick" in potency—similar in power to the shaped charges we'd been supplied at SEAL Team Two to destroy nuclear weapons.

I wanted a powerful explosion—something that would destroy the whole town with its concussion and also vaporize the cans of BWR. The deadly anthrax would be scattered over a hundred square miles of northwestern Afghanistan. But not for some days, if things went according to my design.

When I'd finished stuffing and tamping, Nasty and Wonder inserted a pair of electronic detonators into the neck of the shell casing. Tommy, who'd been playing with the radio, attached an improvised remote-control firing device. We ran the antenna up to the surface, strung it along the ground, and ran it up the mosque's minaret. Then we filled the pit in again.

We'd be leaving now. We packed our gear, loaded all the tango paperwork into sacks, and clambered aboard a trio of Toyota Land Cruisers. Exfiltration would be reasonably simple. We'd move south down the ravine, following the stream to the Jalalabad-Asadabad highway, then swing north to Sarkani—about twenty-five klicks. At Sarkani, we'd veer south before we reached the town proper, then link up with a gravel road that crossed the Pakistani border at a lightly manned checkpoint. We'd have no problems— and if we did, we were carrying enough firepower to decimate an entire company.

From the border, we'd go through the Nawagi Pass and slip down into Peshawar. From there—we'd improvise.

There was a small rise three klicks south of the camp. I held up my hand and our vehicles stopped just long enough for me to set the electronic detonator to ninety-six hours and turn the switch to ON.

I jumped down and made my way up a small rise one hundred yards from the road and concealed the transmitter behind an outcropping of small rocks.

I wiped the dust from my hands, returned to the vehicle, jumped in behind the wheel, and gunned the Land Cruiser's engine. It was time to move.

Chapter

20

SEVENTY-SOMETHING HOURS AFTER WE CROSSED THE PAKISTANI BOR-
der we hauled ourselves over the barbed-wire fence of the FAMFUC
into Mick Owen's waiting arms. How did we do it? you ask. How
did six wanted men travel halfway around the world without
getting caught? The answer, my friends, is depressingly simple. We
did it the same way terrorists do it.

In the Third and Fourth World, you can buy your way across
borders—and besides, nobody really cares, just so long as you have
lots of things stamped in your passport for them to examine. In fact,
Marcinko's First Law of Travel states that the more backward the
society, the more stamps they'll put in your passport.

In Europe, there are no borders anymore. It's easy to go from city
to city, country to country. There are no thorough passport checks,
no visas or travel permits necessary. Society is open. That makes it
easy to move—for good guys and for bad guys as well.

But the system, you say. All those computers. All those modern
identification methods—what about them?

Well, gentle reader, all the computers and all the sophisticated
systems in the world are only as good as the people working them.
And when the people working them don't pay attention, shit
happens.

You want an example of such a clusterfuck? Okay. Remember when a couple of F-15s shot down a pair of NATO Blackhawk choppers in northern Iraq a few years back? Despite the fact that there was an AWACs plane flying overhead, and that everyone supposedly knew the IFF—Identification Friend/Foe—signals, the F-15s smoked the Blackhawks. That's the perfect example of shit happening, of things falling through the cracks because attention isn't being paid to detail (either that or it was a case of cold-blooded murder).

But Iraq was a military operation you say, and military operations are always subject to Murphy's Law. Okay, take Sheikh Omar Abdel-Rahman—please. If the name doesn't ring a bell, he's the blind Egyptian fundamentalist cleric who was charged as the mastermind behind the bombing of New York's World Trade Center.

Consider this: even though Rahman was listed by the Department of State as a terrorist suspect, he got a U.S. entry visa when he applied for one.

How'd he do that? Simple. Instead of applying in Cairo, Paris, Rome, or London, where all visa applications are checked on a computer database, Rahman traveled to Khartoum, Sudan. Sudan may be one of the main centers of world terrorism according to most of the world's intelligence agencies. But obviously, it's not a place where the State Department was concerned about terrorism. How do I know that? Because the agency hadn't bothered to install the antiterrorism computer database there.

Bottom line? The consul went through a months-old loose-leaf book and looked for Rahman's moniker—which wasn't there—checked his name with the resident Christian in Action gumshoe, who didn't see anything amiss, and then stamped his visa U.S. Government Approved.

No prob, Sheikh Omar—go to it. Blow up our whole fucking country if you want to.

Well, we coasted through the cracks by going hi-diddle-diddle, straight down the middle, too. We flew first-class from Peshawar to Paris, caught the train to the Channel ferry, and slipped into Britain with the rest of the EC day-trippers.

We got to the FAMFUC by 1140. Mick's watchers had put Brookfield's house under surveillance an hour after I'd transmitted from Afghanistan. So far, however, it had been a bust—Brookfield was following his normal schedule of meetings with government officials, lunches at one of his clubs, and afternoon paperwork. There had been no suspicious meetings, no phone calls, no nothing. "Why can't we just go in and bust the son of a bitch?" I wondered aloud.

Because, Mick said, when you have as many friends in high places as Ishmael, Lord Brookfield, it's a great way to end a career.

"But the embassy's been secured."

"Not exactly," said Mick.

What the fuck was going on?

He explained that he'd passed a message through channels, and that the Threatcon had been raised from Alpha to Bravo. But that since there had been no direct evidence, the State Department had refused to go any further. "The regional security officer told me the ambassador didn't want to make a fortress out of the embassy," Mick said. "There was very little I could do."

"What about Special Branch?"

"We've doubled outside surveillance, set up additional vehicle barriers, and put no-parking signs up all over Grosvenor Square. But without any concrete evidence, it's hard to make a case against Brookfield—or anybody else."

"What about the BWR?"

"Have you actually seen him with it?"

I had to admit that I hadn't. Mick was right—the unhappy truth was that every bit of evidence I had on Brookfield so far was circumstantial. There was nothing concrete. His security man, Todd Stewart, had met with Azziz in Cairo. That could be sloughed off as Todd's doing. The meetings with the Pakistani officers in London could be put down to intelligence gathering. Ditto the confabs with Marcel Mustache in Nice. Lord B kept himself at arm's length. And knowing his smooth operational style, he'd probably weasel his way out of any charges I brought against him.

As much as I hated to admit it, Mick was right—we'd have to wait until we could connect him posolutely and absitively both with the terrorists and with the anthrax.

Speaking of which, I asked Mick what he'd done about the six canisters of BA-PP3/I I'd sent back through Colonel Angelotti. The news was good: since the anthrax spores used in the BWR had been developed by the Soviets back in the mideighties, there was already an antitoxin for it. Moreover, Mick's epidemiologists were confident that the drug's plague component could be combatted with massive doses of tetracycline. Mick was keeping the BWR under wraps—no sense letting anyone, especially Lord Brookfield or his friends in the intelligence community, know we had the stuff. We knew Brookfield's sources were good, so there was no reason to tell anyone we were holding BA-PP3/I, or what we knew about it.

And what of the five companions—nationality British—with whom Brookfield had arrived?

Of them, there was no trace whatsoever after they'd cleared customs.

Of course there was no trace, or contact. I believed I knew why, too—because those "Brits" were really Americans. To be precise, they were the American tangos we'd missed in Afghanistan. And I knew—just knew—that they were about to hit the embassy.

Why? Because it was exactly the sort of thing I would do. It was an inviting target. Security was lax—the huge loading dock on the building's west side provided an inviting target for infiltrators. And the embassy was in every sense of the word a public building. Every day, hundreds of applicants lined up on the building's south side to apply for visas to visit or emigrate to the United States. Americans by the scores marched through the metal detectors and bulletproof Plexiglas of the main entryway on Grosvenor Square to visit consular officers or commercial attachés. The Brits also held regular meetings there, with resident attachés from agencies ranging from the FBI and the U.S. Customs Service to DIA and No Such Agency.

Moreover, the embassy was situated in one of the most bustling areas of London: two blocks from the city's biggest shopping district, Oxford Street; only a few blocks from New Bond Street and its pricey boutiques, auction houses, and art galleries; a few hundred yards from Park Lane, one of the city's most heavily traveled streets. If the BWR canister was exploded on the building's roof, it would infect all of central London.

I may have been on the wrong end of a murder indictment, but it was still my duty to tell Pinky that the balloon was about to go up. So I used the FAMFUC's scrambled cellular network to place a call to CINCUSNAVEUR from the messy room Mick used as his office.

"Admiral Prescott's office."

I didn't waste time on niceties. "Tell him Dick Marcinko's on the line."

He picked up in a flash—so agitated he sounded like a tape being run backward. He threatened. He fulminated. He ranted and raved. When he finally stopped to catch his breath (or wipe the drool off his chin), I interrupted his tirade. "Look, asshole, all this screaming isn't going to get you anywhere."

That only set him off again. Finally, I'd had enough.

"Listen, cockbreath—"

That quieted him down. I heard him slap his palm over the receiver and listened to him as he shouted something into the next office. "You can't trace this call, Pinky, so don't even try."

I could almost see him roll his eyes in frustration. "Now, listen, Dick—"

"No, you listen to me. We've got problems here. Not bullshit problems, real ones."

He interrupted me and started to rant again, so I hung up on him. There wasn't time to waste—especially on idiots like Pinky.

When unable to go through, go around. I called Hans Weber's extension. A strange voice answered. I asked for Hansie and was told he'd been transferred.

"Where?"

"Back to the U.S. He's TAD in Norfolk for the next one hundred and eighty days. Handling the restricted-duty personnel for the master chief at arms."

Talk about your world-class fuckings. Hansie had been royally screwed. He'd been assigned to baby-sitting at Norfolk; put in charge of the screwups, misfits, malcontents, and chronic troublemakers confined to the base. Worst of all, he was working for another command master chief—probably a nitnoy no-load by-the-book asshole, too. This was Pinky fucking Prescott's handiwork, no doubt about it—Pinky's revenge against Hans for the help he'd given me. Another black check mark went up next to the good admiral's name in the mental notebook I carried.

I called the embassy and asked for the RSO—the Regional Security Officer. He'd left last night, I was told, on home leave.

"Let me talk to his assistant."

"She's out to lunch. May I leave a message?"

Out to lunch was right. Oh, sure—tell her to straighten her seams and touch up her lipstick because she's about to be attacked by a mean bunch of tangos. "No—I'll call back."

I tried my old girlfriend Nancy's extension at the CIA's office. It was busy. I dialed the Marine duty desk. No answer. *No answer?* What the hell were these people up to, anyway?

I tried the ambassador's office. No one picked up there, either.

Frankly, I was getting frantic and said as much to Mick. He was in no position to operate—without an official call-up from the Home Office, he couldn't mobilize his troopers.

I wasn't impressed. I knew from experience how easy it is to foil basic precautionary measures—I'd done it hundreds of times with Red Cell. "Let's raise the ante," I told him.

Mick agreed. He dialed the commander of London police's D-11 unit. D-11 is the metropolitan police's SWAT team. Unlike almost all other British police units, the constables on D-11 are armed. They carry pistols and have access to weapons ranging from submachine guns to sniper rifles. Mick suggested that D-11's CO contact Special Branch and work out a rapid-response contingency plan.

Mick shrugged at me. "Not much more I can do right now, mate."

I stood up and stretched, peering through the dirty window toward the two-story concrete kill-house a hundred yards away. "What about picking Lord Brookfield's ass up off the street, clapping him in a padded room out here, and letting me have a go at him?"

Mick's expression told me it wasn't an option.

"You're getting soft in your old age."

"Maybe—but you're only a transient. I have to live here, y'know?"

"Sure, sure." I grabbed the phone again, dialed CINCUSNAVEUR, and asked for Randy Rayman's extension. He picked up after three rings. "Plans and Policy, Commander Rayman."

"It's Dick Marcinko." I heard the intake of breath. I could just see him reaching out for the intercom button to let someone with more stripes than he know I was on the line. "Listen, asshole—"

Randy started to say something, but he was interrupted by a loud Klaxon horn at his end of the conversation. I heard two rapid five-*ougah* bursts, then the phone went dead.

Aboard a ship, five blasts of the Klaxon horn means battle stations. In a land-based facility, it means that you have just gone to a wartime footing.

"Well, fuck me," I said to Mick. "We've been worrying about the wrong damn building. The goddamn tangos just hit North Audley Street—CINCUSNAVEUR." Serious as the situation was, the thought of Pinky Prescott as a hostage brought a wry smile to my face. It occurred to me in passing that perhaps I could make a serious mistake when Green Team went in after the bad guys.

Most people look at buildings and see architecture. I look and wonder how to best destroy them. That's how I'd evaluated CINCUSNAVEUR's hundred-year-old building when Pinky had clapped Nasty Nicky Grundle in chains a couple of weeks ago. So, it didn't take long to formulate a tactical plan of action with Mick. In fact, it took longer to ensure that my men and I wouldn't be arrested when we showed up on-site.

But after fifteen minutes on the phone to COBRA—the Cabinet Office Briefing Room—team, Mick managed to convince the powers that be to let us participate. His logic was incontestable: we were an American Navy hostage-rescue unit. We were on scene. No one knew the building better. And those were our guys in there.

So, after holding up my right hand and promising to turn myself in as soon as the crisis was over (I crossed two fingers behind my back), Green Team and Mick's Pagoda Troop of thirty choppered from the FAMFUC, landed just north of the Hyde Park police station, and took a roundabout approach to Grosvenor Square. We arrived on-site at 1455 and went to work immediately.

The Brits had already evacuated the Marriott. That's where we set up our command post. It was convenient. The hotel is actually contiguous to CINCUSNAVEUR—you can get from one roof to the other. In fact, the Marriott's basement kitchen abuts CINCUSNAVEUR's boiler room, too. There is a common wall—made of Victorian brick laid six feet thick. Waiting for us was Sir Aubrey Hanscomb Davis and his monocle. He would be the MOD monitor.

Sir Aubrey didn't look happy to see me. In fact, he refused to speak to me directly. Instead, he did his communicating through Mick. That was all right with me—I didn't need his brand of pompous self-righteousness just now.

Another double-breasted, chalk-striped suit was in attendance, too. It belonged to the Home Office undersecretary for terrorism, a sallow-faced, lanky 44-extra-long named Sir Roderick Townley. He performed better than he looked—he'd already had the telephone trunk lines to CINCUSNAVEUR diverted. That was good—we could reach out and touch anybody inside, but they couldn't get an outside line. That also meant there would be no calls to the press for these tangos, no interviews with asshole TV anchors, radio talk-show hosts, or print reporters. They'd speak only to us—on our schedule. Unless, of course, they were carrying cellular phones, in which case they'd be able to talk to whomever the fuck they wanted to. I asked Sir Roderick if we could get a cellular-jamming unit on-site. He said he'd already sent for one—just in case.

Simultaneously, we had the London police set up a wide cordon sanitaire. Mick took an A-to-Zed map and drew a thick red rectangle that went from Marble Arch to the northwest, down Park Lane, across Mount Street, north along Davies Street to Oxford Street, and back to Marble Arch. "Nobody inside those lines," he instructed the police inspector assigned as his liaison. No way was a single TV camera going to get any pictures of us doing our work.

Mick had learned that lesson during Operation Nimrod at Princes Gate, when BBC cameras captured the whole rescue on videotape and broadcast it live. I knew that CINCUSNAVEUR had a satellite dish on its roof. It got CNN, Sky News, BBC, ITV—the whole panoply of twenty-four-hour news services. It would be easy for the tangos to keep tabs on us if we let even a single camera through our boundaries.

What do I hear, an argument out there? So, you think the public has a right to know. Well, I agree with you—it does. And as soon as we'd finished our work, the goddamn networks could interview anybody they wanted to. But not now. Not when lives were at stake and a single careless word by some idiot correspondent could cause innocent people to die.

Almost as if they'd been monitoring our conversation, we received word that CNN and the *Daily Mirror* had hired a chopper, which was trying to get close enough to use one of their 1,000mm lenses—the ones they use to spy on topless Royals in the Bahamas. I ordered a police chopper aloft to intercept and arrest the sons of bitches, and if that didn't work, shoot 'em down. I also made sure that we used only scrambled communications from here on in. No journalist asshole was going to intercept my messages.

But the press had to be informed.

Well, that's why God invented men who wear suits—to stand

there and rock on their heels and say nothing. Which is exactly what Sirs Aubrey and Roderick did. We set up a press center at the Park Lane Hotel—almost half a mile from our operations center. Every half hour on the half hour, Sir Roderick or Sir Aubrey, accompanied by an inspector from the Metropolitan Police Department, shambled to the microphone and mumbled four or five minutes of gibberish, took another five minutes of shouted questions, then shuffled off to Buffalo again. They looked miserable. Well, fuck 'em—they didn't have to like what they were doing, they just had to do it.

1522. Mick and I got down to serious planning. You want to react immediately in cases like this. But I knew from experience that we'd do better if we proceeded one step at a time.

Detail number one was the perimeter. As soon as we'd established that, we positioned our three SAS sniper teams. In a perfect world, I'd have used SEAL Team Six snipers because I believe they're the world's best. But there were no SEAL Six snipers here, and my guys hadn't shot lately, while the SAS teams had been doing more than 100 long shots a day at the FAMFUC.

One pair went atop the roof of the hotel directly across the square from North Audley Street—a 150-yard shot. Another team looked down on CINCUSNAVEUR's western facade—a 50-yard shot. And we set the third team atop a building one hundred yards north, looking down at the rear windows and smokers' door. While the snipers moved into position, we assembled medical units and fire trucks on Brook Street, just below the Square, so they'd be well out of the tangos' line of sight but readily available to us. The preliminaries completed, we turned our attention toward necessity number one: the gathering of intelligence—learning the same basics they teach at both DIA and journalism school: who, what, when, where, how, and why.

We had fragmentary intelligence about what had happened from a hysterical Navy wife who'd been coming out of the medical unit just as the takedown took place, and the young Marine lance corporal security guard who'd managed to get her and her eighteen-month-old out of the building through a hail of gunfire. He'd taken a round through the lung, but he fought the pain and told us what he knew. I squeezed his shoulder and told him he'd done good.

The Marine's story told me that we were up against professionals

—they'd Kept It Simple, Stupid. A clean-shaven young man with a Navy ID card and a regulation haircut showed up at the main security barricade—a six-by-eight-foot cage of seven-eighths-inch bulletproof glass, you'll recall. He was admitted. He stopped long enough to stick his head through the open door into the security cage and ask for help finding a warrant officer in the personnel office. As the duty sergeant reached for his building locator, the visitor shot him in the back of the head. Then he hit the release button, which allowed three other colleagues who'd been loitering just outside the front door past the barrier.

The trio had submachine guns under their coats and carried huge duffel bags over their shoulders. But that didn't keep them from moving fast. Before anyone could react, they killed three more Marines, wounded the civilian security guard in the information booth, and took control of the ground floor.

That was the Marine's story. I asked for a description of the perps. He went blank. "I just don't remember, Captain. They were just guys—three white, one black."

The Navy wife didn't have much more to add. She'd been too terrified, she said, to remember anything but the sound of the shots, the screaming, and the Marine who put himself between the tangos and her and dragged her and her baby outside.

So there were at least four of 'em inside. There could be more, of course; Navy IDs were easy to obtain if you knew how, and another half dozen—hell, another dozen and a half tangos—could have filtered in without being noticed. Remember the "smokers' door" on the alley? Any self-respecting tango would have picked up on it the very first time he walked around the building.

Four was too few. I figured they had to have at least eight to ten inside. The size of the building and the number of occupants—120 so far as we could tell—required that many.

Well, there were ways to find out. CINCUSNAVEUR, if you remember, has security cameras in the hallways on each floor and mounted high atop the outside walls. Those cameras were hooked up to a central unit that sits in the security room on the ground floor. But—and I wasn't altogether sure that the tangos knew this—the system had been designed with a passive link to the security cameras at the embassy across the street.

Which meant that if we played with enough patch cords, we could see what was happening inside CINCUSNAVEUR by looking at screens in the embassy. Better still, we could run another six hundred yards of cable and set up our own screens at the Marriott.

There were no mikes in the security system, however, so we'd have to find ways of getting audio sensors inside the building. That wouldn't be hard. Sensors can be dropped down plumbing vents. They can be planted on outside walls. They can be drilled into the target building itself. Parabolic mikes can pick up the vibrations that the human voice makes in glass windows. Other, more sensitive devices can listen through a foot of steel and stone.

Our most difficult task would be ascertaining what was happening on the fifth and sixth floors. That was where most of the command's top-secret materials are located. One hoped that, even as the Klaxon horns went off, the NAVOPS people on five were shredding and burning as much as they could behind their cipher-locked doors.

And if the tangos weren't carrying detasheet explosives—ten-by-twenty-inch sheets of plastic explosive, which you can precut for use on door hinges, locks, and bolts—it might take them hours to get past the heavy steel doors of the CINCUSNAVEUR communications center. By which time the men inside could use the saws and bolt-cutters cached inside to cut through the heavy bars on their windows, climb up to the roof, and escape by coming over to the Marriott.

It was time to divvy up the responsibilities. Working with Mick Owen made that job easy. As big a C²CO as Geoff Lyondale had been, Mick was efficient, and we worked together seamlessly. He knew that the most important thing was a successful op. Everything else—ego, rank, glory—was forgotten.

Okay, we'd need communications in the operations center. Mick took care of that. And we'd need an intelligence-slash-negotiation team. I assigned Tommy Tanaka to lead it. And we'd need an assault team. That would be my responsibility.

That was the one thing Mick and I argued about. His view was that I'd be best used in the command post, playing orchestra conductor to this band of lethal instrumentalists.

I disagreed. First, I knew the building as well as any man alive. That gave me a great tactical advantage. Second, my team—Green Team—was built around my lead-from-the-front style. I'd trained with my men. I'd forged the unit integrity that allowed us to act as one. No way was I going to let my shooters ever go over the rail without being there myself.

In any hostage situation, the primary issue is intelligence. My three primary questions were, how many friendlies were in the building, how many tangos, and—most significant—where the hell was the fucking container of BWR. Sure, we'd want to know where the friendlies were being held and how we could get to them. Sure, we'd want to know the number of tangos. But the primary goal was to isolate the BA-PP3/I and neutralize it before they could set it off.

Determining the answers to those questions was the hard part. Once we had the facts in hand, assault wasn't going to be much of a problem. Getting in would be easy. I had a number of choices. I could tunnel from the sewer lines that ran parallel to CINCUSNAVEUR along North Audley Street. I could cut through the roof. Or I cold abseil down and come in on the first, second, third, or fourth floors.

Since time was crucial (get the bad guys before they blow the BWR), my initial instinct was to send four teams at once. Alpha would go through the sewer. It would blast a four-by-four-foot hole through a foot and a half of basement wall with a series of ribbon charges and work its way upstairs. Responsibilities: basement levels one and two, and the ground floor. Bravo would cut through the roof, drop into the comm center, and work its way down. Responsibilities: fifth and sixth floors. Charlie and Delta would abseil down opposite ends of the building, bust through the unbarred fourth-floor windows, and work their way down to the first floor, sweeping tangos as they went. First priority for each team was the BWR canister. Once we discovered where it was, we'd realign the assignments.

My guesstimation was that the assault could be completed in less than six minutes. That was critical—especially in light of the anthrax. Back in 1980, it had taken Mick's Pagoda Troop eleven minutes to clear the Iranian embassy at Princes Gate because of Murphy fuckups and missed timing—and they hadn't been worried about a goddam canister of BWR that could kill half the population of London.

Something else had occurred to me as well, although I didn't mention it to anyone. It was this: these tangos had staged a complicated hostage-taking operation on North Audley Street when all they really had to do to bring the city to its knees was camouflage the BWR in a box from an Oxford Street store, drop it off at the cloakroom of the Marriott or the message desk at CINCUSNAVEUR, then explode it by remote control. There was an element or two missing here, and if there'd been time, I would have head-shedded the subject. But there was, as usual, no time.

I ran my assault plan past Mick, who liked what he heard. He simply nodded and said, "Building blueprints?" He wasn't one to mince words when time was a factor.

"On their way."

"Video?"

"Ten minutes." We had the embassy communicators working on it.

He nodded. "Good."

We'd appropriated the Marriott's dining room as our ops center. The dining tables had been pushed together to make work areas. Tommy T's intel work group had taken over the corner of the room. Tommy, wearing a headset, was working the phones. An SAS Mike the Psych—that's a combat-qualified shrink—worked with him, trying to glean a psychological profile of the bad guys. Communications took up the opposite corner. In hostage rescue, communications is as important as intel. You have to be able to speak to everyone—whether to give a sniper the green light or talk to your breaching teams as they go through the doors or—well, you get the idea.

Duck Foot and Rodent were downstairs, busy making demolition charges. SAS supplied the raw materials, but they didn't have the recipes I'd need here.

To cut through the roof, I'd use an Arleighgram, a trick I'd learned from Arleigh MacRae, the legendary Los Angeles Police Department demolitions man who'd designed hundreds of charges —from the ones LAPD teams used to break into crack houses to sophisticated explosives that could take a door off its hinges without disturbing the frame.

Arleigh had once been asked to design something to go through a flat, metal-reinforced roof so that an LAPD SWAT team could drop in on some hostage takers. He'd devised a wonderful entry tool, which SEAL Team Six had named the Arleighgram in his honor. It used the same kind of three-hundred-grain flexible charge—PETN plastic explosive contained inside a seamless, L-shaped (or inverted-V) lead sheath—used by SEALs and Frogmen for years. This kind of charge will penetrate two-inch-thick steel plate if it's used right.

What Arleigh had done was focus the explosion by taping the charge to an inner tube filled with water. It was so KISS simple I'd kicked myself for not having thought of it first. You placed the charge against the target. When it exploded, the water served as a tamping agent, which resulted in an explosion that blew a neat circular hole the size of a manhole cover into the target.

We'd use the Arleighgram to blow a hatch in the roof, then we'd drop straight down and wreak our havoc. Doom on you, Mr. Bad Guy.

For the basement, we'd employ the same kind of flexible explosive, but set it up as a ribbon charge. Here's how. You lay out the size of the hole you need to blow. In our case it was four by four. Then you find a piece of Styrofoam insulation sheet half an inch thick. Using the foam as a template, you tape the charge to the foam and attach all your blasting devices. That way you don't stand around wasting time while a couple of your guys place the charge, tape it to the target wall, set the detonators, and ignite the fuse, while the bad guys stand around and shoot at you.

Hostage rescue cannot take a lot of time. So what you do is prepare everything beforehand. That way, when you're ready to go, you slam the Styrofoam template into position, blow the fucking thing, go wham through the hole, and shoot the bad guys. Keep It Simple, Stupid.

1603. We had video. We gathered around the screens and punched up the pictures floor by floor. The situation was about what I'd expected. Empty hallways and stairwells. Office doors open. The subbasement was cleared. Good. No one in the holding cell. The cafeteria was empty. They'd moved everyone upstairs. That also was in our favor. Ground floor. The doors were barricaded and booby-trapped—rectangles of C-4 taped to them. That was okay, because we had no intention of staging a frontal assault.

Some of the hostages had been secured in the big second-floor conference room. We couldn't see everything, but it appeared as if there were about forty of 'em there, hunkered on the floor, hands behind heads.

I could make out Pinky Prescott because he was in the front row. From the look of it—he was sitting by himself; the closest hostages had scrunched themselves as far away from him as they could— he'd peed in his pants. Typical.

There was one camera in the basement hallway opposite the cafeteria. I could see a bunch of hostages there, too. That would be a hard target because there were no windows and only one approach: straight up the middle of the road. Damn. We punched up the upper floors. The fifth-floor ops center had been breached—the door was open. But the hallways to the sixth-floor comm center were empty and the heavy steel doors were closed.

We called in on the comm center's secure line and got an answer from a very scared but coherent petty officer first class radioman named Steve Werner, who told us the six guys up there were secure for the time being, that all the classified paper was being shredded as fast as they could do it, and they had the code machines wired to self-destruct.

That was impressive. They could have spent their time trying to escape—cutting their way onto the roof or out through one of the barred windows. Instead, they were doing the job. I let Petty Officer First Class Werner know it.

"Shit, sir, that's what we're trained to do."

It was nice to see that in this new, see-me, feel-me, touch-me, heal-me Navy, there were some old-fashioned fleet sailors left. I told Werner to hang on—that the cavalry would be coming soon. It was a lie, of course—we were in no way ready to stage our assault. But it was important to keep the kid's spirits up.

I saw something in the hallway. "You guys have any weapons up there?"

I heard a verbal shrug. "Well, there's supposed to be a forty-five somewhere—but I never saw it."

"Too bad."

"Why's that, sir?"

"Because you're about to have visitors." I squinted at the six-inch monitor to the left of my nose. There was indisputable movement in the sixth-floor hallway. A figure in a gas mask and flak jacket was making its way to the thick steel door. "You've got hostiles outside, Werner."

There was a pause on the line, then his voice came back at me. "Roger that, Captain. I can hear 'em."

Now a second and third figure came down the hallway. They were carrying duffel bags. As soon as they set the bags down and started to unload, I saw what they were up to. "Werner—get away from the door."

The tallest of the three men outside unrolled a length of flexible explosive from a spool. He ran it around the perimeter of the steel doorframe and taped it into position—shit, there was enough explosive there to take the fucking roof off. The second man attached a pair of ten-by-twenty-inch pieces of detasheet to the surface of the door. The third, moving efficiently, attached pencil-shaped electronic detonators to the two explosive charges and set their timing devices. The job was completed in less than 10 seconds, and the trio withdrew rapidly—scampering down the hall out of camera range.

They reappeared in the fifth-floor stairwell and hunkered down. Two explosions erupted one right atop the other.

The line went dead and the screen in front of me went blank, obscured by the thick, opaque ball of smoke that now filled the sixth-floor hallway. In my earpiece, I heard one of the sniper teams tell me that the windows on the sixth floor north side had just exploded outward.

Two of the sixth-floor cameras were out of commission—nothing but snow on the screens. The one that was left gave me a long shot down the hallway, looking toward the blasted door from above the fire stairs. It was through that lens I saw the assault team again as it crossed below the camera and made its way toward the comm center.

They were wearing their gas masks. Instead of duffel bags they carried submachine guns. They worked their way through the smoke to what had been the comm center door. The heavy steel must have been blown five yards inside the room from the look of things.

As the smoke was exhausted by what was left of the efficient ventilation system, I was able to see what had happened even though the camera angle was bad. What I could make out wasn't pretty. In fact, it looked like the fucking number two turret of the *Iowa* after the accident that killed forty-seven sailors.

The power of high explosive is enhanced when it's set off in a contained area. CINCUSNAVEUR's comm center was, in effect, the equivalent of a steel safe built inside a brick building. So when the door was blown inward and then the second—killing—charge went off, the energy caromed around the room, just as the explosion aboard the *Iowa* had devastated the inside of the steel gun turret. And just like aboard the *Iowa*, the possibility of survivors here was nil, too.

Six more brave Americans had been sacrificed while doing their duty. The three perpetrators were dead men so far as I was concerned. We watched silently as the trio advanced into the comm center, their guns at the ready. One must have seen movement because we could see him swing his MP5 around and squeeze off a burst.

The feeling of impotent helplessness was absolutely overpowering. I wanted to do something—now.

Mick squeezed my upper arm. "We'll have our chance," he said, his face grim.

Chapter

21

1822. THE STRANGE THING WAS, THEY WERE MAKING NO DEMANDS. That really concerned me. For one thing, all the tangos we'd killed back in Afghanistan had lists of demands. For another, terrorists are always making demands—release their buddies from prison or they'll kill hostages. Get them a plane or a bus or a car or they'll drop a pregnant woman out a window. Get them $2 million in cash or they'll send you a body part. Put their demands on the TV news or they'll maim somebody. But not these guys. From them, not a word. It made me real uneasy. I wondered what they were waiting for.

We could see them go about their business with grim efficiency—clearing the floors, dividing the hostages between the big second-floor conference room and the basement cafeteria. We were able to identify ten of them—I'd been right that they needed more than four to secure a building the size of CINCUSNAVEUR. The tangos all dressed alike: Nomex hoods, coveralls, and flak jackets in your basic dark color.

1900. Somebody up there got smart. Floor by floor, the TV cameras went dark. They were cutting the transmission cables on all the interior cameras, leaving only the outside perimeter on-line. I looked at the snow on my TV screens. Well, it had been fun while it lasted. It was time to fall back on plan B. In minutes, we'd assigned six teams of SAS "moles" to place audio sensors so we could try to keep tabs on our T's.

Meanwhile, we stayed silent, too. We busied ourselves with tactics and strategy. Hostage situations are all alike, and all different. You can use the same dynamics, but the tactics must shift with the territory. Planes are easy because they are all alike. Structure, door placement, cockpits, don't change much from, say, a 747B to a 747E. Buildings, however, are all unique. Each one has a different plan, a new layout. Most of the time in situations like this one you go in essentially blind—operating from plans that are outdated, or nonexistent. We were lucky. I knew CINCUSNAVEUR well. And we had the up-to-date plans.

So, with the bad guys bottled up and quiet, we head-shedded, drew diagrams, and problem-solved. We also cleaned and oiled our weapons one last time. We'd all use Heckler & Koch's MP5 submachine guns as our room-clearing brooms. The handguns were another story. When it comes to CQB—Close Quarters Battle—SAS uses the Browning High Power 9mm pistol, a single-action, virtually foolproof design that's more than half a century old.

We SEALs, however, train with double-action semiautos. To make sure we didn't operate at a disadvantage, Mick supplied us with his newest gadget: 9mm Glock 19s, equipped with both Trijicon combat night sights, and Crimson Trace laser sights. I'd always been leery of laser sights because they had to be bolted, strapped, or snapped onto a gun, which meant—Murphy's Law working at its usual 100 percent efficiency—that they'd come off when you needed them most.

These Crimson Trace sights were unlike any I'd ever seen before. They'd been tooled especially for Glock frames by a Portland, Oregon, aerospace company. The sights fit flush into the frame, allowing us to shoot with our normal two-handed combat grip, instead of trying to wrap our hands around something cumbersome attached to the trigger guard. The brilliant red five-milliwatt laser beam made snap shooting easy—cutting through smoke and darkness like the proverbial knife. I wish he'd had similar sights for the MP5s, but nothing's ever perfect.

We loaded dozens of magazines with SAS's hostage-rescue

rounds: CBX's frangible low-penetration ammunition. It's a SWAT-type load that brings a man down but won't pass through his body and hit the hostage behind him. And we checked and double-checked our equipment to make sure it was in good order. There'd be enough Murphy when we went in. I didn't want to worry about whether or not the ropes would hold or the breaching charges were wired correctly.

I'd had floor-by-floor scale models of CINCUSNAVEUR constructed in the Marriott's bar. The entry teams went over them again and again. My guys knew the building. But Mick's SAS troopers did not. There couldn't be any mistakes.

We'd hit in four six-man teams, augmented by the sniper units. The normal MO in an SAS hostage rescue is to pump scores of CS tear-gas canisters through every window at the instant the rescue goes down, then send six or eight two-man teams in to clear the target room by room. Here, gas would not do us any good because the bad guys were wearing gas masks (we could still try to disorient them using flash-bang grenades, however). And two-man teams were insufficient to work through such a large building with the speed we'd need.

So I'd revised my plan. My first thought had been to cut through the roof with an Arleighgram and work my way down, clearing the top two floors as I went. Now, with the comm center devastated, I reworked the scenario. I'd still go through the roof. But instead of wasting time on the top two floors, I'd lead my men straight down to the conference room, where the majority of the hostages were being held.

The fact that the bad guys had put all of their hostage "eggs" in two baskets—or in this case, one conference room and one cafeteria—was both good news and bad news. The good news was that we knew where the Americans were being held. The bad news was that if they were wired with explosives, we could lose the whole batch the instant the first flash-bangs came through the windows. I mean, Pinky was expendable—but what about all those valuable enlisted men who actually worked for a living?

The first report of communications came at 2232. They had a cellular phone inside, and they were using it to make an international phone call to Geneva. How did I know that? Because the passive cellular monitor Sir Roderick had installed had caught them as they punched the international access code, then 41, Switzerland, then 22, the Geneva area code. What the hell was in Geneva?

They let the phone ring five times. When no one picked up, they dialed another number—this one in Cairo. Now I was really confused.

"Mick—can we trace those international numbers?"

"Sure."

I studied the digital readout and read them off to him. He scribbled everything down and handed the sheet of paper to a sergeant, who was back in less than half an hour with results. The Geneva number was a leased cellular phone—the kind you rent at airports for $50 a day plus calls. The other number was a ditto— except it was a Cairo exchange.

I was confused—for about half a minute. Afghanistan. Tangos. Plane tickets. Travel documents. Maps and drawings. Lists of demands. I'd brought them back and handed them over to Mick for analysis, but things had happened so fast here that there'd been no time to get the results.

Now, I didn't need any analysis. I knew all too well what was happening.

"Mick—"

It all made perfect sense. The tangos weren't making demands because it wasn't on their schedule to make demands—yet. This was, I explained, but one part of a six-part operation. The guys inside were going to hook up electronically with the other five groups. Then, when they were tied together, they'd make their demands known.

But not just to us here in London—they'd be dealing with the whole fucking world.

Except—doom on you, tangos—Demo Dickie and his band of merry marauders had stymied their plans.

This group was the one that had departed before I'd hit the terrorist camp. They didn't realize their compadres were dog meat—that there'd be no answer when they dialed Geneva, Cairo, Moscow, or wherever.

That gave us an upper hand—we knew something they didn't. It also meant that we had to act quickly, before they realized that there would be no linkup.

"Wonder."

"Yo." Obviously, he was in a good mood because he was wearing rose-colored lenses in his shooting glasses.

"How do you make somebody think their cellular isn't working?"

"Simple. Jam the frequency."

"Yeah—but I want them to think there's a problem with the phone. Otherwise, they'll waste the hostages and set off the fucking anthrax."

"You got a point, Holmes." Wonder's head swiveled left-right-left, right-left-right, while he pondered the possibilities. "Grid failure," he finally pronounced. "We cut the power to the grid where all the local repeater stations are located. The phones'll go dead."

That sounded pretty good to me. But Wonder wasn't satisfied yet. He frowned and drummed his fingers on the table, then shook his head. "Nah—bag that shit."

"Why?" It sounded good to me.

"Because cellular systems are set up to restart themselves—to go around electrical problems. They switch automatically from dead lines onto a working power grid. Like when there's a power blackout at home—there may be no electricity, but the phones still work."

He was right. "So?"

He crossed his arms in a passable imitation of Jack Benny. "I'm thinking, I'm thinking." Then, a huge, shit-eating grin spread slowly across Wonder's face. You could watch it unfold, like a sunrise. "Natural gas. A natural gas explosion would kill the repeaters. No way they could come back on-line for a while."

His knuckles rapped a paradiddle on the tabletop. "Here's what we do—take one of the Brits' EOD trucks. You know—one of their bomb-disposal units. Okay, we drop about three pounds of C-4 inside and set it off—but we leave the top lid open so the blast'll channel straight up into the atmosphere where it won't hurt anything, but the fucking thing will sound like a goddamn gas main going *ka-boom*. If that doesn't convince the assholes there was a fucking explosion, nothing will. Then you jam their cellular—play 'em a recording that the system's down. They'll believe it." He looked at me with a self-satisfied grin. "Whaddya think?"

What did I think? I thought the boy was sick. I thought he was twisted. I knew he was brilliant.

Mick wasn't wasting time. "Consider it done." He took Wonder by the earlobe and led him away to supervise the maneuver.

It was a clever ploy. If we could convince the news media that other terrorists were striking in London at the same time as our boys at CINCUSNAVEUR, we could disorient them and use their confusion to our advantage.

2352. The explosion must have awakened all of metropolitan London. It was big. And just as we'd hoped, there were immediate bulletins. The IRA actually took credit for the "bombing" in a phone call to Channel Four. The airwaves were filled with erroneous reports about casualties, all fed by Sir Roderick and his team of briefers.

Our tangos nibbled the bait—the first thing they did was try to find out what the hell was happening. They must have panicked because guess what number they dialed. Okay—let me tell you. What came up on our digital readout was a phone that rang on the bedside table at Brookfield House in Hampstead.

I love it when bad guys screw up. Now, we had concrete evidence—admissible evidence—of a connection between the tangos and Lord Brookfield. His ass was mine. I asked Mick to keep Brookfield on ice for me—and to cut his communications. He sent a troop and a Metropolitan Police squad up to Hampstead with orders to bottle the place up tight.

Meanwhile, the bad guys played and played with their telephone. Of course, they never completed any calls because we were jamming their equipment. What they got was a lot of beeps, bells, and electronic hiccups, as well as an unctuous recorded message, which explained that cellular links were down because of an "unforeseen incident" (I liked that!), and that it might be some hours until they were restored.

I checked in with our SAS eavesdroppers, who told me the tangos had swallowed the bait—they'd debated amongst themselves and decided to hold off doing anything until they could make contact with at least one of the other groups. That made me breathe a bit easier: we'd bought ourselves some time. Not a lot of time. I knew the bad guys would get impatient within a few hours. But at least we now had a window of opportunity—and I wasn't about to let it slam closed on my fingers.

I set things in motion. H hour would be 0400, when resistance would be at its lowest. You had to figure that the tangos were exhausted. They'd been on edge all day and were probably operating on pure adrenaline now.

I'd been along this road before. When I commanded Red Cell, I learned that security troops are easy to wear down. Why? Because base commanders seldom provide their security people any bench strength. That means that the first string can be on its feet for days and days without any rest.

While the defense sweated, Red Cell was pacing itself—probing here and there, then going back to the motel for a cold beer, a hot shower, and a few hours of shut-eye. They were ragged, exhausted, and frustrated. We were rested and well fed—we even had time for pussy.

I knew we'd have to keep the tangos on edge. But I wasn't about to make the mistake the FBI did during the Waco siege, when their attempts at disorienting psy-ops merely served to make the Branch Davidians all the more resolute. So, instead of doing things that said "Psychological Operation in Full Swing—prepare yourselves to be boarded" to the tangos, I went with subtlety. There were no choppers swooping overhead or loud atonal music played on rock-band loudspeakers—some of the things that the FBI tried (and failed with) in Waco.

Tonight, police cars with loud *ougah-ougah* sirens blasting would drive by CINCUSNAVEUR in a random but never-ending procession. To make sure the tangos developed migraine headaches, I sent a team of Special Branch police constables dressed in overalls into the street half a block away and had them play chopsticks—using half a dozen jackhammers on steel plates to make the music.

Meanwhile, we plugged our ears and took combat naps. I set the alarm for 0245.

Before an op, everyone feels a certain amount of gut-wrenching, sphincter-puckering nervousness. I don't care how seasoned, proficient, and competent you may be, how cool you are under fire, or how many times you've gone shooting and looting. Until you're actually over the rail and the bullets are flying, you're going to experience a few butterflies.

So there was the usual unusual silence as we strapped and buckled ourselves into our assault gear. The only sounds I heard were the rip of Velcro straps being adjusted and readjusted, the metal *slaap* of submachine-gun bolts as the men slapped them and let them fall forward, and the scuffing of boots shuffling on the floor. Each man was lost in his own thoughts; each was preparing himself mentally for the tasks ahead.

I looked over at Wonder as he checked each round before loading it in his Glock magazine. His lips were moving as if in silent prayer. No rosary for him, though: he was going over the sequence of events until he had it down cold. Rodent counted cadence on his fingers. He, too, was making mental notes. Nasty Grundle worked the length of abseil rope, checking it for flaws. The intensity of the moment showed on his face. Duck Foot tightened the laces of his high-top boots and then, satisfied with the way they felt, tied the ends in double knots and cut the excess cord. No way would his shoelaces hang up on a protruding nail or ledge.

The solitary sulker was Tommy Tanaka, walking wounded. Intellectually, he understood that the hole in his thigh was bad enough to keep him from coming with us. The work would simply be too physically demanding, and there was no way I was going to risk the mission to satisfy his ego. He knew that. He understood it. But the SEAL in him chafed and bitched—he felt as if he were deserting us, and he let us know it. I would have liked nothing better than to say, "Tank—let's go." But being a CO means putting the mission ahead of everything else. So I let him curse me out. There was nothing to do but take the heat.

We wore British assault equipment: Nomex fireproof coveralls and balaclavas, and SF10 respirators with integrated goggles that could be used in conjunction with SAS's CT100 communications rig. Over the top of the coveralls, we strapped ourselves into ceramic body armor—more than twelve pounds per man, but worth it, as the reinforced plates we wore can defeat even the most advanced rounds. We used the British AC100 composite helmet as our cover because they were built to accommodate both the respirator and communications gear. A Velcro patch on the front of the vest held the two-inch mike-control button—big enough so that it could easily be pressed with a forearm.

I would have preferred SEAL Team Six communications. We've miniaturized our comms more than the Brits have, so we don't have to carry as much weight per man. But—as Mick put it succinctly—

"buggers can't be choosers—and you assholes are the poor buggers here."

I tell you, the man's all heart.

Mick and I ran the revised sequence one last time. No tunnels through the sewers, or Arleighgrams through the roof. We were going to Keep It Simple, Stupid. My SEALs and I would be the tip of the spear. We'd go over the Marriott roof to CINCUSNAVEUR, make our way high above the security cameras' ability to focus, let ourselves down the side of the building to the sixth floor just behind the cornice camera on the building's northwest side, cut through the bars silently, and make our way surreptitiously down to two, checking as we went for the anthrax. When we were in position, four SAS teams would hit the building simultaneously. Their assignments: rescue the hostages in the basement, and neutralize all tangos between the basement and the second floor. As SAS hit, my unit would move on the conference room and take down the hostage holders there.

It was so KISS it would probably work. Unless, of course, we couldn't get through the bars on six and had to abseil down to five, where we might run into a few tangos, which would spoil the surprise, which would allow the bad guys on two to hose the hostages. You get the idea.

0344. We made our way up to the Marriott's roof, climbed out, and began the crossing sequence. If it was cold, I didn't know it: between the four layers of clothes and the pucker factor, I was sweating heavily. I heard Tommy T's voice in my earpiece, telling me that it was all quiet on the western front. I liked getting good news.

The ladder we were going to use to make the crossing was a twenty-two-foot aluminum (or, as they say in London, alu*minium* job—giving us two feet of security at each end. The feet and top were wrapped in foam and taped so that they wouldn't scrape on brick and give us away.

Things had been going too well so far. Mother Nature, knowing how well I like a challenge, had called in some rain. What had, half an hour ago, been a mild drizzle, now gained in intensity, moving up the scale to moderate downpour. It's amazing how slippery an aluminum ladder can become when it's soaking wet, and you are wearing thirty-five pounds of equipment and carrying thirty more. I went first. Instead of walking across from rung to rung, much like you'd do on a rope bridge, I was reduced to hands-and-knees crawling, trying to balance my gear, my weapons, as well as all my other sundry supplies, while the goddamn ladder shook and quaked beneath me as if King fucking Kong was jostling one end.

Who was it said getting there is half the fun? Please tell me—I'd like to shoot the optimistic cocksucker.

Once I crossed, things got easier. I held the far end in place while the others crossed. Unable to restrain himself, Tommy T had come out on the roof just after I crossed over, and he held the far end of the ladder while Duck Foot, my favorite mountaineer and the last man in the stick, sauntered across the slippery metal with nary a second thought.

I saluted Tommy with my middle finger and gave him a silent signal to get the hell back inside. He gave me a Fuck You Very Much double bent-arm wave—it looks like a SEAL version of the Funky Chicken—and withdrew. Good—I needed him inside, on the radio, keeping me informed. He had to keep tabs on the security cameras and audio monitors so I'd have some idea about what the bad guys were up to.

We made our way single file, just below the ridgeline of CINCUSNAVEUR's roof, one foot at a time probing the wet slate so that our progress wouldn't be interrupted by any slip-sliding. It was not fun. The fucking roof was encrusted with bird crap, which made the already-wet stone even more slippery. One false step, and someone would roll off the edge and slam down seven floors. And where would our element of surprise be then?

Halfway to our goal, the roof line changed. The top of the building had been reinforced to hold three huge air-conditioning units that cooled the comm center below. We worked our way around them, making sure not to disturb the dozens of sensitive antennas and satellite dishes placed in clusters.

Below, two police cars raced north on North Audley Street, their ready electronic horns blasting atonally. I peered over the top of the roof, toward the square. I couldn't see them, but I knew that at least one SAS sniper team was following our progress through their 6X42, night-enhanced scopes. It did me a lot of good to know that we had some reinforcements out there.

0356. Above the northwest cornice. With Nasty and Wonder holding my feet, I wormed my way down to the edge of the roof, right above the security camera. It was pointed east—down the alley. No security camera covered the southern front of the building. I knew that because I'd recommended having one installed when I'd brought Red Cell through London a few years ago to do a security study at the request of the admiral. Of course, the four-striped admiral's aide to whom I'd posited my report promptly 'posited it in the round file. Why? Because he held the title of security coordinator and believed that the discovery of even one chink in his precious Maginot Line might ruin his chances for selection to admiral.

I windmilled my arm and they drew me back up the canted roof. We uncoiled two thirty-foot lengths of nylon rope and looped them around the base of an air-conditioning unit. The end of one rope I took in my hands so I could tie it to the window bars. The other rope was attached as a safety line to the abseil belt cinched tightly around my waist.

Headfirst I went over the edge of the roof, Nasty and Wonder again holding my feet and Duck Foot and Rodent paying out the safety line. The barred window was four feet below the gutter, and by the time I reached it, I felt like fucking Spider Man—except that he, as a cartoon character, has the advantage of sci-fi suction-cup gloves, while I wore real-world Nomex that slipped on the wet surfaces.

Quickly, I took the rope and looped it around the bars with two half-hitches. I was able to get off a muffled "Okay" by pressing the transmit button on my right tit against the wall of the building, and I watched as the rope tightened against the bars. Good—they'd tie it off up there.

I let go and swung free. Did you know that working upside down can make you light-headed? Well, friends, it can, and does. In some perverted corner of my mind, all I wanted to do now was swing like a goddamn pendulum, back and forth for a few minutes, because it seemed like fun to do.

I shook my head to clear it and got back to work. Around my waist was a ballistic nylon fanny pack, which I now unzipped. Secured inside was a small pressurized bottle, to which was attached a three-foot length of hose. The hose ended in a small version of an acetylene cutting torch. There was a built-in igniter, too.

There are times when you want to get inside somewhere without using a shotgun or an explosive charge to blow a door, because the sound will give you away. My old friend Chargin' Charlie Beckwith had first ordered this minitorch cutting tool for Delta Force back in the eighties. It is still in use today with CT units all around the world.

I turned the valve, pointed the nozzle away from me, and hit the igniter. The thing came to life with a *fwoomp*—a brilliant blue-white point of light. Quickly, I started on the farthest bar.

The goddamn thing cut through steel like the proverbial hot knife through butter. But it took about seventy seconds to go through each bar—two thirty-five-second cuts. There were eight bars. That was almost ten minutes of cutting time, and we were less than three minutes from H hour. Doom on Dickie. I hit the tit transmitter to let Mick know I was about to be behind schedule and got a gruff "Roger" for my efforts.

Fucking Brits always want to be on time—well, let *him* come out here and hang by his heels for a while.

The work was hot and uncomfortable. My arms were sore, my hands hurt inside the gloves, and the heat was beginning to take effect on my respirator—I could feel it coming through the rubberized fabric. The weight of the composite helmet was almost unbearable now. It only weighs 925 grams—that's just over two pounds. But it was strapped tightly around my chin, which jammed the respirator, mike, and earpiece up against my face and neck. It gets uncomfortable when worn for long periods of time—and that's standing right-side up. I was doing an imitation of a sleeping bat. So, the whole cumbersome apparatus was like a five-pound weight pulling on my neck while I hung upside down. I was going to look like a fucking giraffe before this sorry episode was over.

Six bars down, two to go. I was sweating like—well, like me. Do I sweat heavily? Is the Pope Polish? I could feel the perspiration build. It started between my toes, ran up along my legs, over, around, and through my crotch, seeped upside my waist and back, oozed under my armpits gaining strength and bouquet as it wended its way up my neck, an inexorable, inevitable, unavoidable stream that ran over my Adam's apple, up my chin, and straight into my big, wide, spaghetti-sucking nostrils, making me choke and gag.

Dickie wanted relief. Dickie wanted a break. *"But you're not gonna get one,"* said the Froglike growl of Chief Gunner's Mate/Guns

Everett E. Barrett, in my brain. *"Remember how it was back on Vieques Island? You wanted to lie on the beach and drink beer. Instead, I made you clamber up the goddamn coconut palms to pick fronds so you could weave hats. Why? Because it gave you a sense of self-discipline. Remember when you showed me your spit-shined boots, and I made you spit-shine the soles, too, because he who shines only half a shoe is only half a man? That gave you perseverance. Remember when you were hung over and I made you run all those miles in soft sand wearing a twenty-six-pound wet kapok vest to shape your timber? Now listen, Petty Officer Second Class Marcinko, you worthless geek: I didn't do all of that goddamn character-building for nothing. So, get the fuck back to work. You don't have to like this shit, you just have to do it."*

As always, the chief was right. I scrunched my neck muscles to ease the strain and kept at it.

Which was fine, until I ran out of acetylene just as I started to make the final cut. I watched the flame sputter out six inches from my nose and mouthed a curse at the gods of war who'd left me hanging (literally, I must remind you) high and dry. No way was I going to be screwed out of my revenge. I dropped the torch and took the bars in my hands, wrenching them violently, screaming obscenities into my respirator mask. I didn't give a shit—the fucking thing was going to *move.*

It didn't budge. That was good-grade steel. I twisted my body, trying to get myself more purchase and leverage. I slid my hands behind the grate, nudged my shoulder into the narrow space between grate and window, and heaved. I could feel things popping in my back, but this was no time to give in to my body. I wrenched at the bars again.

This time I felt a hint of "give." And yeah, if it weakened, even ever so slightly, I knew in my soul that the fucking thing was *mine.*

And it finally gave. I twisted it back and forth until I pulled it loose. I was exhausted. I couldn't get my fingers to release the bars. Finally, I was able to pry them from the metal, and someone above me pulled the grate up and sat it on the roof. Then Wonder and Grundle retrieved me. They pulled me up. I lay on my back, burnt out, gasping, hyperventilating, and totally drained—and we hadn't even begun our mission yet.

Every bone, every piece of cartilage, every joint in my body, burned and ached and spasmed. I was a wreck. I pulled myself to my knees and made the silent signal for "circle the wagons." It was time to move out. I pressed the send button attached to my chest and let Mick know we were finally on our way.

0412. Rodent took point. He went down the rope, cut silently through the shards of glass, slipped inside the comm center, checked for booby traps, trip wires, and other possible hazards and, discovering none, took a defensive position at the far side of the room to cover the rest of us as we made our way down and in.

We spread out. Even though it was important to get down to where the hostages were being held on two, I wanted to comb through as much of the debris here as possible to make sure that the tangos hadn't hidden the canister of BWR and a chunk of C-4 up here. It would have been a perfect place to set off an explosion—because the anthrax would have been carried directly all over metropolitan London. We went over the room inch by inch. I saw that, as I'd suspected, the wounded comm center personnel had been executed with shots to the head. I made a silent vow to the corpses that I'd even the scores.

Nothing. We made our way down the hallway, moving in the single-file "train" we knew so well. Rodent took point, his suppressed MP5 at the ready. Nasty Grundle, the breach man, equipped with an H&K shotgun, followed slightly behind his left shoulder. I followed, four feet behind Grundle. Then came Duck Foot. Wonder provided rear security. The sixth-floor stairs came just after the hallway swung left. We stacked, and Rodent went ahead. He gave the all-clear signal, and we followed.

We moved down the stairwell slowly, working our way in the darkness foot by foot. It was a reverse of Cairo—now we moved down riser by riser, checking for trip wires and other deadly pitfalls. We cleared the fifth floor in a matter of minutes. The offices had been ransacked. Three bodies were in the ops center—Randy Rayman was one of them. He'd gone down with a pistol in his hand, although he hadn't fired a shot.

Of course he hadn't. He wasn't a shooter. He may have been nice, kind, and well-groomed. But when it had come down to the nitty-gritty, he couldn't pull the trigger. My men always got bad fitness reports from officers like Randy, who thought they were ash-and-trash misfits, rogues, even scum.

But my men and I could—and did—pull the trigger when we

had to. That's why the Navy needs us. They might not like us—but they need us.

There was no anthrax here, either. We swept down the stairs to four. It was clear. We crept to three. Empty. This was going too smoothly for me. Was I being mud-sucked?

Mr. Murphy made his long-awaited appearance in the stairwell between two and three. Rodent tsk-tsked into his mike and called me forward. I went for a look-see.

Nice. I had to hand it to them. Six treads, each with a pressure mat, made it impossible to proceed. The handrail and banister had also been booby-trapped.

It was a well-thought-out bottleneck, a choke point I would have been proud of.

But I wasn't proud—I was frustrated. I crooked my gloved hand and Wonder and Grundle presented themselves front and center.

"Nu?"

Wonder shrugged. "We go over it, or we go through it."

"Through?"

"Blow it up, Dickhead."

That was not an option—we were too far away from the hostages to do that and be able to reach them before the tangos began waxing 'em.

Duck Foot elbowed his way up for a look. I could barely see his eyes behind the respirator mask. But he gave me a thumbs-up and went to work.

He went back to three and rigged a rope line from the fire door down toward our position. He drew the rope tightly around the banister above the booby traps, then flung it—ever so carefully—down below the pressure pads and explosives.

He extracted a length of fish line and a hook from his thigh pocket, knotted the hook and snagged the rope, which he brought back up around the explosives.

Then, he tied the rope off, stored his fish line and hook, and gave me a thumbs-up.

If he'd had tits on his back, I would have married him then and there. In four minutes he'd built us a bridge. It was narrow. It was precarious. But it would work.

Duck Foot went first because he was the best climber. At the bottom, he reversed himself to make sure the landing wasn't booby-trapped. It wasn't. So Rodent followed, then Wonder, then Nasty, then me. Why did I go last when I always talk about leading from the front? Because I have the biggest butt—so if anyone was going to trip the explosives, it would have been me.

We set ourselves up. I worked the radio to let Tommy know we were—finally—in position. I could hear the relief in his voice.

"Minus fifteen seconds," he told me.

We hunkered down and waited, counting. This was make-or-break time. We knew what had to be done—the question was whether we could beat the clock.

There is nothing that quite describes the madness and chaos of a hostage-rescue assault. Speed and surprise are the two keys to success. Disorienting the hostage takers is paramount. So flash-bang devices are important because of the amount of noise and light they create. Gunfire, too, can be of help.

There were explosions as Mick's troopers came through the first-floor windows. The instant we heard the flash-bangs come through the second floor, we moved.

I led the way. I tossed three flash-bangs ahead of me and shielded my eyes as they went off. I moved through the rising smoke.

A tango blocked the hall. I brought him down with a three-round burst. I saw another. I shot him, too. A third man appeared, and Nasty cut him in two with a blast from the shotgun. Unit fucking integrity—we knew where each other's fields of fire were so we could literally shoot over one another's head without incident.

With Stevie Wonder at my heels I rushed the hall, heading for the conference room. The others would clear the other offices as they followed.

As I hit the heavy wood door and tossed my last flash-bang, things started to move in slow motion. I could pick out the hostages, sitting, hands clasped behind their heads, in a clump at the far side of the room, below the big windows that looked out on Grosvenor Square. I screamed at them not to move, not to get up, to suck the floor, but my voice was squelched by my respirator—not to mention the 185 decibels of the "bang" portion of the device.

It went off with an incredible boom—the concussion broke glass, showering the room with deadly shards. The orange-white explosion hit like a goddamn firestorm. Sparks flew everywhere. The drapes above the big window started to smolder—in a matter of seconds they'd caught on fire.

But the device did its job—the asshole holding an MP5 had dropped to his knees, his hands moving toward his ears because he hadn't had any hearing protection.

But he was wearing body armor, so I stitched him upside the head with a three-round burst. April fool, motherfucker.

I cut to my right, my back to the wall, and moved around the perimeter of the room. That was the prearranged plan. Wonder would be performing the same choreography on the opposite side. Our field of fire was always the same, forty-five degrees, which gave us an overlapping kill zone without shooting either ourselves or the hostages.

I put my back into the corner of the room and slid ninety degrees south. "Wonder—corner!"

"Yo. Roger." He'd made the turn, too.

Two three-round bursts from Wonder's side. Then two more. He was earning his money today.

I wanted to clear the goddamn room fast. There were too many unanswered questions. Where the fuck was the BWR container? Had they wired the hostages? But we had to proceed by the numbers.

At least things were going well for Mick's lot. I heard the radio chatter and knew they'd secured the basement. No anthrax container, and all the hostages clear.

They were sorting them out now—rushing them out the building, flinging them prone on the street, and going over them one by one to make sure no bad guys were among 'em.

I saw something going on at four o'clock. Two shapes through the smoke. I let the MP5 drop on its sling, reached down, and brought up my Glock—but they'd disappeared. I moved like a fencer, sliding along the wall foot by foot, through the fog, the laser cutting a swath around me right-left, left-right.

Movement again. A shape in front of me. No time to aim. The laser touched the shadow and I fired twice, *ba–blam*, then dropped into a prone position.

Two inches above my head, three rapid shots vaporized the wood paneling. Shit. This asshole was good. He'd either tracked the muzzle flash or the laser.

Things were getting precarious. I knew that if I moved into the center of the room Wonder might, could, and would take me for a hostile and wax my nasty Slovak ass.

But there was really no other way to take this one down. So I dove five, maybe six feet into the room—dinging my elbows and knees nicely on the parquet floor in the process—rolling to my right (his left), came up on one sore knee, and hit the laser sight. He was four feet away, still calmly shooting at the wall where I'd been.

Gotcha! I was Admiral Horatio Fucking Nelson. I was John Paul Fucking Jones. Because I had the cockbreath broadside in my sights. *Ready your cannons.* All the frustrations I'd experienced in the past hours—hanging upside down, cutting the goddamn bars, wrenching my back out—threaded their way out of my brain, flooded through my nervous system, and dumped into my arms and hands, down into my right index finger, which staged the Glock's six-pound trigger. *Aim your cannons.* Oh, I was pumping—a steady 140 at least. *Fire your cannons.* But I held the fucking gun steady enough to put three shots into him. Head, neck, and armpit. He dropped in his tracks.

I put one more in his head to make sure he wouldn't get up. Like Admiral J. P. Jones, I hadn't begun to fight yet, either.

I heard Nasty on my earpiece. He, Duck Foot, and Rodent had their rooms cleared. Now they were moving toward us.

This was the ticklish part. See, you're going at top speed. In fact, it's taken me longer to tell this all to you than it took to do it. Plus, the more bodies you add, the more confusing it gets.

But what the fuck—I could use some help. We had forty or so hostages huddled here, and they were beginning to make the wrong noises—like they wanted to get out. I called them in, letting them know—more or less—where Wonder and I were.

"Nasty—blow the windows."

That would help vent the place, so we could see what the hell we were doing.

I heard four quick blasts of Grundle's H&K breaching shotgun, and the smoke started to clear. When it had gone from cumulus to cirrus, I ripped the respirator from my face and shouted, "Everybody down—facedown on the fucking floor."

The hostages didn't seem to think I was talking to them, so I hosed the wall four feet above their heads with my MP5. They sucked parquet.

"Spread-eagle—hands and feet out—out, out!" I kicked at a recalcitrant body to make sure my directions were being followed to the letter. The hostages lay on the floor, facedown, spread-eagled. I radioed Tommy to send reinforcements quick.

Now we moved among them, our weapons at the ready. Rodent, Nasty, and Duck Foot stood watch, Glocks aimed, triggers staged, lasers pointed at vital parts, as Wonder and I frisked the hostages one by one, stem to stern.

There is no way to be either gentle or genteel when you're doing this. When I commanded Red Cell, we taught the base security commands how to frisk someone correctly. Women security operatives, for example, are often squeamish about frisking men's crotches. They can't be. Neither can men be shy about working around a woman's breasts and crotch.

Believe me, it isn't sexual harassment, it's life insurance. Many's the time my men would conceal a .22 or a grenade in their Skivvies because they knew women officers wouldn't want to grope them. Many's the time we used a woman to carry weapons for us because we knew the sailors doing the frisking wouldn't touch her tits.

Who was a hostage and who was a tango? There was no way of knowing for sure. So we worked everyone over, searching for weapons, explosives, and booby traps. Everyone—even those people I knew.

I let Wonder have fun with Pinky—he was halfway to giving him a goddamn proctoscopy by the time I waved him off.

Pinky didn't see anything funny about the situation, either. No sooner did we get the tape off his mouth than he began making a pain of himself. He started yelling and screaming for someone to come and arrest me.

By now, gentle reader, you will have realized—even so, it pains me to admit this—that perhaps I'm not the world's most tender, understanding, empathetic chap. Perhaps you've noticed I'm not big on Phil Donahue huggie-cuddily-touchie-feelie shit.

But I gotta tell you, even my sandpaper sensitivities were bruised by Pinky's rude, unthoughtful, intemperate outburst. I mean, here I'd just saved his ass. We'd come a long way to do it, too—halfway around the world, give or take a few hundred miles. We'd just performed a successful, I might even say virtually letter-perfect, hostage-rescue takedown.

So far as I knew, we hadn't lost a fucking hostage—I glared at Pinky—hadn't lost one *yet*, that is. But here, as if to tempt me toward mayhem, was this pompous three-star asshole—who'd been so scared a few hours ago that he'd pissed in his pants—braying at all and sundry to come and clap me in irons, drag me away, and shut me in a cell pending some sort of summary court-martial where he'd have all the votes.

Such lack of tact made me despair, especially when you consider that Pinky was allegedly an officer and a gentleman.

So I brought the subject up. "Really, Pinky, that's no fucking way to say thank you" is how I phrased it.

And, since there was further work to do, *and* since I'd made my feelings known, and since there was nothing left to say (and since Pinky chose to ignore me), I took my normal direct—some might even call it rogue—approach. I wheeled, set him up with my left hand, and—*whop!*—coldcocked the son of a bitch.

I watched as Nasty dragged him out by the feet, his head going pitter-patter on the wood floor. If there'd be hell to pay, I was more than willing to risk it. What could they do—fire me?

Nah—I had fire insurance. It was buried underneath my kitchen floor.

0532. The building was declared clear. Mick and I stood in the ground-floor foyer, which still smelled of cordite, CS gas, and stale sweat. My face was grimy. I'd bloodied my nose at one point, my lip was split, and my elbows and knees felt as if I'd just played all the Stanley Cup games in the last decade at once.

And that was the good news. The bad news was that, despite a top-to-bottom search, despite my guys and Mick's going over CINCUSNAVEUR inch by bloody inch, there was no canister of anthrax on the premises.

We'd been rused, used, and abused. To put it in SEAL terms, we'd been goatfucked, but good.

Of course we had been. Remember, gentle reader, when I said not so long ago that there was something wrong about these fuckers not making any demands? Well, it had nagged at me all night. The tangos we'd killed in Afghanistan all carried lists of demands. These guys had no such lists on them. Now, I realized why. They were a diversion. This whole op was a diversion. Just like all those terrorist bombings in Europe had been diversions—diverting attention away from the preparation for the attack on the *Mountbatten* that killed CNO and Sir Norman Elliott. There'd been five attacks in a week—and no demands made. Well, these assholes hadn't made any demands either. So, somewhere out there, there was another shoe waiting to drop.

Said shoe dropped just as I was about to suggest that Mick and I take the men and find ourselves twenty or thirty gallons of good ale. Sir Aubrey Hanscomb Davis picked his way gingerly through the debris, taking care not to spoil the shine on his bench-made cap-toes.

His monocle hung like a bull's-eye in the center of his chest. He carried a cellular phone in his hand. His expression was grim—as sour as if he'd sucked a pound of lemons.

He grimaced and handed me the phone. "There's a call for you," he said by way of dour explanation.

I pressed the button on the phone and put it to my ear. "Marcinko."

"You are an intensely nettlesome fellow," the voice at the other end said in an oh-so-proper Oxonian drawl. "It's time to put a stop to this charade. I'm waiting for you and Sir Aubrey. Please come alone and unarmed—or there'll be anthrax all over London."

When you're given such an exclusive invitation, the only possible response is a positive one. "Sounds good to me. You are calling from Brookfield House, aren't you?"

When he didn't answer, I continued, "I'll be there in half an hour. But do you mind if I clean up first, old chap? I'm a bit, ah, gamey at the moment—spilt a lot of your chaps' blood, it would seem, and it's all over me."

"Not-at-tall," Call Me Ishmael replied through clenched (but perfect) teeth, "I b'lieve hawf an hour would still be an acceptable schedule." He pronounced it the British way—shed-yule.

I didn't give a rusty you-know-what he b'lieved. "Frankly, Lord B, I think your shed-yule is about to turn to skit. But don't worry. I'll be along as soon as I can manage."

Chapter

22

TODD STEWART MET US AT THE DOOR, HIS LONG HAIR TIED DOWN WITH A wide strip of Hunting Stewart tartan. We were told His Lordship was waiting for us in the first-floor drawing room. But first, there would be certain formalities.

Quickly, Todd ran his hands over Sir Aubrey's bespoke suit. Finding nothing, he turned his attention to me.

As promised, I'd showered and changed clothes—getting them from the suitcase from Rogue Manor, which I'd stored in the Marriott's baggage room before this whole chain of events had begun. I still wore my assault boots. But I now sported pressed jeans, a polo shirt with the SEAL Team Eight logo on the left breast pocket, and an H&K promotional sweatshirt, the back of which featured a huge cartoon of GSG-9 shooters ripping the hell out of some nasty-looking fundamentalist Islamic tangos.

My jeans were held up by a wide, ornately tooled brown leather pistol belt, cinched with the five-inch, solid-sterling SEAL Team Six buckle I'd received as a parting gift from my men when I left the command to create Red Cell—the original of the replica currently on display at the UDT/SEAL Museum. It was the size of a rodeo trophy-buckle: a huge oval of hammered silver, on the surface of which was carved the SEAL Budweiser sitting atop the Roman numeral VI.

Todd started at the top. He fingered the neck-band of my shirt and retrieved the straight razor taped to the back of my neck. "Nasty, nasty," he chided.

Then he worked his way round my sides. "You're tickling me, chum," I told him.

"Hard cheese, mate." He continued, his fingers walking my rib cage, back to front, front to back. He plucked the Montblanc ballpoint out of my breast pocket and opened it up to discover the one-shot trigger apparatus and single .22-caliber hollowpoint round inside. He tsk-tsked and dropped the pen into his own blazer pocket.

He ran his hands around, then inside of my waistband, plucking the Emerson CQC6 folder from above my right hip and slipping it on his own belt. "You won't be needing this anymore."

He then worked his way south. He turned my front pockets inside out and patted the rear ones to make sure they were empty. He looked through my wallet. Then he slipped his hands down along the outside seams of my jeans, around the tops of my boots (removing the Gerber boot knife from the right one, and the Mad Dog Frequent Flyer from the left), then back up my inseam to my crotch, which he squeezed, then tapped with a cupped hand.

I coughed.

Satisfied, he stood back and admired his handiwork. "You're clean," he pronounced.

"And soft as a baby's bottom," I added.

It didn't draw even a hint of a smile. Todd pointed up the stairs. "This way," he said, leading the way.

Talk about your morose Scots. The man had no sense of humor.

Neither, for that matter, had Sir Aubrey. Monocle Man's dour countenance hadn't changed a whit since we'd climbed into his Bentley for the long haul up to Hampstead, accompanied by a quartet of Metropolitan Police outriders and two SAS bodyguards.

He'd sat silent in the left corner of the rear seat as we'd careened around Regent's Park, past Swiss Cottage and Finchley Road, up Fitzjohn's Avenue, through a narrow alley to Hampstead High Street, where we'd pulled up in front of the police station a block and a half from Brookfield House. Shoulders hunched, we'd walked together past the police roadblock, behind which television cameras and curious onlookers were held at bay, toward the Regency villa into which I'd broken only weeks ago.

Well, he had cause to be upset. *He'd* been the one to give Lord Brookfield a top-secret clearance and allow him inside Her Majesty's government. This turn of events served him right, if you ask me.

Where I come from, it's the accepted practice that people have to earn their security clearances. They don't get 'em simply because they have a title in front of their name or happened to have gone to the "right" school. That kind of old-boy-network thinking has screwed the Brits up before.

You want an example? Okay—how about Kim Philby? Harold "Kim" Philby, the son of a famous English explorer, is the perfect example of Britain's old-boy system gone wrong. A rich, stuttering alcoholic, Philby was one of Britain's top spooks, recruited out of Cambridge with several of his friends.

He worked with the Americans during and after World War II, rising to the top levels of the British intelligence service. Then, in 1951, he was forced out of the SIS because he was suspected of being a double agent. Even so, he was still accepted and dealt with by many still in government—right up until the day in January 1963 that he disappeared from Beirut, defected to the Soviets, and turned up in Moscow as a highly decorated KGB colonel. Not only was Philby dirty, but three of the Cambridge boys recruited with him—fellow SIS stars Donald Maclean, Guy Burgess, and Anthony Blunt—were also KGB agents.

We made our way to the first-floor drawing room with its ornately painted ceiling and Aubusson rugs. Brookfield was waiting for us. He was dressed in a tattersall check shirt with French cuffs, a striped knit silk tie, gray flannel trousers, and a heavy tweed hacking jacket. His cap-toe shoes were brown suede. He looked like nothing less than an advertisement for Burberry.

He stood silent as we entered the room, his arm resting on the shelf of the intricately inlaid mother-of-pearl Syrian wedding chest. "So glad you could come," he said evenly. He indicated a striped Regency sofa opposite where he stood. "Please be seated."

Sir Aubrey and I plunked ourselves down side by side, like a couple of uncomfortable seventh-graders at our first dance. Todd took up a position directly behind me. His presence made the hair on the back of my neck stand up. I rose. "If you don't mind," I said, "I'd prefer to stand."

Brookfield looked at me, his green eyes piercing. "Not at all," he said.

There was a period of silence. I could hear the ticking of a clock somewhere in the house. Then Brookfield opened one of the topmost cabinet doors of the Syrian chest and withdrew an olive drab canister—just like the ones I'd retrieved from the radwaste facility at *Numéro Douze* outside Nice. The canister was sealed. But around the outside of the bottom was wrapped a single strand of flexible ribbon charge. Into the charge, a pencil-sized electronic blasting cap had been inserted through the lead sheathing.

Now I realized that wires from the blasting cap ran from the canister and inside Brookfield's tweed hacking jacket. I looked closely. He was holding the self-powered detonator in his right hand.

What we had here was a living, breathing explosive device. There was absolutely no way I could reach Brookfield before he'd be able to set off the charge and propel the deadly anthrax all over north London.

The smug look on Brookfield's face told me he knew that I knew what he'd accomplished.

"You have to accept the fact that I am ready to die," he said by way of explanation. "I told you, Captain, that jihad had already claimed more than two million martyrs."

"Yes," I said. "And that it might require two million more."

"Precisely. You know, then, that I am absolutely serious. Absolutely committed to my cause."

"Yes, I believe you are." I paused. I realized that he was setting the pace of this meeting, and that Sir Aubrey was allowing him to do so. That put Lord B in control—which was not in my interest. It was time to shake things up a little—not to mention get down to business. "Okay, Lord Brookfield, why did you summon us?"

"Although I am quite willing to die, I am not sure this is quite the time or place. There is work left to do."

"I'm sure there is," I said, moving slightly in his direction. "But not by you."

As I moved, Todd Stewart shifted, too. He put himself between me and Brookfield.

The young nobleman motioned his bodyguard aside so he could face me directly. "We'll see about that," Brookfield said. "You are a worthy adversary, Captain. I must admit that it concerned me—not being able to contact my teams. Which is why, at the last minute, I did not allow this"—he tapped the canister of anthrax—"out of my possession."

I'd been right—the tangos at CINCUSNAVEUR were a diversion. He'd held the BWR back. I edged to my left. Todd mirrored my move. I looked at Brookfield and balled my fists. "You son of a bitch."

"Captain—no." Sir Aubrey rose to his feet and spread his hands, palms up. "Let us hear what Lord Brookfield has to say."

"Thank you, Sir Aubrey." Brookfield inclined his head toward the monocled spook. "I will be brief. The fact is, sir, that despite the advantages I was given, despite my birth, and my position, I was never seen by any of you as anything more than an outsider."

"I say—" Sir Aubrey's monocle plopped onto his chest. "I must protest."

"It doesn't matter." Brookfield's voice took on a resigned, even fatalistic tone. "You may protest, but it's true. I may have been the son of an English nobleman—all you saw was one of those rich Arab boys come to England to become educated. I read and write Greek, Latin, Hebrew, and Aramaic, not to mention French, German, and Italian. I speak, read, and write Arabic—more than most of your scholars can do. You allowed me into your homes, your clubs, your government. But basically, you all saw me as . . . nothing more than a privileged wog. Fortunately, I was able to deflect your prejudice and use it to my advantage. It deepened my commitment to all Islamic people. It made me strive toward my destiny of leadership."

It was time for plan A: Marcinko subtlety. "What horse puckey," I interjected. "What horse shit."

Brookfield looked as if I'd slapped him across the face. *"What?"*

"You're just another can't-cunt whining no-load shit-eating asshole. You blame everyone else for your problems. Well, fuck you. You had all the advantages—money, education, position, connections—but all you can do is snivel, like some snot-nosed schoolboy whose hankie isn't ironed the way he likes it. You're just a pussy, Lord B. A fucking pussy."

By the time I finished, Brookfield had regained his composure.

"You are trying to provoke me. It will not work, Captain." He withdrew a huge linen handkerchief from his left trouser pocket and wiped at his brow. "You know, in the Bekáa Valley, as a hostage, I read the Holy Koran for the first time. I'd read it twenty times before—but never really understood what it was telling me."

Okay—on to plan B. I broke into his monologue again. "And what, pray, did it tell you?"

He brushed my sarcasm aside. "That redemption was within my grasp," he said, his expression tranquil. " 'God promises those who believe in him lush gardens irrigated by cool waters where they will live forever in great houses, graced by God's presence.' "

I looked at Lord Brookfield and edged an inch or so in his direction. "You recite Allah's promise to the true believers."

He looked coolly back at me. "I choose to think of it as the Prophet's promise to martyrs. The following verse, Captain, says, 'Make war on unbelievers and hypocrites. Deal with them mercilessly.' "

I moved again. "With terror? Through biological warfare?" Todd Stewart held his ground as I spoke.

"If that is what it takes," said Brookfield. "These canisters are simply a means to an end."

I moved once more. "That end being?"

"Islamic unity. Islamic unity cannot be bought, as the Saudis and others have tried to do. It cannot be achieved through coexistence with the West—as those who have been subsidized by your country to make peace with Israel will discover. It must be earned—earned through struggle and redemption. It can be fulfilled only by following my plan."

His plan was wholesale biological warfare. So far as I was concerned, he'd obviously gone over the edge. What he was saying made no sense, and I told him so, edging another few inches closer without attracting anyone's attention.

"Not to you, perhaps," Brookfield said, his eyes bright. "But the chaos that will come as a result of these canisters will show my Moslem brothers once and for all that the West is vulnerable—that it can be defeated. There have been victories in the past—but nothing on such a massive scale."

I was about to contradict Brookfield again, but before I could, Monocle Man entered the dialogue. "We suspect, sir," he said deferentially, "that there are other anthrax caches in Britain."

That was news to me. Mick had briefed me pretty goddamn thoroughly, and he hadn't said a word about any anthrax other than the six canisters I'd taken from *Numéro Douze* and sent back.

Sir Aubrey continued, "If you would give me their locations, and your word as a gentleman that you will not employ them against us, we may be able to reach some sort of agreement."

Brookfield's lips drew back in a smile. "My word as a gentleman?" he asked rhetorically. "I say, Sir Aubrey, that's good."

Sir Aubrey shrugged. "I was instructed to ask."

"I'm sure you were."

Brookfield was crazy. No doubt about it. And things were getting out of hand. It was time to deal with reality. "Look," I said, "let's cut to the chase here."

Brookfield peered at me. "What?"

"Cut to the chase—get on with it. You've told us about your Pan-Islamic vision. Okay, message received. And you've explained that you don't care very much for people like Sir Aubrey here. Well, frankly, I agree with you. He's an asshole—stiff upper lip and all. But the bottom line here, Lord B, is that so far as I'm concerned, you're a fucking tango. Cut the martyr shit. Bag the intellectual rhetoric and the fifty-dollar words. To me, you're just another perp trying to hurt innocent people—millions of them. The proof's right here in front of my big Slovak nose: you've wired yourself to the goddamn anthrax. That means you'll set it off if we don't meet your demands. Okay, Lord B—what do you want?"

"You're always very direct, aren't you, Captain?"

"It saves time."

He grinned malevolently. "I expect so." He shifted, turning his body toward me. "As you say, I've wired myself to this canister of extremely hazardous material. What I want is safe conduct for myself and for Sergeant Stewart here. We will leave aboard my own plane. Our destination isn't important. The fact that we will be allowed to fly undisturbed is."

I knew he wasn't finished. "And?"

"And when we arrive wherever we will arrive, I will—my word as a gentleman, Sir Aubrey—let you know where other similar containers are located."

Monocle Man nodded. "How many containers are there?"

"Six," said Brookfield.

Now I realized what Sir Aubrey was up to. He was sending me a message: there were no six containers.

Why? Because I had sent the six BWRs in question to Mick Owen, courtesy of Colonel Angelotti.

The lightbulb that went off above my head was so bright that I wondered whether or not everyone else in the room could see it. When no one reacted, I surmised that the epiphanies in question were mine alone.

Epiphany one: Mick Owen had been briefing Sir Aubrey all along.

Epiphany two: Lord Brookfield had no idea that Marcel Mustache's trip to Dorsetshire had been canceled because of death, caused (albeit accidentally) by yours truly back at *Numéro Douze*. In fact, if Lord B had checked up on his accomplice, he'd have been told that one Monsieur André Marcel Dall'au had checked in, stayed two nights, and left—right on shed-yule. That's how I'd set it up with Mick from Italy.

Speaking of which, there was epiphany three: I'd been set up. Again. I was the cheese in the trap. The bait. The lure. The decoy. The patsy.

I realized why, too—do you?

No? Let me explain quickly. Lord Brookfield was too highly placed, and too well-connected, to be dealt with by the class-conscious Brits. He was part of their power structure, and bringing him down would be evidence that it was completely rotten from the inside. Instead, they turned a rogue American—me—loose on him.

While I was having my epiphanies, Sir Aubrey kept talking. I stopped thinking and started listening. "Where are they, Lord Brookfield?" he was asking.

Brookfield smiled. "You know I can't say anything until later." He shifted his body. "It occurs to me, Sir Aubrey, that you should come with me. That way, as soon as I've reached my destination, I'll give you your information."

Frankly, I'd had enough. CNO, as good and brave a man as ever lived, had been murdered by this asshole. Howie Kaluha, too, was dead, a casualty of the chase. Now, Brookfield was threatening to take more innocent lives unless he got his way. So far as I was concerned, whatever I did to stop him would be justified.

So, as Brookfield shifted, my hand moved to my belt buckle. I reached three fingers under the bottom edge and withdrew the .357-caliber derringer that had been custom-fitted when the buckle was made.

The gun's a Davis D-38, cut down to an overall length of just over three inches. It holds two .357 cookie-cutter rounds—customized, high-explosive, shock-trauma loads perfected by Doc Tremblay as last-ditch man-killers. They're called cookie cutters because they cut through tissue the way a cookie cutter cuts through dough.

I fired twice from a distance of just under four feet, aiming at Brookfield's shoulder.

The rounds hit him—one in the shoulder, the other in the upper chest. They connected with a *thwomp* that knocked him backward off his feet. I saw the incredulous expression on his face as, instinctively, he squeezed the detonator button to set off the anthrax.

Except he couldn't squeeze the button, because his arm had been blown two feet away.

There are three elements to a cookie-cutter round. The first is the knifelike cutter, which opens a huge wound channel. Then comes a small charge of plastic-based explosive, which widens the path. Finally, a third charge implodes, causing tremendous, lethal trauma. The whole process takes less than three one-hundredths of a second. If you're not killed by the initial shock, you die from loss of blood.

Brookfield collapsed, the socket where his arm had been attached pumping blood onto the floor at a healthy rate. That meant the rounds hadn't cauterized the artery. Too bad for him.

I would have liked to watch him bleed, but there was Todd Stewart to deal with. He'd launched himself at me—almost horizontal—an SAS stiletto aimed at my throat.

Bob Spear, who designed the Field Fighter, has a theory about weapons defense that I also subscribe to. We call it C-3 defense. I put it to use now.

The first C is contact. So, I didn't try to grab the weapon as Todd came at me. I blocked him with my shoulder and hit the back of his neck with my elbow, deflecting him as he careened past me. He went down.

It was time for C-2—control. I hit him with a chair, which stunned the son of a bitch for about half a second. It was enough for me to jump his bones and kneel on him, trying like hell to get both of my hands on the wrist that held the knife.

Todd was not being cooperative. He was a strong asshole, too. We rolled around for a while, each of us trying to gain the advantage. I kneed him in the groin. He returned the favor. I bit—taking much of his ear off. He got a hand around my throat and tried to crush my Adam's apple.

I fought free, loosed my left hand, broke his nose, and tried to claw his eyes out.

The stiletto came around. He nicked me good, too—right through the upper right arm.

But it gave me the opening I'd been waiting for. I broke his thumb, snapping it back alongside his big wrist. That got his damn attention. He looked at his arm, an expression of dumbfounded amazement on his face.

I hit him in the face with a closed fist—smashed his nose twice, then rolled over, kneed him half a dozen times rapidly in the groin, as if I were stretching wall-to-wall carpet, then wrested the knife out of his damaged hand.

Time for C-3—counter. I countered by sinking the stiletto into him just below the solar plexus. There was an audible hiss as it perforated his diaphragm.

That brought him to a full stop. I rolled him onto his stomach, snapped his neck from the rear, then flopped over and lay on my own back, exhausted.

Believe me, there have got to be easier ways of earning a living.

But not as challenging, right? It took a few minutes, but I finally struggled to my knees, then my feet.

Sir Aubrey was on the phone, looking as pleased as the fucking cat who ate the canary.

He cupped the receiver. "Good work, Captain. I'm sure your CNO would have been proud of you."

That was nice to hear. Nobody'd mentioned CNO in a while, and it was good to know that a few of us still remembered him. It was, after all, CNO who'd put this whole convoluted chain of events in play by sending me to Cairo.

There were a bunch of questions I'd have liked to ask Sir Aubrey right then—like, whether he'd been the one to leak the Cairo op to Pinky, knowing Pinky would put me on the run and I'd be forced to prove my theory about Lord B's being a tango on my own, thus allowing the Brits to remain at arm's length from the op, while still controlling me through Mick.

But I knew better than to ask, because I knew Monocle Man would never answer me truthfully. It just wasn't his style.

Sir Aubrey finished his conversation and rang off. He turned to me. "It seems, Captain Marcinko, that you broke Admiral Prescott's jaw in two places."

I shrugged. "Too bad."

"That it's broken?"

"No—that it's only broken in two places." I heard action downstairs. "Police?"

The Brit shook his head. "SAS. This thing has to be handled quietly. Too many sensitive ramifications, y'know."

I knew all too well.

Sir Aubrey screwed his monocle into place. "So, Captain, what's next?"

"A lot of Bombay gin on the rocks, Sir Aubrey, a few pints of bitter with Mick, and then I'm going to take my men and go home, if it's all the same to you."

"Home?" That actually brought a smile to his face. "But what about your Admiral Prescott? He's not going to let you off the hook so easily this time."

I shook my head. "Don't be too sure about that, Sir Aubrey. I'm confident Admiral Prescott and I will come to an understanding."

"You will? After all of this, I'd think your differences were completely irreconcilable."

"Sir Aubrey, that's because you don't know Pinky the way I know him."

After all, I knew something about Pinckney Prescott III, Vice Admiral, USN, that Sir Aubrey didn't.

I knew I still have his fucking NIS file.

Glossary

Admirals' Gestapo: what the secretary of defense's office calls the Naval Investigative Services Command. See SHIT-FOR-BRAINS.
AK-47: 7.62x39 Kalashnikov automatic rifle. The most common assault weapon in the world.
AMEMB: AMerican EMBassy.
APC: Armored Personnel Carrier.
ARG: Amphibious Ready Group.
Arleighgram: highly effective shaped ribbon explosive charge designed by Los Angeles Police Department EOD expert Arleigh MacRae. Used to blast through roofs.
ASW: Anti-Submarine Warfare.
A-Team: basic Special Forces unit of ten to fourteen men.
ATF: Antiterrorist Task Force, or Ambiguous (Amphibious) Task Force.
A/VCNO: Assistant Vice Chief of Naval Operations.

BA-PP3/I: real bad shit. See BWR.
BDUs: Battle Dress Uniforms. Now that's an oxymoron if I ever heard one.
BIQ: Bitch-In-Question.
blivet: a collapsible fuel container, often used in SEAL missions.

BLU-43B: antipersonnel mine currently in use by U.S. forces.

BOHICA: Bend Over—Here It Comes Again!

Boomer-class: nuclear-powered missile submarine.

brick: SAS slang for patrol.

BTDT: Been There, Done That.

BUPERS: naval BUreau of PERSonnel.

BURT: Big Ugly Round Thing.

BWR: (pronounced beware) Biological Warfare Rat-shit.

C-130: Lockheed's ubiquitous Hercules.

C-141: Lockheed's ubiquitous StarLifter aircraft, soon to be moth-balled.

C-4: plastic explosive. You can mold it like clay. You can even use it to light your fires. Just don't stamp on it.

C²CO: Can't Cunt Commanding Officer. Too many of these in Navy SpecWar today. They won't support their men or take chances because they're afraid it'll ruin their chances for promotion.

CALOW: Coastal And Limited-Objective Warfare. Very fashionable acronym at the Pentagon in these days of increased low-intensity conflict.

cannon fodder: see FNG.

CAR-15: Colt's carbine-sized .223 assault weapon.

Christians in Action: SpecWar slang for the Central Intelligence Agency.

CINC: Commander IN Chief.

CINCLANT: Commander IN Chief, AtLANTic.

CINCLANTFLT: Commander IN Chief, AtLANTic FLeeT.

CINCUSNAVEUR: Commander IN Chief, U.S. NAVal Forces, EURope.

clusterfuck: see FUBAR.

CNO: Chief of Naval Operations.

cockbreath: SEAL term of endearment used for those who only pay lip service.

Combatmaster: palm-sized .45-caliber pistol made by Detonics, often used during undercover assignments.

CONUS: CONtinental United States.

cosh-and-carrys: British spook slang for snatch-and-grab operations.

CQB: Close-Quarters Battle—e.g., killing that's up close and personal.

CQC6: Ernest Emerson's titanium-framed Close Quarters Combat folding knife.

Crimson Trace: state-of-the-art laser sights engineered especially for Glock pistols.
CT: CounterTerrorism.

D-11: London Metropolitan Police CT/SWAT unit. Armed bobbies.
DDS: Dry Dock Shelter. The clamshell unit put on subs to deliver SEALs and SDVs.
DEA: Drug Enforcement Agency.
DEFCON: DEFense CONdition.
DEVGRP: Naval Special Warfare DEVelopment GRouP. Current designation for SEAL Team Six.
detasheet: olive-drab, ten-by-twenty inch, flexible, PETN-based plastic explosive used as a cutting or breaching charge.
Dickhead: Stevie Wonder's nickname for Marcinko.
diplo-dink: no-load cookie-pushing diplomat.
DIPSEC: DIPlomatic SECurity.
dipshit: can't cunt pencil-dicked asshole.
dirtbag: the look Marcinko favors for his Team guys.
DITSA: Defense Technical Security Administration—the guys who try to keep complex, dual-use technology out of the bad guys' hands. They are often stymied by State Department diplo-dinks and Commerce Department apparatchiki.
du-ma-nhieu: (Vietnamese) go fuck yourself. See DOOM ON YOU.
doom on you: American version of Vietnamese for "go fuck yourself."
Draeger: great German rebreathing apparatus.
DREC: Digitally reconnoiterable Electronic Component. NSA's top secret computer chip that allows it to decipher all U.S. military codes.
dweeb: no-load shit-for-brains geeky asshole, usually shackled to a computer.

EC-130: electronic-warfare-outfitted C-130.
ELINT: ELectronic INTelligence.
EOD: Explosive Ordnance Disposal.

FAMFUC: FAMiliarization Facility/Urban Combat.
Fart Cart: Marine-pilot slang for A-4 Skyhawk.
Field Fighter: Bob Spear's massive all-purpose combat knife. Great for eviscerating tangos, or cooking kabobs.
FIS: Flight Information Service.
flash-bangs: disorientation device used by hostage-rescue teams.

FNG: Fucking New Guy. See Cannon Fodder.

Foca: Italian minisub built with SpecWarriors in mind.

foreplay: hold on Brigitte, here it comes.

FORTE: Fast On-board Recording of Transient Experiments satellite. New, still top-secret, multispectral, thermal-imaging spy-in-sky bird that can track radioactive matter with great precision.

four-striper: captain. All too often, a C²CO.

frags: fragmentation grenades.

Frequent Flyer: composite knife made by Mad Dog Knives that can get through any airport security procedure with the exception of a head-to-toe frisking.

FUBAR: Fucked Up Beyond All Repair.

Glock: reliable 9mm pistols made by Glock in Austria.

goatfuck: what the Navy likes to do to Marcinko. See FUBAR.

GSG-9: *Grenzschutzgruppe-9.* Top German CT unit.

HAHO: High-Altitude, High-Opening parachute jump.

HALO: High Altitude, Low-Opening parachute jump.

HK: SEAL talk for the ultrareliable pistols, assault rifles, and subma-chine guns made by Heckler & Koch, a German firm. SEALs use H&K MP5 submachine guns in various configurations, as well as H&K-93 assault rifles, MSG-90 sniper's rifles, or H&K USP and P7 9mm, .40-caliber, and .45 ACP pistols.

Huey: slang originally for Bell's AH-1 two-bladed helicopter, but now refers to various UH-configuration Bell choppers.

HUMINT: HUMan INTelligence.

humongous: Marcinko dick.

Hydra-Shok: extremely lethal hollowpoint ammunition manufactured by Federal Cartridge Company.

IBS: Inflatable Boat, Small—the basic unit of SEAL transportation.

ICS: Joint Intelligence Community Staff. The guys at 1776 G Street who (allegedly) coordinate intelligence operations.

IED: Improvised Explosive Device.

Incursari: Italian Frogman unit based at La Spezia.

inshallah: (Arabic) God willing.

Japs: bad guys.

Jarheads: Marines. The Corps. Formally, USMC, or Uncle Sam's Misguided Children.
JSOC: Joint Special Operations Command.

KATN: Kick Ass and Take Names. Marcinko avocation.
Ketamine: Dr. Nostradamus's best knockout potion.
KH-11: NRO's spy-in-the-sky satellites, now superseded by KH-12s.
KISS: Keep It Simple, Stupid. Marcinko's basic premise for special operations.

Lacrosse: latest-version eye-in-the-sky NRO spy satellite with upgraded capabilities.
LANTFLT: AtLANTic FLeeT.

M16: basic U.S. .223-caliber weapon, used by the armed forces.
Mad Dog: Paulden, Arizona, bladesmith Kevin McClung, whose Frequent Flyer composite knife is carried by Marcinko SEALs.
MagSafe: lethal frangible ammunition that kills but does not exit the human body. Favored by some SWAT units for CQB.
Mod-I Mark-0: basic unit.

NAVAIR: NAVy AIR Command.
NAVSEA: NAVy SEA Command.
NAVSPECWARGRU: NAVal SPECial WARfare GRoUp.
Navyspeak: redundant, bureaucratic naval nomenclature, either in written nonoral, or nonwritten oral modes, indecipherable by nonmilitary (conventional) or military (unconventional) individuals during normal interfacing configuration conformations.
Nexis: private database.
NIS: Naval Investigative Service Command, also known as the Admirals' Gestapo. See SHIT-FOR-BRAINS.
NMN: No Middle Name.
NRO: National Reconnaissance Office. Established August 25, 1960, to administer and coordinate satellite development and operations for the U.S. intelligence community, currently headquartered in a secret, $310-million, 1-million-square-foot compound off Route 28 behind Dulles International Airport outside Washington, D.C. Very spooky place.
NSA: National Security Agency. Snoop-'n'-spook complex at Ft. Meade, Maryland. Known within the SpecWar community as No Such Agency.

NSCT: Naval Security Coordination Team (Navyspeak name for Red Cell).
NSD: National Security Directive.

OBE: Overtaken By Events—usually because of the bureaucracy.
OOD: Officer Of the Deck (he who drives the big gray monster).
OP-06-04: CNO's SpecWar briefing officer.
OP-06B: assistant deputy CNO for operations, plans, and policy.
OP-06D: cover organization for Red Cell/NSCT.
OP09N: commander, Naval Criminal Investigative Command.
OpSec: Operational Security.
OXY-NG: U.S. Divers first-class bubbleless underwater breathing apparatus used by SEALs.

P-3: Orion sub-hunting and electronic-warfare prop-driven aircraft.
PDMP: Pretty Dangerous Motherfucking People.

RPG: Rocket-Propelled Grenade.

SAS: Special Air Service. Britain's top CT unit.
SATCOM: SATellite COMmunications.
SBS: Special Boat Squadron. Royal Marine commando unit with CT responsibilities.
SCIF: Special Classified Intelligence Facility. A bug-proof bubble room.
SEAL: SEa-Air-Land Navy SpecWarrior. A hop-and-popping shoot-and-looter hairy-assed Frogman who gives a shit. The acronym stands for Sleep, Eat, And Live it up.
Semtex: Czecho C-4 plastic explosive. Used for canceling Czechs.
SERE: Survival, Evasion, Resistance, and Escape school.
SH-3: versatile Sikorsky chopper. Used in ASW missions and also as a Spec Ops platform.
shit-for-brains: any no-load pus-nutted pencil-dicked asshole from NIS.
SIGINT: SIGnals INTelligence.
Simunition: Canadian-manufactured ammo using paint bullets instead of lead.
SLUDJ: top-secret NIS witch-hunters. Acronym stands for Sensitive Legal (Upper Deck) Jurisdiction.
SMG: submachine gun.
SNAFU: Situation Normal—All Fucked Up.

SOCOM: Special Operations COMmand, located at MacDill AFB, Tampa, Florida.

SOF: Special Operations Force.

SpecWarrior: one who gives a fuck.

SSN: nuclear sub, commonly known as sewer pipe.

STABs: SEAL Tactical Assault Boats.

SUC: Marcinkospeak for Smart, Unpredictable, and Cunning.

SWAT: Special Weapons And Tactics police teams. All too often they do not train enough and become SQUAT teams.

Syrette: self-injection dose, usually of morphine.

TACBE: TACtical BEacon. Homing device.

TAD: Temporary Additional Duty (SEALs refer to it as Traveling Around Drunk).

Tailhook: the convention of weenie-waggers, gropesters, and pressed-ham-on-glass devotees that put air brakes on NAVAIR.

TARFU: Things Are Really Fucked Up.

TECHINT: TECHnical INTelligence.

THREATCON: THREAT CONdition.

tiger stripes: the only stripes that SEALs will wear.

TIQ: Tango-In-Question.

Trijicon: maker of the best radioactive night-sights for SEAL weaponry.

TTS: Marcinko slang for Tap 'em, Tie 'em, and Stash 'em.

tube: Brit for subway. See UNDERGROUND.

UGS: Unmanned Ground Sensors. Useful in setting off claymore mines and other booby traps.

underground: London subway. See TUBE.

UNODIR: UNless Otherwise DIRected. That's how Marcinko operates when he's surrounded by can't cunts.

USP: Heckler & Koch's ubiquitous semiautomatic Universal Self-loading Pistol, which comes in 9mm, .40-caliber, and .45-caliber.

Walther: good, very concealable German handgun, commonly bought in .380 ACP, although professional triggermen prefer a .22-caliber Walther PP, or PPK.

wanker: SAS slang for male organ.

wanna-bes: the sort of folks you tend to meet at *Soldier of Fortune* conventions.

weenies: pussy-ass can't cunts and no-loads.

Zulu: Greenwich Mean Time (GMT) designator used in formal military communications.

Zulu-5-Oscar: escape-and-evasion exercises in which Frogmen try to plant dummy limpet mines on Navy vessels, while the vessels' crews try to catch them in *bombus interruptus.*

INDEX

All entries preceded by an asterisk (*) are pseudonyms.